They're rugged, tough Aussie men –
and they're drop-dead gorgeous!
Meet the…

MASTERS
OF THE
Outback

Three top authors bring you three
passionate tales of powerful romance
and exotic adventures set under the
sizzling-hot Outback sun!

MASTERS
OF THE
Outback

MARGARET WAY
BRONWYN JAMESON
MELANIE MILBURNE

M&B™ and M&B™ with the Rose Device
are trademarks of the publisher.
Harlequin Mills & Boon Limited, Eton House,
18-24 Paradise Road, Richmond, Surrey TW9 1SR

MASTERS OF THE OUTBACK © Harlequin Books S.A. 2010

These novels have been published in separate, single volumes in the
UK as follows:

Outback Man Seeks Wife © Margaret Way, Pty., Ltd 2006
Quade: The Irresistible One © Bronwyn Turner 2003
Her Man of Honour © Melanie Milburne 2007

ISBN: 978 0 263 87473 0

009-0710

Harlequin Mills & Boon policy is to use papers that are
natural, renewable and recyclable products and made from
wood grown in sustainable forests. The logging and
manufacturing processes conform to the legal environmental
regulations of the country of origin.

Printed and bound in Spain
by Litografia Rosés S.A., Barcelona

Outback Man Seeks Wife

MARGARET WAY

Margaret Way, a definite Leo, was born and raised in the subtropical River City of Brisbane, capital of the Sunshine State of Queensland. A Conservatorium-trained pianist, teacher, accompanist and vocal coach, she found her musical career came to an unexpected end when she took up writing – initially as a fun thing to do. She currently lives in a harbourside apartment at beautiful Raby Bay, a thirty-minute drive from the state capital, where she loves dining *al fresco* on her plant-filled balcony, overlooking a translucent green marina filled with all manner of pleasure craft – from motor cruisers costing millions of dollars and big, graceful yachts with carved masts standing tall against the cloudless blue sky, to little bay runabouts. No one and nothing is in a mad rush and she finds the laid-back village atmosphere very conducive to her writing. With well over one hundred books to her credit, she still believes her best is yet to come.

Look out for Margaret Way's exciting new novel, *Australia's Most Eligible Bachelor*, available this month from Mills & Boon® Romance

familiar excitement surging through her veins. She loved these special days when the closely knit but far flung Outback community came together from distances of hundreds of miles to relax and enjoy themselves. Many winged their way aboard their private planes. Others came overland in trucks, buses or their big dusty 4WD's sporting the ubiquitous bull bars. Outsiders joined in as well. City slickers out for the legendary good time to be had in the bush, inveterate race goers and gamblers who came from all over the country to mostly lose their money and salesmen of all kinds mixing with vast-spread station owners and graziers.

Picnic race days were a gloriously unique part of Outback Australia. The Jimboorie races weren't as famous as the Alice Springs or the Birdsville races with the towering blood-red sand-hills of the Simpson Desert sitting just outside of town. Jimboorie lay further to the north-east, more towards the plains country at the centre of the giant state of Queensland with the surrounding stations running sheep, cattle or both.

It was early spring or what passed for spring; September so as to take advantage of the best weather of the year. Today's temperature was 27 degrees C. It was brilliantly fine—no humidity to speak of—but hotter around the bush course, which was located a couple of miles outside the small township of Jimboorie. It boasted *three* pubs—what could be sadder than an Outback town with no pub, worse no beer—all full up with visiting guests; a one man police station; a couple of government buildings; a small bush hospital manned by a doctor and two well qualified nurses; a chemist who sold all sorts of things outside of pharmaceuticals; a single room school; a post office that fitted neatly into a corner of the craft shop; a couple of shoe and clothing stores; a huge barn that sold just about everything like a city hyper-dome; the office of the well respected Jimboorie *Bulletin,* which appeared monthly and had a wide circulation. The branch office of the Commonwealth Bank had long since been closed down to everyone's disgust, but the town continued to boast a remarkably good Chinese restaurant and a bakehouse famous for the quality of its bread and its mouthwatering steak pies.

This afternoon the entire township of less than three thousand—a near boom town in the Outback—was in attendance, including the latest inhabitants, the publicans, Vince and Katie Dougherty's six-month-old identical twins, duly cooed over.

The horses, all with thoroughbred blood, were the pride of the competing stations; proud heads bowed, glossy necks arched, tails swishing in nervous anticipation. This was a special day for them, too. They were giving every indication they were ready to race their hearts out. All in all, though it was hidden beneath lots of laughter, back-slapping and the deeply entrenched mateship of the bush, rivalry was as keen as English mustard.

The Jimboorie Cup had been sponsored in the early days of settlement by the pioneering Cunningham family, a pastoral dynasty whose origins, like most others in colonial Australia, lay in the British Isles. William Cunningham second son of an English upper middle class rural family arrived in Australia in the early 1800s, going on to make his fortune in the southern colonies rearing and selling thousands of 'pure' Merino sheep. It wasn't until the mid-1860s that a branch of the family moved from New South Wales into Queensland, squatting on a few hundred thousand acres of rich black plains country, gradually moving from tin shed to wooden shack then into the Outback castles they eventually began to erect for themselves as befitting their social stature and to remind them of 'Home'.

Carrie's own ancestors—Anglo-Irish—had arrived ten years later in the 1870s with sufficient money to take up a huge run and eventually build a fine house some twenty miles distance from Jimboorie House the reigning queen. In time the Cunninghams and the McNevins and the ones who came after became known as the 'sheep barons' making great fortunes off the backs of the Merinos. That was the boom time. It was wonderful while it lasted and it lasted for well over one hundred years. But as everyone knows for every boom there's a bust. The demand for Australian wool—the best in the world—gradually went into decline as man-made fibres emerged as strong competitors. The smart producers had swiftly switched to sheep meat production to keep afloat while still maintaining the country's fine wool genetics from the dual purpose Merino. So Australia was still riding on the sheep's back establishing itself as the world's premium exporter of lamb.

The once splendid Jimboorie Station with its reputation for producing the finest wool, under the guardianship of the incredibly stubborn and short-sighted Angus Cunningham had continued to focus on a rapidly declining market while his neighbours had the good sense to turn quickly to diversification and sheep meat production thus optimising returns.

Today the Cup was run by a *group* of station owners, working extremely hard but still living the good life. Carrie's father, Bruce McNevin, Clerk of the Course, was one. Natasha Cunningham's father another. Brad Harper, a relative newcomer—twenty years—but a prominent station owner all the same, was the race commentator and had been for a number of years. One of the horses—it was Number 6—Lightning Boy was acting extra frisky, loping in circles, dancing on its black hooves, requiring its rider to keep a good grip on the reins.

'He's an absolute nothing, a nobody,' Natasha Cunningham continued the contemptuous tirade against her cousin. She came alongside Carrie as she moved nearer the white rails. Flemington—home of the Melbourne Cup—had its famous borders of beautiful roses. Jimboorie's rails were hedged by thick banks of indestructible agapanthus waving their sunbursts of blue and white flowers.

'He certainly knows how to handle a horse,' Carrie murmured dryly.

'Why not? That's all he's ever been, a stockman. His father might have been one of us but his mother was just a common little slut. His father died early, probably from sheer boredom. He and his mother roamed Queensland towns like a couple of deadbeats, I believe. I doubt he's had much of an education. Mother's dead, too. Drink, drugs, probably both. The family never spoke one word to her. No one attended their wedding. Shotgun, Mother said.'

She *would*, Carrie thought, a clear picture of the acid tongued Julia Cunningham in her mind. Carrie thoroughly disliked the pretentious Julia and her even more snobbish daughter. Now she knew a moment of satisfaction. 'Well, your great uncle, Angus, remembered your cousin at the end. He left him Jimboorie.'

Natasha burst into bitter laughter. 'And what a prize that is! The homestead is just about ready to implode.'

'I've always loved it,' Carrie said with more than a touch of nostalgia. 'When I was little I thought it was a palace.'

'How stupid can you get!' Natasha gave a bark of laughter. 'Though I agree it would have been wonderful in the old days when the Cunninghams were the leading pioneering family. So of course we're still important. *My* grandfather would have seen to Jimboorie's upkeep. He would have switched to feeding the domestic market like Dad. But that old fool Angus never did a thing about it. Just left the station and the Cunningham ancestral home fall down around his ears. Went to pieces after his wife died and his daughter married and moved away. Angus should never have inherited in the first place. Neither should James. Or Clay as he calls himself these days. No 'little Jimmy' anymore. James Claybourne Cunningham. Claybourne, would you believe, was his mother's maiden name. A bit fancy for the likes of her.'

'It's a nice tribute to his mother,' Carrie said quietly. 'He can't have any fond memories of your side of the family.' What an understatement!

'Nor we for him! But the feud was on long before that. My grandad and great-uncle Angus hated one another. The whole Outback knows that.'

'Yes, indeed,' Carrie said, long acquainted with the tortured saga of the Cunninghams. She angled her wide brimmed cream hat so that it came further down over her eyes. The sun was blazing at three o'clock in the afternoon. A shimmering heat haze hovered over the track. 'Look, they're about to start.'

'Oh goody!' Natasha mocked the excitement in Carrie's voice. 'My money's on Scott.' She glanced sideways, her blue eyes filled with overt malice.

'So's mine,' Carrie answered calmly, visibly moving Scott's two carat diamond solitaire around on her finger. Natasha had always had her eye on Scott. It was in the nature of things Natasha Cunningham would always get what she wanted. But Scott had fallen for Carrie, very much upsetting the Cunninghams, and marking Carrie as a target for Natasha's vicious tongue. Something that had to be lived with.

Three races had already been run that afternoon. The crowd was in fine form calling for the day's big event to begin. There was a bit of larrikinism quickly clamped down on by Jimboorie's resident policeman. The huge white marquees acting as 'bars' had been doing a roaring trade. Scott, on the strapping Sassafras, a rich red chestnut with a white blaze and white socks, was the bookies' favourite, as well as the crowd's. He was up against two fine riders, members of his own polo team. No one had had any prior knowledge of the riding skills of the latest arrival to their far flung bush community. Well they knew *now,* Carrie thought. They only had to watch the way he handled his handsome horse. It had an excellent conformation; a generous chest that would have good heart room. The crowd knew who the rider was of course. Everyone knew his sad history. And there was *more!* All the girls for hundreds of miles around were agog with excitement having heard the rumour, which naturally spread like a bushfire, Clay Cunningham, a bachelor, was looking for a wife. That rivetting piece of information had come from Jimboorie's leading publican, the one and only Vince Dougherty. Vince gained it, he claimed, over a cold beer or two. Not that Clay Cunningham was the only bush bachelor looking for a wife. In the harsh and lonely conditions of the Outback—very much a man's world—eligible women were a fairly scarce commodity and thus highly prized. As far as Carrie could see all the pretty girls had swarmed here, some already joking about making the newcomer a good wife. Perhaps Clay Cunningham had been unwise to mention it. There was a good chance he'd get mobbed as proceedings got more boisterous.

He certainly cut a fine figure on horseback though Carrie didn't expect Natasha to concede that. The black gelding looked in tip-top condition. It had drawn almost as many admiring eyes as its rider. A fine rider herself—Carrie had won many ladies' races and cross country events—she loved to see good horsemanship. She hadn't competed in the Ladies' Race run earlier that day, which she most likely would have won. She was to present the Jimboorie Cup to the winning rider. Her mother, Alicia, President of the Ladies Committee and a woman of powerful persuasion, had insisted she look as fresh as a daisy and as glamorous as possible. A journalist and a photographer from a popular women's magazine had been invited to cover the two-day event with a gala dance to be held that night in Jimboorie's splendid new Community Hall of which they were all very proud.

A few minutes before 3:00 p.m. the chattering, laughing crowd abruptly hushed. They were waiting now for the starter, mounted on a distinguished old grey mare everyone knew as Daisy, to drop his white flag…Carrie began to count the seconds….

'They're off!' she shouted in her excitement, making a spontaneous little spring off the ground. A great cheer rose all around her, lofting into the cloudless cobalt sky. The field, ten runners in all, literally leapt from their standing start. The horses as was usual were bunched up at first. Then the riders began battling for good positions, two quickly becoming trapped on the rails. The field sorted itself out and the horses began to pound along, hooves eating up a track that was predictably hard and fast.

When the time came for the riders to negotiate the turn in what was essentially a wild bush track, half of the field started to fall back. In many ways it was more like a Wild West gallop than the kind of sophisticated flat race one would see at a city track. The front runners had begun to fight it out, showing their true grit. Scott, his polo team mates and Jack Butler, who was Carrie's father's overseer on Victory Downs. Clay Cunningham's black gelding was less than a length behind Jack and going well. Carrie watched him lean forward to hiss some instruction into his horse's ear.

'Oh dear!' Carrie watched with a perverse mix of dismay and delight as the gelding stormed up alongside Jack's gutsy chestnut, then overtook him. Jack, who would have been thrilled to be among the frontliners, was battling away for all he was worth. At this rate Clay Cunningham was a sure thing, Carrie considered, unless Scott could get some extra speed from his mount. Scott was savagely competitive but the newcomer was giving every indication he'd be hard to beat. One thing was certain. Clay Cunningham was a crack rider.

Natasha, too, had drawn in her breath sharply. The possibility Scott could be beaten hadn't occurred to either woman. Golden Boy Harper, as he was popularly known, was captain of their winning polo team and thus had a special place in Jimboorie society.

'Your cousin looks like winning,' Carrie warned her, shaking her own head. 'Damn it, *now,* Scott! Make your move.' Carrie wasn't sure Scott was riding the right race. Though she would never say it, she didn't actually consider Scott had the innate ability to get the best out of a horse. He didn't know much about *coaxing* for one thing.

Natasha belted the air furiously with her fist. 'This shouldn't be happening.'

'Well it *is!*' Carrie was preparing herself for the worst.

She saw Scott produce his whip, giving his horse a sharp crack, but Clay Cunningham was using touch and judgment rather than resorting to force. It paid off. The big black gelding had already closed the gap coming at full stride down the track.

'Damn it!' Natasha shrieked, looking ready to burst with disappointment.

Carrie, on the other hand, was feeling almost guilty. She was getting goose bumps just watching Clay Cunningham ride with such authority that Scott's efforts nearly fell into insignificance. That feeling in itself was difficult to come to grips with. The fast paced highly competitive gelding, like its rider, looked like it had plenty left in reserve.

Carrie held her breath, still feeling that upsurge of contrasting emotions. Admiration and apprehension were there aplenty. Sharp disappointment that Scott, her fiancé, wasn't going to win. Elation at how fast the big gelding was travelling—that was the horse lover in her she told herself. That animal had a lot of class. So did its rider. There was a man *determined* to win. After the way Jimboorie had treated him, Carrie couldn't begrudge him the victory. She liked a fighter.

Two minutes more, just as she expected, Lightning Boy flew past the post with almost two full lengths in hand.

What a buzz!

'Oh, well done!' Carrie cried, putting her hands together. For a moment she forgot she was standing beside Natasha, the inveterate informer. 'I wonder if he plays polo?' What an asset he would be!

'Of course he doesn't play polo,' Natasha snapped. 'He's a

pauper. Paupers don't get to play polo. Where's your loyalty anyway?' she demanded fiercely. 'Scott's your fiancé and you're applauding an outsider.'

'*Insider*,' Carrie corrected, looking as cool as a cucumber. 'He's already moved into Jimboorie.'

'For now.' Natasha made no effort to hide her outrage and anger. 'Just see if people deal with him. My father has a great amount of influence.'

Carrie frowned. 'What are you saying? Your family is readying to make life even more difficult for him?'

'You bet we are!' Natasha's blue eyes were hard. 'He'd be mad to stay around here. Old Angus only left him Jimboorie to spite us.'

'Be that as it may, your cousin must intend to stick around if he's looking for a wife,' Carrie said, really pleased that after a moment of stunned silence the crowd erupted into loud, appreciative applause and even louder whistles. They were willing to give the newcomer a fair go even if Natasha's vengeful family weren't. 'Well there you are!' she said brightly. 'No one rated his chances yet your cousin came out the clear winner.'

'We'll see what Scott has to say,' Natasha snorted with indignation, visibly jangling with nerves. 'For all we know there could have been interference near the fence.'

'There wasn't.' Carrie dismissed that charge very firmly. 'I know Scotty doesn't like to lose, but he'll take it well enough.' Some hope, she thought inwardly. Her fiancé had a considerable antipathy to losing. At anything.

'I'll be sure to tell him how delighted you were with my cousin's performance,' Natasha called quite nastily as she walked away.

'I bet you will,' Carrie muttered aloud. Since she and Scott had become engaged, two months previously, Natasha always gave Carrie the impression she'd like to tear her eyes out.

A tricky situation was now coming up. It was her job, graciously handed over to her by her mother, to present the Cup. Not to Scott, as just about everyone had confidently expected, but to the new owner of historic Jimboorie Station. The Cunningham ancestral home was falling down around his ears and the once premier cattle and sheep station these days was little more than a ruin said to be laden with debt. In all likelihood the new owner would at some stage sell up and move on. But for now, she had to find her way to the mounting yard for the presentation and lots of photographs. Come to that, she would have to take some herself. For two years now since she had returned home from university she had worked a couple of days a week for Paddy Kennedy, the founder and long time editor of the *Jimboorie Bulletin*. Once a senior editor with the *Sydney Morning Herald*, chronic life-threatening asthma sent him out to the pure dry air of the Outback where it was thought he had a better chance of controlling his condition.

That was twenty years ago. The monthly *Jimboorie Bulletin* wasn't any old rag featuring local gossip and kitty-up-the-tree stories. It was a professional newspaper, covering issues important to the Outback: the fragile environment, political matters, social matters, health matters, aboriginal matters, national sporting news, leavened by a page reporting on social events from all over the Outback. The rest of the time Carrie was kept busy with her various duties on the family station she loved, as well as running the home office, a job she had taken over from her mother.

Her work for the *Bulletin* stimulated her intellectually and she loved Paddy. He was the wisest, kindest man she knew whereas her father—although he had always been good to her in a material fashion—was not a man a *daughter* could get close to. A son maybe, but her parents had not been blessed with a son. She was an only child, one who was sensitive enough to have long become aware of her father's pain and bitter disappointment he had no male heir. He had already told her, although she would be well provided for, Victory Downs was to go to her cousin, Alex, the son of her father's younger brother. Uncle Andrew wasn't a pastoralist at all, though he had been raised in a pastoral family. He had a thriving law practice in Melbourne and was, in fact, the family solicitor.

Alex was still at university, uncertain what he wanted to be, although he knew Victory Downs would pass to him. Carrie's mother had fought aggressively for her daughter's rights but her father couldn't be moved. For once in her married life her mother had lost the fight.

'You know how men are!' Alicia had railed. 'They think women can't run anything. It's immensely unfair. How can your father think young Alex would be a better manager than you?'

'That's not the only reason, Mum,' Carrie had replied, thinking it terrible to be robbed of one's inheritance. 'Dad doesn't want the station to pass out of the family. Sons have to be the inheritors. Sons carry the family name. Dad doesn't care at all for the idea anyone other than a McNevin should inherit Victory Downs. He seems to be naturally suspicious of women as well. Why is that? Uncle Andy isn't a bit like that.'

'Your father just doesn't know how to relax,' was Alicia's stock explanation, always turning swiftly to another topic.

It had been strange growing up knowing she was seriously undervalued by her father but Carrie was reluctant to criticise him. He was a *good* father in his way. Certainly she and her mother lacked for nothing, though there was no question of squandering money like Julia Cunningham, who spent as much time in the big cities of Sydney and Melbourne as she did in her Outback home.

People in the swirling crowd waved to her happily—she waved back. Most of the young women her age were wearing smart casual dress, while she was decked out as if she were attending a garden party at Government House in Sydney. Alicia's idea. Carrie's hat was lovely really, the wide dipping brim trimmed with silk flowers. She wore a sunshine-yellow printed silk dress sent to her from her mother's favourite Sydney designer. Studded high heeled yellow sandals were on her feet. Her long honey-blond hair was drawn back into a sophisticated knot to accommodate the picture hat her mother had insisted on her wearing.

'I want you to look really, *really* good!' Alicia, a classic beauty in her mid-forties and looking nothing like it, fussed over her. 'Which means you have to wear this hat. It will protect your lovely skin for one thing as well as adding the necessary glamour. Never forget it's doubly essential to look after one's skin in our part of the world. You know how careful I am even though we have an enviable tawny tint.'

Indeed they had. Carrie had inherited her mother's beautiful brown eyes as well. Eyes that presented such a striking contrast to their golden hair. Carrie, christened Caroline Adriana McNevin had *no* look of her father's side of the family. She didn't really mind. Alicia, from a well-to-do Melbourne family and with an Italian Contessa as her maternal grandmother, was a beautiful woman by anyone's standards.

'You're a lucky girl, do you realise that? Scott Harper for a fiancé.' Alicia fondly pinched her daughter's cheek. 'I don't think the Cunninghams will ever get over it. Julia worked so hard to throw Scott and Natasha together.'

As if you didn't do the same thing with Scott and me, Mamma, Carrie thought but didn't have the heart to say. Scott Harper was one of the most eligible bachelors in the country. His father's property ventures were huge. Even Carrie's father had been 'absolutely delighted' when she and Scott had become engaged. Obviously the best thing a daughter could do—her crowning achievement as it were—was to marry a handsome young man from a wealthy family. To prove it her father seemed to have a lot more time for her in the past few months. Could he be thinking of future heirs, not withstanding the fact he had already made a will in favour of Alex? It wouldn't be so bad, would it, to pass Victory Downs on to someone like Scott Harper, rich and ambitious?

Sometimes Carrie felt like a pawn.

Clay was agreeably surprised by the number of people who made it their business to congratulate him. Many of the older generation mentioned they remembered his father and added how much Clay resembled him. One sweet-faced elderly lady actually asked after his mother, her smile crumpling when Clay told her gently that his mother had passed on. He hadn't received any congratulations from the runner-up, the god in their midst, Scott Harper, and didn't expect any. Leopards didn't change their spots. Aged ten when his parents uprooted him from the place he so loved and which incredibly was now his, Clay still had vivid memories of Scott Harper, the golden-haired bully boy, two years his senior. Harper had treated him like trash when he'd never had trouble from the other station boys. For some reason Harper had baited him mercilessly about his parents' marriage whenever they met up. Once Harper had knocked him down in the main street of the town causing a bad concussion for which he'd been hospitalised. His father, wild as hell, had made the long drive in his battered utility to the Harper station to remonstrate with Scott's father, but he had been turned back at gunpoint by Bradley Harper's men.

Clay's taking the Jimboorie Cup from Scott this afternoon was doubly sweet. Soon the surprisingly impressive silver cup would be presented to him by Harper's fiancé. He had been amazed to hear it was Caroline McNevin, whom he remembered as the prettiest little girl he had ever laid eyes on. How had that exquisite little creature grown up to become engaged to someone like Harper? But then wasn't it a tradition for pastoral families to intermarry? His father—once considered destined for great things—had proved the odd man out, struck down by love at first sight. Love for a penniless little Irish girl now buried by his side.

There was a stir in the crowd. Clay turned about to see a woman coming towards him. He drew himself up straighter, absolutely thrown by how beautiful Caroline had become. Her whole aura suggested springtime, a world of flowers. Her petite figure absorbed all the sunlight around her.

She seemed to *float* rather than walk. For a moment an overwhelming emotion swept over him. To combat it, he stood very, very still. He wondered if it were nostalgia; remembrance of some lovely moment when he was a boy. The hillsides around Jimboorie alight with golden wattle, perhaps?

Now they were face-to-face, less than a metre apart, and he like a fool stood transfixed. He was conscious his nerves had tensed and his stomach muscles had tightened into a hard knot. She was *tiny* compared to him. Even in her high heels she only came up to his heart. She still had that look of shining innocence, only now it was allied to an adult allure all the more potent since both qualities appeared to exist quite naturally side by side.

He couldn't seem to take his eyes off her while she consolidated her hold over him.

Caroline had beautiful large oval eyes, a deep velvety-brown. They were doubly arresting with her golden hair. Her skin, a tawny olive beneath the big picture hat, was flawlessly beautiful. Her features were delicate, perfectly symmetrical. No more than five-three, she nevertheless had a real presence. At least she was running tight circles around him.

'James Cunningham!' The vision smiled at him. A smile that damn near broke his heart. What the heck was the matter with him? How could he describe what he felt? Perhaps they had meant something to each other in another life? 'Welcome back to Jimboorie. I'm Carrie McNevin.'

Belatedly he came back to control. 'I remember you, Caroline,' he said, his voice steady, unhurried, yet he was so broad-sided by her beauty, he forgot to smile.

'You *can't*!' A soft flush rose to her cheeks.

'I do.' He shrugged his shoulder, thinking beautiful women had unbounded power at their pink fingertips. 'I remember you as the happy little girl who used to wave to me when you saw me in town.'

'Really?' She was enchanted by the idea.

'Yes, really.'

Her essential sweetness enfolded him. Her voice was clear and gentle, beautifully enunciated. Caroline McNevin, the little princess. Untouchable. Except now by Harper. That made him hot and angry, inducing feelings that hit him with the force of a breaker.

'Well, it's my great pleasure, James, or do you prefer to be called Clay?' She paused, tipping her golden head to one side.

'Clay will do.' Only his mother had ever called him James. Now he remembered to smile though his expression remained serious even a little sombre. Why wouldn't he when he felt appallingly vulnerable in the face of a beautiful creature who barely came up to his heart?

Carrie was aware of the sombreness in him. It added to the impression he gave of quiet power and it had to be admitted, mystery. 'Then it's going to be my great pleasure to be able to present you, Clay, with the Jimboorie Cup,' Carrie continued. 'We'll just move back over there,' she said, turning to lead the way to a small dais where the race committee was grouped, waiting for her and the winner of the Cup to join them. 'They'll want to take photos,' she told him, herself oddly shaken by their meeting. And the feeling wasn't passing off. Perhaps it was because she'd heard so many stories about the Cunninghams while she was growing up? Or maybe it was because Clay Cunningham had grown into a strikingly attractive man. She felt that attraction brush over her then without her being able to do a thing about it. She felt it sink into her skin. She only hoped she wasn't showing her strong reactions. Everyone was looking at them.

Natasha might well continue to denounce her cousin, Carrie thought, but the family resemblance was strong. The Cunninghams were a handsome lot, raven haired, with bright blue eyes. Natasha would have been beautiful, but her fine features were marred by inner discontent and her eyes were strangely cold. Clay Cunningham had the Cunningham height and rangy build— only his hair wasn't black. It was a rich mahogany with a flame of dark auburn as the sun burnished it. His eyes, the burning blue of an Outback sky, were really beautiful, full of depth and sparkle. He looked like a *real* man. A man women would fall for hook, line and sinker. So why wasn't he married already, or actively looking for a wife? If indeed the rumour were true. Something she was beginning to doubt. He had to be four, maybe five years older than she, which made him around twenty-eight. He was a different kind of man from Scott. She sensed a depth, a sensitivity—whatever it was—in him that Scott lacked.

It had to be an effect of the light but there seemed to be sparkles in the space between them. Carrie never dreamed a near-stranger could have this effect on her. Her main concern was to conceal it. Up until now she had felt *safe*. She was going to marry Scott, the man she was in love with—yet Clay Cunningham's blue gaze had reached forbidden places.

Their hands touched as she handed over the Silver Cup to the accompanying waves of applause. She couldn't move, even *think* for a few seconds. She felt a little jolt of electricity through every pore of her skin. He continued to hold her eyes, his own unfaltering. Had her trembling transferred itself to him like a vibration? She hoped not. She wasn't permitted to feel like this.

Yet sparkles continued to pulsate before her eyes. Perhaps she was mildly sun-struck? She had the unnerving notion that the little frisson of shock—unlike anything she had ever experi-

enced before—was mutual. She even wondered what life might
have in store if he decided to remain on Jimboorie? All around
her people were laughing and clapping. Some were carrying col-
ourful balloons. The thrill of the race had got to her. That was it!
Her course was set. She was a happily engaged woman. She was
to marry Scott Harper in December. A Christmas bride.

And there was Scott staring right at her. Too late she became
aware of him. She felt the chill behind his smile. She knew him
so well she had no difficulty recognising it. It came towards her
like an ice-bearing cloud. He was furious and doing a wonderful job of hiding it. A triumphant looking Natasha was by his side,
the two of them striking a near identical pose; one full of an over-
bearing self-confidence. Maybe arrogance was a better word.
Scott as Bradley Harper's heir certainly liked to flaunt it.
Natasha, as a Cunningham, did too.

Now Scott sauntered towards the dais around which the VIPs
of the vast district milled, calling in a taunting voice, 'You'll absolutely have to tell us, *Jimmy,* where you learned how to ride
like that? And the name of the guy who loaned you his horse. Or
did you steal it?' He held up defensive hands. 'Only joking!'

As a joke it was way off, but Clay Cunningham held his
ground, quite unmoved. 'You haven't changed one little bit, have
you, Harper?' he said with unruffled calm. 'Lightning Boy was
a parting gift from a good friend of mine. A beauty, isn't he? He
could run the race over.'

'Like to give it another go?' Scott challenged with an open
lick of hostility.

'Any time—when *your* horse is less spent.' Clay Cunningham
gently waved the silver cup aloft to another roar of applause.

Bruce McNevin, a concerned observer to all this, fearing a
confrontation, moved quickly onto the dais to address the crowd.
Even youngsters draped over the railings managed to fall silent.
They were used to hearing from Mr. McNevin who was to say a

few words then hand over the prize money of $20,000 dollars, well above the reward offered by other bush committees.

Her father was a handsome man, Carrie thought proudly. A man in his prime. He had a full head of dark hair, good regular features, a bony Celtic nose, a strong clean jawline and well defined cheekbones. He was always immaculately if very conservatively dressed. Bruce McNevin was definitely a 'tweedy' man.

While her father spoke Carrie stood not altogether happily within the half circle of Scott's distinctly proprietorial arm. She was acutely aware of the anger and dented pride he was fighting to hold in. Scott wasn't a good loser. Carrie didn't know why but it was apparent he had taken an active dislike to Clay Cunningham.

Now Clay Cunningham, cheque in hand, made a response to her father that proved such a mix of modesty, confidence and dry humour that time and again his little speech was punctuated by appreciative bursts of laughter and applause. The crowd was still excited and the winner's speech couldn't have been more designed to please. The race goers had come to witness a good race and the Cup winner—a newcomer—had well and truly delivered. Not that anyone could really call him a newcomer. Heavens, he was a Cunningham! Cunningham was a name everyone knew. There was even a chance he might be able to save what was left of that once proud historic station, Jimboorie, though it would take a Herculean effort and a bottomless well of money.

'Who the hell does he think he is?' Scott muttered in Carrie's ear, unable to credit the man 'little Jimmy' Cunningham, the urchin, had become. 'And what's with the posh voice?'

'He *is* a Cunningham, Scott,' Carrie felt obliged to point out. 'It's written all over him. And it may very well be he *did* get a good education.'

Scott snorted like an angry bull. 'His father left here without a dime. Everyone knows that. Angus Cunningham might have sheltered them to spite the rest of his family but he couldn't have

vengeance. She already knew about Scott's jealous nature, but usually he kept it under control. Scott actually disliked even his own friends smiling at her let alone attempting a playful flirtation. It was a terrifying thought he might have intuited her spontaneous reaction to the man Clay Cunningham had grown into. She realised, too, with a guilty pang ever since Clay had told her she used to wave to him in the town when she was a little girl, she had been trying very hard to evoke a forgotten memory.

Goodness, what's the matter with me? she asked her reflection. She was usually very level-headed. She even felt an impulse to start praying the evening would go well. Glancing up at the silver framed wall clock she saw it was almost eight. She really should be on her way. Scott was going to meet her in the foyer It was only a short walk from Dougherty's pub where she was staying to the new Community Hall. The band had been underway for at least an hour, the infectious toe tapping music spilling out onto the street. The band was good. Her mother had arranged for the musicians to come from Brisbane. She started to sing along a little, trying to lift her spirits.

A final check in the mirror. Turning her head from side to side, she saw the sparkling light of her hair combs, one of innumerable little presents from her mother. Her parents were staying overnight with friends. She had elected to stay with Vince and Katie at the pub, as they always looked after her. The pub was spotlessly clean, the food not fancy, but good. She stayed there overnight when she was working for Paddy at the *Bulletin.* It was preferable to making the long drive home, then back again the following morning. Victory Downs was over a hundred miles west of the town—no distance in the bush—but she had to multiply that by four when she worked in town as she mostly did, two days in a row.

She had her silver sandalled foot on the second bottom tread of the staircase when Scott, wearing a white dinner jacket, and looking dazzlingly handsome, swung through the front doors.

'Hiyah, beautiful!' His blue eyes travelled over her with pride of possession. 'I *am* impressed!'

The overhead light glinted on his smooth golden hair and the white of his smile. If they had children—she wanted three, four was okay—they were bound to have golden hair, Carrie thought, holding out her hands to him.

'There's not going to be anyone to touch you!' Scott continued to eye her, appreciatively. She looked as good to eat as a bowl of vanilla ice cream. He'd had a lot of girls over the years but Carrie was unique.

'You look great yourself!' she told him, sincerity in her velvety eyes.

'All for you.' He'd had a few drinks: now, he badly wanted pull her into his arms. He wanted to race her back upstairs, strip that pretty white dress off her, throw her down on the bed and make violent love to her. Only he was afraid of what might happen. Carrie, by his reckoning, had to be the last virgin over fifteen left on the planet. If that weren't astonishing enough, she wanted it to remain that way until they were married. Could you beat it! He would *never* have agreed, only he saw her resolve was very strong. Or maybe she was playing it smart, teasing the living daylights out of him. She was his fiancée yet he had to keep his hands off her. Well, within limits. It was excruciatingly frustrating—more torture—when she filled him with such lust as he had ever known. Not that he had taken a corresponding vow of celibacy. He got release when he wanted it. Most girls were his for the asking including that bitch Natasha Cunningham. He'd had an on and off relationship with her for years. She was mad for him—and he knew it.

But it was innocent little Caroline McNevin he had always wanted. He guessed he had started to want her from when she was a yummy little teenager with budding breasts. He'd confidently thought virginity was a relic of the Dark Ages. He'd been stunned when Carrie told him she wanted to remain a virgin until their wedding night. At first he'd been sure it was a damned ploy to keep him interested, on a knife's edge. As a ploy it certainly worked, but then he came to realise she was fair dinkum. It was impossible to believe! But, boy, wouldn't he make up for the long hungry years of deprivation! Their wedding night couldn't come soon enough.

They had scarcely made it into the packed hall with huge silver-blue disco balls suspended from the ceiling like glittering moons, when Scott's grip on her arm tightened. Carrie let out a surprised little whimper. 'Hey, Scott, you're hurting!'

'Sorry.' He shifted his arm to around her waist, hauling her close to him. 'That bastard has had the nerve to show up,' he ground out, his eyes quickly finding Clay Cunningham's rangy figure across the room.

So it wasn't going to be a happy evening! Carrie's heart began to thump. She lifted her eyes to Scott's tight face. 'Scott, please settle down. We're here to enjoy ourselves aren't we? Everybody will be watching. Clay Cunningham has a perfect right to be here. I expect there would be a lot of disappointed girls if he hadn't shown up. Surely you're not looking for trouble?'

'He'd do well to steer clear of me,' Scott gritted, unable to conceal a flare of jealousy so monstrous it startled even him. He tried to calm himself by sheer will power. So far as he was concerned it was Cunningham versus *him!* Across the packed hall Cunningham was standing head and shoulders above a group of silly giggling females. One let out a burst of ecstatic laughter, obviously thrilled there was an eligible bachelor in their midst. A man, moreover, who had expressed his desire to find himself a wife. Hadn't they heard, the little fools, Jimboorie House was falling down? Didn't they know Jimboorie Station would never be what it was again? Or would any man do? Girls fell in and out of love so fast. They were like kids with some wonderful new toy.

All right, Cunningham was handsome. Scott was honest enough to admit that. All the Cunninghams were. Even Natasha. And Cunningham had that look about him, he recognised, of a fine natural athlete. How had that little weed of a kid who he'd loved slapping around turned into this guy? Scott wasn't even sure he could take Cunningham in a fight, even though he was a good amateur boxer, a welterweight champion at university. The fact Cunningham had beaten him for the Cup Scott took as a scalding defeat. And he'd been beaten so *easily!* That was what stunned and humiliated him. He was used to being king pin. To cap it off his fiancée had presented Cunningham with the Cup. He'd watched their eyes, then their hands meet. It had only taken him a second to register the look on Carrie's face. It had filled him with jealousy and unease.

Cunningham had stirred her interest and attention. That wasn't going to be allowed to happen. Carrie was *his*! He owned her. Or near enough. She was wearing his ring.

I mightn't be able to stop you looking, but don't touch, you bastard! Scott swung Carrie into his arms, whisking her onto the dance floor. At least the music was great. It filled up the room.

After each bracket of numbers, the crowd clapped their appreciation. One of the band, a sexy looking guy in tight jeans, a red satin shirt and cowboy boots, took over the microphone to a roar of applause and began to sing, launching into the first romantic ballad of the night; one that was currently top of the charts. His voice was so attractive the dancers gave themselves up to it….

Carrie didn't have the usual succession of dance partners she'd had in the past. Things had changed since she had become engaged to Scott. She realised she was starting to worry that Scott was so possessive. She wasn't *property*. She was a woman, a human being. The last thing she wanted was a stormy married life with a control freak for a husband. But then her thoughts turned to how understanding Scott was about her desire to remain a virgin until their marriage. It pleased her that he was so considerate of her wishes. She had never been one to bow to peer pressure so she hadn't been part of the general sexual experimentation that had attended her university years. She knew some of her fellow students had labelled her a bit of an extremist, but the idea of sex without genuine strong feeling had little appeal for her. It was *her* body that would be invaded after all. Men came from a different place. Most of them she had found, saw sex as satisfying an appetite like food and drink. At the same time they were notoriously quick to pin cruel labels on their willing female partners. Carrie thought there was not only a moral standard, but a health standard that made fastidiousness matter.

Then again she had to take stock of the fact she had no real conflict with remaining a virgin. There was even the odd moment when she had to consider perhaps she hadn't met the man who could overturn all her defences? Or maybe her libido wasn't of the intense sort? Not that Scott hadn't awakened her romantic desires. He had. She knew about sensual pleasure. But still it had been relatively easy to keep to her vow. Or it had been up until now.

She was momentarily alone. Scott was caught up in settling an argument about some polo match when she heard her name—her *full* name—spoken.

'You dance beautifully, Caroline. Will you dance with me?'

He was standing in front of her, looking down at her from his superior height. The corners of his mouth were upturned in a smile. His dark blue eyes held a current of electricity that bathed her in its glow.

She managed to smile back. It felt like taking a risk. A tremble shook her body. The music…the laughter…the voices…oddly started to recede. She knew her lips parted but for the smallest time—maybe a few seconds—no words came out.

'Caroline?'

The oxygen came back to her brain. 'Yes of course I will,' she said, unaware a nerve was pulsing in the hollow of her throat.

His arms came around her. He held her lightly yet his arms enclosed her. Letting him hold her—she knew—vastly increased the risks.

She couldn't relax. Not there and then. He was, she realised, gifted with sexual radiance and he was using that gift. Consciously or unconsciously? She couldn't tell.

She tried to distract herself by looking at the sea of happy, excited faces around them.

'I know, I'm too tall for you.' Clay's voice was wry. 'And I'm not much of a dancer. Never had time to learn.'

'No, you're fine.' Indeed, it seemed to her he moved with natural ease and rhythm.

'And you're kind.' He pulled her in a little closer and she lifted her hand higher on his shoulder. She could feel the strength in it; the warmth of his skin. He wasn't formally attired like Scott . He wore a beige coloured linen jacket over a black T-shirt and black jeans. A simple outfit, yet on him it looked very sophisticated. He would have absolutely no difficulty finding a wife. In fact, the frenzy had already started. It was her role to watch. Never let it be forgotten she was taken!

She realised she was luxuriating in his clean male scent, redolent of the open air, of fragrant wood smoke. Inhaled, it left her with a feeling akin to a delicious languor. The overhead disco lights dazzled, throwing out blue and silver rays over the swirling crowd, their faces and clothes streaked with light.

For long minutes they danced without speaking, he leading her expertly for all he claimed he couldn't dance. She was beginning to feel a degree of trepidation at the forces set loose by their physical contact. She didn't want it. She certainly didn't need it. She didn't even understand it. Her reaction wasn't *normal*. She couldn't allow herself to think it was akin to being in a state of thrall!

Be careful with this! A warning voice said.

There was a pressure behind Carrie's rib cage. Could he incite emotion as easily as he could incite his high mettled horse to victory? She feared that might be the case. It was even possible he could be looking at *her* as a conquest? Retribution for the way he had been treated? A perverted desire to win over Scott Harper's fiancée? She saw how he had won the Cup. His was a powerful determination and maybe she was next on his list? Only time would prove her right.

Meanwhile he was making her feel decidedly odd. It was as if she were someone else. She couldn't allow that. She had to be herself, yet the feel of his arms around her had deep chords re-sounding within her. His hand on her back could even be playing her like a master musician. What was he really thinking?

'You look very beautiful,' he said. His voice, which was resonant and deep, had considerable emotional power.

Carrie took a quick breath, thinking she wasn't going to give him any help.

'Harper is a lucky man.'

Now she tilted her head to stare into his eyes. 'What went wrong between you two? It seems strange—you were both so young when you moved away, yet I sense a history between you and Scott. An animosity that still clings.'

The flash in his eyes was as blue as an acetate flame. 'Scott Harper used to like to scare me when I was a kid.'

She felt shame on Scott's behalf. 'It still matters?'

He shrugged. 'You saw how your fiancé was. I'm sure he'll be right with us any moment now. Do you mind that most of the guys here, though they're dying to dance with you, are keeping their distance?'

That hit home. 'I *do* realise,' she said, more severely than she had intended, 'but Scott is my fiancé.'

He nodded. 'A pity'

'A pity he's my fiancé?' Now she was really on the defensive.

'How do you know I don't want you for myself?' He unfolded a slow smile, keeping his tone light.

Hectic colour swept into her cheeks, enhancing her beauty. 'I'm sorry, Clay, but I'm taken.'

'Have you set a date for the wedding?' he asked, with interest.

'Why aren't *you* married?' she countered, aware something potentially dangerous was smouldering between them.

'Because I believe a man has to be able to provide for a wife before he embarks on matrimony.'

She realised she was becoming agitated. She had to rein herself in. 'The rumour around town is you're looking for a wife. Could that possibly be right?'

His smile was self mocking. 'You might very well see me on the doorstep of the *Bulletin* some time soon. I understand you're Pat Kennedy's right hand woman. You can help me run an ad. "Bush Bachelor Seeks A Wife!" You could advise me what to say, maybe help me read through what replies come in.'

'You're joking!' She felt an odd anger.

Clay's blue, blue eyes were alight with what? Devilment? A taunt? He was still holding her lightly but she was starting to feel she couldn't breathe.

'I couldn't be more serious,' he replied. 'I want a wife beside me. I want children. I've been so flat-out working all my life, I've had little time to play the courting game. Besides, eligible young women aren't all that easy to find. I thought an ad might work. It would certainly speed things up.'

He was obviously waiting for her response.

It came out soft but tart. 'Why don't you simply walk up to one of the girls here?' Carrie challenged him, wishing she was older, taller, more experienced. As it was she was a little afraid of him.

He wasn't smiling. 'Forgive me, but it's hard to see past you.'

That transfixed her. She, so light on her feet, a lovely dancer, missed a step, nearly causing him to tread on her toe. 'Must I remind you that I'm taken?' she said as though he had broken a strict rule.

'So you are!' His voice was deeply regretful.

What should she do? Walk away? Abandon him on the dance floor? She didn't *want* to. At the same time she knew she had to.

Run, run away! Far from temptation!

'Give yourself plenty of time to make sure it's going to work.' He steered her away from a whirling couple.

'Is that a warning?' This man was deliberately casting a spell on her. To what end?

'I don't see the two of you together,' he said.

'How can you possibly judge?' Despite herself she began to compare him with Scott. It was something she couldn't control. 'You don't know me and you don't know Scott. We have a fine future ahead of us.'

'Why, then, the fright in your eyes? If he's the love of your life?'

There was such a whirring inside her. It was as though some part of her hitherto not properly in working order, suddenly sprang into life. 'Why are we talking like this, Clay? It's getting very personal and private.' Not to say out of order.

'I told you. I don't have much time. Besides, I feel I could talk to you far into the night.'

'You've just told me why.' She pointed out, not without sarcasm. 'You're lonely.'

'It's possible that's part of it,' he agreed smoothly.

Carrie sucked in her breath; waited a moment. 'I must tell you I wouldn't have agreed to marry Scott if I didn't love him.' Now her voice sounded stilted.

'As I said, Harper is a very lucky man.'

This was too much. Just *too* much. She couldn't play this game if that's what it was. Dancing with him wasn't the same as dancing with Scott. Or any other man for that matter. She could feel the blood beating in her throat, in her breasts, in the pit of her stomach. She had never been so breathtakingly conscious of her own *flesh*.

The same tipsy couple almost careened into them. Clay's arm tightened around her as he swiftly drew her out of harm's way.

She knew it was well past the time to break away, but she made the excuse to herself that would only draw attention to them. So change the subject quickly! 'You're not planning to leave, then?'

'Caroline, I've just arrived,' he replied, mock-plaintively.

'Everyone calls me Carrie.' She spoke as if to correct him when in reality the sound of her name on his lips was like a bell tolling inside her.

'I'm not everyone,' he said quietly. 'Carrie is pretty. Caroline suits you better.'

'What if I say I want you to call me Carrie?'

'All right, Carrie.' He smiled. 'I'll call you Caroline whenever I get the chance.'

It was totally unnerving how dramatically he was getting to her. 'I used to think when I was little that Jimboorie House was a palace.'

'So did I.' Again his glance like blue flame rested on her.

'You have more than a trace of an English accent. Where did that come from?'

He looked over her blond head. 'From my mother I guess. She was Anglo-Irish and well spoken—and lovely. My father's appallingly cruel family had no right to treat her the way they did. They turned all their fury on *her* because my father abandoned them for her. The accent would have been reinforced by long contact with my late mentor who was English. I became very close to him.'

'Was he the one who presented you with Lightning Boy?' She wanted to know all about him.

He nodded. 'Yes, he was. He handed Lightning Boy over a couple of months before he died.'

She read the grief in his glance. 'What did you do? Did you work for him?'

'I was proud to,' he said briefly, his tone a little curt. 'My boss and mentor.'

'Are you going to tell me his name?'

'No, Caroline.' He refused her. At the same time his gaze gathered her up.

'I'm sorry.' She glanced across the dance floor at all the glowing, happy faces. This would go on into the wee hours. 'I won't intrude. I'm just glad you met someone who treated you well.'

'I can't recall many others.' His expression was openly bitter.

'Are you going to make us all pay for wounding you?' she asked, thinking he had been hurt a great deal.

He ignored her question. 'I'd like to take you out to Jimboorie. Would you come?'

Her heart jumped. Agree and there'd be trouble. *Big* trouble.

'Look at me,' he invited quietly. 'Not away. Would you come, Caroline?'

A back-up singer in the band launched into a romantic number. 'How do you see me?' she countered. 'As someone whose freedom is being curtailed?'

'Is it?' He studied her so intently he might have been trying to unmask her.

That put her on her mettle. 'I'd be delighted to come,' she said shortly, consoling herself she had been driven to it.

'Good. I confess I find a woman's views necessary.'

'Is it your intention to put in your ad that Jimboorie House is falling down?' She met his eyes.

'Certainly. It's the right thing to do,' he replied smoothly.

'But it's not in the utter state of decay it appears to be from the outside. The best materials were used in its construction. The finest, stoutest timbers. The cedar came from the vast forests of the Bunya Bunya Mountains. The house itself is built of sandstone. There *is* a tremendous amount of restoration to be done—I can't deny that—but somehow I'll get around it.'

'Perhaps you should say in your ad that you're looking for an heiress?' she suggested, bitter-sweet.

'Now that's a great idea.' His face broke into a mocking smile.

Unnoticed by either of them Scott Harper, who had been further detained by two of his father's friends wanting to know if he thought his team could continue their unbeaten polo season, was quickly canvassing the crowd.

The blood flooded into his face the moment he saw them together. He drew in his breath sharply, catching his bottom lip between strong teeth and drawing blood. How could Carrie possibly do this thing? She knew how he felt about Clay Cunningham. All his childhood antipathy had returned but one hundred times worse. He made his way towards them, threading a path through the dancers, some of them, marking his expression, getting out of his way.

Just look at her, Scott inwardly raged, his jealousy violent and painful. Her beautiful blond head was tipped right back as she stared up into Cunningham's eyes.

This is wrong, all wrong. Let her go!

His progress was stopped when a woman got him in a surprisingly strong arm-lock. 'Scotty, you're not ignoring me are you, darling?'

He swung, catching the hateful expression of malice on Natasha's face. 'You can't let your dewy little fiancée have a bit of fun, can you?' Her voice dropped so low he could barely hear her. 'And she *is* having fun, isn't she?'

'Let go, Natasha,' he rasped. If she'd been a man he would have hit her, so tense was his mood.

'Sure. One dance and we'll call it a night.' She stepped right up to him, a stunning figure in violet banded in silver, putting both hands on his shoulders. 'Don't make a fool of me now, Scotty,' she warned. 'I've kept my mouth shut up to now, but things can change.'

'You're a real bitch! You know that?' he muttered, contempt built into his voice. Nevertheless he retained enough sense to draw her into his arms.

'You don't say that when I'm making you happy.' Natasha, a tall woman, stared with hard challenge into his eyes.

'I should never have started with you,' he said.

A shadow fell across her blue eyes. 'You told me once you were in love with me. I'm still in love with you.'

'Why don't you get over it?' he suggested harshly.

'Easier said than done, Scotty. Don't get mad at me. I'm your friend. I've loved you far too much and far too long. You've made a big mistake getting yourself hitched up to Carrie McNevin. You haven't got a damned thing in common. And how ridiculous is that virgin bit?' Her lips curled in a sneer.

'Shut up,' Scott hissed violently, in the next minute thankful the dance music had changed to something loud and upbeat. Why had he ever told Natasha about Carrie and himself? He was a thousand times sorry.

'Watch it!' she warned, an answering rage in her eyes. 'You don't want people to see how jealous you are my cousin is fascinating your beloved little virgin. I have to admit he scrubs up pretty well. That's the Cunningham in him, of course. Why don't we sit this out for a while? Or we could go outside?'

'Forget it,' he said bluntly.

Her expression was both wounded and affronted. 'What is it she's got? I'm beautiful, too. Is it the hunt? The thrill of the chase? Once you've had her you won't want her anymore.'

'You don't understand *anything,*' Scott said, shaking his head as if to clear it. 'Carrie appeals to the best part of me. When I'm with her I remember I have a soul.'

That affected Natasha more than the cruellest rebuff. 'You fool!' she said.

Scott gave up. In the middle of the dance floor he dropped his arms from around her and walked away, leaving Natasha feeling hollowed out, gutted. Why did she love Scott Harper? It dismayed and humiliated her. She was well aware of his character flaws, which that little innocent Carrie wasn't. Living through this engagement was a long nightmare. She knew Scott had used her up—she had let him, was still letting him—but damn if he was going to throw her away. Maybe it was about time she had a little talk with darling Carrie even if she risked having her own life torn apart.

Carrie danced twice more with Clay Cunningham. It was driving Scott crazy, but he couldn't seem to do a damn thing about it. Cunningham set the pace. Other guys lined up to dance with her. He was drinking too much and he knew it. Alcohol was flowing like water from a bubbling fountain. His mind swirled with crazy thoughts.

Get Carrie on her own.

She had denied him for far too long. They were engaged now. It was his right to have her whether with her consent or not. In his experience girls said *no* all the time when what they really meant was *yes, yes, yes!* He could have any girl he wanted. Natasha Cunningham. Why did he want Carrie so desperately? There was even a strong chance she didn't go for sex. That would be a disaster. Sex was as essential for him as breathing air.

It didn't take him long to come up with an idea. He could tell her he had something for her in the SUV. A little present. Women loved being given presents, though to be honest, Carrie was no gold digger. But couldn't she feel his pain, his desire? No, she was oblivious to everything except remaining a *virgin.* Scott's anger turned ugly, a red mist swirling before his eyes. He remembered the expression on her face as she'd looked up at Cunningham. What *was* it exactly? Curiosity, a deep interest? More than that. A *craving* for something she had never had. Scott only knew she had never turned such a gaze on him. His face darkened.

Finally he had her to himself. They crossed the street with Scott holding her firmly by the arm. 'No, I won't tell you. It's a surprise!' he said in a playful voice he dredged up from somewhere.

She turned to him, puzzled. 'Why did you leave it in the car, Scott? Is it big?' She laughed a little although she was uneasy, concerned Scott had had far too much to drink. Not that he was the only one. The whole hall was filled with tipsy people, singing, dancing, chanting, full of high spirits that would last through until dawn. She couldn't worry about them but she was afraid Scott might make something of a spectacle of himself with his father around. Bradley Harper just wouldn't understand. Usually Scott held his drink well, but tonight was different. He was slurring his words. He never did that.

It was dark under the shadow of the trees that ringed the town park. The gums were smothered in blossom. There was a lovely lemony scent in the air. A little way in the distance she could see couples strolling arm in arm through the park, their bodies spotlighted by the overhead lighting. Others had moved off to cars either to catch a nap or indulge in a spot of canoodling. The big question was, why didn't she want Scott to make love to her? Saying he'd had too much to drink wasn't answer enough. She was going to marry him in three months time. My God, she should be ravenous for his lovemaking. She was so perturbed tears sprang to her eyes.

'Let's sit in the back for a moment,' Scott said, opening up the rear door and all but pushing her in.

'I don't know,' she wavered. 'We shouldn't stay.'

'You're not a bit of fun, are you?' Scott climbed in beside her, turning to her and cupping her face hard with his hand.

'What's the matter with you, Scott?' She shook her head vigorously to free his grip. 'You're in a mood.' It couldn't have been more obvious now.

'Thanks to you,' he said bitterly, abandoning all pretence.

'I've no idea what you mean!' She tried to defend herself. 'Where's the present?' She couldn't have cared less about any present. She just wanted this over.

'What do you know?' he laughed. 'I forgot to bring it with me.'

'Ah, Scott!' She tried hard to fight down her dismay.

'You don't want to be here with me, do you?' he accused her, his hot temper rising.

'Not when you're making me nervous,' she answered truthfully.

'Kiss me.' His voice grated harshly.

She could smell his damp breath, heavy with bourbon. She tried to draw away. 'We have all the time in the world for kisses. Not *here*, Scott. Our parents expect us to set a certain standard.'

'Damn them!' he said violently, getting his arms around her. 'You tell me you're a virgin, but I'm worried you're *not!* You females are full of wiles.'

He sounded terrible, hardly recognisable. A different Scott from the one she knew.

'I refuse to have this discussion now, Scott,' she said quietly, though she was starting to shake inside. 'Let's go back to the hall. Please.'

'Why don't I find out right here and now?' he responded, making his intentions very clear.

She hit him then, a cold spasm of dread causing a real ache in her stomach. It was absolutely spontaneous, her cracking slap to the side of his head. 'I don't lie, understand?' she panted. 'I demand respect from you, Scott!'

He gripped her delicate shoulders, all male force and threat. 'Now isn't that the strangest thing of all! Little Carrie McNevin attacking me.' With a grinding laugh he hauled her to him, hard and tight, crushing her body against him. 'You're *mine,* Carrie. You better believe it. I'm sick to death of holding off. Can't you feel me.' He forced her hand down to his powerful erection. 'I'm mad for you! What is making love anyway, a big mortal sin?'

He cranked up his offensive. He was half on top of her, shoving his tongue deeper and deeper into her mouth. Carrie almost gagged.

'Now we're talking!' he crowed in triumph, his hand buried in the front of her dress, his fingers clamping on to her breast. 'You're the freshest, sweetest girl in the world,' he grunted. 'You made me a promise, Carrie. You accepted my ring. Now accept *me!*'

Quick as a striking snake his other hand was under her skirt, while he rammed her body back into the seat.

'Stop, Scott. *Please.*' She was forced to beg, but she was damned if she was going to scream.

'Relax, you're going to love this.' His hungry hand was at the top of her panties.

'Dammit, I said *stop!*' Carrie cried, cursing her own stupidity. She was frightened of his brute strength. Drunk or not, he was physically in control. Even his weight was relentless. She could never get clear of him.

It was time to think, not give in. The day hadn't arrived when she was going to lie back and take it. Not like *this* anyway. This wasn't love. This was catastrophe. Rape. She let her body go slack, seemingly quiescent, as his hand plunged between her legs. He was moaning now. Moaning with a kind of fierce animal pleasure, primal in its mindlessness.

It was now or never. Carrie gathered herself, fiercely ignoring that his hand was going where it had never gone before. There wasn't much of her but she was fit. And she was an expert horse-woman with strong legs and knees. She waited her moment then when his fingers were about to thrust into her, she rammed one of her knees hard into his sensitive scrotum.

He *howled*! He actually howled! The sound was wild and appalled. Sexual passion turned to a stunned rage. 'God, you bitch!' He lifted a hand to hit her, only the contempt in her voice stopped him in his tracks.

'Don't hit me, Scott. Don't even attempt to go there.'

'You bitch!' he repeated, thinking she needed teaching a lesson. Some part of him was ashamed, the rest was in a whole lot of pain. He let out another moan, rolling across the seat away from her and hunching over, clutching his throbbing parts.

With a dazzling turn of speed Carrie was out of the SUV and on to the grass. Anger burned inside her. She tried desperately to straighten her clothing. What motivated men to behave the way they did? It was a very big question that had never been answered.

A voice called sharply from the other side of the street. 'You all right, Caroline?'

She could have died from humiliation. Clay Cunningham. This was a nightmare. What was she supposed to do, wave? Call out her fine handsome fiancée had just tried to rape her? 'I'm okay. It's nothing,' she answered, her mouth so dry she could barely form the words.

Clay didn't seem too impressed with that. He strode across the street, moving towards the parked vehicle. He watched in disgust as Scott Harper, holding his crotch staggered out of it. 'Mind your own bloody business, Cunningham,' Scott gritted, his voice full of hate and loathing.

'Sorry.' Clay Cunningham had made the transformation from Mr. Nice Guy to one tough looking character, powerfully intimidating. 'I'm not the kind of guy who walks away from a lady in distress. Come over here, Caroline,' he instructed.

'Don't do a damn thing he asks you,' Scott snarled her a warning.

That really bugged her. She responded by running around the front of the vehicle, clearly making her choice. When she was on her own maybe she'd have a good howl herself, but for now she had to get away from Scott. At least until he came to his senses. That she was running to Clay Cunningham was just one of life's great ironies.

'You've torn your dress,' he said, his eyes moving swiftly over her. The light from the street lamp revealed to him the stress on her delicate face. The bodice of her gown had fallen so low it disclosed the rising curves of her lovely high breasts. One of the thin straps that held it was ripped, the other fell off her shoulder. He watched her straightening it.

'I'll get her another one,' Scott lurched towards them, ready and willing to do battle. 'Why don't you get the hell away from here, Cunningham? Do you really think you're capable of stealing *my* fiancée?'

'Where do you want to go, Caroline?' Clay asked, ignoring Scott.

'I can't go back into the hall,' she said, fighting down her humiliation. She had lost one of her hair combs. She couldn't retrieve it. Not now. It would have to stay in the SUV. 'You can walk me back to the hotel if you would. I'm calling it a night.'

'Don't go, Carrie,' Scott called to her with great urgency. 'Let's start remembering *I'm* your fiancé.'

'I thought that meant I could trust you, Scott,' she retorted, as though he were beneath contempt. 'I don't want to talk about this.'

'If you walk off with *him* our engagement's finished! That's right, finished!' he shouted, as if she were about to make the worst mistake of her life.

'Then let's get it over with!' Carrie didn't go to pieces—

though she felt like it. She tugged at the diamond solitaire on her finger, then when it was off, she threw it directly at him. 'You might like to give this to Natasha. She's got a reputation for making out in cars.'

My God! For a shocked moment Scott went cold. Did Carrie *know* about him and Natasha? 'Hey, come on,' he cajoled, trying to get a grip on himself. 'Natasha means nothing to me.'

When did you find out? he wondered, but didn't dare ask.

Carrie, however, still had no idea of the secret liaison between Scott and Natasha that continued right into their engagement.

'Be careful you don't stomp on the ring,' she warned. 'It will do another turn. Good night, Scott.'

'Carrie, don't go!' He reverted to pleading as she and Cunningham began to move off. 'I love you. I've had so much to drink.'

Clay Cunningham intervened. 'There's no need for everyone to know, Harper. Keep your voice down.'

'You talkin' to *me*?' Still hurting, Scott made a maddened charge forwards, full of bravado, fists flying, ready to show Cunningham a thing or two. His mind inevitably flew back to the way he had knocked Cunningham down when they were kids. He could take him now. Cunningham was a good three inches taller, but he was heavier and he'd had years of training.

'Oh for God's sake, no!' Carrie was fearful they would soon have an audience ready to cheer a fight on. She couldn't help knowing some people would enjoy seeing Golden Boy Harper get a thrashing.

Only Clay Cunningham didn't want any fight. He threw out a defensive arm to block Scott's vicious punch. At the same time he threw a single punch of his own. It landed squarely on the point of Scott's jaw as he knew it would. Scott staggered back in astonishment, trying desperately to recover from the effects of that blow. Only his legs buckled, then went out from under him as he fell to the grass groaning afresh.

'You've hurt him,' Carrie said, in a sad and sorry voice, but not feeling encouraged to go to her ex-fiancé.

'He'll live,' Clay assured her in a clipped voice. 'The fight's over. Let's get out of here, Caroline, before we draw a crowd.'

This was a turning point for Carrie. Her life could go in one of two directions. With Scott. Or without him.

CHAPTER THREE

'SO WHAT exactly happened?' It was ten o'clock the next morning. Carrie and her mother were sitting in a quiet corner of the pub having coffee which Katie had served with some freshly baked pastries.

'I don't want to go into it, Mamma,' Carrie said carefully.

'But darling, I need to know.' Alicia leaned forward across the bench table. 'One moment you were there, the belle of the ball. Next time I looked you and Scott were gone. Did you have an argument? I wouldn't be surprised if you did. Scott has a jealous streak and you did appear to be enjoying yourself with Clay Cunningham, who incidentally, is an extraordinarily attractive young man with a strong look of his father. He disappeared as well and he didn't come back.'

'Scott and I did have a few words,' Carrie confided, unwilling to upset her mother.

Alicia frowned slightly. 'Scott's hopelessly in love with you, darling. You *are* putting him under quite a bit of pressure.'

'Are you suggesting I sleep with him, Mamma?'

Alicia glanced away. 'Who would blame you if you had that in mind? You *are* engaged. You're to be married in December.'

'So I should feel free to jump into bed? Or rather Scott should feel free to force me into sex?' Carrie took several hot, angry breaths.

'Gracious, darling, that's not what he tried to do?' Alicia looked extremely dismayed. 'Everything has been going so very well.'

Carrie began to spoon the chocolate off her coffee. 'He was drunk, Mamma. I've never seen him like that before. Losing to Clay Cunningham set him off.'

'That's one of his little failings,' Alicia said, thanking God it wasn't a whole lot worse. 'Scott's a bad loser.'

'I don't know that we should count that as a *little* failing,' Carrie said. 'In many ways Scott has been spoiled rotten. His mother idolises him—'

'Heavens, she couldn't love him more than your father and I love you.' Alicia looked at her daughter dotingly.

'Does Dad love me?' Carrie asked bleakly. *Lord, did I really say that!* 'I'd really like to know. He *wants* to love me, he tries hard to love me but it seems to place too much of a burden on him.'

'Sweetheart, you shock me. Please don't talk like that.' Alicia's beautiful eyes filled with tears. 'Your father is a very reserved man. You know that. He doesn't know how to be demonstrative. You have to take it into account.'

'I assure you I have done. For years.' Carrie couldn't let go of the mountain of pain that was inside. 'Why did you marry him? You're very different people.'

Alicia laughed shakily. 'I suppose we are.' She didn't attempt to deny it. 'But we were very much in love.'

'Well, that's good to hear. Actually Dad loves you to death! He tolerates me, because I look like you.'

Alicia's dark eyes grew wide with shock. She bowed her graceful head. 'Carrie, you're upsetting me, darling.'

'That's certainly not my intention,' Carrie reached out to take her mother's hand. 'There couldn't be many fathers who would bypass their only child—a lowly daughter—for their nephew who's nowhere near as smart as I am, could there? Alex would be the first to admit it. I'm not even sure he *wants* Victory Downs.'

Alicia's voice was heavy with irony. 'He will when he's old enough. I console myself you don't need it darling. You're going to marry Scott. You will be so well looked after. His will be a splendid inheritance.'

'*His* inheritance, not mine, Mamma,' Carrie pointed out. 'Even the Japanese government is driven to pass a law to allow the little princess to become Empress in due course.'

'And so she should!' Alicia said emphatically, when she had to all intents and purposes given up the fight to have Carrie inherit the McNevin station. 'Now regards Scott. Give him time to apologise for his less than acceptable behaviour last night. I know he will. He's mad about you, Carrie.'

'Why exactly?' Carrie asked, staring at her mother, waiting for her answer. 'It's becoming as much a mystery to me as you and Dad. Scott worked very hard to sweep me off my feet. He was determined to and he succeeded. You welcomed him as a prospective son-in-law, so did Dad. At long last I'm in Dad's good books. He's been much more relaxed with me since the engagement, hasn't he? I pleased him, made him proud. It was a good feeling. For a while.'

Alicia's hand on her coffee cup was shaking. 'Don't make any hasty decisions you might come to regret,' she warned. 'A devil gets into the best of men from time to time.'

'You sound like you know what you're talking about. Actually you sound like you led a secret life, Mamma,' Carrie said, surprised to see her mother's cheeks fill with warm colour. It was so unlike her to blush.

'My past is an open book,' Alicia declared, spreading her hands. 'I can't say I came to my marriage a virgin. You could teach me a thing or two about abstinence, my darling, but I only had one lover—before your father. When I finally got out of a Catholic boarding school there was no stopping me. I was ravishing in those days. All the boys were in love with me.'

'I bet!' The number of men who had fallen in love with her

mother was legendary, but Alicia had never been known to have affairs. That would have killed the husband who worshipped her. 'You know you're a dark horse, Mamma,' Carrie said simply. 'Who was he?' It occurred to her, her mother might have a whole host of secrets hidden away.

Alicia put her hands together as if in prayer. 'Good gracious, darling, I'm sorry I mentioned it. No one had what your father had to offer.'

'And what was that exactly? A well-respected name? Money? A historic sheep station?' Carrie asked. She couldn't say it—she didn't even want to think it—but her father could be a very boring man, given to the silent treatment.

'Not to be sneezed at,' Alicia said briskly. 'There are more important considerations than romantic love in marriage. Love is a madness anyway. And so short-lived! There's no such thing as eternal passion I'm afraid, my darling. Any fool can fall in love. It takes time and hard work to grow a successful marriage. It is a bit like gardening. Putting down good strong roots. Your father and I mightn't appear as demonstrative as other couples but we understand one another. We'll stay together.'

There had to be something about her parents' relationship she couldn't see. 'Can you imagine life without him?' Carrie asked, knowing however much she looked like her mother she had an entirely different temperament and approach to life. Where did that come from? she wondered, certainly not her father.

'What a question! This coffee is a bit strong and it's going cold. Look out for Katie. We'll order more. Your father is in splendid health. So am I.'

But Carrie persisted. 'Did Dad ever make you feel breathless with excitement? Under a spell?' There was something in her mother's eyes that was troubling her. 'Did he ever make you feel you could do something utterly rash? Be powerless to stop yourself?'

'Please…please, Carrie.' Alicia clutched the table as if the whole world had started to spin. 'The emotions you're describing can cause a lot of pain. Even ruin lives that were once full of promise. You're in a very unsettled mood aren't you, my darling girl?' she asked, worried Carrie might be thinking of calling the engagement off.

Carrie began to confirm her worst fears. 'I don't think I want to marry Scott and leave you behind,' Carrie said, staring back at her beautifully groomed mother who always looked that way. 'I've had the feeling recently he'd like to chop me off from my family. He wants me all to himself.'

Alicia stifled a deep sigh. 'And who could blame him! But that first hectic flush will pass. Your father and I will be very much in the picture. Count on it. We're looking forwards to becoming doting grandparents.'

Carrie's voice was shaky, her small face tense. 'I feel differently about Scott today,' she said, thinking of his hard, hurting hands on her body.

Concern flew into Alicia's face. 'Oh darling, give yourself a little time. He shocked you with his demands, did he?'

'He did,' Carrie said grimly.

Alicia's honeyed speaking voice turned icy cold. 'Really! Would you like your father to have a word with him?'

'God, no.' Carrie was appalled.

'It wouldn't bother me to speak to him,' Alicia said, itching to do it.

'Please, no, Mamma '

'Men aren't saints, my darling.'

'I never thought for a moment they were!' Carrie answered.

'You're a beautiful *and* sexy young woman, Carrie, even if you don't see it. In many ways you're unawakened. Of course I respect your decision to remain a virgin. Probably a very smart move with someone like Scott.'

'Smart moves had nothing to do with my decision,' Carrie pointed out, with a trace of admonition.

'Of course not. I don't really know why I said that. My advice is, if it wasn't all that bad—my God, I'm sure we're not talking rape—forgive him if you can. If you can't—' Alicia threw up her elegant hands '—your father and I will always back your decision.'

'*You* will,' Carrie said. 'I don't know about Dad. I think he'd be bitterly disappointed if I went to him and said the engagement was over.'

'But you're not going to do that, are you, darling?' More than anything Alicia wanted to see her daughter make a good marriage. Scott Harper mightn't be perfect but he had a lot going for him. 'One can understand his being in serious need of sex,' she pointed out gently.

'Be that as it may, whatever happened I dealt with it,' Carrie said. 'And Clay Cunningham came along at the right moment to back me up.'

Alicia drew in a sharp, whistling breath. 'Clay Cunningham? Now I do feel rather sorry for Scott. So Clay Cunningham rescued you like a true hero?'

Carrie on the other hand sounded suddenly *pleased*. 'He knocked Scott down.'

'Good God! I must say he had to wait a long time to do that,' Alicia laughed shortly. 'It's no secret Scott put Clay in hospital when they were boys.'

'I had no idea Scott was such a bully,' Carrie said. 'Or I didn't know until last night.' Now she sounded bitter and angry.

'You used to wave to Clay whenever you saw him in town,' Alicia suddenly recalled. 'You didn't wave to everybody.'

'He told me I used to wave,' Carrie said. 'I don't remember at all.' She didn't add she'd been trying very hard to.

'He was a handsome boy. Now a striking young man. That red in his hair he got from his mother, though she was pure

Titian. I only saw her once or twice. She was so pretty. An English rose. I wanted to befriend her but your father was very much against it. He sided with the Cunninghams. So did most people. Reece was to marry Elizabeth Campbell. It was as good as written in stone.'

'It shouldn't have been,' Carrie said, acutely aware of her own change of heart. 'You might as well know, Mamma, I gave Scott his ring back.' No need to say she had pitched it at him.

'Darling!' For one extraordinary moment there was a gleam of satisfaction in Alicia's eyes. 'He must have received one hell of a shock, being, as he is, God's gift to women. *My* only concern is for *you*. If you don't want to marry Scott Harper, there's just one thing to do. Tell him. But first give him a chance to apologise. To tell you he deeply regrets causing you pain. I'm sure he'll do just that.'

Katie appeared from the direction of the kitchen and Alicia held up her hand. 'Yoo-hoo, Katie, Carrie and I would love two more coffees. The little pastries were delicious.'

'Glad you liked 'em, Mrs. Mac!' Katie called cheerfully.

Just as her mother had predicted Scott, looking pallid beneath his tan and deeply troubled, sought out his ex-fiancée. The diamond solitaire was in his shirt pocket. No way could he let Carrie go out of his life. She was perfect. What girl ever was or would be again?

It was another brilliant day. A big barbecue lunch had been organised in the park to start at 1:00 p.m. Afterwards entertainment had been arranged for the kids, clowns and games, kites and balloons, rides on the darling little Shetland ponies and for the older, more daring kids, rides on two very aristocratic looking desert camels.

Carrie was helping out at the tables when Scott approached her. 'Carrie, could I talk to you, please?'

'It's okay, love, go right ahead. We're fine here,' one of the women on the committee called to her, giving Scott a coy wave.

'Last night was a nightmare,' Scott began wretchedly. He took Carrie's arm, drawing her along a path beneath a canopy of white flowering bauhinia trees like a bridal walk. 'I can't tell you how sorry I am any of that happened. I've been agonising about it and I reckon someone had to have spiked my drink. I've never been so out of it in my life.'

'The question is will you be out of it again?' Beautiful as the day was, sorry as Scott seemed, Carrie wasn't ready to forgive. She had come very close to being violated. Scott's assault on her had caused revulsion and a sense of inner devastation. She had trusted him. She knew it was a struggle for him no sex before marriage but she sincerely believed it was worthwhile for both of them. Her mood of desolation was further deepened by the knowledge he had been on the point of hitting her and from the look on his face, hitting her very hard. Physical violence horrified her.

'I swear by all that's holy, I'll never force myself on you again,' Scott said, sounding miserably abject. 'It was all the alcohol, Carrie. That and seeing you in Cunningham's arms. It drove me right off the edge.'

'Why exactly?' Carrie asked. 'We were enjoying a dance in front of hundreds of people. You didn't catch us in some compromising position.'

'It was the look on your face,' Scott said. 'It had a closeness about it you never give me.'

'Nonsense,' Carrie said firmly, though she felt herself under scrutiny. 'You're a frighteningly jealous person. Now I think about it, a domineering sort of man.' *Like your father,* hung in the air.

'What is it, Carrie?' Scott groaned. 'You need me to be perfect? Near inhuman? I'm madly in love with you. I'm a man of twenty-nine, nearly thirty, and you don't want me to touch you? Do you know how hard that is?'

'Yes, I do,' she said quietly, her reaction to Clay Cunningham taking over her mind, 'but I was proud of your sense of discipline, your consideration of my wishes.'

'You can't forgive me for *one* mistake?' Scott just stopped himself from turning ugly.

'That one mistake showed me you're not the man I thought you were,' Carrie said, brushing a spent white bauhinia blossom from her shoulder. 'You were even going to hit me. Don't deny it. You were going to slap me very hard. That was *bad,* Scott. Is that what you do when a woman doesn't give consent?'

'Oh God, Carrie!' Scott's voice was a heartfelt lament. 'I wouldn't really have hit you. I think maybe I thought about it for half a second.'

'Wrong. You were about to do it. Somehow I was able to stop you. Perhaps it was the disgust in my voice.'

Quite simply it had been. 'Carrie, I can't really remember last night,' he said. 'I can't be certain I hadn't been given some drug.'

'Did you take something?' She glanced up at him, knowing there was nowhere designer drugs hadn't reached.

'Carrie, stop punishing me,' he said. 'I love you. I'm desperate to marry you. I'll never deliberately cause you pain again. I beg you. Give me one more chance.' His eyes were extraordinarily intense. 'Is that too much to ask of the girl who's supposed to love me? You can't abandon me for one mistake.'

'Two bad mistakes.'

'We're getting married in December,' Scott pressed on. 'I've tried. God, how I've tried!'

This at least was true. Despite herself Carrie found herself moved by his obvious pain and contrition. 'Oh, Scott,' she sighed in a dispirited kind of way. She had a big problem now deciding she had ever loved him. A problem that hadn't really existed before Clay Cunningham came back into their lives.

'Please, darling.' Scott fumbled for the diamond solitaire in his pocket. 'A commitment has been made, Carrie. We can sort this out. Everyone is so happy we're together. My parents, your parents. Your dad and I are good mates. He thoroughly approves me of as a son-in-law.'

Wasn't that the truth! An outsider if asked might have said Scott was Bruce McNevin's offspring rather than his daughter.

'Let me prove to you all over again how much I love you,' Scott said ardently, lifting her hand and pushing his ring home on her finger. 'I'm nothing without you.' He lifted her hand to his mouth and kissed it tenderly. 'Say you forgive me.'

Carrie shook her head. 'That's impossible for me to say today, Scott.' She had never felt so dejected, so unsure of herself to the point of tears.

'It's your father. He's coming towards us,' Scott told her swiftly, seeing Bruce McNevin hurrying towards them across the grass. 'Don't let me down.'

'Ah, there you are, you two!' Bruce McNevin, having witnessed that heart-warming little moment between Carrie and Scott, called to them in a voice that was almost affectionate. A big concession for him. 'I've organised a corner table for all of us near the fountain. Your mother and father, Scott, Alicia and I and you two lovebirds.' He eyed them both with wry amusement. 'Goodness, from the look of you both, you must have been up all night.'

'Darn nearly sir.' Scott flashed his prospective father-in-law a respectful smile. 'Thanks for organising the table. I can tell you we're definitely hungry.'

Clay stayed in town for three reasons: as the winner of the Jim-boorie Cup; to get to know people; and to avail himself of the magnificent barbecue lunch free to all. Or so he told himself. Why he *really* stayed was to keep a watchful eye on Caroline. She had well and truly aroused his protective streak which was always near the surface when it came to vulnerable women. Now he wanted to see how she was going to handle an ex-fiancé who was determined to fight his way back into her good books.

The worst of it was, Harper appeared to have succeeded. Though Clay did his best not to look too often in their direction he had noted Caroline was not only wearing her big solitaire again, but Harper was sitting close beside her, in the company of both sets of smiling parents. As to be expected theirs was the best table set under the trees near the playing fountain.

Last night he had escorted Caroline back to Dougherty's pub where she was staying. He had asked if she were okay, then when she said she was, he said a quiet good-night watching her walk up the stairs to the guest bedrooms. He had longed to stay. To offer a few words of comfort—he had even wanted to rush into some good advice—but he could see how upset and vulnerable she was. The torn skirt of her beautiful dress and the ripped shoulder strap made him so angry he felt like going back outside to find Harper and give him the thrashing he deserved.

Caroline wouldn't thank him for that. She wanted the incident kept as quiet as possible. It was quite a miracle they had made it back to the pub without anyone paying them any particular attention. Caroline had tucked the torn shoulder strap into her bodice and her skirt was long and swishy concealing the rent. Such damage spoke for itself.

Harper had attacked her. Attacked the young woman he professed to love—his wife-to-be! Child, and man, Harper was a born bully. And what was it about anyway? Obviously Harper had wanted to make love to her—just as obviously she had said no. Any man in his right mind would have accepted it. Harper, alcohol driven, had nevertheless revealed the inner man. He had forced her only in this case he had underestimated his fiancée's fighting qualities. A woman at bay, even a pocket-sized one, could inflict damage if she were able to overcome her fear and get in a telling kick where it hurt most.

Clay felt proud of her. Like a big brother. Best to think of it like that. After all she'd used to wave to him from when she was a toddler until she was about six. And what a beautiful little girl she had been.

For another two hours he had sat across the street from the pub keeping an eye on the entrance just in case Harper took it into his mind to try to get Caroline alone again. He hadn't showed, though Clay was struck by the fact at one point in the night he had seen Harper in the distance having what looked like a serious disagreement with his cousin, Natasha. Impossible to miss her tall, willowy figure and the light was shining on her violet dress. Natasha might have been his cousin, but she wanted no part of Clay. On the other hand, why had Natasha been engaged in a violent argument with Harper? She couldn't have been acting on Caroline's behalf. Clay had gained the strong impression during the course of the afternoon and evening Caroline and Natasha weren't at all friendly. Yet a strong link existed between Natasha and Harper. How else could both of them have been filled with such anger? Clay had to admit he found that troubling.

Surrounded by 'family' Carrie was feeling hemmed in. She was tormented by her complex emotions. Had she really agreed to give Scott a second chance? She didn't think so, yet why was she seated at this table as if nothing had happened? Her mother had given her a quick, surprised glance after registering the diamond solitaire was back on her finger. Alicia didn't say anything but she patted Carrie's arm gently. Two lovers had had a fight and made up. It was much easier not to rock the boat. Alicia was in excellent spirits as was her father.

Why am I doing this? Carrie wondered. Was she in such desperate need of her father's approval? The deep reserve of his lifelong manner with her, the distancing, the lack of response, had caused her much grief and pain. She was sure that was why her mother had sent her away to boarding school early. Her mother gave her plenty of love and affection, cared for her as a mother should, but it was never enough. Her mother told her pretty much daily, 'I love you.' Her father—and she had racked her memory—had *never* said it. Surely that was wrong, wrong, *wrong!* Instead of disturbing her less, it disturbed her more and more as she grew older. It suddenly occurred to her, before her engagement to Scott Harper her existence hadn't had much significance for her father. Now with blinding clarity she saw that her father's approval rated higher than Scott's love.

That was immensely disturbing.

Across the green parkland she glimpsed Clay Cunningham seated at a table with the very attractive McFadden sisters, Jade and Mia. They were really sweet girls. The whole family was nice. The sisters sat on either side of him looking thrilled to be there. Several other young people she knew, including the girls' younger brother Aidan, made up the number at the table. If Clay Cunningham was desperate to find himself a bride he had arrived in town at the optimum time. It would be another year before the town saw such a gathering. As she expected, given Clay Cunningham was such a stunning man, both sisters were flushed with excitement as was Susie Peterson of the big blue eyes sitting opposite him. Susie leaned across the table to say something to him, which made them all laugh.

Carrie almost laughed herself. No need to help him out with his Bush Bachelor advertisement. He actually had three eligible young women hanging on his every word. If he were serious about finding a bride he'd better make the most of this glorious opportunity. After today they would all go their separate ways; home to pastoral properties all over the vast State. Distance was a big factor in the difficulties confronting those wanting to form meaningful relationships. Distance and back breaking sunup to sundown hard work that left precious little time for play.

After lunch Carrie helped out with the children's races. Even if she said so herself she had a talent with kids. They always welcomed her around. Afterwards she took a turn leading the little ones mounted on Shetland ponies around the sandy oval, the ponies perfectly behaved if not the kids. It was good to be able to make her escape from the 'family.' Though she had tried her hardest she'd found lunchtime oppressive. Once she had caught Scott's mother, Thea, looking at her with an odd expression in her eyes. A kind of what's-going-on-here? Mrs Harper's enmity would be deadly if she decided to go ahead and call off the engagement.

To her surprise she saw Clay Cunningham take a turn at leading around the older kids in saddlelike rigs aboard the camels. These domesticated camels came from a Far West property. Camels were such intelligent animals, Carrie thought. Not indigenous to the continent, they had been brought to Australia along with their Afghan handlers in the early days of settlement. Camels had been used on the ill-fated Burke and Wills expedition, by other explorers, miners, telegraph line builders, surveyors, station owners, tradesmen of all kinds. Camels had been *the* beasts of burden all over the Outback. Now they numbered around three hundred thousand, the healthiest camels on the planet. To Carrie's mind their heavy, long lashed eyelids gave them a benign look but she knew in the wild they could be dangerous.

There was no danger today. The camels couldn't have been more docile and obliging. They didn't even mind the excited little sidekicks they were getting from the children, predictably the boys, to spur them on. She was reminded how Scott had used his whip on Sassafras when Clay Cunningham had 'talked' his horse home.

She had a breather from Scott. He had gone off with her father to try their hand at flying the big, wonderfully painted and decorated kites too difficult for youngsters to handle. She could see one swooping up and up in the sky. It really had been a flawless day.

Aidan McFadden approached her, giving her a big smile. 'I'll take over from you now, Carrie. You must feel like a rest from this lot?'

'I sure do.' Carrie returned the smile. 'A cold drink will go down well. Thanks, Aidan. It's been a great weekend, hasn't it?'

'As far as I'm concerned the new guy Clay Cunningham put on the best show. Boy can he ride!' Aidan's open expression registered admiration. 'Do you think he'd mind if I took a look at the old homestead sometime? I was going to ask him. He sat at our table for lunch. He's a nice, easygoing guy. Do you really think he will stay? I hope he will. Only old Angus Cunningham left Jimboorie in a woeful state.'

'He had a breakdown after his wife died,' Carrie said. 'Then his daughter left him. He was a sad, sad man. Clay told me he wants to stay, Aidan. Why don't you simply ask him if you can visit sometime? Unless he's disappeared.' She glanced around the area.

'No, he's still around.' Aidan grinned. 'He can't shake Jade and Mia. Is it true he's looking for a wife? Or is that a bit of a joke? We didn't like to ask him but I can tell you the girls want him for themselves.'

'He can only pick one.' Carrie smiled back, but she felt a prick of something very much like misery.

'Then it's Jade!' Aidan called hopefully after her.

Clay Cunningham had won the McFaddens over it seemed.

One of the committee ladies met her with a home-made lemonade in a tall frosted glass decorated with a sprig of mint. 'Thank you so much, Carrie. You're always such a help. The kids love you.'

'I love them,' Carrie answered truthfully, accepting the very welcome drink. 'Where's Mamma?'

'Talking to Thea Harper the last time I saw her. The wedding's not far off now. You'll make the most beautiful bride,' she gushed.

Carrie smiled but could not answer. Was it possible she was having the first of a sequence of panic attacks?

'Hi, Caroline!' a deep attractive male voice called. A voice she now thought she'd know anywhere.

She paused, turning her head. 'Hello there, Clay.'

'How are you today?' He caught up to her, the both of them moving spontaneously towards an empty park bench.

'Very unsettled,' she admitted, sinking gratefully onto the timber seat.

'I couldn't help noticing Harper is forgiven.' He glanced down at her slender, polished fingers. The diamond solitaire was blazing away in a chink of sunlight.

'Everyone is just so happy we're engaged,' she said.

He knit his mahogany brows. 'Everyone but you.'

She risked a direct glance into his face, bewilderment surging into her voice. 'I used to be happy. Or I thought I was. Maybe I was just basking in everyone's approval.'

'What does that mean exactly?' The question was intense, far from light.

'God you know all about approval and the lack of it, Clay,' she said raggedly. 'I can't talk about it. It's disloyal to my family.'

'What about Harper?' he asked in a taut low voice. 'Hell, Caroline, you're not a schoolgirl. You're a woman. What are you afraid of? You weren't afraid last night. You were astonishingly gutsy. What's happened to change that?'

She didn't answer for a moment. She took a long draft of the lemonade, moving her tongue into a curl. It was delicious and refreshingly cold. 'I was very angry with Scott last night. I'm still not happy about him, but he came to me this morning and—'

'Swore he'd never use force on you again?' he interjected. 'You believed him?'

She had the strong impression he was disgusted. 'May I ask why it's any of your business, Clay?'

'You may ask but I might be less inclined to answer.' He gave a humourless laugh. 'Think of it as I'm catching up with a friendship that never had a chance to get started. I was a pretty lonely kid, living on the fringe of things. My father dishonoured by his own people. My mother spoken about as if she were nothing more than a wayward little tramp. In reality she had more class than any of them. But it broke her as time went on. It might seem like a small thing but I saw the way little Princess McNevin always gave me a wave as a bright spot in my blighted childhood.'

'I can't remember.' She stared at him out of sorrowful doe eyes.

'Sounds like you've been trying?' His voice had a tender but challenging note.

'I know I *will* remember,' she said, clinging to the idea. 'It's going to happen all at once.'

'When can you come to Jimboorie?' he asked, with some urgency because Caroline was never on her own for long.

'It's not a good idea.' In fact it could cost her a good deal.

'Caroline, you *promised,*' he reminded her, his eyes a blazing blue against the bronze cast of his skin.

'Scott hates you.'

His handsome face bore an expression of indifference. 'That's okay. I can live with it. I don't exactly admire him. He's a bully. Man and boy. What days do you come into town for Pat Kennedy?'

She could see he wasn't going to let this alone. If the truth be told she badly wanted to accept his invitation. 'Make it next Friday,' she said. 'I'll meet you at the *Bulletin* office at 10:00 a.m. Would that suit?'

'No, but I'll be there.' He gave her a smile that made a lick of fire run right down to her toes.

'Then another day?' she suggested quickly.

He shook his head, his thick mahogany hair, lit by rich red tones. 'Friday's fine. The sooner the better. Are you going to tell your folks?'

She laughed as if it were an insane thing to ask. 'Oh, Clay, they won't even notice I've gone. Well, my father won't.'

He wanted to touch her cheek but he knew he shouldn't. 'What's the problem with your father? There appears to be one.'

'Maybe I'll tell you sometime,' she said. 'Oh, God!' she muttered, under her breath. 'Here he comes now with Scott.'

Clay rose immediately to his impressive height. 'Don't panic, I'll go. You will turn up?'

She trembled and he saw it. 'Yes. 10:00 a.m. at the office,' she repeated.

'What I'd really like to do is stay and meet your father. Ask him why he turned against the man who was once his friend?'

'Now's not the time for it, Clay!' She looked at him with a plea in her eyes.

'Don't walk into the trap,' he warned, touching a forefinger to his temple before striding away.

CHAPTER FOUR

THEY had been driving for well over an hour. There hadn't been much conversation between them, rather an intense *awareness* that made any comment deeper than normal, a potential minefield. She had not removed her engagement ring. She offered him no explanation and he didn't ask for one, yet she carried the conviction he would before the day was over.

She'd told her mother where she was going…

'Darling, is that wise?' Alicia had shown a level of concern, bordering on alarm.

'Wise or not I'm going,' Carrie had replied. 'I really want to see the old house. When I was little I thought it was a palace like the Queen lived in.'

'And you want to see Clay Cunningham.' Alicia didn't beat about the bush.

'I like him,' Carrie said. What she failed to say was he had an extraordinary effect on her. It was something she had to keep secret. Even from herself, but Alicia's expression suggested she knew all the same.

There was Jimboorie House rising up before them. Once the cultural hub of a vast region, it stood boldly atop a rise that fell away rather steeply to the long curving billabong of Koona Creek at its feet. It was to Carrie, far and away the most beautiful home-stead ever erected by the sheep barons who became the landed gentry. It was certainly the biggest, built of sandstone that had weathered to a lovely soft honey-pink. It lofted two tall storeys high, the broad terrace beneath the deep overhang of the upper level supported by imposing stone columns, which were all but obscured by a rampant tangle of vines all in flower. The great roof was tiled with harmonising grey slate that had been imported all the way from Wales. The whole effect was of an establishment that would be considered quite impressive in any part of the world, if only one narrowed one's eyes and totally ignored the decay and the grime.

The mansion was approached by a long driveway guarded by sentinel towering gums. This in turn opened out into a circular driveway with a once magnificent fountain, now broken, in the centre. The gardens, alas, were no more but the indestructible bou-ganvilleas climbed over every standing structure in sight. A short flight of stone steps led to the imposing pedimented Ionic portico.

Clay drove his 4WD into the shade of the flowering gums, the low trailing branches scraping the hood.

'What it once must have been!' Carrie sighed. 'It's still beau-tiful even if it's falling down.'

'Come see for yourself,' he invited, with a note in his voice that made her doubly curious.

Carrie stepped out onto the gravelled driveway, a petite young woman wearing a white knit tank top over cropped cotton drill olive-green pants, a simple wardrobe she somehow made glam-orous. Their arrival disturbed a flock of rainbow lorikeets that had been feeding on the pollen and nectar in the surrounding euca-lypts, bauhinias, and cassias all in bloom. The birds displayed all the colours of the spectrum in their plumage, Carrie thought, fol-lowing their flight. The upper wings were emerald-green, under wings orange washed with yellow, beautiful deep violet heads, scarlet beaks and eyes. They presented a beautiful sight, chattering shrilly to one another as they flew to another feeding site.

A sprightly breeze had blown up, tugging at her hair which she had tied back at the nape with a silk scarf designed by aboriginal women using fascinating traditional motifs. 'What does it feel like to be back?' she asked him, filled for a moment with a real sadness for what might have been.

'Like I've never been away,' Clay answered simply, though his face held myriad emotions. 'This is precisely the place I belong.'

'Is it?' His words touched her deeply. She looked across at his tall, lean figure. He was dressed simply as she was, in everyday working clothes—tight fitting jeans, and a short sleeved open necked bush shirt. Dark, hand tooled boots on his feet gave him added stature. He had a wonderful body, she thought, starting to fear the effect he had on her. At her deepest level she knew a man like this could push over all her defences as easily as one could push over a pack of cards. It was something entirely new in her life. She wondered could she resist *him* as she was so able to resist Scott? At heart, she was beginning to question herself. Was her decision to remain a virgin until marriage brought about by sheer circumstance? It seemed very obvious to her now she didn't love Scott in the way a woman should love the man she chooses to marry. Everyone else saw him as a solid choice. Did that automatically make for a good marriage?

As for Clay Cunningham? She didn't have a clue where their friendship would lead. In short he presented a dilemma. Carrie's nerves stretched taut as her memory was overrun by images of her father and Scott as they joined her yesterday only moments after Clay had moved off. Both handsome faces wore near identical expressions. Anger to the point of outrage. It chilled her to the bone. She wasn't a possession, a chattel. She was a grown woman with the right to befriend anyone she so chose.

Her father didn't think so and made that plain. 'Better you

don't have anything to do with him, Carrie,' he'd clipped off, his grey eyes full of ice.

'Why not?' She had never in her life answered her father quite like that before. A clear challenge that brought hot, angry colour to his cheeks.

'I wouldn't have thought I had to tell you,' he reprimanded her. 'He's bad news. Just like his father before him. You're an engaged woman yet it's quite obvious he has his eye on you.'

She had waited for Scott to intervene but he hadn't. Best not get on the wrong side of Mr McNevin. At least until he and Carrie were safely married.

'That's carrying it a bit far, Dad,' Carrie had said. 'Clay just came across to say hello. I like him.'

Her father looked pained. 'People talk, Carrie. I don't want them to be talking about *you*.'

'You're very quiet today, Scott?' She hadn't bothered to hide the taunt. 'Nothing to add?'

He shook his golden head. 'As far as I'm concerned your father has said it all.'

That earned him Bruce McNevin's nod of approval.

Clay took her arm as they climbed the short flight of steps to the portico and on to the spacious terrace. 'Careful,' he said, indicating the deep gouges between the slate tiles. 'Just stay with me.'

Guilt swept through her. *Why, why, why did she want so much to be with him?* This was all too sudden. She had the mad notion she would have gone with him had he asked her to take a trip to Antarctica.

The double front doors towered a good ten feet. They were very impressive and in reasonably good condition. When she had *really* looked from the outside, she had seen the large numbers of broken or displaced tiles on the roof and the smashed glass in the tall arched windows of the upper level. Some of the shutters, once a Venetian green, were hanging askew. Panels of glass in the French doors of the lower level were broken as well and replaced with cardboard.

The effect was terrible. Some of the damage could have been caused by vandals. The smashed glass in the doors and windows for example. Six months had elapsed since Angus Cunningham's death and the arrival of his great-nephew. It could have happened then although the talk in the town was Jimboorie House was haunted by the late Isabelle Cunningham. No one had the slightest wish to encounter her.

Clay opened one door, then the other, so that long rays of sunlight pierced the grand entrance hall.

As far as Carrie was concerned, the entrance hall said it all about a house. 'Oh!' she gasped, as she stepped across the threshold. She stared about her with something approaching reverence. 'I've always wanted to see inside. It's as noble as I knew it would be.'

Her face held so much fascination it was exquisite! Clay thought. 'I'm glad you're here, and you're not disappointed.'

Something in his tone made Carrie's heart turn a somersault in her breast. She didn't look back at him—she didn't dare—but continued to stare about her. After the mess of broken tiles on the terrace she was thrilled to see the floor of the entrance hall, tessellated with richly coloured tiles was intact. In three sections, the design was beautiful, circular at the centre with equally beautiful borders.

'What a miracle it hasn't been damaged.'

'The house isn't in any where near as bad condition as everyone seems to think,' Clay commented with a considerable amount of satisfaction. 'Which is not to say a great deal of money won't be spent on its restoration.'

She stood in the sunbeams with dust motes of gold. 'It would be wonderful to hear your great-uncle actually left you some money?'

'He had it,' Clay said, surprising her.

'He couldn't have!' Carrie was completely taken aback. 'How could he have had money and let the homestead fall into ruin let alone allow the station to become so rundown?'

'He no longer cared,' Clay told her, shrugging. 'Simple as that. He cared about no one and nothing. He only loved one person in his entire life. That was his wife. After she died he slowly sank into a deep depression. She's supposed to haunt the place, incidentally. My mother claimed to have seen her many times. Isabelle died early. Thirty-eight. No age at all! I wouldn't like to think I only had another ten years of life. She was carrying Angus's heir who died with his mother. Their daughter, Meredith, the firstborn, spent most of her time at boarding school, or with her maternal aunt in Sydney who, thank the Lord, loved her. Meredith was never close to her father after her mother died. No one was. Uncle Angus locked everyone out.'

'Yet he took you in? You and your parents?'

'It was only to spite the rest of the family, I assure you,' Clay said, the hard glint of remembrance in his eyes. 'My father worked like a slave for little more than board for us all. Angus kept my father at it by telling him he was going to inherit Jimboorie. Meredith didn't want the place. Mercifully she married well. Her aunt saw to that. When Angus finally admitted he fully intended to sell up, my father decided it was high time to move on.'

'What happened to your father?' Carrie asked, positioning herself out of the dazzling beam of light so she could see him clearly.

His face became a tight mask. 'He was helping to put out a bushfire, only he and the station hand working with him became surrounded by the flames.'

'Oh, Clay!' Carrie whispered, absolutely appalled. No one knew this. At least she hadn't heard anything of Reece Cunningham's dreadful fate. 'How horrible! Why should anyone have to die like that?'

The corners of his handsome mouth turned down. 'To save the rest of us I suppose. I had to concentrate on his heroism or go mad. My mother spent the rest of her life having ghastly nightmares. The way my father died left her not only bereft but sunk in a depressive state she couldn't fight out of. That fire destroyed her, too. I know she actually prayed for the day she would die. She truly believed she would see my father again.'

'Do *you?*' she asked with a degree of trepidation.

'No.' Abruptly he shook his burnished head. 'Still I can't help but wonder from time to time.'

'Mystery, mysteries, the *great* mystery,' she said. She lifted her head to the divided staircase. Of polished cedar and splendid workmanship it led to the richly adorned overhanging gallery. The gallery had to have a dome because natural light was pouring in. Either that or there was a huge hole in the roof. The plaster ceilings, that once would have been so beautiful, were badly in need of repair.

'Does the gallery have a dome?' she asked, hoping the answer was yes.

'It does,' he said, 'and it's still intact. The bedrooms are upstairs of course. Twelve in all. The old kitchens and the servants' quarters are the buildings at the rear of the house. We'll get to them. Let's move on. There are forty rooms in the house all up.' He extended his arm to the right.

More tall double doors gave on to the formal dining room on their left, the drawing room to their right. Neither room was furnished. The drawing room was huge and classically proportioned. The once grand drapes of watered Nile-green silk were hanging in tatters.

She was both appalled and moved by the badly neglected state of the historic homestead. 'Where do you plan to start first?'

she asked, her clear voice echoing in the huge empty spaces. 'Or are you going to leave that to your wife?'

'I'll have to,' he said, amusement in his voice. 'I'll be too busy getting the station up and running.'

'So what are you going to run?' Her voice lifted with interest.

'A lean commercial operation geared for results,' he answered promptly. 'Jimboorie's glamour days are over. Beef is back. There's a strong demand. I'm going to run Hereford cattle. Angus couldn't envisage any other pursuit than running sheep even when the wool industry was in crisis.'

'Are you going to tell me where you acquired your skills as a cattleman?'

He nodded. 'I actually got to Agricultural College where I did rather well. Then I worked on a cattle station rising to overseer.'

'Would I know this station?'

'Oh, come on, Caroline,' he gently taunted her. 'You would if I told you.'

'So you think if you confide in me I'll tell everyone else?' She was hurt he didn't trust her but she made a huge effort to hide it.

'I don't think that at all. Not if I told you not to. It's just that it's difficult to talk about a lot of things right now.'

She turned away from him. 'That's okay. It's not as if we're *friends.*'

'It's not easy to make a true friend,' he said sombrely. 'What *are* we exactly?'

'We're in the process of becoming friends,' she bravely said.

'So you'd befriend me and rebuff your fiancé? It's back on again, I take it?' His tone was sardonic, if not openly critical.

'It's just a mess, Clay,' she said, that tone getting to her.

His brilliant blue eyes seemed to *burn* over her, making her skin flush. 'Well you can't disregard it. It's your life's happiness that's on the line. Are you so afraid of increasing the discord between yourself and your father?' he asked with considerable perception. 'He's obviously an extremely difficult man to please?'

She glanced away through the French doors at the abandoned garden. The wildflowers, shrubs and flowering vines that had survived lent it colour as did the hardiest of climbing cabbage roses, a magnificent deep scarlet, in full bloom over an old pergola. She had seen many pictures of Jimboorie House in its prime so she knew there had been a wonderful rose arbour. 'My father is difficult about some things,' she answered at length. 'He's a good father in others. I don't know why I'm telling you. I feel I know you.'

'You do know me,' he replied. 'You're the little girl who used to deliver the sweetest smile and the wave of a little princess, remember?'

'May I ask you a personal question?' She turned to face him, held fast by the extraordinary intensity of his gaze.

'You can try.' He smiled. 'And what would it be? Have I ever been in love?' His voice held amusement.

It wasn't her question, but she stared back at him, aware she badly wanted to know. 'Have you?'

'Caroline, I told you.'

That smile was *magic*. Few smiles lit up a man's face like that.

'My lifestyle left very little time for romance,' he explained again. 'There was a girl once. She got spooked by my lack of money. All she had to do was give me a little time.'

'Do you still love her?' The muscles in her slender throat tensed. She told herself it would be wonderful to have a man like Clay Cunningham love her. Something she knew she would agonize over later.

'No.'

'Are you sure?'

'Absolutely positive,' he said. He didn't tell her, nor would he, he'd already dated falling in love from the moment he'd laid eyes

on her, albeit rashly. He had already discovered she was the
fiancée of Scott Harper, the bully boy of his childhood. Still
was, for that matter. She wore Harper's ring. Maybe the death of
his mother and returning to Jimboorie had put him in a very vulnerable state of mind. That's why he wanted a wife, a wife and
children, a family of his own to love. Having a family of his own
had somehow developed into a passion. Caroline McNevin could
too easily become a passion. A *doomed* passion. Unless she
found the strength to break away from Harper.

Carrie moved on. 'I love the fireplace,' she said. The chimney
piece was constructed of flawless white Carrara marble. Instead
of the usual large gilded mirror to hang above it—any mirror
would probably have been shattered—was a very elegant over-
mantel in the same white marble. Judging from the staining left
on the marble, it seemed a painting had once hung there and on
other places around the walls.

'It would take a great deal of furniture to fill this room alone,'
she marvelled, finding it easy to visualise the drawing room
restored. She loved houses; beautiful houses like this. Clay was
quite correct in saying the interior wasn't in any where near as bad
condition as everyone thought. At least as much as she had seen.

'A lot of the original furnishings, paintings, rugs, objets d'art,
you name it, are in storage,' he said, further surprising her.

'Really?' Her dark eyes opened wide. 'On the property, you
mean? One of the outbuildings?'

He shook his head. 'Great-Uncle Angus wasn't so steeped in
grief he didn't make sure nothing of real value was left here to
be stolen. There's a warehouse full of it in Toowoomba.' He
named a city one hundred miles west of Brisbane, the state
capital, lying on the edge of the Great Dividing Range and
famous for its spring carnival of flowers.

'I think you could safely say your great-uncle Angus fooled
the world,' she said wryly. 'Have you seen what's in there?'

'Not as yet, but I have the inventory. I'll make the trip to Too-woomba some time fairly soon. Want to come?'

'Aren't you the bush bachelor looking for a wife?' She gave him a look.

'Most definitely,' he retorted. 'We could talk about what I should put in my ad along the way.'

'You have a devil in you, Clay Cunningham.'

He absorbed her slowly with his eyes. 'Most men do, but *you'll* never stumble on mine, I promise. You speak of loving Harper, but I don't think you do.'

She had learned that in stages. 'Off-limits, Clay,' she warned moving into the huge handsome room that was obviously the library. Cedar bookcases were set in arcaded recesses all around the room, but the collection had gone. A book lover, she prayed it had gone into storage.

'Perhaps you're a little too accustomed to doing what you believe will please everyone?' he questioned, his voice resonating with a certain sympathy.

'Is that a good reason to get married?' She felt wounded.

'It happens a lot,' he said. 'I had no difficulty sensing you badly need to please your father. That desire must be far from new.'

She stopped abruptly. 'You sense far too much. What is it you want from me, Clay?' Without meaning for it to happen—her momentary weakness shocked her—tears filled her eyes.

He stared down at her in dismay. 'Caroline, don't do that,' he implored, slowly rubbing a hand across his tanned forehead. 'I've got plenty of self-control, but your tears might prove my undoing.' In reality he saw himself on the very edge of a yawning chasm. If those tears spilled onto her cheeks, he might plunge into that chasm, taking her with him, his arms enclosing her, cradling her, his mouth closing over hers to muffle her cries.

Oh God, Caroline, stop it! When he was with her his every perception was intensified.

'Meaning what?' She tried valiantly to blink the tears away.

'You know perfectly well what I mean.' His handsome face was grim. 'Why do your eyes contain tears anyway? They're no protection against me. The reverse is true. It seems to me you want to cry from sheer necessity. You're unhappy. You feel caught in a trap. You can get out of it if you're strong.'

Was she strong? She'd thought she was. Now she turned her head away from him and the tremendous temptation he presented. 'It's impossible overnight.' Her hands were shaking. She lifted one to clasp the silk scarf at her nape. She pulled it free, suddenly irritated by the knot of material on her neck.

'No, it's not,' he answered roughly, watching her hair uncoil into long golden skeins. It radiated light like a halo around her head. He couldn't help himself. He moved nearer, lifting a hand and curling a long shining lock around his fingers. It felt like silk, sweetly scented. He tugged on the thick lock very gently edging her towards him.

'Don't *do* this, Clay,' she warned, knowing they had both reached a turning point that was far from unexpected.

'Look into my eyes and tell me that,' he said. His hand moved to the mass of her shining hair pulling her head back so he could stare into her face. 'Caroline?'

'I must be mad,' she murmured.

'I know. So am I.'

Now the tears did seep from her eyes. What she saw in his face was sexual ardour of a nature she had hitherto never even glimpsed. It wasn't crude lust. Lust she had come to despise. There was real *yearning* there, as though he believed she might be the one to cure his deep-seated griefs. She, in turn, was spellbound by the concentration of pure desire that burned so brilliantly in his blue eyes.

She didn't so much go along with it. She surrendered herself to it, deferring to a stolen moment in time. 'This may well be a serious mistake!' The streams of passion that stormed through her veins offered proof.

He nodded solemnly, one hand cupping her face with a tenderness that was profoundly moving. 'You're so small!'

'I'm a woman,' she said. 'A woman of nearly twenty-four.'

'A very serious young woman who has to put a few things right.'

'That's how you see it?' she whispered, her eyes on his clean cut mouth.

'Don't *you*?'

Before she had time to react—did she really have the strength?—he lifted her as though she weighed no more than a child and carried her to one of the recessed alcoves, setting her on top of the solid cedar cupboard, which supported the ceiling-high bookshelves.

'Caroline McNevin, you are *so* beautiful!' He trailed one hand down over her cheek, her throat, lightly skimmed the low-necked front of her tank top that gave a tantalizing glimpse of the upward curves of her breasts.

Her body ached. There was pain, she was learning, in desire. 'Why are we doing this, Clay?'

'It's all I've wanted to do since you walked back into my life,' he confessed.

Her eyes were very dark, her expression strange. 'When kissing me is strictly forbidden?'

'By whom?'

'God help me, not *me*!'

Her words chimed in his mind. He lowered his head, while Carrie closed her eyes, dizzy suddenly with the level of sensuality.

His powerful, lean body stood directly in front of her. Without thought—all she wanted was to get as close to him as possible—she brought up her slender legs to wrap him around. It was something she had never done before but her inhibitions were melting like a polar thaw. Her fall from grace—the full rush of it—

stunned her. If indeed fall was what it was. But she had promised to marry another man, for all the decision to make a clean break from Scott was fast overtaking her.

She could pay heavily for this moment out of time. They *both* could. But Carrie was powerless to stop what had already started. The sense of having been caught up in something far beyond the power of either of them to control was strong in her. Fate, destiny, something preordained?

Gently, so *gently* at first, he touched his mouth to hers. A communion. Yet the effect was so overwhelming it drowned her in a wave of the most voluptuous heat. She had never experienced such a powerful sexual reaction. It caught at her breath so it emerged as a moan.

'I'm not hurting you?' He drew back a little.

'No!'

The flame and the urgency of their coming together seemed to devour her. No flutter of conscience troubled her then. His kiss was so deep and so passionate there was no question of denying him what he sought to take from her. No question of denying herself such excitement, such a tremendous physical exhilaration.

She had never dreamed a kiss could be like this.

Never!

At that dangerous moment she was his for the taking. She was *pressing* herself against him with absolute abandon. All the world was lost to her. Instead of her habitual ingrained caution she felt only a magnificent generosity. She was offering herself, shamelessly, ultimately inciting him to take as much as he wanted from her. She was acutely aware he was powerfully aroused but she had no thought of withdrawing herself or calling a stop. Desire such as this was a revelation. It was the most potent of all intoxications and she was drinking it from his mouth.

Why would she call a halt to such a storm of wanting? For all she knew it might never happen again.

'Caroline!' He gasped out her name, getting one hand to her hair that was tumbling all around them in golden sheets.

She realised with a shock he was trying to hold her off.

Oh, God!

Absolute bliss turned to blinding mortification.

His dark head was bent over hers as he smoothed the hair away from her flushed face. 'You know where this is going?' His voice was as taut as a bow.

Wasn't she inviting it? God help her, she was practically begging him to make love to her. She took a deep breath, then pushed him away, one hand flat against his chest.

'I'm sorry.'

'Don't be.' He, too, had been unable to diminish the scale of all that he felt for her.

The whole extraordinary episode couldn't have taken more than a few minutes yet she felt she would remember this encounter until the day she died. 'It's all right. I'm all right,' she said. It took a while—she was cautious she wouldn't slip into a faint she was so dazed—but she was able to slide off the cupboard bench, onto the floor. 'I wanted that as much as you,' she said, her voice full of confusion and regret, 'but we have to watch ourselves from now on.'

A week later Carrie was working in a rather desultory fashion on station accounts when her mother rushed into the office, looking violently upset.

Gripped by panic, Carrie sprang to her feet. 'What is it, Mamma?' For a moment she experienced pure dread. Had something happened to her father? Was her mother ill? Had she received some terrible news? Blows had a relentless way of coming right out of the blue.

'It's Scott,' Alicia gasped, sounding quite breathless.

'What's happened? Has he been hurt?' Carrie began to

imagine all sorts of horrendous things. Station accidents were all too common. Even fatalities. She had only seen Scott once since the Sunday of the picnic races. A Scott so repentant, so painfully anxious to please her, she'd found it extremely difficult to say what she needed to say; what desperately needed saying.

Scott, I want out of our engagement!

But the way Scott had acted made her feel breaking their engagement would be too terrible for him to bear at that time. Had she been blinded to the true depth of his love for her? Had she not seen how much he cared? Had she blamed him too severely for that terrible night? She couldn't forget the sight of his hand upraised to her. His excuse was that he was drunk. People acted out of character when they were under the influence of alcohol. Pity for him was part of her self-enforced silence. He had treated her so carefully, as though she were utterly *precious,* and in the end she had let him drive away without saying one word of what was going round and round in her head.

The need for decisive action. It was causing her many a sleepless night. She had the awful feeling once she broke her engagement the recent harmony between herself and her father would break down overnight into icy rejection. Once the thought would have terrified her. But she was a woman now. She was well-educated. She would have to live separate from her parents. That meant she would have to leave her beloved home, the *land* she loved and seek a life for herself in the city. There were far worse things.

Now she led her mother to a chair. 'Mamma, sit down. Here have some water.' Swiftly she poured a glass from the cooler and put it into her mother's hand. 'Scott's been injured, hasn't he?'

'They've *both* been injured,' Alicia said bitterly. Alicia set down the glass of cold water so forcibly it was a wonder it didn't break.

'Both?' Carrie stared at her mother vacantly.

'Scott and that sly, underhanded bitch, Natasha Cunningham,' Alicia said and thrust back a long strand of her hair.

Carrie was stupefied. 'Mamma, what are you talking about? What happened? Where? Why were they together?'

Alicia looked at her daughter with pitying eyes. 'Because he's been seeing her on the side, that's why!'

Carrie couldn't seem to take it in, though she was staring at her mother, hard. 'Scott has been seeing Natasha?' she repeated. Given the way Scott had been behaving towards her—the way he always labelled Natasha 'a bitch'—Carrie found it impossible to believe. Only a few days ago Scott had been literally down on his knees telling her how much he loved her, his voice filled with a I-can't-live-without-you fervour. 'How do you know? Who told you?' Carrie demanded, wondering if there were a possibility her mother had got things wrong.

'The way they found them told the story.' Alicia reached for the glass and drained it as if she were parched to the point of severe dehydration.

'What on earth do you mean?' Carrie's even temper started a slow boil. 'Who found them? Where were they? Spit it out. Mamma, for God's sake! I bet it's all over the district already. Were they in his SUV?'

Alicia clapped her hand to her mouth as though she was about to be sick. 'They careened right off the road and plunged into Campbell's Crossing. It was Ian Campbell who found them. They've already been airlifted to hospital.'

'My God!' Carrie's voice was flat with shock. 'How bad were their injuries?'

'No one knows yet,' Alicia said, forcing herself to steady down. 'Scott was in a worse state than Natasha, I believe.'

Carrie released a devastated groan. 'We must ring the hospital to find out.'

'Carrie, love, did you hear what I told you? Did you take it in? They were *together*. Scott has betrayed you. We all know he and

Natasha were an item one time, but everyone thought it was over. What fools we've all been. Obviously their affair has never left off.'

'I can't understand this,' Carrie said and she couldn't. 'I've been agonising over finding the best moment to tell Scott our engagement is off. I felt desperate to let him down lightly. Now I learn he's been seeing Natasha behind my back all the while. It doesn't make a bit of sense!'

'Doesn't it?' Alicia laughed grimly. 'She was giving him what *you* wouldn't,' she said, bluntly. 'It was just sex.'

'Just sex!' Carrie's voice soared to the ceiling. 'You seem to know a hell of a lot about sex, Mamma.'

Alicia laughed even more bitterly. 'I'm a married woman.' Suddenly tears surged into her eyes. 'Oh, Carrie, what a terrible mess!'

Carrie looked past her mother towards the door. 'I'll have to find out what condition they're both in,' she said. 'I can't stand here wondering. Does Dad know?'

Alicia raised her golden head, looking utterly drained. 'He's the one who told me. He's shocked out of his mind.'

'He never thought to come to me.' Carrie's feeling of wretchedness increased. 'After all, I am supposed to be Scott's fiancée. But Dad came to you. As always.'

'He's dreadfully upset.' Alicia made excuses for her husband. 'Naturally he would come to me, Carrie, and allow me to break the news to you. He was being thoughtful. He's only just got the news directly from Ian Campbell. Your father thought the world of Scott.'

'*You* didn't, Mamma,' Carrie pointed out, without emotion. 'You wouldn't have been too upset if I broke off the engagement.'

Alicia shielded her face with her hand. 'I'm your mother. I wanted to see you marry well. Scott Harper is a great catch. *Was* a great catch.' Her voice broke.

'I pray to God he still will be,' Carrie said, her expression badly strained. 'But not for *me*. Why didn't I recognise what was behind all those snide remarks Natasha used to make? The outright malice in her eyes? I put it down to jealousy. Understandable, when she must have been in love with Scott at one time. Now it appears she's never given up on him. Maybe they were going to continue their affair right into our marriage? I'm a complete fool and I've only just found out. Surely *someone* realised what was going on?'

Alicia lifted her hand, her expression stony. 'They erected a pretty good smoke screen, the two of them,' she said with utter contempt. 'I daresay some of his mates would have known what was going on. They'd think Scotty was entitled to a bit of fun on the side.'

'*Fun?*' Carrie's voice rose again. 'Fun, for God's sake, *fun!* Well it's not fun now.'

CHAPTER FIVE

HER father was remarkably solicitous. He treated her as if she had been in the accident; as if she were breakable when she didn't feel breakable at all. The town treated her the same way. One would have thought Scott and Natasha had been involved in separate accidents so determined were people not to mention their names in the same breath.

But they *had* been together. There again, no one would tell her what it was about the accident that had so compromised them. Had they been found stark-naked? She rather doubted that. Was Natasha in a state of undress? She finally got it from Paddy when she called into the *Bulletin* office to see him in person—they had spoken on the phone—and ask for time off.

'Needless to say out of respect we won't be printing the full story,' Pat Kennedy told her, studying her face closely. He loved this girl. She was as dear to him as the granddaughter he had wished for but never had.

'At last we get to it,' Carrie sighed, her dark eyes full of misery. 'Tell me, Paddy. Get it over. I guess twenty-four isn't too late to find out you're a gullible fool.'

'You're no fool, my girl,' Paddy said, then added with sudden fierceness, 'it's that fiancé of yours who's the fool. I don't understand this whole business actually. I could have sworn Scott was madly in love with you. No pretence, he couldn't wait to marry you.'

'That's all over, Paddy.'

'He's still in the induced coma?'

Carrie gulped down tears. 'Yes.' Ever one to visualise she had a clear picture of Scott lying in a hospital bed, hooked up to monitors. He had been badly concussed—the great fear being of brain injury—with a broken collarbone, multiple lacerations and two broken ribs. All Carrie wanted was for him to open his eyes again and talk to someone. His mother. She didn't want to be the one but as far as she was concerned all was forgiven. She had no wish for him or Natasha to suffer, though Natasha wasn't the one to worry about right now. Natasha had been lucky. Compared to Scott she had come through relatively unscathed. No broken bones but severe bruising and multiple lacerations that nevertheless were not considered serious enough to leave scars. Carrie was glad of that. Natasha Cunningham was a beautiful woman—if not a beautiful person.

Carrie had spoken to Scott's distraught mother the day of the accident. Thea Harper, after all, was to have become her mother-in-law. All Carrie could do was offer comfort in the face of a mother's agony. Thea was nearly out of her mind with worry, as well she might be. Scott was not only her only son, he was her only child. Both of them had chosen to put Natasha's presence in Scott's SUV to one side. There was enough to worry about without following through on that issue. Time enough for that.

'Are you going to give Scott a chance to tell his side of the story?' Paddy asked, his normally twinkling blue eyes troubled. 'That Cunningham girl is trouble. I've long said so.'

'So what's the full story,' Carrie asked wearily.

Paddy, seasoned journalist, close friend and mentor, with all the wisdom of a fulfilled life, at seventy-three, coloured up. 'It seems Natasha wasn't wearing her, er, shirt. Or her bra,' he added with a shake of his silver head.

Carrie was past shock. 'That seems extraordinarily wild, even for Natasha. Or was it night-time?'

'Must have been,' Paddy said briefly. 'You're going to visit him?'

'Regardless of what they were up to, it's high time I did,' Carrie said. 'I'll look in on Natasha while I'm at it. We've never been friends but I've often thought there's something sad and lost about her. That's why she behaves so badly.'

'Dreadful crowd,' Paddy tutted though he was kind about most people. 'Cruel what they did to Reece and his young family. I've met Clay. He used to be 'little Jimmy Cunningham' back then. I would have met him at the picnic races only for my old mate, Bill Hawkins's funeral in Brisbane. Clay came into the office last week to make himself known to me. I must say he appears to have turned out splendidly.'

Carrie kept her eyes downcast. 'He's a wonderful horse-man. It was quite thrilling to see him win the Cup.'

'Scott must have hated that?' Paddy spoke wryly, showing his understanding of Scott's nature.

'He didn't take it too well,' Carrie agreed. 'Was there some feud in their childhood, Clay and Scott? If so it's carried through to now.'

Paddy's face creased up. 'Scott was a bit of a bully in those days, Carrie,' he settled for, deliberately not mentioning the time Scott Harper had fiercely knocked a younger, smaller child to the ground. 'He chose to pick on Jimmy—I mean Clay—every time he saw him in town. People took sides in those days. Even a child would have been affected. Reece was going to marry Elizabeth Campbell after all. Not that they were engaged. It was just taken for granted. Enter one lovely little English-Irish girl—I never knew which—with blazing Titian hair, and that was that! Elizabeth and Thea Harper were friends. Naturally they turned against Reece and more particularly the young woman he fell in love with.' Paddy's well rounded voice was thin with regret. 'Awful the things that were said about that young woman. Not a single rumour that was sustainable. But mud sticks.'

'I'm wondering how long this particular piece of mud is going to stick?' Carrie sighed. 'I pray for Scott's rapid recovery but I can't marry him, Paddy. I had decided not to even before *this*.'

'Look, who would expect you to?' Paddy asked. He had never thought Golden Boy Harper was half good enough for Carrie.

Carrie stared sightlessly at the wall clock. 'When it happened, Dad was shocked out of his mind. He thought the world of Scott.'

'Yes, isn't that odd?' mused Paddy.

'*You* didn't?' Carrie turned her gaze back on her friend and mentor. He had never said a word against Scott.

Paddy looked embarrassed. 'Well, he's a handsome young fella. He's much admired in certain quarters. He's certainly going to be very rich, but I didn't really see you two as compatible, Carrie. Scott doesn't have your depth of character.'

'Oh, Paddy,' Carrie sighed. 'What depth of character? I'm not much of a judge, am I? Do you think it would be okay if I took this week off? I have to make arrangements to travel to the hospital. What I was going to tell you was, Dad seems to be doubling back on himself. An injured Scott is somehow working his way back to being reinstated in Dad's good books. I can *feel* it! Lately I've been wondering if Dad didn't think my getting myself engaged to Scott was the best thing I've ever done.'

Paddy shook his head. He had to bide his time to speak to Carrie in depth. He had never liked Bruce McNevin any more than he had approved of Scott Harper for Carrie. McNevin, a man of considerable reserve and a dreadful snob, was in Paddy's opinion, a controlling person. In some way he controlled his beautiful, outgoing wife. God knows why! He had long sought to control his daughter as though without his guidance her beauty would cause her to run off the rails. It was all very odd!

Both parents had acted as though the sooner Carrie was married off to a young man they judged right, the better.

Carrie stayed to have a bite of lunch with Paddy and afterwards walked down to the local super market—to stock up on a few items for which her mother had given her a list. It was as she was leaving the huge barn, pushing a laden trolley—why was it one always bought so much more than was on the list?—that she ran in to Clay.

'Hi, I'll take that.'

Her heartbeat stumbled, then staggered on. She watched as he took charge of the trolley. She hadn't spoken to him—neither of them had made contact—since that day on Jimboorie when they had gone into each other's arms. Ecstatic, then, afterwards trying to push away.

'How's Harper?' he asked, following her lead to the parking bay.

'Stable when I rang this morning.'

'And Natasha, my wayward cousin?'

'She'll be coming home. I pray to God they'll both be coming home soon.'

'So how do you feel about it?' he asked, starting to load the provisions into her 4WD.

'I'm just thankful they're alive, Clay. Other than that I feel like a complete fool.'

Clay paused in what he was doing to look down at her. There were faint shadows beneath her beautiful eyes as though she'd slept badly. 'You haven't heard yet what he has to say? I take it at this point you're not *unengaged*?'

'It's a difficult moment to announce the wedding's off,' she countered. 'The town has decided to pretend Natasha's presence in Scott's SUV was quite innocent. She was accompanying him on some journey out to Campbell's Creek a well-known beauty spot for lovers. And at *night*!'

'You don't buy the innocent story?'

She looked away from him, a pressure building up behind her rib cage. 'My mother told me not long after it happened it *wasn't*. She's dreadfully upset. So is my father. Both of them were thrilled when I got engaged to Scott.'

'In God's name, *why*?' There was a lick of anger in his brilliant blue eyes. 'It sounds to me like you were almost railroaded into it.'

She raised a delicate shoulder in a shrug. Let it drop. She realized now there was more than a grain of truth in it. 'Not anymore,' she said. 'When Scott is fit enough I'm going to tell him—'

'For the *second* time—'

'Our engagement is over.' She was wearing a wide-brimmed straw hat, protection against the hot rays of the sun but now a strong gust of wind blew it from her head.

Clay caught it, twirling it in his hand. 'Pretty!' he said, feeling both happy and sad. Something about wide-brimmed straw hats and lovely little faces beneath them made him want to laugh and cry if ever a man was allowed to cry. His mother with a redhead's porcelain complexion, had always worn big shady hats in the sun.

'If he wants to be with Natasha he's welcome to her,' Carrie was saying, sensitive to the changing expressions on his face. *What* was he thinking about?

Clay handed her hat back to her. 'Put it back on. You have the most beautiful skin. I'd say Scott will probably take the line Natasha came onto him. I think that's the sort of thing he would do. The point is, whatever arrangement he had with Natasha, he wants *you*.'

'Maybe for a while.' A little bitterness seeped out. 'But that's not going to happen, Clay.'

'I wish I could believe you,' he smiled ironically.

'What's it to you anyway?' The breathless feeling was increasing. She had never stopped thinking about this man even with everything else going on in her life.

'For a highly intelligent young woman that's a very stupid question,' he said tersely.

She had to breathe in deeply as she looked up at him. His strong features were drawn taut.

'Clay, I'm not taking anything away from…from what happened that day on Jimboorie,' she burst out emotionally. 'I fell…'

'*We* fell…' He corrected, shoving his hands deep in the pockets of his jeans lest he reach out and grab her.

'Are you going to keep interrupting me?' she asked a little raggedly.

'Yes.' He nodded. '*We* fell…'

'Fathoms deep in…*fascination,*' she said, her dark eyes enormous in her face. 'It's not love, Clay. It can't be love. We barely know one another. I've known Scott for most of my life.'

'So?' He pulled at the knotted red bandanna around his bronze throat as though he, too, were having difficulty breathing. 'You got engaged. You pleased your parents, his parents. But he certainly didn't make you happy. Are you going to admit it?'

She looked up at the blazing blue sky—the colour of his eyes—as if looking for an answer. 'I can't abandon him until he's out of hospital and safely home. He could have been killed or condemned to live life in a wheelchair. He could still take a turn for the worse.'

'I hope to God he doesn't,' Clay said, with utter soberness. 'This guy seems to be able to project guilt on you. Are you sorry about *our* time together?' He tilted her chin up. 'Tell me. I'm not here to harass you, Caroline. But I'm not going to stand by and watch you get locked into a bad situation. On your own admission your parents are coming around to dismissing the rumours or ignoring them altogether.'

'Who told *you*?' she asked, curious to know.

'Someone who was there,' he said in a clipped voice.

'Surely not one of the Campbells? You know the story. Your father was supposed to marry Elizabeth Campbell.'

His blue eyes were spangled with silver in the glare. 'Sounds like a lot of railroading goes on in this part of the world. My father told me the only woman he ever wanted to marry was my mother. If you'd have seen them together you would have known how much they loved one another.'

'They both died young,' Carrie lamented.

'Young enough,' Clay said. 'My father never used his name, Cunningham. That's just between you and me. Cunningham was too well-known and he wanted no part of his family anymore. We were the Dysons. Dyson was his second name. We kept ourselves to ourselves. After my father was killed, my mother and I were even more quiet.'

'My heart goes out to you, Clay.' Indeed all of her went out to him.

He could see the sympathy and understanding in her lovely face. 'Don't get upset, Caroline. You know what happened the last time. Do you feel like a cup of coffee?' He was desperate to prolong his time with her.

'I have to get going, Clay,' she made her excuse, seeing station women she knew wheeling out their trolleys and waving to her, eyes curious. She waved back. So did Clay.

'You don't want us to be seen together? Is that it?' His dark-timbred voice turned hard.

'No, I don't mean that.' She shook her head. 'I feel I must visit Scott in hospital. I have to make arrangements. It's a duty I can't avoid.'

He stood there looking down at her, picturing them both back at Jimboorie. 'If you want I can drive you to Toowoomba,' he said. 'Natasha mightn't love me as a cousin should but I've been thinking of calling in to see her. She might need a bit of support. I bet her family are very unhappy with her. Cunninghams *hate* scandals. When would you want to go or did you intend to fly? Are your parents going with you?'

A whole new excitement opened up. Temptation. Danger. 'Not

at this stage. We're all caught in a maze of moral dilemmas, I'm afraid. But I feel I *must* see Scott. I would never forgive myself if anything happened to him. He's been a big part of my life. God, Clay, I was going to marry him in December.'

'Marry *me* instead,' he found himself blurting out when he could well be ruining his chances by speaking out so precipitously. But, hell, wasn't he a better option than Harper?

Carrie's knees nearly gave way from under her. 'You can't be serious?'

His handsome head blocked out the sun. 'I've never been more serious in my life,' he said, flying in the face of caution. 'I wasn't joking when I said I wanted a wife and family. I do. I fully intended to advertise for the right woman. I'd thought it over carefully, came to that decision. Then along came *you*.'

'At what point did you think I might suit?' She feigned a kind of anger.

'Don't get angry,' he said. 'The last thing I intended was offence. Does it matter at what point?' Hadn't he wanted her *instantly*? But to tell her was really to risk frightening her away. 'I think we could make a go of it, Caroline. You'd never feel trapped with me. You love Jimboorie and the old homestead. I've seen that with my own eyes. We could restore it. I'm sure you know all about that side of things.' She was the sort of girl he'd dreamed of but doubted he'd ever find.

Bees were buzzing in a nearby flowering bottle brush or was it a sound in her head? 'Clay, you can't speak to me this way.' She clenched her hands together in agitation.

'Why not?' He lowered his resonant voice lest it float all over the parking area. 'This is a serious proposal. One I'd be honoured if you'd consider. I'm not stone-broke like everyone seems to think. Miracles do happen in life. I've no great fortune, but quite enough to be going on with. I could make a good life for you. I'd dedicate myself to it.'

'You'd marry a woman you didn't love?' She stared up at him, knowing his dedication wouldn't be enough for her. Scales had been lifted from her eyes. She wanted a man who would love her passionately. As passionately as she loved him. Love that would be there to stay.

'You were going to marry a man you didn't love,' he pointed out very quietly.

She felt like she was being swept along in a turbulent stream. 'Clay, I can't possibly consider this. It would take more than I'm prepared to give. Besides, I'm in an impossible place in my life. Haven't you enough admirers already? You could have had your pick of a dozen at the gala dance?'

'What, pretty little teenagers who don't yet know their own minds?'

'There were others!'

'Stop, Caroline,' he said. 'I understand you're in a difficult place. I daresay your parents wouldn't be happy about me, but I know we can make a real go of it. I can't put it better than that. Except to say I'm as strongly attracted to you as you are to me. Okay, it's not love. You say you can't fall in love right away. But what we have is *good*.'

She couldn't deny it. What they had was beautiful. No one could take that kiss away, but exposing her heart with all that had happened to her seemed an ominous thing to do. Her fellow shoppers would probably think she was flirting with Clay when Scott was lying comatose in a hospital bed.

Knowing what sort of person Carrie was, the other women shoppers *weren't* thinking that at all, but Carrie found herself burdened by unwarranted guilt.

'When are you wanting to leave?' Clay asked, oblivious of anyone now but Carrie.

'Tomorrow morning,' she said. 'It would be a three-hour drive even moving!'

'I'll take you,' he said.

'So how would we meet up?' she asked shakily. God, she wanted so much to be with him when she didn't even know if she could handle it. Her whole philosophy of life was coming under bombardment. It was as though a volcano lying dormant within her was showing perilous signs of erupting.

'What the hell, I'll drive out to Victory Downs,' Clay decided. 'I'll get an early start. What have we got to hide anyway? I'm going to see my cousin. You're going to see your ex-fiancé. No need for me to come in and meet the folks,' he said with extreme dryness. 'You can come out to the car.'

Carrie shook her head. She just couldn't face her father's opposition. It would be like a great icy wind from Antarctica. 'I'll meet you in town. I'll park here.'

'What time can you make it?' He didn't like the idea of her making all these long drives.

'Eight o'clock. Is that too late?'

'Eight's fine. Put in a few clothes. You'll be tired. We might as well stay in Toowoomba overnight.' His blue eyes looked directly into hers. 'Trust me, Caroline. We'll be fine.'

Did she trust him?

That wasn't the question at all. The answer was and it came right away. Did she trust *herself?*

When she found Scott's room, his parents were already there, seated at their son's bedside.

'Carrie, dear!' Thea Harper rose at once, coming to hug and kiss her. 'I'm so glad you're here.'

'Carrie!' Even Bradley Harper's severe face broke into a smile. 'Thanks for coming. How did you get here?'

'Drove,' Carrie said, cutting off the conversation by moving quickly towards the bed. 'How is he?' She bent over Scott's prone frame, gently, even tenderly, taking his hand. 'Any change?'

'They've wound down the drugs,' Thea Harper said, in a shaky voice. 'They're waiting for him to come out of it.'

Carrie lowered herself into the chair Bradley Harper drew up for her close to Scott's head. He looked very young and handsome. Sleeping quietly except for the monitors. 'He's going to be all right,' she said.

'Oh, God, he has to be!' Thea Harper suddenly started to sob.

'Thea, stop that,' her husband commanded. 'You're wearing yourself out. Scotty's going to be okay now Carrie's here.'

Please, please, please, don't put this on me, Carrie thought, something like panic crawling across her skin.

How was she supposed to feel when Scott had been continuing an affair with his old flame? Ready to forgive and forget? It seemed so. As far as the Harpers were concerned she and Scott were destined for marriage no matter what! The Harpers adored their only child so much they were prepared to make any sacrifice for him including *her*. If, God forbid, Scott were to be confined to a wheelchair they would still expect her to go through with the marriage. If she loved him, she would. Now she fully understood she didn't love him.

The Harpers, sick and exhausted, had gone off to have coffee leaving Carrie still sitting by Scott's bed. She, too, had shut her eyes as a headache pressed down on her temples, although she was still gently holding his fingers.

'Carrie?'

Her eyes flew open. She hadn't imagined that. Scott had spoken, sounding perfectly lucid. 'You're awake. Oh, thank God!'

'What happened?'

His dilated pupils seemed impossibly large. 'It's okay. You're all right,' she patted him reassuringly. 'You're in hospital. You were in an accident. You were badly concussed. Hang on, I have to get a doctor in here.' She rose from her chair.

'Don't leave me,' Scott called. 'Don't ever leave me.'

Carrie flew out to the nurses' station, her mind swirling with crazy thoughts of flight.

The Harpers were ecstatic. 'It was *you*!' Thea Harper, laughing and crying gave Carrie all the credit. 'He heard your voice. He felt the touch of your hand.'

'He was ready to come out of it, Mrs. Harper,' Carrie said, aware Scott's doctor was studying her with a close but friendly eye.

'No, *you* were the miracle!' Thea maintained, hugging Carrie yet again, her exhaustion lifted. 'You, Carrie McNevin. You're an angel.'

An angel, imagine!

'Look I'll have to shoo you all out for ten minutes or so,' the doctor said. 'You can come back one at a time and say your goodbyes. This sleeping beauty might have awakened, but he's still in need of plenty of rest.'

'We'll go,' Bradley Harper said, putting an arm around his wife. 'Love you, son!' A hard, tough man, he declared it in a strong, emotional voice. That hurt Carrie. She doubted her father could ever say that to *her*. Certainly not in that voice. 'We'll be back later,' Brad Harper said.

'Don't go, Carrie,' Scott appealed to Carrie, his eyes glassy. 'I need you here. Carrie?'

She looked at the doctor unsure what to do. 'She can come back later,' the doctor said. 'Settle back, young man. You want to get out of here as soon as possible, don't you?'

'Can't wait. Everything is going to be okay, Carrie,' Scott said and it seemed to her there was full comprehension in his eyes. 'Kiss me before you go.'

She bent over him, touching her lips to his temple. 'I'll come back later, okay?'

'I love you,' Scott said, as though there were no other woman in the world.

* * *

The Harpers were waiting for her down the corridor. Thea reached out to hug her yet again. 'You're really a godsend, Carrie. *You* are the one he needs.'

The pressure was getting scary. 'We should talk about that, Mrs. Harper, but not today,' Carrie said. 'Are you going to look in on Natasha? She hasn't been discharged yet.'

'Of course we're not going to look in on that scheming young woman,' Thea said. 'She's done nothing but throw herself shamelessly at Scott.'

'It appears I was the only one who didn't know that,' Carrie said quietly.

'My son loves only *you*, Carrie,' Brad Harper told her in a voice that defied her to disagree. 'Natasha Cunningham meant nothing to him.'

'Actually she did, Mr. Harper,' Carrie said, inside objecting to his domineering tone. Why did men want so much power over women? 'But let's not spoil the moment. Scott is going to make a full recovery.'

'Thank God!' the Harpers declared in unison. 'Come and have a coffee with us, Carrie,' Thea invited. 'We're drowning in it but we can have tea.'

'Thank you, Mrs. Harper, but I intend to look in on Natasha,' Carrie said, letting them make what they liked of that.

'Good! Give her what for!' Brad Harper advised, his weathered face grim.

Natasha Cunningham was not in bed. She was sitting in an armchair looking out the window, her back to Carrie. No one else was in the room. Clay must have gone, although they had made arrangements to meet up late afternoon.

'Natasha, it's me, Carrie,' she said in as gentle a voice as she could muster.

A moment of stunned silence, then, 'What the hell are *you*

doing here?' Natasha responded roughly. She thrust up and turned around as if prepared for confrontation.

'I would have thought that obvious,' Carrie said. 'I came to see how you are. Knowing what your family is like I thought you could do with a friend.'

'Ain't that the truth!' Natasha was half laughing now, but she looked terrible. She was white and drained, her eyes bloodshot and red rimmed as though she had never stopped crying. The right side of her face was black and blue all around the jawline. Lacerations were clearly visible on her lower neck and arms. She wasn't in hospital garb. She was wearing a T-shirt and loose linen trousers that hung on her. Always bone thin, she had lost even more weight.

'Thank God you got out of it as well as you did,' Carrie said. 'Please sit down again. You don't look so good.'

'How's Scotty?' Natasha asked, leaning over as though her stomach ached. 'I dared not go near his room.'

'I was about to tell you. *When* you sit down. Preferably lie down.'

'Okay, okay.' Natasha waved a hand irritably, but she went back to the bed. 'How is he?' She stared Carrie right in the eye.

'You know he's been in a medically induced coma. He's fully conscious now. He recognises everyone. The fractured clavicle will keep him quiet for a couple of months and he can forget polo for a while longer, but he'll heal. His doctor is expecting him to make a full recovery. His youth and fitness will be a big help.'

There was an unbearably intense look or gladness and relief on Natasha's face. Then she burst into violent tears. 'It was all my fault. Everything is my fault.'

Carrie could only feel pity. 'Are you well enough to talk about it or should we let it go?' Her very nature was preventing her from feeling the ill will towards Natasha she thoroughly deserved.

'You must be furious with me. Furious and disgusted.'

Natasha dashed her tears away with the back of her head. 'I'm a bitch. A real bad bitch. I've gloried in it.'

'No, you haven't.' Carrie shook her head, suddenly convinced it was true. 'Somehow I think you've been pushed into that role. I'm not furious with you. I don't exactly understand why. By rights, I should be.' Carrie reached inside her handbag for some clean tissues, which she passed to Natasha. 'Did you have an argument? Was that it? Scott lost control of the wheel?' She could well see it happening. Natasha was such a volatile young woman.

'Do you love him, Carrie?' Natasha didn't answer Carrie's questions but asked one of her own. 'He's a real bastard you know.'

'But *you* love him,' Carrie pointed out, doing her own ignoring.

'God knows why! I've always loved him. I've tried, but I could never get myself free of him. He took *my* virginity, you know. I might have held on to it longer if not for him. And he wasn't too gentle about it, either. Scotty only thinks about *himself.*'

'It certainly looks like it,' Carrie agreed. 'And you've been with him all this time?'

Natasha wept afresh, charcoal smudges beneath her eyes. 'He's as mad as he can be for you, but you wouldn't come across. He told me. I could barely stop laughing. I, unlike you, couldn't keep away from him. Not that he ever turned me down. Sex is very high on Scotty's agenda.'

'A little bit *too* high, if you ask me,' Carrie said, crisply.

Natasha nodded as though they were two friends having a serious discussion. 'He even wanted it the night of the dance when he had that fight with Clay.'

'Oh my Lord!' Carrie groaned softly. 'And that's the man I got myself engaged to! How utterly blind I've been.'

'Don't sound so shocked.' Natasha picked up a few white grapes and popped them in her mouth. 'He needed comfort. He knows I can give it to him. None of this little bit of loving stuff like you dish out.'

'Thanks for sharing that with me, Natasha,' Carrie said. 'You're one underhanded pair and it's starting to show.'

Natasha laughed. 'You're a very dull person, Carrie. Face it. I have more than a few tricks.'

'Of course you have,' Carrie said. 'Even then Scott isn't all that interested in you.'

'*You* don't love him,' Natasha cried, mortally stung.

'You'd have been ready to do violence had I truly taken your man.'

'You bet!' Natasha wiped her mouth with the back of her hand. 'I'd have skinned you alive.'

'Only I wouldn't stoop to prostituting myself with another woman's fiancée,' Carrie said flatly. 'Has Clay been to see you?'

She didn't expect to see a smile break across Natasha's face. 'You know my cousin's a really nice guy when you get to know him. One of the *good* guys. I didn't get to know too many of them. Scott got in the way. Clay would never tell a woman to get herself an abortion.'

Carrie felt like an avalanche had hit her. *Abortion!* She could even feel herself turn pale.

'I'm sorry, Carrie,' Natasha burst out. 'I'm really and truly sorry. You're a good guy, too. You've always been nice to me even when I've been a pig.'

Carrie hardly heard her. 'You're pregnant?' she asked, astonished now Natasha hadn't caused it to happen long before this.

Natasha's answer came right away, not without a trace of triumph. 'I am.'

'Even through the accident?' It was a mystery to Carrie.

'Strong little beggar,' Natasha said, fondly.

'How far along are you?'

'Ten weeks,' Natasha said, patting her flat tummy.

'Did you tell Clay?'

'God no!' Natasha looked astounded by the question. 'Of

course I didn't. What's it got to do with him? Strewth, he was acting like *you're* the love of his life. What's with you anyway that the guys get so carried away?'

'*You're* the one who got carried away, Natasha,' Carrie said, her expression firming. 'Either that or you decided to resolve the situation. I wouldn't put it past you.'

'It wasn't like that,' Natasha said.

Carrie shook her head. 'You have a gnat's sense of what's right and wrong, Natasha. And Scott suggested you get an abortion?'

'Not suggested, dear. Scott's not like that. It was a command. It's *you* he wants to marry. I'm beginning to wonder if you little virgins aren't the smartest of us all.'

Carrie ignored the comment; instead she asked, 'What are you going to do about the baby?'

Natasha touched her stomach tenderly again. 'I don't know yet. This will be a great, great scandal unless I pack up and leave home in a hurry.'

'Do your parents know?'

Natasha shook her dark head vehemently. 'Come off it, Carrie. We're talking the world's most sanctimonious people. It's just you, me and Scotty. And the doctor who examined me, of course and he's not talking.'

'You must keep the baby, Natasha,' Carrie said, trying hard to deal with all this. 'It's precious new life you're carrying. This is *your* child. You'll regret it all the days of your life if you allow yourself to be talked into an abortion. Your little one has put up a fight for life so far.'

'That he has. It's a boy, I know. Scotty's son.' Natasha stretched out a leisurely hand for more grapes, her expression showing maternal pride.

Carrie's head was swimming so badly she might have been drunk. There was an ache in her heart. A worse ache in her head.

'So you'd better get Scotty to marry you,' she said, somehow finding the strength to stand up. 'I wouldn't touch him with a barge pole.'

CHAPTER SIX

THEY sat in a quiet corner of a little restaurant at the top of the Range, a twinkling world of coloured lights spread out across the city beneath them.

'No appetite?' Clay asked, having watched her toy with the delicious food.

'I should have stuck with the entrée,' Carrie said, putting down her knife and fork. 'The food's great, but life's getting too much for me.' Her dark velvety eyes registered sadness.

'Scott's going to make a full recovery,' he pointed out. 'That must take a lot of the burden off you.' He hoped to God it did. Maybe then she could tell Scott to let go.

'It does,' she admitted.

'Is there something you're not telling me?'

'Yes.' He was just so perceptive, she dipped her head.

'Thought so.' He let his eyes rest on her. She was wearing a bare little black top with a multi-coloured, multi-patterned gauzy skirt that almost reached her ankles. Her beautiful long hair braided away from her face shone pure gold in the candlelight. Her skin had an equally lovely gold tint. He had never seen any woman he thought more beautiful. No woman to touch her.

'Obviously it's very much upset you?' He topped up her glass of white wine.

'Thank you.' She raised her glass and took a long sip. 'This is in complete confidence, because I trust you.'

Warning bells began ringing inside his head. 'Just so long as you're not about to tell me you're going to marry Harper in December?' His eyes sizzled over her.

'I'm *not* going to marry Scott,' she said and shook her head. 'Chances are when he's fit enough—or even before then—he'll be marrying Natasha.'

Clay sat back, astonished, though Carrie had delivered the news quite matter-of-factly. 'Now that's the very *last* thing I expected to hear.'

'She's pregnant,' Carrie explained, still in that quiet even tone. 'I had to tell someone. I couldn't keep it to myself. Natasha is pregnant with my ex-fiancé's child.'

'God!' Clay was genuinely stunned. 'Doesn't she know about contraception?'

Finally Carrie released a long-baffled sigh. 'Being Natasha I'd say she took her chances. She could even have been trying to push her luck. Who knows? The fact is, she's carrying Scott's child.'

'Then he must marry her,' Clay said as though there were no other course open to the man.

'He told her to have an abortion.'

Clay couldn't disguise his contempt. 'Doesn't that say everything you need to know about Scott Harper? His *own* child and he's ready to destroy it? Natasha can't listen to him. Times have changed so much. She'll get through and she'll adore her baby.'

'I hope so,' Carrie said, thinking the essence of the Cunninghams was their coldheartedness. 'There aren't too many families like yours.'

'They're not *my* family,' Clay retorted, his voice peppered with loathing. 'Nor will they ever be in my mind. I gather Natasha doesn't get along too well with her parents. It doesn't make sense to me, these rich people. They have everything and they have nothing. Then again Natasha is getting looked after so well financially she'd never leave home.'

Carrie drank her wine slowly. 'I would say that's because of Scott.' Natasha wasn't far off thirty and on her own admission she hadn't really looked beyond her first lover.

'The bastard!' Clay exploded, then apologised.

'No need, you're spot on. Scott has always been in the picture.'

'Poor Natasha!' Clay said. 'Though she doesn't seem to have much going for her in the way of morals. But she was nice for the time I was with her. Quiet and introspective. Now I know why. In a way it's the same for her as you. Harper caught both of you into a trap.'

Carrie tasted the bitter truth. 'I'm thinking Natasha turned the tables on him.'

'You said it's over?' Clay caught the tips of her fingers across the table.

'It's over,' she said, reacting to the thrill of his hand on hers.

'But you haven't told him?'

She averted her dark eyes. 'When he's settled back at home Scott and I will be having a serious talk.'

'I'm really happy to hear that,' Clay said, not looking happy at all. 'He surely doesn't think Natasha is going to do as he says?'

'He'd have to be forced to marry her,' Carrie gave her opinion. 'I don't think his parents would force him to do anything. Especially after his accident which apparently Natasha caused.'

'I'm sure she didn't plan it. I guess he went ballistic when she told him.'

'I would say his reaction would be fairly strong.'

'Anyway, that's their problem. Natasha's child is the Harper's grandchild. Surely that means everything to them? Their *grandchild*? The Cunninghams aren't nobodies. Natasha's parents would adjust overnight. So would the town if Scott and Natasha were to marry.'

'Nothing would surprise me,' Carrie said, 'but I have the awful feeling some of the scandal will stick to *me*.'

'You're the innocent party,' Clay said.

'That won't stop it. It never does. I don't feel like I'm walking on solid ground any more.'

'I can understand that,' he said quietly. 'You're in shock. You have to give yourself a little time, Caroline.'

'*You* have to give me a little time.' She looked into his eyes, sealing the rest of the world off.

'I'd give you all the time in the world if only we had it,' he replied. 'I know what's in my head already.' He could, and perhaps should, have said what's in 'my head and my *heart*.' It was true enough, but she still wasn't absolutely free of Harper. 'I know it came out all wrong the last time. I startled you. I see now I could hardly fail to do so, but I'm here for you, Caroline, once Harper is out of the way. I seem to have been alone for so much of my life. It wasn't only my father who left me. My mother left me as well after he was killed. Neither of them returned.'

She pressed her hands against the heat in her cheeks. It flamed through her whole body. 'What if you found you couldn't love me? *After* marriage, for all your best intentions it just didn't happen?' It was a legitimate fear.

All Clay wanted to do was rain kisses on her face, her throat, her breasts, down over her whole body to her toes as beautifully formed as were her slender fingers. Fingers that were doubly pretty because she wasn't wearing Harper's ring. When had she taken that off?

'I refuse to believe it couldn't happen,' he said. 'Didn't a fire burn inside you when I kissed you?'

She was almost ready to tell him his kiss had awakened her to full life only she held back. 'This is the wrong time for a courtship, Clay,' she said. 'You know it's funny, but sometimes, I badly want to call you James,' she confessed.

'So you can call me James when we marry.' He gave her the smile that so easily melted her heart.

'I think it's time to take me back to the hotel,' she murmured, just that little bit scared of so much emotion. When she was with Clay she wasn't prim and proper Carrie. She was someone else.

'Do you intend seeing Harper again in the morning before we return?' he asked, somehow sensing what was actually in her mind. He, too, was overwhelmed by the powerful attraction that had overtaken them. He had wished for the right woman. It had happened. But he could see she was so unguarded she could snap.

'I don't want to, but I will.' Carrie spoke more firmly. 'Hospitals aren't the best places to deliver bad news. And it *will* be bad news for Scott and his parents. Scott has lived his life thinking he can have any girl he wants. For whatever his reasons he's hell-bent on marrying me. Perhaps it was because I wasn't giving him what he wanted? I had to be absolutely *his* and marriage was the only way? Who knows? He was only using Natasha when she lay in bed with him. I feel sorry for her. Nevertheless at this point he's too sick to tell him what I think of him. That will have to wait.'

'So we're going around in circles?' Clay realized he had to accept that. He gestured to the waiter for the bill.

'It's a bit like that.' Briefly Carrie met his gaze.

She was standing quietly in the foyer, admiring the exquisite flower arrangement—this after all was the Garden City of Queensland—while Clay settled the bill.

He joined her after a moment and took her arm. They were barely out the door when they were confronted by a well dressed middle-aged couple about to enter the restaurant. It was the Harpers, even though Carrie had been given to understand that Bradley Harper was returning home, leaving his wife staying with a friend who lived on the Range.

Carrie felt so guilty she might have been caught in the exe-
cution of a serious crime.

The Harpers, too, looked startled.

'What on earth are you doing here, Carrie? And with *him*?'
Shock quickly turned to outright aggression as Bradley Harper addressed her in his deep, gravelly voice. He snapped a furious
glance over Clay who stood, a tall, quiet presence by Carrie's side.

'Good evening, Mr and Mrs Harper,' Carrie said in her
usual courteous manner. 'You remember Clay, don't you?
Clay Cunningham?'

'Yes,' Thea Harper said briefly, incapable of arranging her
face into a smile. She was pale with dismay. 'What are you
doing here together, Carrie? I don't understand. Scott's still lying
in hospital and you've had dinner with this young man? I really
can't believe it. Not *you,* Carrie. You always conduct yourself
so well.'

'I hope I'm still doing that, Mrs. Harper,' Carrie said. 'Clay
is my friend. Nothing more.' That wasn't true but they didn't have
to know. 'Many things have changed since before and after
Scott's accident. I'm so glad he's going to make a full recovery
but Scott knows in his heart our engagement is over. It just wasn't
the right time to make that perfectly plain to him at the hospital.
I'll delay our talk until he's well enough.'

The Harpers stood staring at her. 'You're not *serious*? You
can't be, Carrie,' Thea Harper moved forward to lay a hand on
Carrie's arm. 'You're overreacting surely? My son adores you.'

'That's not true, Mrs. Harper,' Carrie said very gently. 'I don't
want to distress you. I know how upset you and Mr. Harper have
been, but Scott really is involved with Natasha. I'll allow him to
tell you about it himself.'

Bradley Harper broke in so violently he must have reached
breaking point. 'Involved with Natasha Cunningham, rubbish!
There are always women like Natasha Cunningham in life. What

I want to know is, what's been going on between *you* two?' His expression turned ugly.

Clay spoke for the first time. 'Have a care, Mr. Harper,' he said in a very quiet, controlled sort of voice.

'What was that? Speak up?' Bradley Harper, a powerful man, began to square up, looking at the six-foot-three, superbly fit young man as though he were an insect to be crushed underfoot.

'You heard me perfectly well the first time,' Clay said. 'We're in public, remember? I suggest you back down. And you might apologise to Caroline. She's the injured party here.'

'*Caroline?*' Harper's expression froze. 'She's not *Caroline*. She's Carrie. Don't get smart with me, son!' Bradley Harper warned, his beefy, still handsome face flushed with blood. 'I saw off your father. I'll do the same for you.'

'I wouldn't bank on that.' Clay's alert stance and sombre tone would have convinced anyone. 'As I understand it you didn't see off my father, as you call it. Your men saw him off your station at gunpoint. You didn't appear at all. I'm not like my father anyway. My father was a *gentle* man. I'm not.'

A rush of contemptuous laughter broke from Bradley Harper's mouth. 'Why you arrogant young bastard!' That peculiar smile broadened as he threw a rage packed right hook, which Clay blocked so effectively the older man went staggering back. Like father. Like son.

Both women were utterly dismayed. 'Please. Please stop it!' Carrie begged. This wasn't what they wanted. Other people were coming out of the restaurant, staring at them, whispering.

'You'll be sorry for that!' Bradley Harper snarled at Clay after he righted himself and regained a little control. 'How dare you lay a hand on me? Do you even have a clue how powerful I am?'

'You're not above the law, Mr Harper,' Clay reminded him, in a voice that held a natural authority. 'What you attempted was assault. *I'll* lay charges if you ever attempt anything like that again. Believe me, I only stopped you because of the ladies and the fact I knew you'd come off badly.'

The tears were spilling down Thea Harper's face. 'Brad, please! You're making a spectacle of us.' She'd had the feeling all along it wasn't a good idea for Brad to bring her here. Now *this*!

'*These two* are making the show,' Bradley Harper corrected her with surprising venom.

'I'm sorry, Mrs Harper.' Carrie, who was trembling badly, took Clay's arm to move him away. She could feel the tension right through his body—the desire she supposed, to pummel Bradley Harper as he had pummelled Scott. There were old issues that had to be settled here, though she knew it wouldn't be Clay who would make the first move. He'd simply finish it.

Neither of them said a word all the way back to the hotel where they were staying.

'I feel like a drink,' Clay said softly, when they entered the hotel lobby. 'Care to join me?'

'I'll sit for a while,' she said, too upset to go up to her room. 'I feel very shaky. He's an awful man, Brad Harper.'

'Of course he is.' Clay led her into the well-appointed lounge where a few guests were seated at the small circular tables. 'You can count your lucky stars you won't be getting him for a father-in-law after all.'

'Mrs Harper is okay.' She sank into a plush banquette, resting her back against it. 'She's easy enough to get on with, but she's right under his thumb, poor woman. He's such a domineering man. Even Scott is intimidated by his father.'

'Bag of wind,' Clay said, dismissing the powerful and ruthless Bradley Harper. 'What can I get you?'

'I don't especially want anything.' Yes, she did. She wanted his arms around her.

'What about a brandy and ginger? You want something to settle you down. I'm for a single malt whiskey. Don't move from this spot. I'll be back in a moment.'

Her mother and father would soon get the news, Carrie thought, watching Clay walk over to the bar. When he arrived there, he turned and looked back at her. Even at a distance his eyes *burned* an electric-blue.

She gave him a little wave, conscious women at other tables were looking at him as well. And why not? He was a marvellous looking man. She hadn't planned on falling in love with him. Yet here she was with him. She saw him give the order to the bartender, then he returned to the table, settling his tall, rangy frame into the banquette beside her.

Carrie drew great comfort from his nearness. Comfort and a kind of bliss that flushed her skin and made her look as though she were lit from within.

'What's with the Harpers always throwing punches?' he asked, wryly. 'Wild punches, I might add.'

'They see themselves as men of action,' Carrie said, with a crazy impulse to lay her head on his shoulder.

'Better to think first and act later,' Clay said, looking towards the waiter who was approaching with their drinks.

Carrie took not a sip, but a gulp of her drink. Things were getting right out of hand. The encounter with the Harpers had really thrown her. Her drink was cold and the shot of brandy added depth to the sparkling ginger ale. 'Mrs Harper won't lose any time ringing my parents to let them know they've seen me with you,' she said, one part of her admiring the paintings around the walls. 'They'll do it tonight.'

'It's always best to say exactly what you're doing, Caroline,' he told her quietly. 'You're a grown woman not a child. You could have told your mother I was giving you a lift.'

'I did,' she said.

'Well, that's not so bad then?' He studied her pure profile. 'Would she tell your father?'

Carrie shook her head. 'No. I'm beginning to think there's lots my mother doesn't tell my father. Sometimes I can't figure Mamma out. She does things I know she doesn't want to, to please Dad.'

'Lots of wives would do that.'

'Mamma does it for a *living*,' Carrie said. 'It's all coming to a head, isn't it?'

'It has to, Caroline. You have to get on with your life. Whether I'm in it or not remains to be seen.'

'Sure you don't want to run that advertisement?' she asked, tilting her head to stare into his eyes.

'Only if you write it up for me.'

'Let's see, how would it go?'

'You're the journalist,' he reminded her.

'Photojournalist,' she corrected with a little smile. 'I take photos for the *Bulletin* as well.'

'I'm certain you'll take a good one of me. Now where were we?'

'Bush Bachelor, twenty-eight, never married, very fit, owns his own pastoral property, is looking for a wife aged between—?'

'Twenty-four and twenty-eight,' he filled in, in a helpful tone of voice. 'Under twenty-four too young to really know their own mind, over twenty-eight older than me. Twenty-four for preference. Petite. Must be a golden-blonde with velvety-brown doe eyes. A countrywoman, loves the land, an excellent horse-woman, interested in restoring a historic homestead, eventually having kids, two or three, must be able to guarantee a daughter who looks just like her. Let's see, what else?'

'You don't need me at all,' she said. She took another little swallow. Even tried a smile.

'Oh, yes, I do. Haven't I just described you?'

'Maybe I was the first one your gaze really fell on?' she suggested. 'Maybe knowing I was Scott Harper's fiancée had something to do with it?'

'What is that supposed to mean, Caroline?'

The question was dead serious. 'Didn't Brad Harper fire up when you called me Caroline?' she remarked, ignoring his question. 'You'd think that wasn't allowed.'

'Answer the question, please.' He gently tapped the back of her hand.

'Maybe you felt like taking something of his?'

He kept looking at her until she looked away. 'Actually I'm fine with that, but the thought never crossed my mind. I saw the connection as a huge complication. I definitely wanted to get to know you better, but there you were, engaged.'

The air around them seemed on the point of igniting. 'I'm sorry,' Carrie apologised.

'So you should be. But I'll forgive you. This one time.'

'It could just as easily have been someone else. One of the McFadden sisters,' she persisted. 'Jade or Mia. Both of them are very attractive and good company. They're station people. They're good riders. Jade and I often battle it out for first place in competitions. They certainly gave the impression they were attracted to you.'

'So we've narrowed it down to the McFadden sisters and *you*.'

Inside she was deeply, *deeply,* shaken. 'I can't see clearly about myself, Clay. You've got to heed it. What I do see is a twenty-four-year-old woman who was about to marry a man who continued to sleep with other women—I bet there were others—while we were engaged, then he impregnated one. Finally to cap it off a man who told another woman to get rid of his own child so he could still marry me. What kind of a fool did he think I was? What kind of a fool am I for that matter?'

'What kind of a callous bastard is he, don't you mean?' Clay responded, with frightening calm. 'Countless people have been deceived, Caroline. Men and women. They give their trust only to have it trampled underfoot. One doesn't have to be a fool for that to happen. It happens right across the board.'

'Trust is so very important,' she said quietly. 'It is to me yet it's so easy to lose faith. What happens then? Does one turn into a cynic, never trusting anyone again?'

'You know what they say! Life's a gamble. Love's a gamble. We come through with courage and a dollop of daring.'

'And there's another thing about me,' she said. 'I don't know my own mind. I'd be devastated if I'd truly loved Scott. Obviously I didn't. I just thought I was in love with him.'

'So when did you wake up to the fact you weren't?' he asked dryly. 'Did it just happen one morning?'

She turned her head slightly. 'The fact I could so easily be attracted to you was a tremendous eye opener. What if it had happened *after* I married Scott?'

'No need to worry about it,' he consoled her. 'You're not going to marry Scott. We might leave the rest of that drink.'

'Are you saying I've had too much?' There was a little flash in her dark eyes.

'Perhaps the tiniest little bit. You had very little to eat and that confrontation with the Harpers upset you.'

'Didn't it upset you?'

'I wanted to hit that man,' Clay admitted, his handsome face taut. 'I wanted to hit him so badly, but he's too old to hit. And then there were you women. Women don't like violence.'

'You're right about that!' she wholeheartedly agreed. 'I'm apprehensive about what my father is going to say.'

'He's very tough on you in his way, isn't he? Why *is* that?' He studied her, a beautiful, refined young woman any father would be proud of. He was quite unable to understand it.

Carrie suddenly picked up her glass and clinked it against his in a funny little gesture. 'Our personalities are incompatible?' she suggested, with a brittle little laugh. 'There's something about me he doesn't like? I suppose it can happen.'

'Leave home, Caroline,' he advised. 'It's time you did.'

'Victory Downs isn't going to be mine, anyway,' she sighed. She didn't want the rest of her drink but she had it anyway.

'How's that?' A vertical line appeared between his strongly marked brows. 'You're an only child. Who else can take over?'

'My cousin, Alex, will inherit. He's still a student.'

'Good God!' Clay found himself appalled. 'So what's your little lot?'

'Did you think I was an heiress?' she asked, outright challenge glimmering in her eyes. 'Did you think you just could land an heiress? You didn't put that in the ad.'

'Caroline, I couldn't care less if you were penniless,' he said a little curtly. 'It's *you,* the woman, I'm interested in.'

'That's what they all say.' He was quite right. She was just that tiny bit intoxicated. 'I'll be "well looked after" I've been told. Besides, I was to marry Bradley Harper's heir. That was considered a compelling reason for matrimony.'

'How very mercenary,' he said with contempt.

'Only I'm not marrying anyone,' she said.

They took the lift to Carrie's floor walking down the quiet, empty corridor to her room. There they paused while Carrie hunted up her keycard.

'You seem to be taking an awfully long time,' he said, an attractive wry note in his voice.

'Damn, where is it?' She knew she had it. 'I know!' She sank her hand into the deep hidden pocket in her skirt.

'Here, give it to me.' He took the keycard from her, opening up the door. 'Good night, Caroline,' he said.

'Goodness, you sound as if you have a very pressing engagement elsewhere. Are you that anxious to get rid of me!' She pushed past him and entered the comfortably furnished room, switching on more lights. Am I about to make a fool of myself? she thought. Why not? He already knows I am.

'Come here,' he said gently, standing just inside the door.

She spun about. 'There's nothing going to happen, Clay.'

'What makes you suppose there was?' His blue eyes gave off sparks.

'The way you're looking at me for one thing,' she said, trying to keep her emotional equilibrium and losing the battle. 'I'm a virgin. Did I mention that? It's a joke these days.'

He stayed where he was. He wasn't smiling. 'Why wouldn't a woman keep herself for the man she truly loves?'

'For fear she mightn't find him and life is flying by. I'm sorry, Clay. I'm trying to tell you I'm not a good judge.'

'You're tired,' he said. 'Exhausted.'

'We both are. Do you want to sleep with me in this bed?'

He didn't say anything for a moment. He just wanted to look at her. 'I don't think I'd be doing much sleeping,' he said, finally. 'I told you, Caroline. There's no pressure.'

'That's something else!' she said raggedly, doing a half spin. 'Scott was ready to wait. Next thing he's trying to rape me.'

Clay remembered that night very clearly; the way he had felt. 'Don't remind me! That would never happen to *any* woman with me, Caroline. You know that. Come on now, you're tired and upset. You'll get over all this. It's been pretty full on, one thing after another.'

'And another to face,' she said, leaning wearily against an armchair.

'I'm driving you back to Victory Downs tomorrow,' he told her firmly. 'We can get your 4WD picked up from the town and delivered to the station. I don't want you pushing on home.'

She wasn't looking forward to it, either. 'There'd be fireworks, Clay,' she warned.

He wasn't worried for himself. 'Your father's temper wouldn't bother me any more than Brad Harper's. I didn't think your father gave way to emotion anyway, he looks so darn buttoned up.'

For a moment Carrie looked quite lost. 'I should have said iceworks, not fireworks. Dad freezes you out.'

'I'm driving you home, Carrie,' Clay repeated. 'Right to your door. Now come here.'

Adrenaline shot into her bloodstream. All her senses lifted and began to soar. 'What for?'

'I want to kiss you,' he said simply, not taking his eyes off her. 'I want to take your *kiss* with me to bed.'

What else could she do? Every cell in her body demanded it. She walked towards him as if she couldn't keep away.

His arms were around her, his hand at the back of her neck, taking the weight off her head. He was so much taller he was lifting her, enveloping her. He bore her weight so easily her feet were clear of the ground.

'Caroline!' he breathed, over her head.

Then his marvellous mouth came down on hers. She was so hungry, *greedy* to keep it there. What had happened to that *absent* part of her? The part Scott had never been able to reach? Did she only come alive through this man? The pleasure he gave her was so sensual, so limb melting, she thought as she collapsed against him. At any rate she relaxed into a posture of utter submission waiting for him to open her up like a flower.

All her defences were tumbling. She gathered nectar from his open mouth, kissing and nibbling at those cleanly defined, upraised edges as she went.

They were breathing as one.

It was an agony and an ecstasy to kiss and be kissed like this. The one counter-balancing the other. Agony. Ecstasy. But she wanted more. Much more. She realised now she was desperately in need of love. She wanted *everything* a man and a woman in love did together. It was impossible to resist longing such as this. Such was the nature of passion…

Next thing she knew she was lying on the bed, her eyelids closed tight. She was listening to the rapid-fire beating of her heart. It seemed to be shaking her entire being. She lifted a hand to contain her wild heart, slowly opening her eyes.

Only to discover Clay was gone.

CHAPTER SEVEN

CLAY'S big 4WD hummed along the highway, its shadow racing after them. A heat haze rose off the never ending black ribbon of road, shimmering in the air in front of the bonnet. The Great Dividing Range that stretched five thousand kilometres from the tropical tip of Cape York in Far North Queensland to the magnificent stone ramparts of the Grampian Ranges in Victoria, loomed to their left, a formidable barrier between the lush eastern seaboard and the vast Outback. The dry, *dry,* land that had taken the lives of early explorers and many an adventurer without trace. Today the Range looked spectacular, Clay thought, its rugged slopes hyacinth-blue in the blazing heat. It was another brilliantly fine day and the huge Spinifex plains were beginning to reveal themselves in wild golds and greens with broad domed, stunted trees dotted here and there over the countryside.

They had long since left the beautiful Darling Downs region with its wonderfully fertile agricultural land, travelling through the fruit and wine zones, the golden Granite Belt and the cotton fields with their high yielding quality crop, out past the gas and oil regions into the real Outback and the sheep and cattle stations.

'Okay?' Clay asked, glancing down at the blond head stirring on his shoulder.

'Oh, I'm sorry!' Carrie straightened abruptly. 'I must have dozed off.'

'You did,' he smiled. 'That's okay. I liked it.'

'I didn't get much sleep last night,' she explained, putting a hand to the thick plait at her nape. That was an understatement. Apart from an initial hour or two she hadn't slept at all she was so overwrought.

'You're worrying about what's going to happen when you arrive home?'

Carrie nodded.

'The authoritarian father,' Clay sighed. 'I'll make sure I'm not like that. I hate to ask but doesn't your mother ever take your side?'

'Of course she does,' Carrie protested. 'She's a wonderful mother.'

'She makes up for your father's distant kind of parenting?'

'I've told you too much, Clay,' she said.

'You have to tell someone,' he said. 'Besides, I worked it out for myself.'

'Why did you go off and leave me?' she asked. 'Last night, why did you leave me?'

'Right now, Caroline, you're immensely vulnerable,' he said quietly. 'You have an ex-fiancé who betrayed you— He is *ex,* by the way?' He gave her a sidelong glance.

'I told him this morning,' she said. 'I know I said I wasn't going to until he was out of hospital, but I changed my mind after the events of last night. It was only the briefest visit to convince myself he was physically, at least, on the mend. And he is.'

'What did he say?'

'Nothing. He expected it. Why wouldn't he?' she said without bitterness.

'Just checking,' Clay replied. 'I know what a tender heart you have. I left you, Caroline, because I just can't bear to do anything to hurt you. By the same token it was the *hardest* thing I've ever done.'

'I was beginning to think I was frigid,' she said.

He laughed aloud. 'Well, you got *that* wrong. You're *perfect* to make love to.'

'Maybe I never knew what making love meant,' she said.

Just under an hour later they were driving over a grid beneath the huge sign supported by two massive posts that marked the entrance to the station. Victory Downs.

Carrie shifted uneasily in the passenger seat. She hated confrontations but she knew there was one coming up. As for Clay who drove so calmly and efficiently beside her, it was as he said—he was well able to take care of himself.

They swept along the wide driveway lined by magnificent she-oaks. Flocks of woolly white sheep were off in the distance. Kangaroos hopped leisurely towards the silver line of the creek. An eagle soared overhead. Station horses grazed in the home paddocks.

Home. But for how much longer? She didn't understand why her father was leaving the station to her cousin Alex and she never would. It almost seemed as if he were telling her to get married or get thrown out! Her father's delight in her engagement seemed to perfectly express his feelings.

After about a mile they came on the homestead.

The dominating double storeyed central section, the original house, was Georgian in style but single storey wings had been added on later. The whole effect was of order and serenity. The paint on the decorative shutters gleamed as it did on the white ornamental wrought iron. The homestead and the surrounding lawns and gardens, irrigated by bore water, were beautifully maintained—in sharp contrast to the tremendous neglect the once 'Princess of the Western Plains' Jimboorie House had suffered. Carrie loved her home, but in her eyes it lacked the sheer sweep and romance of Jimboorie.

'Here we go!' Clay said, laconically, bringing his 4WD to a halt in the shade of a spreading bauhinia.

Around the side of the east wing two splendid Scotch collies came flying, their long silky near orange coats streaming in the wind.

'Here, boys!' Carrie called, patting her knees.

Clay's handsome face lit up. 'What beautiful creatures!'

'Prince and Blaze,' Carrie told him proudly. 'You won't get better than them. They're working dogs. They'll be pleased to meet you.'

'I'll be pleased to meet them.'

Excitedly the dogs welcomed Carrie home, then turned to sniffing the newcomer who bent to scratch one then the other behind the ear. 'Shake hands.' Clay gave the order to the older dog, Prince.

'He mightn't do it. He doesn't know you—' Carrie broke off laughing, as Prince obediently presented Clay with a paw.

'Good boy!'

Carrie looked past Clay to see her mother coming down the verandah steps towards them. 'You're home, darling,' she called, her face wearing a welcoming smile. 'Good trip? Clay, how nice to see you again.' Smilingly Alicia put out her hand to this stunning young man who so recently had entered their lives like a comet.

'How are you, Mrs McNevin?' Clay responded, shaking hands and looking down into Alicia's beautiful face, that scarcely bore a trace of ageing. Caroline was destined to look like this in maturity, he thought. He had been introduced to the McNevins briefly after he had won the Cup. Alicia had been gracious to him then, but he hadn't expected the friendly greeting he was getting now.

'I'm well, thank you, Clay,' Alicia said. 'I'm sure you'd like to come in and have something to eat after that long trip.'

Carrie's eyes sought her mother's. 'Where's Dad?' she asked carefully.

Alicia was totally relaxed. 'He and Harry Tennant have flown off to Longreach for a meeting. Your father won't be back until tomorrow afternoon.' In other words, the all clear. 'Come into the house,' she invited. 'It's hot standing in the sun. So how did you find Scott?' she asked Carrie as they walked towards the homestead, the dogs trotting quietly by their side.

'It's all very upsetting, Mamma,' Carrie said. 'Didn't Thea Cunningham get in touch with you?'

Alicia smiled tersely. 'She certainly did. I'm not sure now if I didn't tell her off, poor woman. She idolises that boy. In a way she's ruined him. But enough of that. Come in and freshen up then we can sit and relax.'

Clay stayed on for an hour of conversation that skirted any difficult issues. Afterwards both women saw him off.

Alicia slipped an arm around her daughter's waist as they walked back to the house. 'Do you know, I can't remember when I met such a charming young man. And so well spoken. I like him very, *very* much.'

'You liked Scott, remember?' Carrie pointed out with a touch of irony.

Alicia's beautiful eyes clouded. 'I had no idea he was so full of deceit.'

'You haven't heard the half of it, Mamma,' Carrie said.

'Good God there's not more?' Alicia asked in dismay. 'Thea couldn't wait to recount your meeting outside the restaurant in Toowoomba. She said Clay threatened to knock Bradley down. I must confess that shocked me though sometimes I think Brad Harper needs flattening.'

'I didn't think Mrs Harper told lies,' Carrie said, angrily. 'It was Mr Harper who threw a punch at Clay. He blocked it and told Mr Harper not to try it again. That was it!'

'She seemed to think *you* were to blame. You'd let them all down.'

They had reached the verandah. Now both sank into planter's chairs. Carrie looked straight ahead. 'Natasha is carrying Scott's child,' she said baldly.

Alicia who had eased back into her chair sat bolt upright. 'What are you saying?' She stared at Carrie, a dazed look on her face.

'Natasha's pregnant. Believe it,' Carrie repeated harshly.

A bewildered look passed across Alicia's face. 'What sort of an abject low life is he?' she demanded to know.

Carrie sighed deeply. 'I daresay Natasha contrived it. Needless to say with his help. She's mad about him.'

'Dear God!' Alicia shook her head slowly from side to side. 'I take it his parents don't know?'

'I wouldn't like to be Scott when he tells them.' Carrie bit on her lip hard. 'Mr Harper would be a pretty violent sort of man once he gets going. He loves Scott, but he expects him to toe the line. Scott, by the way, told Natasha to have an abortion.'

'That was his solution, was it?' Alicia asked in utter disgust. 'Get rid of his own child? God, haven't *you* been lucky? And haven't your father and I been colossally stupid? You're well out of it.'

'You think I don't know that?' Carrie said. 'Dad thought Scott was perfect for me. He'll be shocked. Does he know Clay was with me in Toowoomba?'

'No, and we won't tell him,' Alicia said.

'Is that a good idea?'

'It's the best one I can think of at the moment.'

'I should probably tell the truth. Dad runs too much of my life.'

'He means well, Carrie,' her mother said. 'He'll be really upset about the whole sorry business. But it's Scott who's the villain here, not Clay. Your father has to get over his misconceptions.'

Carrie considered. 'He's too rigid in his ways. I don't think he's ever going to approve of Clay. He's set his mind against him.'

'Not so different to how he treated Clay's father,' Alicia said in a tight voice. 'But what the heck! You're a woman now. You can do as you please.'

'Maybe the day will come when *you* can, too, Mamma,' Carrie said meaningfully and closed her fingers around her mother's.

When Carrie returned to the homestead at noon for a bite of lunch—she had teamed up with the vet doing his morning rounds—her father had returned home. She could hear his voice upraised in anger as she mounted the front steps. Her father rarely raised his voice. It simply wasn't necessary. Arguments with his wife were exceedingly rare, but they were having one humdinger of an argument now.

Carrie hesitated, uncertain whether to go back outside or find her way up to her bedroom through a side door.

'How could he *do* this? How could he spoil everything,' Bruce McNevin was asking in a rage. 'Here you are able to wind any man—any man at all—around your little finger and Carrie can't hold onto her own fiancé. I thought she'd be married in December. I thought we'd have our lives to ourselves.'

'What a dreadful thing to say, Bruce,' Carrie heard her mother reply, her voice full of pain.

'All right I'm sorry. I've done my best, Alicia. God knows I've tried. But she's not *mine*. How can you expect me to love her? I've tried all these years to love her but I *can't*. She's not my blood. Why do you think I've left the station to young Alex. He at least, *is*.'

Carrie reached for something to hold on to.

Click, click, click! It all came together. *She's not mine!*

A trembling began right through her body. A profound sadness filled her eyes. Nonetheless, she didn't step backwards, but forwards. She was devastated, but to her wonderment, not demolished. *She's not mine!* Hadn't such a thing been implied by his behaviour all these years?

'Shut up and keep your voice down,' Alicia ordered in a voice akin to the sharp crack of a whip. 'Carrie will be home soon.'

'She's home *now.*' Carrie found herself in the kitchen, where her parents or her mother and the man she thought was her father faced each other across the table like combatants in a deadly battle. 'Would someone like to explain to me what I just overheard?'

Alicia's face went paper-white. 'Carrie, darling!' She rushed to her daughter who stood stricken but resolute in the open doorway.

Carrie held up her hand, warding her mother off. 'Who exactly am I, Mum? Is there anyone in this world who hasn't betrayed me? My father all these long years isn't my father at all. So *who* is? I'm not going anywhere until you tell me.' Her dark eyes bore into her mother's. 'That's if you *know*?'

Bruce McNevin stood watching Carrie with such an odd look on his face. 'Please don't speak to your mother like that,' he said. 'I'm sorry you had to hear that. I'm just so terribly upset.'

'*You're* upset?' Alicia rounded tempestuously on her husband, unleashing one of her stunning tennis backhands. 'You miserable bastard!' she cried. 'You miserable whining cur! You *swore* you'd never tell her.'

Bruce McNevin stood as stiff as a ramrod against the blow, the imprint of Alicia's hand clear on his cheek. 'I didn't tell her. She overheard. This was just supposed to be between you and me, Alicia.'

'God!' Alicia moaned. 'I don't want to live with you anymore, Bruce. You've killed whatever feeling I had for you. Carrie is my daughter. I love her best in the world. Far more than I could ever love you.'

'But you never loved me, did you?' Bruce McNevin's grey eyes glittered strangely. 'I've been the one who's done all the loving.'

Carrie intervened, saying what she had to say as if it were enormously important. 'You don't know the first thing about love. You don't even know about simple compassion. You're a cold man. You think only of yourself. God, it must have been so hard for you fathering a child that wasn't yours. Why didn't you tell Mum to have an abortion?'

A white line ringed Bruce McNevin's tight mouth. 'She *wouldn't* have it, that's why!'

Alicia shook her head, her eyes full of grief. 'Never, never!'

'So who's my father, Mum?' Carrie ignored the tears pouring down her mother's face. 'Or is it as I said. You don't know.'

'She's knows all right,' Bruce McNevin burst out furiously. 'But she couldn't marry him. He was married already. I was the poor fool who took her to the altar.'

'It was all you ever wanted.' Alicia rounded on her husband with utter contempt.

'I loved you then. I love you now,' Bruce McNevin's grey eyes turned imploring.

'Totally amazing!' Alicia gave a broken crow of laughter. 'You actually believe it. This marriage is *over,* Bruce. All these years I've lived with your emotional blackmail. Now it's out in the open.'

His answer was full of fear. 'You don't mean that. You'll never leave me, Alicia. It would be very wrong and dishonourable. I've been good to you, haven't I? I've tried my best with Carrie, but the way she looks at me! It's like she's always *known.*'

'I guess some part of me did,' Carrie said. 'Now I don't give a damn which one of you leaves. All I need to know is the name of my real father, then I'm out of here.'

'Where to? You have nowhere to go.' Alicia made another attempt to take her daughter in her arms, but Carrie would have none of it.

'Oh, yes, I have,' she said.

'I hope you're not talking about Cunningham?' Bruce McNevin's breath escaped in a long hiss.

'None of your bloody business,' Carrie said, enunciating very clearly. 'Who's my father, Mum. I *must* know.'

'You're crazy!' Bruce McNevin said.

'Shut up, Bruce!' Alicia looked positively dangerous. She turned her head towards her daughter. 'I can't tell you, Carrie. Maybe one day.'

'One day very soon.' Carrie was adamant. 'Understand? Now tell the truth if you can, Mamma. Did my *real* father know about me?'

Alicia's white face flushed deeply. 'I never told him.'

'He had a right to know.'

'Yes, he did,' Alicia admitted, revealing the depth of her old anguish.

'What would he have done, do you think?'

'He'd have bloody well wrecked his marriage,' Bruce McNevin suddenly shouted. 'A *good* marriage, mind you. Two small children. Two boys. I never had a son,' he cried, his voice full of bitterness.

'Nothing wrong with *me*, Bruce,' Alicia said. 'You never would see a doctor.' She turned her attention back to her daughter. 'I couldn't tell your real father I was pregnant, Carrie. I couldn't do it to him,' she confessed, brokenheartedly.

'No, but you could do it to *me,*' said Carrie. 'That makes you a ruthless person. I should hate you, Mamma. I'm not sure I don't right now. You were supposed to protect me. Not deliver the two of us up to this man.' Her gentle voice was harsh.

Alicia collapsed into a chair, crumpling up over the table. 'Please don't go, darling. Don't leave me,' she sobbed. 'We'll go together.'

Carrie shook her head. 'You have your husband. You've stuck it out with him all this time. I *am* going to find my father. With or without your help.'

'He'll never recognise you as his daughter,' Bruce McNevin told her, the expression on his face half scorn for Carrie, half misery for himself. 'Not even now when his wife is dead. Scandal can't touch a man like that.'

'Oh, yes, he will.' Alicia's tears abruptly turned off. 'I know that much about him.'

'Then perhaps when you're ready you'll give me his name,' Carrie said. 'I don't intend to embarrass him. I just want to see him with my own eyes.'

'You have seen him, you little fool!' Bruce McNevin had totally lost his habitual cool. One side of his face was paper-white, the other flushed with blood. 'All you have to do is watch television.'

'What's he talking about, Mum?' Carrie asked.

'Go ahead. Tell her,' Bruce McNevin dared his wife.

'Is he some television personality?' Carrie asked with something like amazement.

'No, no, nothing like that!' Alicia shook her head. 'He's an important man, Carrie.'

'Oh, listen to her! He's an *important* man. And I'm not?' Bruce McNevin glared at his wife.

'Oh, shut up, Bruce,' she said yet again. 'I wish to God you'd just been *kind*. I'll tell you when I'm ready, Carrie. Please don't ask me now.'

Carrie could see the trembling in her mother's hands. 'Okay,' she sighed, her heart torn. 'Now I hope you don't mind if I throw a few things in a bag. It won't take me long. I'll get the rest of my things picked up.'

'Carrie, no!' Alicia jumped up, her voice full of emotion. 'Please stay. We'll work something out.'

'Not anymore, Mum.'

'Let me handle this, Alicia,' Bruce McNevin said, striding after Carrie as though she were deliberately causing her mother unnecessary pain. 'Where are you going, Carrie? Answer me.'

'Sorry, Mr McNevin.' Carrie turned with great severity on the man she had called father. 'You've given your last performance. You've waited for this a long time. You wanted me out? Be thankful. I'm going!'

When she arrived at Jimboorie, a red sun was sinking towards the jewelled horizon. Carrie stepped out of her 4WD, which one of their employees had brought back from the town only that morning, looking up at the great house. There was the glow of lights inside. She had parked right at the base of the flight of stone stairs, now she leaned into the vehicle keeping her palm pressed flat on the horn.

I'm on the run, she thought. *I'm a fugitive. A profoundly wounded woman.*

At least Clay was at home. She felt in her jeans pocket for the folded note paper she intended to present to him. He would understand what it was. It was her response to the advertisement for a wife he'd never placed. Surely he'd told her she would fit the bill? She had nowhere else to go. And nowhere else she wanted to be.

Clay's tall rangy figure appeared on the verandah. 'Caroline, what's up?'

She gave him a pathetic little wave, feeling pushed to the limit, yet in the space of a nanosecond the vision of herself as a child waving to him while Clay, the handsome little boy, waved back flared like a bright light. For weeks and weeks she had searched the archives of her mind for that cherished memory. Now like some miracle it presented itself, bringing her a moment of happiness.

Clay lost no time covering the distance between them, moving through the portico and taking the steps in a single leap.

'I've just remembered waving to you when I was a little girl. Isn't that strange?'

'Strange and beautiful,' he said, staring down at her 'That meant a lot to me, Caroline.' He spoke quietly, gently, seeing her disturbed state. 'What's happened?'

She looked up at him a little dazedly. 'I've left home and I'm never going back.'

He absorbed that without comment. 'Come inside the house,' he said, tucking her to his side. 'You're trembling.'

A parched laugh escaped her lips. 'How come nothing shocks me to the core anymore?'

'You're *in* shock, that's why,' he pointed out, already feeling concern he could have been a cause of the family fallout.

From somewhere furniture had appeared in the drawing room; a huge brown leather chesterfield and two deep leather armchairs. A carved Chinese chest acting as a coffee table stood on a beautiful Persian rug all rich rubies and deep blues. She looked at the comfortable arrangement with a little frown on her face. 'Where did these things come from?'

'Out the back,' he said, offhandedly. 'There's more in store in Toowoomba. So are you going to tell me?' He led her to an armchair, waited until she was seated. 'What happened? Did you have an argument with your father?'

'What father?' she said.

Clay's face darkened. 'He surely couldn't have told you to go?'

Carrie shrugged. 'No, I did that all by myself.'

'Look, would you like coffee?' Clay suggested. 'I've got some good coffee beans. Won't take me a moment to grind them and put the percolator on.'

'I'll come with you,' she said, her movements almost trancelike.

Furniture had been moved into the enormous kitchen as well. It hadn't been there on her visit. He really was settling in. A long refectory table adorned the centre of the room with six carved wooden chairs, Scottish baronial, arranged around it, three to each side. The seats were upholstered in luxurious dark green leather. The huge matching carver stood at the head of the table. 'Expecting guests?' she asked, starting to drag out one chair. God, either it was *heavy* or she had lost her strength.

'*You're* here,' Clay pointed out, directing her to the carver instead, with its substantial armrests. A big man, it suited him fine. It nearly swallowed her up.

'This is a marvellous kitchen,' she said, looking around her. 'Or it could be. These chairs really belong in a dining room, you know.' She ran her hands along the oak armrests. 'Were they shipped out from England? They're antique. Early nineteenth century, I'd say.'

'Plenty more where they came from,' he said, busying himself setting out china mugs. 'While you were visiting Harper, I took a look at what was in storage. My favourite things were still there. Things I remember from when I was a child. There'll be more than enough to furnish the ground floor. I don't know about upstairs. Twelve bedrooms takes a bit of furnishing. At least I have a bed.'

'That's good,' she said wryly. 'Somewhere to rest a weary head. You might want to take a look at this.' She stretched her right leg so she could remove the folded notepaper from the pocket of her tight fitting jeans.

'What is it? Hang on a moment, I'll just grind these beans.'

Carrie covered her ears, counting to about twenty.

A few moments later, the percolator on the massive stove, Clay took the seat right of her. 'So what's this?' He unfolded the crumpled paper, looking at it with interest.

'It's not my best effort. I just had enough time to get down the facts,' she explained, very carefully, very precisely.

He turned his head to stare into her large, almond eyes. She was hurting badly but she wasn't going to say. 'Is this what I think it is?'

'Read on,' she invited, with an encouraging little movement of her hand.

He began again. 'This is truly *remarkable,* Caroline,' he said when he had finished. 'On the scale of one to ten, I'd give you an eleven. No, wait, a twelve!' He refolded the letter and thrust it into his breast pocket.

'Isn't it good,' she agreed. 'I mean it's so good you won't need to advertise for anyone else.'

'Well, that will certainly save a lot of time,' he said briskly. 'It's all happening around here. I have a firm lined up to fix the roof and a team of tradesmen to do the repairs. They'll be kept busy for months. There's an expert on the environment—a Professor Langley, my old professor—calling some time soon to advise about drought and flood management on the station. He's brilliant. He's bound to know someone to restore the garden.'

'Good heavens, you have been busy.' For a few moments he had completely taken her mind from her own problems. 'Where's all the money coming from?

'*You,*' he said.

She caught the gentle mockery in his eyes. 'I don't come with a dowry, Clay,' she said sadly. 'I daresay I'll be cut out of my ex-father's will without delay. I do have a little nest egg from Nona. That's my grandmother, Alicia's mother. I wish Nona were here, but she went to live in Italy after my grandfather died. You're welcome to that.'

'Why how very sweet of you.' Clay lightly encircled her wrist. 'But such a sacrifice isn't necessary. That money is *yours.* Don't feel bad about not coming with a dowry. I told you Great-Uncle Angus was far from broke. In fact he'd have given Scrooge a run for his money.'

'So he left you the money as well.'

'I guess I was the only one he could think of.' Clay's comment was sardonic. 'One way or another we have enough.' He lifted her hand and kissed it.

'How upset that's going to make your relatives!' Carrie, numb for hours, awoke to sensation. 'They were hoping it was all going to fall down around your ears.'

'Instead of which I get to marry the princess and share the pot of gold,' he said, gazing deeply into her eyes. 'Now tell me what's causing all this suffering? Take your time.'

'Mum had an affair before she was married.' She spoke in a voice utterly devoid of emotion.

Clay's strong hand closed over her trembling fingers. What was coming next just had to be momentous.

'The man I *thought* was my father all these years isn't my father at all.' Carrie gave him a heartbreaking smile. 'Can you beat that?'

'How could they do that to you?' Clay felt the blood drain from his own face.

Carrie shrugged. 'Apparently he was married with two kids, but he wasn't worried about committing adultery. Neither was Mum. He must have been Someone even then. Mum decided she couldn't break up his marriage. She married Bruce McNevin instead.'

'So that explains it,' Clay said, steel in his voice.

'At least Mum didn't consider a termination.'

'Thank God for that!' he breathed, unable to contemplate a world without Caroline. 'So how did this all come out? I mean what provoked it after all these years?'

She pulled a sad little clown's face. 'You know the old saying. Eavesdroppers never hear well of themselves? I could hear them arguing when I arrived back at the house for lunch. They *never* argue. I heard my *father* say, "She's not mine! How can you expect me to love her? She's not my blood!"'

Muscles flexed hard along Clay's jawline. 'Go on. You have to get this off your chest.' He stood up to pour the perked coffee, setting a mug down before her then moving the sugar bowl close to her hand. 'Do you want milk or cream?'

'Black's fine.' She spooned a teaspoon of sugar into the mug and absently began to stir.

'Have another teaspoon of sugar,' he urged. 'You're awfully pale. Wasn't your mother worried about your driving?'

Carrie nodded. 'She begged me not to go but I couldn't stay in *his* house another moment. He's only tolerated me because of Mum. He's still madly in love with her. So what the hell's wrong with *me*? Am I so unlovable?'

Clay felt a rush of anger on her behalf. 'That's the last thing you have to worry about,' he said so emphatically she felt immensely relieved.

'You *really* want to marry me now? I could turn into a pure liability. Well?' she pressed, directly holding his eyes. 'Answer me, Clay.'

'You aren't going to *order* me to marry you, are you?' he asked gently.

'Not unless you want an illegitimate bride. Mum wouldn't even tell me who my real father is. *He* knows.'

'Who, McNevin?'

'Yes. Don't worry, I'll find out.'

'Then what will you do?' he asked very seriously.

'I don't mean to embarrass my real father, Clay,' she explained carefully. 'I just want to lay eyes on him. Can you understand that?'

'Caroline, God!' He was debating whether to pick her up and carry her upstairs. If ever a girl needed loving it was this beautiful traumatised young creature. 'Of course I understand. It's hard to feel *whole* when you only know the identity of one parent.'

'My entire childhood and adolescence lacked *wholeness*,' she said, painfully aware that was so. 'I think I'll be content once I know who my real father is. I can watch him without his being aware of it.'

'What if you're not? What if you're impelled to go up to him and tell him he's your father? He'd have to remember your mother so he'd have to know who *you* are. You resemble her greatly.'

'Clearly I resemble her physically, but not in other ways,' Carrie said, carefully. 'I can't believe she's lied to me all these years. Couldn't she have concocted another story? Couldn't she have married someone else but Bruce McNevin? He's a *mean* man at heart. How could anyone disavow a baby, a little girl, a dutiful daughter?'

'It's no excuse, but I suppose he felt tremendously insecure about your mother,' Clay suggested. 'She's obviously never loved him.'

'Then why didn't she divorce him?' Carrie shot back.

'I can't find an acceptable answer, Caroline.' He stared at her, his eyes full of compassion. 'Who knows what goes on inside a marriage anyway? He must have been doing something right.'

'Not by *me*! But he thought he was the perfect husband. I've even heard him say so.' Carrie picked up her coffee mug again. 'This is good.'

'When did you last eat?' he asked, his eyes moving over her inch by inch.

'Breakfast.' She shrugged. 'I was coming in for lunch when my whole life was shattered. Soon as I heard their voices I knew something awful was going to happen. I think he's actually relieved it's all out in the open. He no longer has to pretend.'

'Should I ring your mother and tell her you're with me?'

'No, Clay, *no*!' She laid a restraining hand on his tanned arm.

'Whatever she's done or *had* to do she loves you, Caroline. She'll be frantic.'

'Don't worry, she won't kill herself,' Carrie said, her voice as dry as ash. 'She knows where I am anyway. I mightn't have told her, but she'll guess. Even my dear old ex-father, guessed I was heading here. That's three ex's in my life. Ex-mother, ex-father, ex-fiancé.'

'Your mother's always your mother, Caroline,' he said. 'Nothing's going to change that.'

Carrie released the gold clasp at her nape so her hair fell heavily around her face. 'Do you realise if all this miserable business with Scott hadn't happened I probably would never have found out?'

'It has occurred to me,' Clay said, thinking however desperate she felt she looked absolutely beautiful. The purity and symmetry of her small features transcended mere prettiness.

'We've all been living a lie,' she said in a melancholy voice. 'I could have married Scott in a few weeks' time.'

'I imagine Natasha would have had something to say about that,' he said dryly.

'Lord, you'd think the accident and all the stress would have triggered a miscarriage.'

'You didn't want that to happen?'

'Oh, my God, no. Dear God, no,' Carrie said. 'Natasha's tough and her baby's tough. They'll have to be. Do you mind my burdening you with all this?'

'Mind, how? Haven't you applied for the position of my wife? I have your application—which I will frame—in my pocket.' There was tenderness on his face and a shadow of physical yearning kept under tight control.

'Well, I don't much care for anyone else,' she said. 'So what's the answer? Or do you want to hear from more women?' She didn't realise it but she sounded incredibly anxious.

'Yours was the winning application,' he said.

'The *only* application.'

'I won't hold it against you. Now as soon as we settle you in I'll have to think about feeding you. By a stroke of good fortune I stocked up the last time I was in town.'

She shook her head. 'I'm not hungry, thank you all the same, Clay.'

'Well *I* am.' He stood up. 'I won't feel happy eating alone. And now I think of it, you didn't mention in your application if you could cook?'

'And you didn't ask.' She smiled weakly. 'I can cook. My mother taught me. I'll never be as good as her. You know *he* didn't want a housekeeper. We have Mrs. Finlay from town come in once a week to do the cleaning. He didn't want *anyone* but Mum I can see that now. And Mum acted as though she *owed* him. What for? For his marrying her when she was pregnant? Is that what Natasha will have to settle for?'

'Don't upset yourself,' Clay said. 'Harper and Natasha will have to solve their own problems.'

Carrie's heart stuttered.

She sat straight up in bed, saying shakily, 'Who's there?'

She looked about her in a dazed panic. Where *was* she?

She waited for full consciousness to kick in. Thank God! She was at Jimboorie with Clay. He had given up his bed for her, a brand-new king-sized ensemble, electing to spend the night in the massive four poster—too big to ever be shifted—in the bedroom just across the hall. They had shared a bottle of red wine over a dinner of tender beef fillet, tiny new potatoes and asparagus—all cooked to perfection by him—and the alcohol had soothed her sending her off to sleep.

The effects had evaporated. She didn't know what time it was but something had awoken her. She willed her memory back to an image.

A slow opening door? A shape of a woman? She was sure it was a woman. Jimboorie House was haunted. Clay's mother had seemed to think so.

Calm down, fool that you are.

Hold down panic. Control the mind. It was only a dream.

She lifted a glass of water from the bedside table; sipped at it, panning her eyes around the huge room, listening intently for the slightest sound. Outside in the night, a full moon was riding high in the indigo sky, its rays washing the room with a silvery light.

But it was impossibly dark in the far corners. A strangeness seemed to be in her and at that moment a supreme wakefulness. She didn't quite know how to handle it. Or herself. One thing she did know with absolute certainty was, she couldn't lie in the semidarkness anymore. She couldn't bear to be alone, either. She wanted love. Plenty of it.

She rose from the bed in that unquiet night, catching the scent of gardenia that wafted from her nightgown She always used gardenia sachets amid her under garments and nightgowns. Her Thai silk robe bought in Bangkok was at the end of the bed, the white background scattered with bright red poppies, the edges bound with ebony. She slipped it on, tying the sash loosely. Her heart was aching afresh as the events of the day flooded back to her mind.

At long last she knew what her inner being had always suspected—the man whose name she bore wasn't her father. All he was, was her mother's husband. Twenty-three years of lying. Could she ever forgive her mother for that? Slowly she made her way across the room, heart fluttering, keeping to the band of moonlight.

What was her excuse for going to him? What would she say when he woke to find her standing beside his bed, staring down at him?

Love me, Clay. I desperately need to be loved.

Need had overtaken her entirely. She felt no embarrassment. just the driving need for comfort that only he seemed able to give.

His door was open. Carrie could hear his gentle, even breathing. She glided as silently as a shadow across the floor towards that massive bed. His naked back was turned to her, one shoulder raised high. She loved the shape of him, the shape of his broad shoulders, the way his strong arms could enfold her. She loved everything about him. And she wanted to learn more. Fate had carried her here to this moment, to this beautiful man. Her life had slipped out of focus. He had the power to put it back in place.

She held her flowing hair back with her hand. 'Clay!'

She thought he might take moments to stir but he was instantly alert.

'God, Caroline!' Fast breathing now. He sat up, thrusting a hand through his hair. 'I was dreaming about you.'

'Isn't it better I'm here?' She let her voice fall to a whisper.

'Did something frighten you?' he asked, with concern. 'I could have sworn you'd sleep through the night.'

'Isabelle's ghost,' she said and even laughed. 'She must walk around the house at full moon. May I get into bed with you?'

'Caroline.' Instantly he was aroused, every nerve throbbing. He dared not think what would happen if she did. 'You know what that means?' he managed to say. 'I couldn't possibly resist you. I just *couldn't*. I'm not strong enough.'

'But I don't want you to resist me,' she said. 'I want you to touch me. I want to touch you.' She reached out and moved her fingers, gently, slowly, over his broad chest letting them tangle in the fine mat of hair.

Clay felt his blood come to a rolling boil. 'Caroline!' he said, taking hold of her wrists. 'What are you trying to do to me?'

'You want me, don't you?'

I want you to be mine forever! 'It's for your protection,' he said, valiantly holding her off, at the same time desperately trying to exert the full force of his will. 'I would let you stay with me. I want nothing more in the world than have you stay with me, but I'm worried. I'm worried about *you*. What might happen.'

'Stop worrying,' she said, pulling away from him gently, to slide off her robe. Then she clambered onto the high bed. 'Can't you understand, Clay. I *need* loving.'

Why tell him *that* when he was wild for her! The very enormity of having her there in the bed beside him, inhaling her fragrance, all but robbed him of his precious self-control.

'So you're going to allow me to take your virginity?' He was already utterly aroused and unable to do a damn thing about it.

'Isn't that your wish?'

'I want you to give it to me. I don't want to *steal* it from you. I care about you too much.'

'Well, I can't wait,' she said. 'I *thought* I wanted to wait. I could have waited easily with Scott. But not with you. It's not all about sex, Clay,' she said reaching out to stroke his face. 'I want *you*. I need you. It's as simple as that.'

'And it has to be this very night, my little runaway Caroline?' he asked with immense tenderness, staring down at her.

'Only you can save me from the pain.'

The blood rushed to his head. She thought herself safe with him. She *was*. But he had to be so gentle when the adrenaline was roaring through his body. He tried to slow himself down by kissing first the side of her neck, then the exquisite little hollow in her throat, moving back to her eyes, her cheeks, her nose, then her lovely mouth. He kissed her again and again, until they were both light-headed, his hands moving irresistibly to her breasts, creamy like roses, their pink tips flaring at his touch. While she moaned softly he let his hand slide down over the smooth tautness of her stomach, downward yet to her secret sex.

Her mouth formed words. She exhaled them.

'My true love,' she said.

It was an utterance that reached right through to Clay's soul.

And he was gentle with her, his fingers feathering over her, his mouth following…

'Do you like that?' He wasn't going to do a thing that didn't give her pleasure.

'Perfect!' she moaned, her back arching off the bed.

'You are *so* beautiful!' He turned her over, making long strokes over her satiny back, cupping her buttocks so smooth and round, pressing his lips to them…

She was yearning for him to move into her, her body was demanding release, but he continued to work his magic on her, inch by inch.

She kept her eyes closed tight.

When he gently worked her clitoris, she made a wild strange sound, like a bird keening. The sensuality was profound. Wonderful and unbearable at the same time. She was panting and gasping with excitement, reaching for him frantically, guiding him to the entrance of her sex.

'Yes!' she cried, overcome by the extraordinary piercing sensations that were running riot in her body. She couldn't control them. They were controlling her.

Clay drew back, laying his palms flat on the bed to either side of her. 'I'll be as gentle as I can,' he vowed.

'You're a *magician*,' she whispered back.

'Am I?'

'Yes!' She was desperate for him to push into her. To *fill* her.

There was a twinge of pain. No more. Then a spreading rapture like life giving rain spreading over the flood plains.

'You're okay?' he whispered urgently against her cheek, striving to keep his own driving needs reined in.

'I *adore* you!' she cried.

Was there ever an answer that could please a man more? He threw his head back with sheer joy and she arched up to kiss his throat. 'Adore you. Adore you. Adore you!'

He couldn't hold back a moment longer. Not after that. Their bodies radiated heat and an incredible *energy*. The whole room was filled with it. It crackled like live wires.

He plunged into her in an ecstasy of passion and she met that plunge, spreading her silken thighs for him. It thrilled him to the core. She was spreading herself wide-open to him, her soul as naked as her beautiful body. His heart swelled with pride, exultation, and an enormous gratitude. He felt *free*. Unburdened of the griefs that had long plagued him.

Neither of them held back. They gave of each other unstintingly. At long last they had discovered something they had never known before.

Pure Desire. Pure Love.

CHAPTER EIGHT

CLAY and Carrie were coming back from a long ramble down to the creek, when they saw Alicia's Land Rover make a sweep around the circular driveway and park, bonnet in, to the shade of the trees. There had been a fantastic, wonderfully welcome downpour of rain around dawn, which had awakened them to more glorious love-making, and now the whole world was washed clean.

'It's Mamma,' Carrie said, unnecessarily, holding Clay's hand tight.

'I'm sure she's only come to see if you're all right,' Clay said, calming her. 'Take it easy, Caroline. Your mother must be under a lot of stress.'

Alicia was waiting quietly on the terrace.

'Why have you come, Mamma?' Carrie started in at once, though her heart smote her at the unhappiness in Alicia's face.

'I *had* to come,' Alicia said.

'Please sit down, Mrs McNevin.' Clay held a chair for her. 'How are things at home?'

'Not good, Clay,' Alicia said, releasing a long sigh. 'And please call me Alicia.'

'I'd be happy to,' Clay said quietly. 'Let's all take a seat.' He put his hand gently on Carrie's shoulder, exerting the slightest pressure. 'Would you two like to talk while I make coffee?'

'I'd be grateful for that, Clay,' Alicia said.

'No problem.' He strode away into the house.

'What a very considerate young man!' Alicia said, sighing as though she'd never had the good fortune to meet one in her life. 'I'm leaving Bruce,' she told Carrie.

'Isn't it about time?' Carrie asked. 'You don't love him, Mum. You've never loved him, have you?'

'Look,' said Alicia, 'give him some credit. When I knew I was pregnant with you I was absolutely desperate—'

'You couldn't tell Nona?' Carrie broke in, not understanding *her* nona was another person to her mother.

'I didn't think I could,' Alicia confessed. 'Your grandmother had—still has—very definite ideas about how a well-bred young lady should conduct herself. She would have been shocked and bitterly disappointed in me. The scandal would have been enormous. It wouldn't have been so bad if I'd been able to marry the father of my child, but I couldn't.'

'Then why have an affair with him?' Carrie asked, sounding stern about it.

'You're in love with Clay, aren't you?' Alicia made a plea for understanding. 'You're in love at last?'

Colour flooded Carrie's cheeks. 'Oh please…Clay's not married.'

'I was mad about him,' Alicia said. 'I truly believe he loved me. Neither of us planned it. It wasn't supposed to happen, yet all it took was a smile. We met at a fund-raiser. I knew who he was, of course—'

'Which is a damn sight more than I do,' Carrie interrupted.

'He noticed me from across the room.' All these years later Alicia's beautiful eyes went dreamy.

'He would. Any man would,' Carrie said, still in that critical voice.

'I'd noticed him back. That's how it started.'

'Easy as that, eh?' Carrie's voice was unwillingly sympathetic. 'When did you start sleeping together?'

'When did you start sleeping with Clay?' Alicia retorted.

'Last night,' Carrie admitted freely. 'And at dawn this morning. It was *wonderful*! Clay has restored my faith in humanity.'

'I hope you used protection?' Alicia went from penitent to concerned mother.

'I'm not going into details,' Carrie said. '*Why* have you come, Mamma? Your husband hasn't threatened you in any way?' The very thought frightened her.

'He's beside himself,' Alicia said.

'I'm quite sure he's blaming me for all this?' Carrie said.

Alicia passed on the answer. 'I want you to come with me to Melbourne, darling,' she said as though it were something both of them simply had to do.

'Melbourne? What for?' Carrie started to picture where her mother would go. To friends? To a hotel?

'For one thing you can't stay here with Clay,' Alicia pointed out quietly.

'Why not?' Carrie turned squarely on her mother. 'I'm going to marry him.'

'And he'll be a wonderful husband, I know.' Alicia took the news very calmly. 'But you want to do it right.'

'Unlike *you*!' Carrie was near tears. But her mother did have a point—Clay was now the owner of Jimboorie Station. He intended to work it. He intended to restore the homestead. He *was* a Cunningham. If nothing else she had to uphold *his* reputation. 'What's in Melbourne?' she asked finally.

Alicia looked sightlessly across the grounds. 'Your *father*,' she said.

'You're back!' Bruce McNevin greeted his wife the moment she walked into the homestead. 'I knew you'd come back. You've got nowhere else to go.'

'I'm only here to do a little packing, Bruce,' Alicia said. 'I'm taking Carrie with me to Melbourne.'

He blocked her way as she walked to the stairs. 'Just how long do you think you can stay with friends?'

'I've almost lost touch with them, haven't I, through you? Let me past, Bruce.'

'Not until we have this out. I'm extremely unhappy with your behaviour, Alicia. You *owe* me. As for Carrie, she's just going from bad to worse. I suppose she was with Cunningham?'

'Why don't you ask them?' Alicia said. 'They're waiting for me in the driveway.'

'They're what?' Bruce McNevin hurried to the front door, looking out. 'How dare they!'

'They don't trust *you* to behave yourself, Bruce.'

'Have I ever laid a finger on you?' He strode back to her looking outraged.

'If you had, I'd have found the guts to move on.'

Bruce McNevin shook his head, something like grief in his eyes. 'I *knew* Leyland's child would split us one day. You surely can't be going to him? You have no place in his life.'

'I know that, Bruce,' Alicia said simply, 'but Carrie does. There have been a lot of changes in society since I was a girl. People are more *accepting*. Carrie wants to meet her father. I'm going to arrange it. Neither of us intend to embarrass him though I know he'll be deeply disturbed.'

'And what about his sons? What are they going to think?'

Alicia spread her hands in an inherited gesture. 'There are secret places in everyone's life. Besides, they're married men now. Or one is.'

'Been checking up on them, have you?' McNevin sneered.

'They're a prominent family, Bruce. The media like to report on prominent families.'

'They'll relish *this* scandal then, won't they? The return of the prodigal ex-lover along with their lovechild. And what about your oh so proper mother? What the hell is she going to think?'

'She's a long way from here, Bruce. I can't worry about her anymore. Or about you. I'm not the panic-stricken girl I once was.'

'My God!' McNevin breathed. 'I love you, Alicia. Doesn't that mean anything to you anymore?'

She met his eyes directly. 'It would have meant a lot had you loved my daughter, too!' Alicia went around him and mounted the stairs.

Clay and Carrie sat waiting for Alicia to reappear. 'I think I should go in,' Clay said. It was he who had insisted on accompanying them back to the homestead, concerned Bruce McNevin might react badly when faced with losing the woman he loved.

'It's all right, Mum's coming out onto the verandah.' Carrie breathed a great sigh of relief. 'She's ready for you to collect the luggage.' They watched Alicia give them a signal then walk back into the house.

Clay restarted the engine. 'I'll drive up to the steps. He might come out, Carrie. Be prepared.' For *anything,* Clay thought, glad he was with them. Even the mildest man could turn dangerous given enough provocation.

Clay was out of the Land Rover when Bruce McNevin strode out onto the front verandah, his manner highly confrontational. 'Ah, it's *you,* just as I thought. I want you off my land, Cunningham,' he ordered.

Clay reacted calmly to the blustering authority. 'I certainly don't want to be here, sir. But Mrs McNevin needs a helping hand.'

'Not from the likes of you,' Bruce McNevin said, suddenly producing a whip.

'I wouldn't think of using that,' Clay warned. 'You'll definitely come off second best. I understand you're upset, Mr

McNevin, but don't push it. I'll just collect what luggage Mrs McNevin needs then we'll be on our way.'

'*Where,* may I ask?' Bruce McNevin said in his most pretentious voice.

'There's plenty of room at Jimboorie.'

'That crumbling heap!' McNevin scoffed.

'You won't know it in six months' time,' Clay assured him. 'Jimboorie House will in time be restored to its former glory. Take it from me.'

'You!' McNevin asked with great sarcasm. 'What, that wicked old bastard leave you a few bob, did he?'

'Actually he did,' Clay confirmed casually. 'He was far from broke as you seem to think. What he was, was a *miser.* Heard of them?'

Bruce McNevin's face was a study. 'You're not *serious*?'

Clay nodded. 'Yes, I am. Excuse me, sir. I'll just collect those bags.'

Clay entered the house without incident. Bruce McNevin waited a moment then stalked down the steps and over to the Land Rover.

Seeing him coming Carrie opened the passenger door and stepped out onto the gravel to confront him.

McNevin's face was dark with anger. 'I'll never forgive you, Carrie, for what you've done.'

'I haven't done anything,' she said. 'It's more what was *done* to me. I have to live with the fact my own mother lied to me all these years. I suppose she *had* to, to stay under your roof. Your precious reputation is very important to you, isn't it? But she had to pay dearly. I was to be passed off as your child, but right from the beginning you never treated me as family, much less an adopted daughter. You mightn't be able to see my scars. They're not visible to the naked eye, but they're there. Things might have been very different had you been a man of heart.'

Bruce McNevin flushed violently. 'I know I fed you, clothed you, housed you, educated you. Don't let's forget all that, my girl. You never wanted for anything.'

'Maybe so and for that I thank you, but I went wanting for a bit of affection,' Carrie said quietly. 'I know you couldn't make it to love. You couldn't love another man's child.'

'How many men do you think could?' he asked with the greatest impatience. 'All those cuckolded men, when they find out through DNA the child they've long parented isn't theirs at all, doesn't the love switch off? You bet it does. That bastard, that father of yours, raped your mother.'

For the first time in her life, Carrie literally saw red. Clouds of it swirled in front of her eyes, almost obscuring her vision. Even now he couldn't leave well enough alone. He was impelled to cause more damage. Blindly she moved a step closer to the man who had treated her all her life with such contained severity and cried out. 'That is absolutely unforgivable. And a blatant *lie*. Your miserable mean way of getting even? I demand an apology.'

'Why, you arrogant little girl!' Bruce McNevin exclaimed, quite shocked by her anger. 'To think you can *demand* anything of me.'

Carrie's heart was thudding violently in her chest. 'It's normal enough in parent-child interactions but then I'm *not* your child, am I? My poor mother is *still* in love with that man even today. There was no rape as well you know. No need when they were madly in love with each other.'

'What a mess! What a bloody mess!' Bruce McNevin groaned, burying his face in his hands.

'A mess that has to be straightened out.' Carrie swept her thick plait back over her shoulder. 'I doubt if I'll be seeing you again, Mr McNevin. So I'll say my goodbyes. I feel sorry for you in a way. But I shouldn't. I can only remember my life as your daughter as being *loveless*.'

Her mother and Clay were already out of the house and coming towards them. Now they joined her, Alicia standing close beside her daughter.

'If you must do this, do it, Alicia,' Bruce McNevin addressed his wife, ignoring Carrie and Clay. 'No good will come of it, I warn you.'

'Well it wouldn't be *you* if you wished us luck,' Alicia said in an ironic voice.

'I don't want you upset and embarrassed, Alicia,' he said. 'I repeat. I love you. I've stood by you no matter what. I'm not perfect. I didn't have it in me to take to another man's child. I'm not proud of it but it's understandable. The thing is I've always stood by you. Take all the time you want, but come back to me. *Please!* We have a good marriage.'

'And you think we'll have a better one without Carrie?' Alicia asked.

'I'm *sure* of it,' he responded.

'Please, Mamma, let it be,' Carrie intervened, glad of Clay's rock-solid support at her back.

'I suppose you think this puts you in the picture, Cunningham?' Bruce McNevin exploded, as he could see his whole life changing. 'Scott's out of the way, so you move in?'

'I don't see that that's any of your business, Mr McNevin.' Clay's tone was perfectly even. It was evident he had no intention of being goaded. 'I'll say good day to you.'

'And good riddance!' Bruce McNevin shouted as Clay moved off. 'Make sure you never come on to my land again.'

'You should take it easy for a while, sir,' Clay advised, half turning and looking over his shoulder. 'You could have a stroke, heart attack, anything.'

'Mind what he's saying, Bruce,' Alicia warned her husband. 'The blood has mounted into your face.'

'So why should I care?' he cried in a distraught voice. 'You're leaving me, aren't you?'

Alicia's beautiful face looked incredibly sad. 'There's nothing left for us, Bruce. I should have done this a long time ago but I didn't have the courage to start again. Our marriage never had a firm foundation. I take a lot of the blame. I'll see a solicitor in Melbourne.'

'To start divorce proceedings?' He closed his eyes then looked up to heaven.

'Of course.'

His expression entirely changed. 'Then don't think for one moment you'll get your hooks into *my* money. *You're* the guilty party. I'll make sure everyone knows that. Mark my words, Alicia, you start this and I'll fight you every inch of the way.'

'Bruce. Goodbye,' Alicia said.

Senator Leyland Richards was having a busy morning. He had flown in from Canberra, the seat of Federal Government, to Melbourne, his home town, the previous evening and he hadn't had a moment to himself since.

Ah, well, this was the life he had wanted, wasn't it?

Fame and fortune.

He sighed deeply, putting off a phone call he knew wouldn't wait. Though his plans, as yet, weren't in the public domain, it was his intention to quit politics after giving twenty-five years of his life to it. He had discussed the matter privately with the Prime Minister; they had agreed on the best time for the announcement and he had received a strong message he was a definite contender for the top diplomatic posting to Washington.

'You're just the man for the job, Leyland!' The P.M. had assured him.

The thing was, though it was far from apparent to his family, his friends, his parliamentary colleagues *and* the P.M. he had lost the driving ambition that had set him on the high road to success. Son of a wealthy legal family—he had himself worked for a few years as a barrister in the prestigious law firm established by his grandfather—his entry into politics was put on the fast track when he married Annette Darlington, the only daughter of Sir Cecil Darlington, a senator at that time. It was in the way he had handled a tricky matter for the Senator that had really brought him to Darlington's attention. From then on it had been plain sailing. He was given to understand Sir Cecil was very impressed with him and his style. Meetings were arranged to interest him in running for a blue ribbon seat he eventually won. Annette, so very sweet and earnest, fell in love with him. And that was that! It was a union of *old money.* A union of Establishment families. The beginning of a good marriage and highly successful career in politics.

It had been two years now since he had lost Annette to breast cancer, a great blow. Annette had made him a wonderful wife and had been a loving mother to their two sons. She had wanted nothing more than to serve him and the boys. Most men would have found that an enormous bonus but he had secretly wanted *more* from her. More of *herself.* He had always been regarded as the perfect husband and son-in-law. God knows he had always tried to be. Less than a year after the untimely death of Annette, the retired Sir Cecil who had adored his only daughter, had suffered a massive heart attack while they were out on his yacht, *Lady Annette II.* Leyland had had an ambulance waiting as they docked, but his father-in-law had died before they reached hospital. Two great blows in as many years.

He'd done his duty by everyone. Doing one's duty was extremely important. Now he felt, despite the honours that apparently were yet in store for him, he desperately needed time to himself. Time to breathe. To sit in the sun. Take the boat out. He was fifty-three now. Surely it was time for a sea change? As it was he was at everyone's beck and call. Only an hour ago his press secretary had popped her head around the door to remind him of a press interview she had lined up for the following morning.

He made the phone call to the Shadow Minister in the Opposition who he definitely didn't admire, but as a natural diplomat he was able to get his message across to the extent a date was made for a round of golf at the weekend. At least the man was a fine golfer.

He was working diligently at some papers when his secretary buzzed him.

'I know you didn't want to be disturbed, Senator,' she said in a low, confidential tone, 'but there's a lady here—she has no appointment—who thinks you might see her.'

A lady? *What* lady? There were no ladies in his life since he'd lost Annette, but plenty who'd like to replace her. 'What's her name, Susan?' he asked. 'What does she want?' Dammit, he didn't really have the time.

'A Mrs. Alicia McNevin, Senator,' Susan said in hushed tones. 'She claims to be an old friend. She's very beautiful.'

Leyland felt something like an electric shock go through him. *Alicia! My God! Would the memory of her ever fade?*

'Send her in, Susan,' he said.

Carrie was so nervous she was almost ill. And she missed Clay terribly. He had become her rock and her refuge.

'Are you *sure* he wants to see me?' she begged her mother.

'He sent the limousine for us, didn't he?' Alicia gently smiled and took hold of her daughter's trembling hand. 'We're having dinner with him at his home, which he intends to hand over to his elder son and young family. Lee has bought a penthouse apartment with fantastic views of the city, Port Philip Bay and the Dandenongs. I understand it's undergone a brilliant renovation. We'll get to see it.'

'You call him Lee?'

'I always called him Lee,' Alicia said.

'And what am I going to call him?' Carrie swallowed hard.

'Just relax, darling,' Alicia advised. 'It will come. Lee is a most charming man. He will put you at ease.'

'Will he now?' Carrie said. 'That remains to be seen. And he wasn't angry you never told him about me?' Her voice was quite shaky, but she so desperately needed reassurance.

Alicia glanced through the window of the moving Bentley, the uniformed chauffeur separated from them by a glass panel, which went up and down at the touch of a button on the console in front of them. 'Well, you know, darling, it's as I told you. He was extremely shocked and very upset. But he rallied.'

'It's a wonder he didn't throw you out,' Carrie murmured, imagining the scene.

'That wouldn't have been at all like him.' Alicia shook her golden head.

Tonight she looked even more beautiful than usual in a sophisticated champagne coloured silk and lace blouse over a tight black skirt, her still small waist cinched with a wide black belt. She'd had her hair done and she radiated a womanly allure on a level her daughter had never seen before.

'I'm sorry he lost his wife.' Carrie's mind was inevitably drawn to the *wife*. She wondered whether Annette Richards had known about her mother. She hoped not.

'He loved her,' Alicia said simply, though her heart twisted.

'Does he know about *you*?' Carrie asked. 'Does he know you're going to divorce Bruce?'

'He knows *everything*!' Alicia said.

Carrie's mouth was so dry she didn't know if she was going be able to speak. This was her *father* she was about to meet. Her *real* father, her own flesh and blood. Her mother, on the other hand, looked remarkably relaxed. Alicia was obviously looking forward to the evening. She had gone to some lengths to look marvellous. Carrie had never laid eyes on her outfit. What had gone on at that meeting? Carrie wondered for the umpteenth time.

Impressive wrought-iron gates led to the Richards mansion, a Tuscan style residence that had known functions and parties galore. The house was designed over four levels, drawing Carrie's eye upwards. Impressive as it was, it lacked the sheer breadth, the size, the glamour of Jimboorie House, falling down or not. Garden beds lay to either side, clipped in the classical style. The gates were open in welcome and the chauffeur guided the Bentley into the huge garage to the right.

'We're here, darling,' Alicia said, touching a hand to her hair. 'You okay?' She was clearly anxious. Carrie looked lovely but austere, like a little saint facing martyrdom.

'I'm fine.' Carrie tilted her chin, wishing Clay were there so she could hold his hand. 'Lead on.'

They stood outside a magnificent front entrance door for barely a moment. It swung open revealing a stunning reception area with tall marble columns and a double staircase with beautiful black and gold balustrading leading to the mezzanine level. It usually stopped most people in their tracks but Carrie saw none of it. Her eyes were rivetted on the tall charismatic man who stood staring down at her, so deeply, so gravely. She had seen him many times on television and in the newspapers never dreaming there could be any possible connection, now she saw him in the flesh before her.

My father! My God!

The realisation didn't come easily. He looked what he was: a powerful, brilliant person, but how would he react to her? Would he entertain her briefly then send her on her way? He had the sons he wanted. The life he wanted, albeit as a widower. Perhaps not for long. Would he swear her to secrecy? A man in his position would surely be desperate to avoid a scandal? Would this meeting even have been possible had his wife still been alive?

She saw him reach out to take her mother's hand. She saw her mother reach up to kiss his cheek, a *special* kiss. 'Lee, this is your daughter,' Alicia said, tears falling gently from her eyes.

Leyland Richards looked down at that lovely, strained young face with its beautiful, haunted doe eyes, despairing that they could never find their lost time. But there was the future! He lifted his arms wide, not making the slightest attempt to hide the raw emotion in his eyes. Indeed his handsome face was suddenly ravaged by a mixture of joy and anguish. This was his daughter. He knew instantly and without doubt.

'Caroline!' he cried. 'Oh, God!' The very breath seemed to catch in his throat.

An enormous lightness seized her. Nothing could hold her back now. This was really her father. She had waited twenty-four years for this. Carrie went into those outstretched arms, feeling them close strongly around her. 'That's my beautiful girl!' her father said.

CHAPTER NINE

I could lose her!

Two weeks went by before Clay started tormenting himself with that frightening prospect. Each day she sounded more and more as though a wonderful new world had been opened up for her. Which of course it had. Her father had done what *he* couldn't. This was what he feared. She was happy living a life apart from him. And it could go on. Perhaps forever! Her biological father hadn't had a moment's hesitation in acknowledging her, she'd told him with enormous gladness in her voice. Clay loved her, so he was able to share in her happiness. But, Lord, he needed her as much as her father. *More.*

Miracles do happen, Clay!

He'd thought one had happened to him. But she was only going to keep him posted. She had been through bad experiences what with Harper, then Natasha and finally the man she had all her life called Father. He'd caught her at a vulnerable moment in time when she was emotionally fragile. That's why she had come to him— actually putting it down on paper—that she would marry him. Maybe now she thought of her promise as just plain *craziness.*

It occurred to Clay in acknowledging her, her father stood to lose much of his unsullied reputation. He would have to know that. His was a household name. Caroline's father was Senator

Leyland Richards, leader of the Upper House. Clay, though not overly struck on politicians of any persuasion, had always admired the man. He was a handsome, distinguished, highly intelligent, highly articulate with a magnetic charm that drew people to him. Senator Richards had long had the reputation for being a man the people could trust. He was also a natural diplomat with an engaging wit that worked well for him in his televised interviews. Women loved him. He got their vote. In short he was just the sort of man Caroline should have had as a father right from the beginning.

Caroline had told him in confidence that Senator Richards intended to retire from politics at the end of the year when he would make his announcement. Who was I going to tell anyway? Clay thought. Bruce McNevin, who must be cursing the day he ever opened his mouth? Clay went over their conversations a hundred times in his head. All too often the line was bad. A lot of work was being done around Jimboorie so he could only take calls at night. Caroline had been gone such a short time, yet she had already met her half brother, Adrian and his wife and young family. The younger brother, Todd, who had won a Rhodes Scholarship to Oxford, was overseas. They were well on the way to becoming one happy family.

Alicia, too, had been welcomed with open arms. Of course Alicia was a stunning woman. Clay was human enough to wonder if Caroline and her mother would have been received so magnanimously had both of them been ordinary people and plain to boot.

By the end of the third week Clay found himself going about his business grim-faced. He missed her unbearably. She may have found her *real* father, but she was in *his* blood, too. He prayed she'd remember that. Absence either made the heart grow fonder or the fond memories faded. Not that she didn't always tell him how much she missed him when she called. But when was she coming home? And where *was* home? He was so lonely without her. He had never known such loneliness. He told himself repeatedly he could scarcely begrudge her this precious time with her father. He was just so worried she might want to stay close to him. Hell, was that so unusual?

Clay worked so hard in an effort to take his mind off his anxieties, he fell into bed each night exhausted to the bone.

By the end of the month he decided to take action. He didn't have to watch every dollar anymore. He would take a trip to Melbourne. He would buy a decent suit and go calling, courting, whatever. Caroline and her mother had moved out of their hotel into the Richards's residence. He had the telephone number and the address. He was hurting so badly he just *had* to see her. If she wanted to remain in Melbourne with her new family he had to face the appalling fact there was *nothing* he could do about it. The very thought made him flinch. Without Caroline, all his plans for the future would be smashed.

They were all over him in the department store where he went to buy some smart city clothes. There was no question it would be extremely easy for a bush bachelor to find plenty of female company in the city but getting a one of them to leave the city for the lonely isolated Outback was another story.

In the end he bought much more than he needed, but the staff seemed hell-bent on outfitting him in a way they considered appropriate. He might have been a sporting icon—they made such a fuss.

You have the most wonderful physique, Mr. Cunningham. Those shoulders!

Thank you, ma'am.

A male staff member, scarcely less flattering, gave him the name of a top hairdresser and how to find the salon. Okay, his hair *was* too long and too thick!

He didn't know himself. He stared in the full-length hotel mirror wondering if he hadn't gone too far. What a change an Italian suit made. Was it really worth an arm and a leg? Where would he ever wear it again? But never mind. He had to look right for Caroline. They hadn't cut all that much off his hair. Just trimmed it and somehow shaped it so it followed the line of his skull. All those people trying to take care of him! He was glad he'd been able to frame his sincere thank yous.

In the hotel foyer he had to be aware he was turning women's heads. He could have laughed aloud. He was no sex symbol. He doubted if they would have looked at him in his usual gear of bush shirt, jeans and high boots. He didn't get the truth of it. He was a stunning-looking man, but he never saw himself that way.

His longing for Caroline was like a hand stretched out to guide him. He had decided on surprising her, not sure she would be at home, but willing to take the chance. She'd told him the Senator was always extremely busy sorting out his affairs but he always managed to make it home for dinner. Why not, with two beautiful women waiting for him! Maybe the Senator and Alicia would revive their doomed romance. They must have loved one another at one time though it would have been a sad thing to break up a marriage, especially when small children were involved.

He took a taxi to the Richards's residence, pausing a moment on the street to look up at the Italianate mansion, four storeys high. The lot would have fitted neatly inside Jimboorie House, he thought, with a surge of pride for the old historic homestead. The workmen he had hired had been going at the renovations hell for leather. It was astonishing what they had already achieved though there was a great deal still to be done. It would all take time and money. With Caroline by his side he had looked on it as a glorious challenge.

A sweet faced maid called Loretta answered the door, telling him Miss Carrie was relaxing by the swimming pool at the rear of the house. She stepped back smilingly to allow him to enter the house. He returned the smile, telling her he didn't wish to be announced. It was a surprise visit. He would walk around the side of the house to the pool, coming on Caroline that way. Loretta grinned at him like a coconspirator.

Following her directions he took the paved path on the western side of the house. A lot of the plants growing to either side were unknown to him. The character of the front and side gardens seemed very classical to his eyes. It was all very beautiful, very orderly, but the only splash of colour was white. Even the flowering agapanthus were white. Clay rounded the end of the rear terrace looking towards a spectacular turquoise swimming pool. The smooth surface was flashing a million sequinned lights. The pool was edged by towering royal palm trees and plushly upholstered chaise longues. A short distance back was a large open living area shaded by a terra-cotta roof with a deep overhang supported by substantial columns. The space was luxuriously furnished with circular tables, rattan armchairs and long rattan divans, again upholstered in an expensive looking fabric.

Sitting on one of the divans, their heads close together, were Caroline and a good-looking young guy, dark haired, bronze tan, wearing blue swim shorts. Clay took a deep calming breath. Then another. Caroline was wearing a brief swimsuit as well with a little bit of nothing over it. Her beautiful hair tumbled down her back. Her skin glowed honey-gold. Her lovely limbs looked wonderfully sleek.

His heart began thudding like Lightning Boy's hooves. He stood perfectly still, watching. Why wouldn't she attract eligible young men? God, hadn't he been struck by her allure, quite apart from her beauty, right off. Why wouldn't this guy who was staring into her face with what seemed to Clay tremendous intensity want her? They were, in fact, closely regarding each other.

Clay's stomach tightened into a tight knot. He braced himself as the guy placed a hand on her shoulder. He'd fallen in love with her. Of course he had. And Caroline was mightily interested in him. He felt lacerated by that.

I'll be damned if I'm going to let him take her away from me!

They were so close to each other. *Too* close. The guy said something that made Caroline laugh; a silvery, carefree peal of laughter.

Clay's built up feelings of anticipation evaporated like creek water in a drought. He was tempted to confront them, find out who this guy was, but he had the dismal idea he might finish up throwing the poor man in the pool. He'd rather die than act the jealous fool.

Clay turned on his heel and walked away. There was no longer any excitement. No longer the sheer magic of seeing her.

Barely ten minutes later Carrie, having had enough sun, was making her way back into the house when she met Loretta coming out onto the terrace.

'Enjoy your swim?' Loretta asked with a coy smile.

'It was lovely!' Carrie said, shaking back her hair.

Loretta's gaze went past her to the pool. 'The gentleman didn't stay long,' she said in a disappointed voice. 'I was just coming down to see if you'd like refreshments.'

'Gentleman? What gentleman?' Carrie frowned.

'Why the young man who came to see you,' Loretta said, eyes wide. 'He was gorgeous!' she added.

'Did he give a name?' There was puzzlement on Carrie's face.

'Sure!' Loretta nodded. 'Couldn't forget it. A nice name. Suited him. Clay Cunningham. Didn't want me to announce him. Said it was a surprise. I directed him—'

Carrie's voice overlapped the maid's. 'What time was this, Loretta?' she asked, urgency in her manner.

Loretta considered, head to the side. 'Not more than ten minutes ago. He was walking around the side of the house to the pool.'

'Well, he never arrived.' He saw *us,* Carrie thought.

She waited not a moment longer. 'Loretta, tell my mother

when she comes home I've gone into town,' she called over her shoulder. 'Tell her I'll try to make it back for dinner.'

It took Carrie under twenty minutes to track down the hotel where Clay was staying, shower, dress and call a cab to take her into the city. Lee had made a car available to her but she didn't want to waste precious time trying to find a parking spot. When she arrived at the hotel she was told by reception Mr. Cunningham wasn't in his room. He had been seen going out perhaps an hour or so before. He hadn't returned.

Carrie retreated to a lounge setting in the spacious foyer ordering a cold drink. Where had he gone? What time was he coming back? Whatever time it was, she was prepared to wait. She was so consumed by her thoughts she almost missed Clay's arrival maybe a half hour later. What alerted her was the ribald comment of one of two young women sitting across from her, sipping highly coloured and decorated cocktails.

'Strewth, would you look at the guy who just walked in?' the one in the sequinned top gasped, putting down her glass and sitting bolt upright. 'Wouldn't I love to wrap my legs around him!'

'We have a Ten!' the other squealed, holding up all her digits.

Carrie's heart catapulted into her throat. She followed the focus of their gaze although it would have been difficult indeed to miss him. It was Clay. He looked absolutely stunning in his city clothes, his marvellous hair barbered to perfection. He had meant to surprise her. Instead, apparently, she had shocked him into leaving.

When the girls saw her staring so avidly, the one with the sequinned top called to her. 'Bet your life someone has already high-jacked him. Wanna come over and join us?'

Carrie stood up quickly, grabbing her handbag. 'Love to, but I can't, sorry. I have to catch up to my fiancé.'

'You mean that drop-dead dreamy hunk of a guy is your man?' the one with the scarlet hair asked.

'Sure is,' Carrie confirmed proudly.

'You're one lucky lady,' Scarlet Hair told her with a wicked grin.

Though she pursued him as fast as her high heels would allow, Carrie saw him disappear into a waiting elevator. She took the next available, glad she knew which floor and which room he was in. Even then he beat her inside his door.

He came at the third knock.

'I missed you at the house,' Carrie said brightly, devouring him with her eyes.

He didn't respond, but stood looking down at her.

'Aren't you going to ask me in?' She had to duck under his arm to get into the room. 'What happened? Why did you leave?' She turned to face him.

He shut the door, leaned against it. 'One's the right answer and the other one isn't,' he said crisply.

'Fire away,' she invited, throwing her handbag down onto the bed.

'Right. One, I was running late for an appointment. Two, I thought I'd give that guy you were being so sweet to some swimming lessons.'

'You were *jealous!*' Carrie gave a little crow of disbelief.

He came away from the door abruptly, all six foot three of him, emanating radiant energy. 'What the *hell* did you expect me to be?' Despite himself Clay suddenly exploded. 'But, hey, I probably had no right. I mean it's not as though we're an old married couple or anything.'

'No,' she agreed, though her heart was fluttering. 'Why don't you try kissing me?' She threw it down like a challenge, moving right up to him and staring into his tense face.

'Why don't I?' He hauled her to him with one arm. 'I'm not enough for you, am I, Caroline?' His blue eyes were so full of emotion they *blazed*.

'I can't tell until you kiss me again,' she said.

He stared at her with those burning eyes, a frown between his brows. 'Do I look like a guy you can manipulate?'

'Manipulate?' She pretended to try the word out on her tongue. 'I don't know what that means!' She knew she was deliberately provoking him but excitement was running at the rate of knots. She was just so *thrilled* to see him and he didn't even know it.

'Of course you know what it means,' he countered harshly. 'Every beautiful woman knows *that*. I didn't aim for your love right off, Caroline. I hoped love would come. But I thought I had your promise. That little letter you wrote me. It said you wanted to be my wife.'

'Well, you didn't take it seriously, did you?' she flashed back. 'You haven't seen me for a month yet you can't even get around to kissing me.'

She actually sounded *aggrieved*.

Clay's strong arms trembled. He'd had enough of her mockery, sarcasm, whatever it was. This wasn't *his* Caroline—what had happened to her?—but he still wanted this Caroline. Madly. Badly. He couldn't look at her without wanting her. He couldn't inhale her fragrance. Clay gathered her up, unprotesting, and carried her back to the deep armchair where he settled her in his lap.

'Go on, kiss me,' she urged, her beautiful dark eyes staring into his, her long blond hair spilling over his arm.

His face tightened into a bronze mask. He wanted to pay her back. Yes, he *did*. But he could never hurt her. Instead he let his mouth move over hers, not punishingly, but letting it convey his deep need of her. His hands moulded her to him. He couldn't make sense of anything. He didn't try. It was the same old magic all over again. Magic that had the power to drain him of his bitter disappointment and anger.

When he finally lifted his head, he saw *radiance* on her face, though her eyes remained shut. 'Caroline?' Surely she couldn't kiss him like that and not love him?

'All right, you've kissed me,' she whispered, opening her dark eyes. 'Now tell me you love me.'

He was moved to reveal his heart. 'I love you,' he said, his voice a deep well of emotion. 'I want you to have my children. I'll love you until the day I die.'

Carrie was trying her hardest not to cry. She sat up a little, holding his face between her hands. 'So why didn't you trust me?' she reproached him.

He shook his head with regret. 'I will from now on, I swear! But God, Caroline, it was understandable, don't you think? I came on the woman I love staring into another man's eyes like he had the answer to all life's problems. A young good-looking guy who had his hand on your shoulder. We'll forget the fact both of you weren't wearing a lot of clothes.'

'Since when do you wear a lot of clothes when you go swimming, my darling?' Carrie asked. 'Haven't I rung you every night? Haven't I told you how much I missed you?'

'Not *enough* apparently,' he said, allowing a deep sigh to escape him. 'I took off before I embarrassed myself. And worse, *you.*'

'Let's face it, Clay,' she said gently, 'you made a mistake. Had you waited I could have introduced you to my half brother, Todd. When he heard about me, he decided on the spot he had to come home to meet me. He's only just arrived. I would have told you tonight.'

Clay threw back his head, stunned. 'Your half brother?' If only he'd phoned ahead he would have been told and saved himself a lot of heartache.

Carrie pressed her lips to his throat. 'My half brother,' she confirmed. 'I can't marry him but I can marry you.'

Clay stared at her until his raging emotions cut back to a simmer. 'I apologise,' he said finally. 'A man in love isn't entirely *sane.*'

'And I accept your apology,' she said, feeling giddy with sheer delight. 'I can't believe you're here with me.' To prove it she hugged him. 'About time, too.'

'And your new family?' Clay questioned, wanting to get things absolutely right. 'You're sure you don't want to stay close to them? We go back to Jimboorie, they'll be a long way away,' he reminded her.

'They're not going out of my life, Clay,' Carrie said. 'That's not going to happen.'

'Of course not,' he agreed, actually looking forward to meeting them. 'But you won't be able to see them on a daily basis or anything like that. There'll just be *me.*'

She took his hand in hers. 'I'm happy with that.' She smiled into his eyes. 'Hey, this reunion has been *perfect,* but my father and my half brothers have their own busy lives. Incidentally they all understand I love *you.* I've told them all about you. You have to meet them.'

'What right *now*?' Clay's voice was a low purr in his throat.

'No, not now.' She pulled down his head and kissed him lingeringly on the mouth. 'But tonight for dinner. I can't wait to show you off. Besides, I haven't quite forgiven you yet. You still have some work to do.'

'Okay,' he said in a smouldering voice, only too willing to prove his love.

'By the way.' Carrie deferred his ardent kisses for only a few seconds. 'We'd better get busy on our wedding plans.'

Clay laughed. 'I say we drink to that!'

'There's a bit more. If we don't, Mamma and Leyland are going to beat us to it, would you believe? Alicia is *still* Alicia, if you know what I mean.'

Clay smiled back at her. 'And Caroline is still Caroline,' he murmured, starting to seriously make love to her.

This was a wonderful outcome to all his hopes and dreams. One lonely bush bachelor had found himself the perfect wife.

EPILOGUE

Jimboorie House
18 Months Later...

THE army of tradesmen—roofers, carpenters, plumbers, plasterers, polishers, painters and wallpaperers, electricians—had all packed up and gone home. At some stage they would return—there was still plenty of work to be done on the many bedrooms of the upper level—but for now restoration work on the mansion had progressed so wonderfully well that Clay and Carrie had thrown it open to the people of the town and the outlying stations. Jimboorie House, once the hub of social life for the vast central plains of Queensland was set to take its place again as the reigning 'Princess' of the vast district's historic homesteads.

This particular gala day, a Saturday, had been set aside as a house warming for the very popular young couple whose splendid home it was and a fun day for all who had been invited. There was scarcely a soul—maybe one or two who had the sense to keep their resentments to themselves—who wasn't thrilled and proud to see 'the old girl' Jimboorie House rise like a phoenix from the ashes. This was *their* heritage after all. Guests were milling around the house now marvelling at what had been done. So absolutely *right*—Carrie and her mother, Alicia, had received hundreds of compliments and congratulations. They had worked closely with the decorators over the long months, demonstrating their own considerable artistic flair and innate good taste.

To Carrie, who couldn't quite believe in her own level of pure bliss, everything was a miracle. Finding Clay, her wonderful husband and her soul mate, was a miracle. Finding her real father another. The fact her and Clay's wishes for a baby had been granted was yet another glorious miracle. She had recently had her pregnancy confirmed. She and Clay were over the moon. So were Alicia and Leyland who had married quietly only a few months before. The fact Senator Leyland Richards had a beautiful daughter from an old twenty-year-plus liaison—the revelation had received wide media coverage—in the end proved no impediment to his diplomatic posting to Washington. Alicia and Leyland had, in fact, delayed their departure to attend the restoration party, making it clear they would visit at every available opportunity. Try to keep them away! Prospective grandparents, they were overjoyed by Carrie's news; Alicia promised she would return home for the birth.

Another stroke of good luck was that Bruce McNevin had very quickly consoled himself by taking a new wife, a rich socialite widow, still young enough to have a child. They were in fact on their honeymoon in Europe. Given their shared history and the fact they would be living in the same district, Clay and Carrie had decided, as they lived in an adult world, some kind of peace had to be made or at the very least an outward show of civility. Carrie hadn't the slightest doubt Bruce still loved her mother, but destiny had planned for Alicia and Leyland to be reunited at long last.

Carrie stood at the French doors looking out over the beautifully restored garden and the magnificent central fountain now playing, smiling quietly to herself.

'Now what's that little smile about?' Clay came up behind her wrapping his arms around her. Carrie was his *life*. Together they had made *new* life. He lowered his locked hands a fraction to press them lovingly against her tummy. 'Love you,' he murmured, the flame of desire never far from his blue eyes.

'Love you,' she whispered back, then gave a little ripple of laughter. 'See out there? I was hoping and praying Natasha and Scott would make a go of it.'

Clay looked out at the young couple who were the focus of her attention. Blond and raven heads together, they were pushing what had to be the Rolls-Royce of prams.

'Well it didn't happen overnight,' Clay remarked quietly, 'but it *is* happening, thank God. Natasha is certainly a different woman.' Natasha in fact had become a routine visitor to Jimboorie saying she was *family* all along.

'Motherhood suits her,' Carrie who was looking breathtakingly beautiful in her trouble-free early pregnancy observed. 'I was wrong all along about Scott. He wasn't going to turn his back on his child.'

'I don't believe his parents were going to let him.' Clay's retort was dry. 'But he seems determined to be a father. So good for him!'

'Well he has an excellent reason to get his life together,' Carrie said. 'Sean is a beautiful little boy.'

'And he'll have another cousin before long,' Clay said, bending his head to kiss his wife's satin cheek. 'God, how happy you've made me, Carrie!' he breathed. 'Supremely happy! You've even with your compassion turned Natasha into a friend. Not content with that, you've caused the Cunninghams to beg forgiveness for past wrongs.'

'It was *you* who did the forgiving,' she reminded him, enormously proud of her husband.

'How could I lock the old bitterness into my heart when I had such love in my own life?' he said simply.

Carrie's soft sigh was eloquent of her happiness. A special radiance emanated from her, visible for all to see. She pressed back against her husband's lean strong body, her head on his chest. 'And the greatest joy is yet to come,' she promised, placing her hands over his on her very gently rounded tummy.

'I didn't think it was possible for you to be more beautiful,' Clay whispered, 'but you *are!*'

And his voice was hushed with awe.

It wasn't until the gala day was drawing to an end that Clay was approached by a young man, around his own age, who thrust out his hand.

'It *is* Clay, isn't it?' The man smiled. 'Clay Dyson? Used to be overseer on Havilah a couple of years back?'

Clay's face broke into a warm answering smile as he recognised Rory Compton, scion of one of the wealthiest cattle families in the Channel Country deep into the southwest. 'Cunningham now, Rory,' Clay said as they shook hands. 'Cunningham is my real name, by the way. How are you and what are you doing so far from home? Not that it isn't great to see you.'

'Great to see you!' Rory responded with sincerity. He hadn't known Clay Dyson all that well, but what he had seen and heard he had liked. 'So what's the story, Clay? And this homestead!' He gazed towards it. 'It's magnificent!'

'It is,' Clay agreed proudly. 'There is a story, of course. A long one. I'll tell you sometime, but to cut it short it all came about through a bitter family feud. You know about them?'

'I do,' Rory answered with a faint grimace.

'Mercifully the feud has been put to bed,' Clay said with satisfaction. 'My great-uncle Angus left me all this.' He threw out his arm with a flourish. 'Caroline, that's my wife and I, have only recently called a halt to the renovations. They were mighty extensive and mighty expensive. What I inherited was a far cry from what you see now.'

'So I believe.' Rory nodded. 'I'm staying at the Jimboorie

pub. The publican told me about the open day out here. I'm glad I came.'

'So am I.' Clay's attractive smile lit up his features. 'Have you met Caroline yet?'

'The very beautiful blonde with the big brown eyes?' Rory gave the other man a sideways grin.

'That's Caroline.' Clay couldn't keep the proud smile off his face.

'I haven't had the pleasure as yet,' Rory said. 'I only arrived about thirty minutes ago, but I'm looking forward to it. You're one lucky guy, Cunningham!'

'*You* should talk!' Clay scoffed, totally unaware of Rory's current situation. 'How's Jay and your dad?' he said pleasantly.

'Jay's fine,' Rory said. 'He's the heir. My dad and I had one helluva bust-up.'

Clay could see the pain behind the level tone. 'That's rough! I'm sorry to hear it.'

'It was a long time coming,' Rory said quietly. 'The upshot being I didn't have much choice but to hit the road. I have some money set aside from my granddad. I guess he thought I might need it sometime. What I'm looking for now is a spread of my own. Nothing like Jimboorie of course. I'm nowhere in your league, but a nice little run I can bring up to scratch and sell off as I move up the chain.'

Clay looked into the middle distance, a thoughtful frown between his brows. 'You know I might be able to help you there,' he said slowly, already turning ideas over in his head. He knew of Rory Compton's reputation as a highly skilled cattleman with more vision than his dad and his elder brother put together. 'Why don't you come back inside. Meet Caroline. Stay to dinner. You're not desperate to get back to town are you?'

'Heck, no!' Rory felt a whole lot better in two minutes flat. 'I'd love to stay if it's okay with your beautiful wife?'

Quade: The Irresistible One

BRONWYN JAMESON

Bronwyn Jameson spent much of her childhood with her head buried in a book. As a teenager she discovered romance novels and it was only a matter of time before she turned her love of reading them into writing them. Bronwyn shares an idyllic piece of the Australian farming heartland with her husband and three sons, a thousand sheep, a dozen assorted horses, assorted wildlife and one kelpie dog. She still chooses to spend her limited spare time with a good book. Bronwyn loves to hear from her readers. Write to her at bronwyn@bronwynjameson.com.

Look out for Bronwyn Jameson's exciting new novel, *Magnate's Make-Believe Mistress*, available in December 2010, only from Mills & Boon® Desire™.

One

Cameron Quade wasn't surprised to see the sleek silver coupe parked in his driveway. Irritated, yes, resigned, yes, but not surprised. Even before he identified the status symbol badge on the car's hood, he'd figured it belonged to his aunt or uncle, one or the other. They probably owned a matched pair.

Who else knew of his impending arrival? Who else had just cause and reason for waving the Welcome Home banner? He'd been expecting Godfrey and Gillian to show up sooner or later but he'd have preferred later. Several years later seemed around about perfect.

As the front door clicked shut behind him, Quade let the weighty luggage slide from his fingers and a weightier sigh slide from his lips. His travel-weary gaze scanned the living area of the old homestead he'd grown up in, then narrowed on a wince.

The place had been unoccupied for twelve months

yet the gleam coming off every highly polished surface was damn near blinding. Someone had been busy but his aunt Gillian wielding a duster? If he could have summoned the necessary energy, he'd have laughed out loud.

As he wandered from room to room he did manage to summon a mild intrigue. The funky R & B tune piping from the stereo—a boy band?—didn't seem like Aunt G.'s taste, although the classic gray suit jacket looped over the hall stand did. As for the flowers—he traced a finger along the rim of a hothouse orchid—yeah, the artful arrangement on said hall stand reeked of her touch.

But the woman in Quade's bedroom, the woman in the classic gray skirt peeling back his bedclothes, was not his father's sister.

No way, no how.

"Come on, come on, pick up the phone!"

The woman's voice—low, smoky, impatient—drew his gaze away from the gray skirt and up to the cell phone clamped to her ear. She raked her other hand through her hair, one sweep from brow to crown that brought the thick dark mass into some sort of order. Temporary, he predicted, watching one curl bounce straight back up again.

"Julia. What *were* you thinking? Did I not specify *guy* sheets? Something practical, no frills?" She wrenched at the bedding, ripping it free from the mattress. "And you chose *black satin?*"

Practically hissing the last words, she flung the sheets behind her. They slithered across the highly polished floorboards to land just shy of where he stood, unnoticed, in the doorway.

"Good grief, Julia, you might as well have left a box of condoms on the pillow while you were at it!"

Quade's brows lifted halfway up his forehead. Black satin sheets and condoms? Not the usual homecoming gift, leastways not from his aunt and uncle. And he wasn't expecting welcome-home gifts from anyone else, especially this unknown Julia, the one copping an earful from the stranger in his bedroom.

"Call me when you get in, okay?"

Correction. *Whose answer machine* was copping an earful.

Equal parts amusement and bemusement curled Quade's lips as the discarded phone skidded across a side table and bumped to a halt against the wall. Still the same blue paint he recalled from his childhood. He'd wanted fire-engine red but his mother had stood firm. Luckily.

His nostalgic smile froze half-formed when the woman leaned across his bed. Holy hell. Quade tried not to stare, but he was only human. And male. And at his lowest point of resistance, completely lacking in willpower. Ten thousand miles of travel did that to a body.

Riveted, he watched her straight skirt ride up the backs of smoothly stockinged thighs. Watched the fine gray material stretch from classic to seam-threatening across a stunning rear end.

It was the first sight to snare Quade's total attention in those thousands of miles of travel.

Hiking her skirt higher, she slid one knee onto the mattress and stretched even farther, and he realized, belatedly, that she was remaking his bed. No, not his childhood bed but the big old double from the guest room—the antique one with the rusty springs. And as she leaned and bent and stretched and tucked, the mattress squeaked and creaked with a sound evocative of another kind of movement, a sound that stoked Quade's warm enjoyment of the scene to hot discomfort.

Hot discomfort as inappropriate as his continued silent observation, he decided with a wake-up-to-yourself shake of his head. He stepped out of the doorway and into the room and asked the first question that came to mind. "Why are you changing the sheets?"

She whipped around in a flurry of fast-moving limbs that put her off the mattress and onto her feet in one second flat. Or, more accurately, onto one foot and one shoe in one second flat. Her other shoe had sailed free midflurry and now lay on its side, stranded halfway between the bed and the discarded sheets. She faced him with one hand splayed hard against her pink-sweatered chest, with her eyes round and startled.

Eyes, he noticed, almost as intensely dark as her hair. Both contrasted starkly with her pale complexion, although her softly rounded face was in perfect harmony with her body.

"I haven't the foggiest who Julia is or why she's been choosing my bed linen," he continued softly, toeing the heap of satin out of the way as he came further into the room, "but I have nothing against her taste."

Her gaze whipped to the phone and back again, and he knew that she knew exactly what he'd overheard, but she offered no explanation, no comment, other than an accusatory, "You're not supposed to be here for another hour. Why are you early?"

She looked annoyed, sounded put out, and there was something about the combination that seemed oddly familiar. Quade tried to place her as he dealt with her objection. "We had a decent tailwind across the Pacific and got into Sydney ahead of schedule. Plus I'd allowed for fog over the mountains but it was surprisingly clear for August. I made good time."

Her attention slid past him, toward the doorway. "You're alone?"

"Should I have brought someone?"

When she didn't reply he lifted a brow, waited.

"We didn't know if you were bringing your fiancée," she conceded. "We decided to play it safe."

Hence the double bed. Hence the black satin and condoms. At least that made some sort of sense, or it would have done if he still had a fiancée to share his bed. As for the rest...

"We?" he asked.

"Julia and I. Julia is my sister. She's been helping me out." Or not helping, if her disgusted glare at the abandoned sheets was any indication.

Again, he felt that inkling of familiarity. Nothing solid, but... Gaze fixed on her face, he came a little closer. "Now we have Julia sorted, that leaves you."

"You don't recognize me?"

"Should I?"

"I'm Chantal Goodwin." She lifted her chin as if daring him to disagree.

He almost did. Hell, he almost laughed out loud in startled disbelief. While at university Chantal Goodwin had clerked in the law firm where he'd worked. Hell, he all but got her the gig but he didn't recall *ever* seeing that spectacular rear end. He did, however, recall her being a spectacular *pain* in the rear end.

"It was a long time ago," she said stiffly. "I dare say I've changed a bit."

A bit? Now there was a classic understatement. "You had braces on your teeth."

"That's right."

"And you've rounded out some."

"Nice way of saying I've put on weight?"

"Nice way of saying you've improved with age."

She blinked as if unsure how to deal with the compliment, and he noticed her lashes, long and dark and natural. If she wore any makeup, he couldn't tell. And in the sudden stillness, the total silence, he realized that the music had stopped. And that a nice warm hum of interest stirred his blood.

"So, Chantal Goodwin," he said softly, "what are you doing in my bedroom?"

"I'm an associate in your uncle's law firm."

"Well, *that* explains you being in my bedroom."

She had the good grace to flush, prettily, he thought. "I also happen to live just across the way—"

"In the old Heaslip place?"

"Yes."

"So, you're making my bed as a neighborly gesture? Kind of a welcome-home gift?"

That pretty hint of color intensified as she shifted her weight from one foot to the other. When *the other* turned out to be the shoeless one, she listed badly to the left. Quade steadied her with a hand beneath her elbow, taking her weight and enjoying the notion that he'd thrown her off balance almost as much as he

was enjoying her pink-sweatered, softly flushing, fe-
male-scented proximity.

Clearing her throat, she pointed beyond his right
shoulder. "Before I fall flat on my face, would you
mind fetching my shoe?"

Quade retrieved it; she thanked him with a smile.
It was no more than a brief curve of her wide un-
painted mouth but it softened her eyes. Not quite
black, he noticed, but the deep opaque brown of coffee...without the cream. That was reserved for her
skin, skin that looked as velvety smooth as those or-
chids in his hallway.

"As I was saying—" She paused to slip her foot
into the shoe. "Godfrey and Gillian wanted your
place habitable before you arrived and because I live
so near, I was...I volunteered."

Ah. His uncle—her boss—had volunteered her for
the job. The Chantal Goodwin he remembered would
have just loved that! "You cleaned my house?"

"Actually I employed a cleaning service. But the
linen's all packed away and I didn't like going
through your father's things. That's why I asked Julia
to buy the sheets."

"Does Julia work for Godfrey, too?"

"Good grief, no." She shook her head as if to clear
it of that staggering notion. "I was running short on
time so she was helping me."

"By buying sheets...?"

"Exactly. Anyway, these ones—" she indicated
the sheets on the half-made bed behind her "—are
mine and because I had to go fetch them, I'm running
late."

"For?"

"Work. Clients. Appointments." With quick hands

she resumed her bed making. "Julia also shopped for groceries. I'm sure you'll find there's enough to get by on. I took the liberty of having your phone connected, and the power, of course."

Quade folded his arms and watched her tuck the plain white sheets into ruthless hospital corners. "Leave it," he said, feeling unaccountably irritated by her seamless switch to business mode.

She straightened. "Are you sure?"

"You think I can't make my own bed?"

Unexpectedly her mouth curved into a grin. "Well, yes, actually. I've never met a man yet who could make a bed worth sleeping in."

Her wry amusement lasted as long as it took their gazes to meet and hold, as long as it took for images of rustling sheets and naked skin and hot elevated breathing to singe the air between them.

"I—" She looked away, off toward the wide bay window and the wild gardens beyond, then drew a breath that hitched in the middle. "I have to go. I'm running so late."

She started to turn, on the verge of fleeing, Quade thought. With a hand on her shoulder, he stopped her and felt her still. He picked up her discarded phone and pressed it into her hand.

Slowly, finger by finger, he wrapped her hand around the instrument. No rings, he noted, with a disturbing jab of satisfaction, just neatly filed nails, unpolished, businesslike. But he felt them tremble, and she retrieved her hand quick smart and took a small step backward. A reluctant step, he knew. Chantal Goodwin didn't like stepping back from anything.

"One thing before you go." He waited for her to turn, to meet his gaze. "You've done a first-rate job here considering you're not a professional house-maid.''

An almost-smile touched her lips. ''Thank you…I think.''

''So, what's in it for you?''

''Like I told you, it was convenient for me to help out, living so near.''

''And this—'' he waved his hand expansively to indicate the whole buffed and sparkling house ''—has to be worth a whole truckload of brownie points.''

One dark brow arched expressively. ''You think?''

''Yeah, I think.''

''Then I'd best go see what I can negotiate.''

This time he let her go although he stood unmoving, listening to the sharp *click-clack* of her sensible heels all the way down the long hallway, around his dumped luggage, and out the front door. Not fleeing, but hurrying off to work, to collect those brownie points.

To further her career. He should have figured that one out without any clues.

Funny how he hadn't recognized her, although in fairness to himself, she hadn't merely changed, she had metamorphosed. Even funnier was the way he'd responded. Hell, he'd been practically flirting with her, circling and sniffing the air. And it wasn't even spring yet.

Scowling darkly, he put it down to sleep deprivation and the complex mix of emotions associated with his homecoming. Combine that with the unexpectedness of finding her in his bedroom, leaning over his bed, and no wonder he'd forgotten himself for a minute or ten.

The next time they met he'd be better prepared.

* * *

Chantal didn't slow down until a passing highway patrol officer flashed his headlights in warning, but even after she eased her pressure on the accelerator her heart and blood and mind kept racing—not because of her near brush with a speeding fine, but because of her brush with Cameron Quade.

With time weren't teenage crushes supposed to fade? In this case, obviously not. Right now she felt as warm and flustered as when she'd first met the object of her teenage infatuation. He had fascinated her for years before that, what with all the retold stories—from her parents via Godfrey and Gillian—of his glorious achievements at the posh boarding school he'd been sent to after his mother died, then at law school, and finally his appointment to a top international law firm.

He'd done everything she aspired to, and everything her parents expected of her. Oh, yes, she'd heard a lot about Cameron Quade even before she met him, and she'd worshiped from afar. Up close he was worth all of the worshiping. Her skin grew even warmer remembering the moment when she'd turned and found him in that doorway. The perfect bone structure, the strongly chiseled mouth, the brooding green eyes and thickly tousled hair.

So long and lean and hard. So unknowingly sexy, so irresistibly male. So exactly how a man should look.

Chantal tugged at the neckline of her sweater and blew out a long breath as she recalled the way he'd looked right back at her. Like she was there in his bedroom for another purpose entirely. What was that all about?

Back in the Barker Cowan days he'd never looked at her with anything but annoyance or dismissal or—on one painfully embarrassing occasion that even now caused her to wince—with blood-freezing disdain.

And didn't he have a fiancée back in Dallas or Denver or wherever he'd been living the past six years? Kristin, if memory served her correctly. He'd brought her home for his father's funeral and she'd looked exactly like the kind of woman Cameron Quade *would* choose as a mate. Tall, stunning, self-assured—the direct antithesis of untall, unstunning, self-dubious Chantal.

She must have misinterpreted that look. Perhaps he'd been even more exhausted than he looked. After all, he hadn't even recognized her. As for Chantal herself…well, her wits had been completely blown away by his sudden appearance. Not to mention what he'd overheard.

Good grief, Julia, you might as well have left a box of condoms on the pillow while you were at it!

Had she laughed it off or explained that she usually didn't go around tossing phones at walls? Oh, no. She'd just stood there staring at him like some tongue-tied teenager…some *lopsided* tongue-tied teenager.

In her mind's eye she saw one low-heeled black court shoe spiral through the air in stark slow-motion replay. She groaned out loud.

Way to make an impression, Ms. Calm Efficient Lawyer!

Especially when making an impression was the whole point of the exercise. Godfrey had asked her to help him out, to check that the cleaners did their job and maybe stock the fridge, but she'd wanted Merindee prepared within an inch of perfection.

To impress the boss's nephew, to impress her boss.

She'd intended to be finished and long gone before said nephew arrived, but then she hadn't counted on the whole bed and sheets debacle...for which Julia had to wear some culpability, she decided, frowning darkly at her cell phone. She punched Last Number Redial and waited nine rings—she counted them—for her sister to pick up.

"Hello?" Julia sounded breathless.

"Were you outside? You better not have run—"

"Relax, sis. You know I'm beyond running anywhere."

In the background Chantal heard a deeper voice, followed by a muffled shush. Her frown deepened. "Shouldn't Zane be at work?"

"Oh, he has been." Julia sounded suspiciously smug. "We're working on our honeymoon plans."

Chantal rolled her eyes. "Good grief. You're six months pregnant. Shouldn't you be working on your nursery?"

Julia laughed, as she did so often these days. "It's been finished for weeks. Where are you, by the way?"

"On my way to work." In fact, she was just passing the Welcome sign at the eastern edge of the Cliffton city limits. "And, thanks to you, I'm running way late."

"Thanks to *me?*"

"You didn't hear the message I left earlier?"

"Sorry, we've been busy." Julia laughed huskily

then added in cavalier fashion, "Well, whatever the prob, I'm sure you'll deal with it."

"The *prob* is those black sheets you bought."

"Oh, no, they're midnight-blue. They *look* black but in the light they have this deep blue shimmer. Very classy but sexy, too, don't you think?"

Chantal didn't think about sexy sheets, at least not consciously. Before Zane Julia hadn't, either, and Chantal was still adjusting to this new mouthy version of her formerly meek and mild sister.

"Now, about tonight..." Julia shifted to a more businesslike tone. "Would you be able to collect the party platters seeing as you're in Cliffton?"

"Well, actually, about tonight—"

"Uh-uh, no way! You are my only sister *and* half of my bridesmaids and you *will* be at my shower."

"I was only going to say I may be running a little late."

"Oh. Then I'll have Tina bring the supplies. But don't be too late and don't forget it's costume."

How could she forget? The other bridesmaid, Zane's sister Kree, had taken complete control of the wedding shower arrangements because, in her words, Chantal's party skills needed serious surgery. A matter of opinion, Chantal sniffed. Some people preferred her quietly elegant dinner parties.

"You won't forget?" her sister prompted.

"No," Chantal said on a heavy sigh. "But I liked this relationship much better when *I* was bossing *you* around."

Julia laughed again then asked, her voice laced with suspicion, "What are you coming as?"

"A lawyer."

Julia groaned and Chantal smiled. "Before I go I should thank you."

"For?"

"Doing that shopping job for me. Sheets aside, you were a big help."

"Don't thank me, just give the man my business card." Chantal closed her eyes for a second and wondered if she could put the card under Quade's door. Or in his mailbox. "Oh, and you might toss in a personal recommendation. If this Cameron Quade saw your garden, he'd know I do good work."

"Look, sis, he may not want to do anything with the old place. He might not be staying."

"You didn't ask Godfrey?"

"I asked but I don't think he knows any more than I do about his nephew's plans."

"Easily fixed. What's the man's E.T.A.?"

Chantal shifted uneasily in her seat. For some inexplicable reason she didn't want to share news of the Cameron Quade encounter with her sister, at least not until she'd come to grips with it herself. "Today some time."

"So, when you pop over to welcome him to the neighborhood, you ask how long he's staying."

Chantal's response fell halfway between a snort and a laugh. *When you pop over.* Huh!

"What? I thought asking questions was what you lawyers did for a living."

"You watch too much television," Chantal replied dryly. Far more of her time was spent on reading and researching and documentation than in courtrooms. She cast a quick glance at the box of files on her passenger seat and felt her heart quicken. Some day soon she hoped that would change, and that the brownie points she'd earned this week would speed the process along.

"So, you'll see him over the weekend?" Julia persisted.

"You don't think this garden design thing could wait, say, until *after* your wedding?"

"No way! I need something to do other than worry about what we'll do if it rains."

"You did have to choose a garden wedding," Chantal pointed out.

"Yeah, yeah, I know. I chose a garden wedding and I chose to wait until spring so my guests would have something to look at other than bare-limbed trees."

"Like your belly?" Chantal teased, and was rewarded with her sister's laughter. Better.

They said their *see you tonights* and disconnected as Chantal braked at the first of three traffic lights in Cliffton's main street. The way her day was going, she'd likely catch every red. Her CD player flipped to the next disc and she remembered the one she'd left in Quade's house. Wonderful. As if she needed another reason to call on her new neighbor...

When you pop over, you ask.

If only Julia knew the half of it!

This morning she hadn't asked any of the questions that needed asking, and she wasn't talking about Julia's garden design aspirations. She was talking questions that had been gnawing away in her mind like a demented woodworm ever since she first heard of Quade's imminent return.

Questions such as, *What's a hotshot corporate attorney like you doing back in the Australian bush?*

And, *Has Godfrey asked you to join his firm?*

Questions whose answers might impact on her own career aspirations. Straightening her shoulders, she reminded herself that she was no longer a gauche teenager with no people skills. She was a mature twenty-five-year-old professional who had worked hard on her inadequacies, on overcoming her fear of not measuring up, at focusing on what she *was* good at, namely, her job.

As such, there was only one option.

Tomorrow she *would* pop over to Merindee and ask her questions.

Two

Two minutes later Chantal swung into the car park behind Mitchell Ainsfield Butt's offices and—thank you, God—found a vacant spot. Maybe her day was about to get better, although she wasn't betting any real money on it.

Juggling keys and phone in one hand, she jammed her briefcase under the other arm and balanced the box of files on one hip. With the other she nudged her car door shut—one of the few instances when a sturdy pair of hips proved an asset, she noted as she crab-walked her load between the closely parked cars.

The back door to the office block swung open just as she reached the stoop. And yes, her luck did seem to have changed for the better. The man holding the door for her, the man taking the box and briefcase and carrying them into her office was Godfrey Butt himself.

"Quite a load," he said, sliding it all onto her desk.

"The Warner files. Since I spoke with Emily I've been doing some further research—"

"Good, good."

Chantal bristled at the interruption, but didn't have a chance to object before he continued.

"And that other little job? Merindee all ready for Cameron's arrival, I trust?"

"Yes, absolutely." She forced herself to smile. "I called in this morning to drop off food and flowers."

"Flowers, eh? Nice touch. I'm sure Cameron appreciates your efforts."

Chantal wasn't so sure but who was she to quibble when Godfrey looked so pleased? Wasn't this *exactly* why she'd worked so hard on that dang house? "Do you have a few minutes, sir? Because I would really like to talk to you about Emily Warner's concerns."

"I was about to go out. Is this urgent?"

"It's important."

"What time frame—today, next week, this month?"

"The last," Chantal conceded reluctantly. "But I would appreciate your input sooner."

"See Lynda about finding some time next week." He was almost at the door before he paused, lips pursed consideringly. "Do you play, Chantal?"

Caught midway through a mental happy dance, his question caught her unprepared. Did she play...what? Then he started to swing his arms in a mock golf shot and the light dawned. Friday. Of course, the partners' regular golf date with People Who Mattered.

As Godfrey completed his follow-through, as Chantal considered the implications of his seemingly casual question, her heart kicked hard against her ribs.

Visions of green fairways and time-consuming strolls and relaxed back-slapping bonhomie with Partners Who Mattered popped into her mind.

"I haven't played in a while," she supplied slowly. How far should she bend the truth? "My game is probably a tad...rusty."

"Take some lessons. The new pro at the Country Club worked marvels with Doc Lucas's swing. When you're up to par, you can join us for a round."

"That would be..." She struggled to find the right description. *Perfect? What I've been waiting for? Terrifying? All of the above?* She swallowed. "Thank you, sir."

After the door closed behind him, Chantal spent several minutes riding a dizzying emotional seesaw. One second she wanted to punch the air with elation, the next she wanted to thwack her head—hard—against the desk. Because Godfrey's invitation came with a proviso.

Once her game was up to scratch.

Once she could be relied upon to spend some time on those verdant fairways of her imagination, instead of watching ball after ball leap into the water trap like lemmings into the sea. That's precisely what had happened the last time she'd attempted the "game." She deliberately inserted quotation marks because the word "game" connoted fun, and there'd been no fun in learning golf under her big brother's tutelage.

"But Mitch lacked the necessary teaching skills," she reminded herself, standing and pushing her chair aside. She never could debate worth a fig sitting down. "Not to mention how he rushed me and bullied me and laughed at my ineptitude. How could anyone learn under such conditions? With a decent teacher and the right motivation, I can learn how to hit that stupid ball.''

Same way she learned everything else. Preparation and practice and patience. With that personal credo, nothing had yet defeated her.

What about sex? a tiny voice whispered.

No contest, she argued. Inadequate preparation, insufficient practice, impatient tutor.

Sinking back into her chair, she reached for the phone and phone book. With receiver clasped between ear and shoulder, she flipped pages, dialed, then opened her schedule. She combed a hand through her hair, grimaced at the overgrown mess, but deleted Make Haircut Appointment. Ruthlessly she X'ed another six items on her To Do list—including Shop For Skirts One Size Bigger—and substituted Golf Lessons, all the while ignoring the nervous palpitations in her stomach.

Sure she hated golf, but she would push that little white ball from hole to hole with her nose if it helped raise her profile at Mitchell Ainsfield Butt, if it helped her earn enough respect to represent clients like Emily Warner. It wasn't that her current work was boring, more like…routine, when what she really craved was a stimulating challenge.

"Cliffton Country Club Pro Shop. May I help you?"

"I hope so," Chantal replied briskly. "I need lessons and lots of them. How soon can I start?"

Twenty-four hours later Chantal was peering through the window closest to Cameron Quade's front door into a still, silent, seemingly empty house. The lack of response to her first dozen raps could simply mean he slept soundly. But, dear God, she did not want him opening the door straight from his bed. Possibly half-dressed, probably bare-chested, definitely ruffled.

Apprehension shivered up her spine…at least she figured it might be apprehension, or indecision, or, God help her, cowardice. Rubbing her hands up and down her arms, she turned and took six steps across the porch before halting her hasty retreat. Retreat? Cowardice? From the nebulous threat of a bare-chested man? No way, José. Last night she had braved a Kree O'Sullivan hosted bridal shower. A bare-chested man should be a walk in the park after that fracas.

The breath she puffed out formed a white vapor cloud of warmth as it met the chill morning air, but with renewed determination she strode back to the door and gave the brass knocker all she had. She figured the strident metallic clanking would carry all the way down to her house, three paddocks away.

Even if he were in the farthest of the sheds out back, he couldn't *not* hear it…could he?

The seconds ticked by. She tapped her foot—in the schmick two-tone golfing shoes purchased three years ago and worn, like the rest of her outfit, a handful of times. Tapping aside, the only other noise she detected was the scuffling of feral chickens in the undergrowth. She turned back to peer through the window one last time, pressing her face right up to the pane in a vain attempt to see around the corner…

"Looking for someone?"

She swung around too quickly. That was the only explanation for her sudden breathlessness, that and the enveloping sense of guilt at being caught in classic Peeping Tom mode. Caught, needless to say, by the very Tom she had hoped to catch a peep of.

He wasn't bare-chested, she noted irrelevantly. He hadn't just left his bed…not unless he slept in a snug-fitting olive polo knit with jeans worn near white in some interesting places. Not unless he was a very vigorous sleeper. For a film of perspiration dampened his brow, and as he came up the two shallow steps onto the porch she felt the heat of recent exertion radiating from his body.

One dark brow lifted, asking a silent question. Or prompting her to answer the one already asked, the one she couldn't quite recall with him standing so close, filling the air around her with body heat.

Looking for someone?

Yes, that's what he'd asked, in that smooth low voice that did strange things to her breathing. She waved a hand behind her, toward the front door. "I tried the knocker and when you didn't answer—" She shrugged. "I had decided you mustn't be home. Or that you were down the back in one of the sheds. Or taking a walk."

"You could tell all that by looking through that little bitty window?"

Wonderful. Now he'd not only caught her snooping, but he'd made her feel like a fool. Straightening defensively, she forced herself to meet his eyes. This morning they looked exceedingly green, as if they'd absorbed the color of the garden at his back. "I could tell by the lack of response. I rang long and loud enough to wake the neighbors."

Mentally she rolled her eyes. *She* was the only neighbor and she'd been awake for hours.

"I heard," he said dryly. "I was around the back, chopping wood."

Which explained the sleeves carelessly shoved up to his elbows and the way his top clung in places, as if to sweat-dampened skin. She cleared her throat, averted her eyes, tried to concentrate on something else. Like the fact he was chopping wood. Dang. She hadn't considered firewood. "I didn't think you'd bother with the log fire."

"And if you *had* thought I'd bother?"

"I would have had a load of split wood delivered."

"Then I'm glad you didn't think of it."

He moved away to lean against one of the pergola's timber uprights. This is good, she told herself, trying not to notice the pull of denim across long muscular thighs and the dark dusting of hair on his bared forearms. Trying to ignore the little jump of response low in her belly.

Concentrate, Chantal. From this distance you can enjoy a nice neighborly conversation and extract the necessary information without it sounding like an interrogation.

"Why are you glad I didn't have firewood delivered?" she asked.

"I enjoyed the exercise."

His gaze rolled over her, taking in her daffodil-yellow sweater complete with crossed-golf-clubs logo, her smart tartan A-line skirt, her thick stockings (it was winter, after all), and the shoes she loved to death. He crossed his arms over his chest—not bare but impressive nonetheless. "Looks like you've got the same thing in mind."

It was her turn to lift her brows in question.

"Exercise," he supplied.

"Yes. I have a golf..." She stopped herself admitting to a lesson. "A game of golf this morning."

He made a noncommittal sound that could have meant anything. Then he shifted slightly and the sunlight streaming between the overhead beams caught his hair, burnishing the ordinary brown with rich hues of chestnut and gold.

Of course he didn't have ordinary brown hair—how could she have even thought it? Inadvertently her fingers tightened...around Julia's business card in her left hand. "My sister, Julia—"

"The bedroom decorator?"

"Actually, she's a garden designer. An absolutely brilliant gard—"

"Was she responsible for the flowers?" he interrupted again.

"No. I brought the flowers."

"And the food?"

Inhaling deeply, she fought her simmering irritation. "Julia brought the food and the first round of sheets. I brought everything else—"

"Except the firewood."

For crying out loud, did the man have a license to exasperate? First he had to turn up looking so...so distractingly male, and then, just when she'd composed herself, he had to interrupt every second sentence.

Chantal impelled herself to breathe in, breathe out, before continuing in a reasonable, patient tone. "Julia adores redesigning old gardens and would love to draw you up a design, if you're interested. If you're staying that long."

A coolness came over his expression. "So, the real

reason for your visit is to find out how long I'm staying."

"I can't say we're not curious because the whole town is agog—"

"And are you visiting on behalf of The Plenty Agog or to satisfy a more personal curiosity?"

Chantal lifted her chin. "I promised to pass on Julia's message about the garden."

"Come on, Chantal. You didn't come here to talk garden design. What is it you want to know?"

"Why do you think I have an ulterior purpose?"

"You're a lawyer."

Affronted, she stiffened her spine. "And you are?"

"An ex-lawyer."

Ex? Chantal moistened her suddenly dry mouth. "So you haven't come home to join Godfrey's practice?"

"Hell, no." He shook his head as if the idea were ludicrous. "Scared I was after your job?"

"I just like to know where I stand," she replied stiffly. And on a more personal level? Yes, she was curious. Yes, she had to ask. "What *are* you going to do?"

"Short-term, as little as possible. Definitely nothing that aggravates me. Long-term, I haven't made up my mind."

"About staying here?"

"About anything."

Chantal's curiosity grabbed a tighter hold. "And your fiancée…?"

"I don't have a fiancée." Expression tightly shuttered, he looked toward her car. "Haven't you a golf game to get to?"

She wanted to stand her ground, she *ached* to stand

her ground, to ask the rest of the questions hammering away in her brain, but he took her elbow firmly and turned her toward the driveway. She had the distinct impression that digging in her heels would have led to a forcible and undignified removal. As it was she had to scramble to keep up with his rangy strides.

"Nice car," he said, opening the door of her brand-new Merc. "A country lawyer must do better than I thought."

Partway into the car, she stilled. It wasn't so much the words as his cynical tone. "You have something against country lawyers?"

"Not if they leave me alone."

He said it mildly but that didn't prevent barbs of irritation blooming under her skin. Before she could form a cutting comment about *this* country lawyer's work prettying up his house, he surprised her by saying, "I didn't picture you ending up back here working for Godfrey."

For a second she was speechless. She hadn't imagined Quade picturing her at all. "How *did* you picture me?" she asked slowly.

"Corporate shark. You still got that bite, Chantal, or did you lose it along with the braces?"

Chantal bared her teeth and he surprised her by laughing. Right there, up close, with only the car door separating them, she felt the effect zing all the way into her bones. Wow.

Still smiling—how could she have forgotten those dimples?—he tapped his watch face. "Don't want to miss tee off."

She lowered herself into the driver's seat and scrambled to regather her wits. No way was she driving off without saying all she'd come to say. "If your heart is set on minimum aggravation, you need help with this gard—"

"I can handle my garden." He closed the door.

She opened her window. "It's going to take more than sweat and muscle to get this mess in order."

"I said I can handle it."

He projected such an aura of confidence and competence, Chantal didn't doubt it. He would chop his own wood and fix his own garden and in between times he would probably round up all the renegade poultry and start an egg farm. Which didn't mean that *she* wouldn't have the last word in this particular debate.

Kicking over the engine, she tossed him a trust-me-I-know-what-I'm-talking-about look. "Julia does wonderful work. If you want evidence, come down and take a look at my garden sometime."

Without a backward glance she spun her car in a tight circle and headed down the driveway, wondering why the heck that last line had sounded like *come up and see me sometime.* When delighted laughter bubbled from her mouth she reprimanded herself severely.

You should be feeling ticked off, Chantal, not turned on. That crack about country lawyers was completely uncalled for. And although you asked your questions, his answers weren't exactly expansive. Doing nothing won't keep a sharp mind like his happy for long, and what then? Do you really think Godfrey won't ply him with offers that would tempt a saint? And Cameron Quade has never been accused of being a saint.

But despite her self-cautioning, despite the fact that Julia's card remained clutched in her hand and she'd again forgotten all about her CD in his player, she found herself turning up the volume of her car stereo and humming along. However the words buzzing around in her brain were very much her own.

She had got the last word in.

She had made him laugh.

He didn't have a fiancée.

Hands on hips and eyes narrowed against the brightening morning sun, Quade watched her drive away. It was only then that he realized he was smiling—smiling in response to that last exchange, in response to her determination to win the last word. She was quite a competitor, Ms. Chantal Goodwin. That much hadn't changed.

The smile died on his lips, gone as quick as a blink of her big brown eyes. If he could expunge the residual buzz of sexual awareness from his body as easily, he'd be a happy man. No, a satisfied man, he amended. The word "happy" hadn't fit his sorry hide in…hell, he didn't even know how many years.

Immersed in the take-no-prisoners race up the corporate climbing wall, he hadn't noticed his priorities turning upside down. He hadn't noticed the lack of enjoyment and he had ignored the lack of ethics. Happy hadn't even figured. It had taken a soul-shattering event to open his eyes, to send him flying home to Merindee. True happiness—the kind you didn't have to think about, the kind that was just there, as natural as breathing—seemed intertwined with his memories of this place, back before his mother succumbed to cancer and his broken father lost all his zest for life.

Twenty years.

Quade scrubbed a hand across his face, then cast his gaze across the rolling green landscape. He had no clue how to pull his life back together only that this was the place to do it. He hadn't lied about his plans. He did intend doing whatever he felt like, day to day, hour by hour. He was going to live in jeans and unbuttoned collars, and sample as much wine as he could haul up from his father's cellar. Who knows, he might even start sleeping upward of four hours a night.

Away in the distance, where the Cliffton road climbed a long steep incline, a silver flash caught his eye. Chantal Goodwin on her way to golf and he just bet it wasn't a hit and giggle weekend jaunt with her girlfriends.

Oh, no, Ms. Associate Lawyer would have an agenda on the golf course same as she'd had an agenda fixing his house and visiting this morning. She hadn't come to tote business for her sister's garden business. Worry about her career had sent her snooping for information.

To find out if *he* was after *her* job.

A short ironic laugh escaped the tight line of his mouth. He didn't doubt that Godfrey would make overtures. He expected it. But uncle or not, benefactor or not, he had no qualms about turning him down. Some time in the future he might feel like putting on a suit and tie and going back to work. But not to the law. Long-term he intended staying clear of all things pertaining to his former profession.

Especially the women.

Three

There she went again. Bobbing up and down and scurrying back and forth like a squirrel gathering stocks for the winter. What was she up to?

Distracted by the distant figure, Quade lifted a hand to swipe at his sweaty forehead but a blackberry thorn had snagged his sleeve. Ripping his arm free, he pushed to his feet and let out a long whistle of frustration. After three hours of hacking and pulling and chopping and cursing, he'd had it with this weed. There had to be an easier way.

Hands on hips, he squinted out across the paddocks to where Ms. You're-Going-To-Need-Help popped in and out of view. He would as soon flay himself with one of these briar switches than admit it to her face, but she was right.

After she'd driven away the previous morning, he'd taken a hard look at the jungle that used to be his mother's pride and joy, and immediately gone searching for tools. But for all the inroads he'd made, there were sections he didn't know how to tackle. And— he glared pointedly at the blackberry outcrop—sections he wished he could take to with a bulldozer. He needed help in the form of expert advice. If said expert happened to be driving said bulldozer, he wouldn't complain...although he couldn't imagine Chantal Goodwin's satin-loving sister at the controls of heavy machinery.

While he enjoyed the fantasy elements of that mental image, Quade watched and waited, but the bright red of his neighbor's sweater didn't reappear. He wasn't surprised. She'd been following the same pattern ever since he first spotted her shortly after lunch. Suddenly she would appear out of the thicket of trees that cloaked the western side of her house, a bright dab of color and motion ducking about on a lush green backdrop, then she would disappear back behind the trees.

What the hell was she up to?

One thing for sure and certain, standing here peering into the lengthening afternoon shadows was providing no clues. Hadn't she invited him down there to inspect her sister's handiwork? And hadn't the small matter of not thanking her for her efforts preparing his house been nagging at his conscience ever since yesterday morning? He could almost see his mother shaking her head reproachfully.

Didn't I teach you better manners than that, Cameron?

Determined to make amends, he hurdled the back fence and set off across the paddocks.

* * *

The thicket of trees he'd been studying on and off all afternoon proved to be a windbreak protecting a good-size orchard, and that's where he found her. There at the end of a soldierly row of bare-branched trees with a golf stick clutched in her hands and a look of such intense concentration on her face that she neither saw nor heard nor sensed his approach.

Dressed in the same cute little skirt as yesterday morning, she stepped up to the first in a line of balls and adopted the stance. After swiveling her hips in a way that caused Quade's mouth to turn dry, she started into her backswing. With his gaze fixed hip height, he saw her lower body lock up and wasn't surprised when she lost the ball way off to the right.

She rolled her shoulders, stiffened her spine and moved on to the next ball. One after another she sent them spraying all over the closely mown pasture that fronted her house.

Suddenly her squirrel-like behavior made sense. She'd been scurrying about collecting golf balls, bringing them back, then hitting them all out there again. Time after time after time. He'd witnessed that same dedication firsthand working alongside her, but golf was supposed to be a game of relaxation. And this *was* Sunday afternoon.

After the last ball rebounded off a tree trunk at least forty degrees off-line, her shoulders dropped again.

"Do I take it yesterday's game didn't go well?" he asked.

Near black with startled indignation, her gaze swung his way. "How long have you been standing there?"

"Long enough."

"Well, there you go." She laughed, but it was a

short, sharp, humorless sound. "You're a firsthand witness to my disproving an old adage. Practice does not always make perfect."

"Ever heard the one about not reinforcing bad habits through practicing them?"

"What bad habits?" she asked warily.

"You're locking up in the lower body. You need to keep loose, relaxed."

Eyes narrowed and faintly indignant, she watched him approach. "You were watching my lower body?"

"Guilty. But in my defense, you are wearing that skirt." Quade allowed himself a pleasurably slow inspection of *that* skirt, before lifting his gaze to meet hers. She did that surprised blinking thing he'd noticed before, the one that made him think she wasn't used to handling flattery. Strange from a woman with her looks.

Then she straightened her shoulders and looked him right in the eye. "So, Quade. I'm sure you didn't come down here to critique my golf swing. What is it you want to know?"

Quoting his words right back at him...how like a lawyer! He almost smiled and it struck him that ever since he walked into her orchard he'd been enjoying himself. A discomforting notion, given the company. "After you left yesterday it struck me that I hadn't thanked you for the effort you put into my house. I know it's belated but thank you."

"You walked down here to say thank you?"

"And to repay you for the cleaning service and shopping."

"Godfrey took care of the accounts."

Quade's lips tightened. This wasn't good enough.

Not the way she deflected his thanks or the way she dismissed his attempt to recompense her. "Fine," he said shortly. "But I do owe you for the time and the inconvenience."

"That's not nec—"

"How about a quick golf lesson?" He rode right over the top of whatever objection she'd been about to make. "We can work on your lower body."

A faint, rosy flush tinged her throat as her gaze fell away from his. Hell. He hadn't meant that kind of work but now *his* lower body responded. "I do mean golf."

"Of course." She lifted her chin. "How do I know that you know what you're doing?"

"Good question."

Did he know what he was doing? Did he really want to tempt himself with hands-on-Chantal-Goodwin lessons? In anything?

But when her expression narrowed with skepticism he took the seven-iron from her hand, grabbed a handful of balls from the pail by her feet and tossed them to the ground. After a couple of idle swings to limber up, he hit one with a macho swagger he'd forgotten he possessed. It felt good.

"Easy as that," he concluded as they both watched the ball soar into the next paddock.

"You're a man. You hit long without even trying."

"Sure, length's important." And he *was* talking about golf, despite the way her gaze flicked down his body. Despite the way his…length…felt compelled to answer for itself. "But it's not the only consideration. Accuracy is crucial."

He illustrated by turning around and knocking the

next ball smack down the center of the gap between two rows of fruit trees.

"You do realize you're going to have to fetch those balls you're hitting all over the countryside."

"Later, but first you're going to hit a few yourself."

He offered her the iron, but she didn't take it. Annoyed by her hesitancy—and, hell, couldn't she have at least acknowledged the sweetness of that last shot?—he folded her unyielding fingers around the handle. They remained stiff, so he wrapped his hands over hers, molding them into a grip. Soft hands, he noticed, with a sinking feeling in his gut. Exactly as he'd feared.

"What have you done to your hands?" she asked, her question hitching a little in the middle.

Quade followed the direction of her gaze, down to where his large hands completely overlapped hers on the iron. For a moment he could only think of that, her soft warm hands under his, wrapped firmly around the hard shaft...

"Your hands?" she repeated.

Dragging his mind up out of the gutter, he noticed the raw scratches. He'd forgotten about the thorns. Standing this close, with erotic imagery pumping through his body, he could be excused for not remembering his name.

"I've been gardening," he said shortly.

"I thought you intended doing nothing aggravating."

"I intended doing whatever I felt like. Today I felt like gardening."

"Gardening or attacking blackberries with your

bare hands?'' She drew a breath, then let it go. ''Have you put anything on those wounds?''

''Such as?''

''Antiseptic. Salve. Peroxide. I don't know what you're supposed to use.'' Her voice rose sharply, aggrieved, and when he looked into her eyes he noticed they echoed her distress. Something stirred deep in Quade's gut, something that wasn't lust.

Something that scared the bejeebers out of him.

He let her hands go and took a quick step backward. Away. ''I guess that means you're not going to play nurse,'' he teased, desperate to lighten the mood.

But the words acquired a sensual weight of their own and hung there between them as her gaze roamed his hands, his forearms, his abdomen. Color rose from her neck to taint her cheeks, and he knew she was thinking about tending his wounds, about touching him in all those places.

This time the heat in Quade's gut *was* lust, pure, simple and so intense it held him paralyzed while he imagined the soft hot caress of her hands on his skin.

She lifted her face to look right at him. Standing this close he could see the black rim of her coffee-dark irises, could feel the allure of their rich depths. Eyes a man could sink right into, he thought, if a man wanted to lose himself. There had been times these past months when Quade had wanted to lose himself, badly, but never to another woman whose only passion was career.

''I'm not much good at playing anything,'' she said finally, and her voice held a husky edge that stroked every place her roaming gaze had missed. ''Nurse, sports, golf.''

Smiling at her wry quip, he took another mental

step backward, although his libido lagged behind. "And your golf swing needs a lot more attention than my scratches. Come on, Chantal." He gestured from the iron in her hands to the golf ball at her feet. "Show me what you've got."

"You want me to just hit it?"

"Yup. Relax and slog it."

"What about the accuracy you mentioned as crucial? What about caressing the ball?"

Quade lifted a brow. "Who's been telling you about caressing the ball?"

"Craig." The admission came slowly, reluctantly. "The local pro."

"Huh." So that's why she was all decked out by Golfers R Us. To impress Craig, the ball-caressing pro. Feeling unaccountably snippy, he watched her go through the same shoulder-rolling attempt at relaxation he'd witnessed earlier. Her white-knuckled grip indicated a distinct lack of success. "Didn't your Craig mention two hands as one?"

"He's not *my* Craig." Adjusting her grip, she stepped up to the ball. "And I usually get that bit right."

Quade stopped her with a hand on her shoulder. Through the plush warmth of her sweater he felt her tension ratchet up a notch and had to stop himself kneading the tightness. "Just relax, no pressure. We'll start without the ball. Transfer your weight," he instructed quietly.

"Like this?"

"Not bad." With a sense of fatalism riding him hard, he moved close behind her, puffed out a breath. Okay, he could do this. Adjust her hands without allowing his to linger. Guide her arms without wrapping his around her waist. Steady the sway of her hips without drawing them snug into the cradle of his. "Can you feel the difference?"

"All I can feel is you breathing on my neck," she murmured in that sense-stroking voice.

Quade closed his eyes for a moment. He decided not to tell her he'd been thinking about putting his mouth on her neck, right there on the delicate pale skin behind her ear.

"How was that?" she asked, finishing off her swing.

"Better, but follow right through."

He kept her at it, correcting, adjusting, suggesting, encouraging. Trying not to admire her determination, trying not to admire anything about her.

"The trick is having your weight in the right spot when you connect with the ball."

Dark gaze hot with frustration, she swung around to face him. "When *do* I get to connect with the ball?"

"When you stop lifting your head."

"Craig said my head position is just fine."

"Craig was probably too busy watching your ass to pay any attention to your head."

Outraged, her eyes widened along with her mouth. He didn't give her a chance to speak. He placed a hand at the back of her neck and directed her head into the correct position.

"Head down, like this, when you strike the ball." The tension in her neck vibrated into his hand. The heat of her skin hummed into his blood. He moved his palm, just a fraction, massaging gently. "You're not relaxing."

With an angry exclamation she swung away from him. "How can I relax with you touching me?"

Holding his hands out, palms up in a conciliatory gesture, he retreated several yards. "Hey, I'm not feeling too relaxed, either, not with that club aimed in my direction."

She lowered the iron she'd been brandishing like a weapon and sighed. "I'm sorry. It's been a long day."

"You're right. But before we pack it in, how about you give that swing one last try?"

She looked dubious.

"I'll stand way over here. No breathing. No instructions." He gestured toward the ball. "Have at it."

When she connected with a solid thunk, when it sailed out in an almost straight trajectory, he could see the delight in her face. In her smile. Felt it shining as brightly as the late-afternoon sunshine, reaching out to wrap him in its warmth. What could he do but smile right back?

"There you go," he said through his smile.

"No need to sound so smug." She swung the club around in several rapid-fire circles, like a gunslinger after a showdown. "I was hitting an occasional decent one before you happened along."

"You were woeful."

"Was not."

Quade laughed out loud—at her belligerence and because he simply felt like it—and when she closed the distance between them and stood smiling up at him, he felt a powerful urge to capture that delight between his hands, to taste it on his lips. When he felt her gaze focus on his mouth, he knew he'd been staring at the source of his temptation.

That full-lipped, soft-textured, smart-talking mouth.

Sobering instantly, Chantal stared up at him. "Thank you."

"My pleasure," he replied with equal gravity.

As she absorbed the shift in mood, everything inside her stilled. He was looking at her as if it *had* been a pleasure, as if he'd enjoyed standing close enough to breathe on her neck, as if he wanted to kiss her.

Now. On the lips.

A wave of longing washed through her, blindsiding her with its intensity, urging her to move closer, to place her hands on the broad wall of his chest. His heart pounded reassuringly loud so she slid her hands higher, up toward his neck.

She moistened her lips. Her lids drifted shut.

Suddenly hard fingers circled her wrists, forcibly removing her hands, setting her firmly back on her feet. When Chantal opened her eyes he was already striding out across the pasture, bending to pick up a golf ball, then moving on. Dang. No, this situation deserved a much harsher word than that old crock. Damn.

Damn, damn, damn, damn, damn.

She'd been a whisper away from his lips, from his kiss. And she had no doubt that Cameron Quade would kiss with the same confidence, the same sure-handed skill, as he'd employed when tutoring her golf swing. Missing out on a kiss like that was enough to make a woman weep, especially a woman who'd never been kissed by a true craftsman. With a heavy sigh, she picked up her pail and stomped off after him.

Had she read him wrong? She didn't think so, although perhaps she'd moved too fast. How fast *was* too fast? Some men didn't like aggressive women…although her lame attempt at a kiss hardly fit that tag. And that girlfriend he'd had at Barker Cowan, that Gina Whatsername in Contracts, she hadn't possessed a passive bone in her long, tightly strung body.

Perhaps she should have grabbed hold of his sweater. Or his face or his hair. Lord knows, she wanted to bury her fingers in that thick dark head of hair. Whatever, her prekissing technique obviously needed as much work as her golf game. Perhaps she should enquire if the local community college ran any classes along those lines. Seduction for Beginners. Or Bedroom Technique 101.

The questions, the answers, the conjecture looped through her brain in gloomily escalating circles the whole time she looped the front pasture, clearing it of golf balls. By the time they met by the side gate into her garden the sun was kissing the horizon with its last rays of light. He dropped a handful of balls into her pail, his expression cool.

"Thanks again," she murmured. "For helping me out with the lower body thing."

"You'll do fine once you learn to relax."

Nodding, she swallowed audibly. Any second now he'd take that big step backward, lift a hand in farewell and saunter off home. The thought filled her with an unreasonable panic. She wanted a chance to make up for her kissing gaffe. She wanted to make him laugh again.

"The way I hit that last ball, I feel I owe you more than a casual thanks." She moistened her dry mouth. "Would you like to stay for supper?"

"Can you cook?" he asked.

"I took lessons."

"And I should be reassured? You told me you took golf lessons, too."

"I haven't poisoned anyone." She paused for effect. And because she couldn't help smiling at his dry answer. "At least not recently."

For several heartbeats she thought he wouldn't respond to her crack, but just as the disappointment sank heavily into the pit of her stomach, he smiled. Full dimples and all. As the impact of that smile danced through her blood, her heart burst into a rumba.

"So tell me, Chantal... Lessons in golf, lessons in cooking. Do you do anything by instinct?"

"I would say no, except I just invited you to supper and I think that might qualify." Her voice sounded low and husky, not at all as light as she'd hoped. "Will you stay if I promise to relax and keep it loose?"

He didn't answer right off and in the tricky twilight his expression was unfathomable. The moment stretched, as taut as the tendons in her fingers where they clutched the pail. Perhaps she should let go the air backing up in her lungs. Perhaps she should laugh and ease the moment. Perhaps she should...

"I don't think that's a good idea," he said quietly.

"Oh." She swallowed a huge lump of disappointment. "Any particular reason?"

"Here's the way I see it—I gave you a golf lesson because I owed you. Then you invited me to supper because you figured you owed me. Next, I'll be asking you out to dinner because I owe you for the supper.'' He paused long enough for her to imagine candlelight and violins, knees brushing under the table, hands touching and retreating across a snowy white cloth. ''Where do you suppose all these favors will end?''

Heart thumping, she moistened her lips and thought about his antique bed all dressed up in satin that shimmered under the midnight moon.

''Better to call us even here and now, don't you think?''

Didn't she think? What *had* she been thinking? If Cameron Quade wanted to start a relationship, there would be women queuing up all the way to Cliffton for the privilege. If he wanted someone sliding between his satin sheets, he would find a woman who knew how to slide, instinctively, not a woman who needed lessons in the basics of male-female relationships.

''Before I go, there is one more thing,'' he continued smoothly. ''You said Julia designed your garden.''

Chantal perked up slightly. ''I did and she did. Do you want to look around? I just happen to have her card in my pocket.''

She extracted the card and handed it over. He pocketed it without a glance. ''How about doing the guided tour tomorrow? It's getting a bit dark now.''

''I won't be home any earlier than this, unfortunately.''

''Working late?''

''Golf lesson.'' She pulled a face.

"No drama. I'll have Julia show me some of her other work."

"I'd reschedule if I could, but Craig's already put himself out to fit me in."

"I'm sure he has." A cynical smile twisted his lips as he turned to leave. "See you around, Chantal."

What did he mean by that? *I'm sure he has.* Said in *that* tone of voice? Was he implying… She lifted her voice enough to carry across the orchard. "Craig has no interest in me other than the fact that I'm paying him to teach me golf."

"If you say so."

"And he does not watch my ass."

He turned, hands on hips, and she could still see that smile, white in the gathering darkness. "Then *he's* an ass."

Four

Doing as little as possible wasn't all it was cracked up to be. Quade arrived at this conclusion six days later, as he prowled around his sodden grounds. His hands itched to grab hold of a shovel or a hoe or a pair of tree loppers, but Julia Goodwin's instructions had been clear.

"Hands off until I say otherwise."

When he objected she'd asked if he really wanted her help or not. He'd unclenched his teeth and agreed to meet with her Saturday afternoon, which, she'd apologetically informed him, was the soonest she could get out there.

"Transportation difficulties," she'd said. "Plus the forecasts are for a wet week."

A less honest man might have blamed his subsequent restlessness on the waiting. Or on the week's unrelenting rain. Or the hollow emptiness of a house he remembered resonating with laughter and redolent with the smell of home cooking.

All of the above could claim some culpability but, in truth, his mood owed as much to self-flagellation for turning down Chantal's invitation. He couldn't cook worth a damn, he couldn't order home delivery out here in the boonies, and he'd turned down a home-cooked meal.

That made him even more of an ass than the short-sighted golf pro.

The long wet week provided plenty of opportunity to appreciate how much he had enjoyed her company—she'd amused him, stimulated him, and irritated him all at once. Yet when she issued that invitation, when she mentioned loosening up and he started to sink into the sultry depths of her eyes, he'd felt a compelling need to get out while he still could. As if she posed some kind of danger.

As if.

Sure, there was something appealing about her combination of soft curves and sharp tongue, something erotically enticing about her silken skin and rich eyes. But Chantal Goodwin was no beauty, not in the big scheme of things. Resisting the attraction was as simple as recalling the single-mindedness of career women with their sights set on the top, as easy as remembering the callousness of Kristin's deceit.

He had called Chantal. She'd not been home. A busy lawyer like her had places to be, hours to bill. That cynical thought kept his feet planted on his side of the fence and a scowl planted on his face, and the latter felt much more at home than the smiles she'd coaxed out of him.

Better to concentrate on whipping his garden into

shape, he decided, not to mention the land beyond, which had fallen into an equal state of neglect. He didn't picture himself as Farmer Jones but he could employ a consultant, same as he was doing to compensate for his lack of gardening knowledge.

The heavy throb of a large engine brought him out of his scowling reverie just as a big black tow truck appeared in his driveway.

Julia Goodwin drove a tow truck?

Quade did a mental double take as the vehicle lumbered to a halt, partly obscured by shrubbery. Expectancy tightened his gut at the sound of a door squeaking open then thudding shut and didn't relent when a woman strode into sight.

She was a slightly taller, even curvier, more stunning version of her sister. Her thousand-watt smile looked capable of lighting every corner of his enormous cellar. And despite all that, Quade's pulse remained slow and steady. If *this* Goodwin sister invited him to supper, he would accept in a heartbeat.

"Cameron Quade, I presume? I'm Julia Goodwin, which you've probably figured out all by yourself."

Smiling back, he offered his hand. "Just Quade."

"Just Quade, huh?" She took his hand and shook it firmly. No tremor, no spark, no heat cascading through his system. Odd, given his extravagant reaction to her sister…but fortunate, given the big stern-faced man who'd followed her from the truck and who now placed a proprietary hand on her shoulder.

"Zane O'Sullivan." He extended his hand over Julia's other shoulder.

"In two weeks' time he gets to be my husband," Julia added.

"Lucky man." Quade met the big guy's gaze,

which happened to be as strong and testing as his grip.

"I think so."

"You *know* so," Julia corrected, turning on her heel in a quick three-sixty appraisal of her surroundings. The action caused her unbuttoned coat to swing open and when she came to a halt with her hands planted on her hips, the tightness returned to Quade's gut with viselike intensity.

Julia Goodwin was visibly, round-bellied pregnant.

Struggling to pull himself together, he forced his gaze up, away, anywhere but *there*. Hell, she wasn't the first pregnant woman he'd seen, not even in the past month, since he'd found out about Kristin. About the pregnancy he'd known nothing about; the pregnancy she had chosen to terminate.

"When are you due?" he asked slowly, and his voice came out strained, as if strangled by the tightness spreading into his chest and up to his throat.

"Early November."

"Is that a problem?" O'Sullivan looked as confrontational as his question sounded. Quade didn't blame him—not when another man had been gawking at his fiancée's belly. It's a wonder he wasn't wearing Zane O'Sullivan's substantial fist in the center of his face.

Quade forced his lips into some semblance of a smile. "No problem. A surprise, that's all."

"Well, hey, it was a surprise this end, too, but of the very best kind. This little one—" Julia patted her middle. "—doesn't stop me doing much. I wish I could say the same for Daddy."

She tempered the cheerful complaint by resting her hand on O'Sullivan's arm and smiling up at him. A four-year relationship and Quade couldn't remember a time when Kristin had looked at him in quite that way. Hell, in the last year she'd barely found time to talk about anything outside of work, and she'd had her own agenda for keeping that channel of communication open.

"I told Zane I'm not doing any of the physical work," Julia continued, "but perhaps you can reassure him? You know, on the digging and lifting front?"

Snapping free of his bitter memories, Quade fixed the other man with a direct look. "I'm only in the market for design and consultancy. I *want* to do all the digging and lifting."

O'Sullivan considered him levelly for a long moment before nodding. "Fair enough."

Satisfied, Quade shifted his attention back to Julia. "You didn't mention the wedding. You're going to be busy."

"Not with Chantal on the team."

"Everything's organized?"

"With the precision of an army maneuver," Julia replied. "And I appreciate something to do other than worrying about the weather."

Quade gestured at the overgrown beds. "You think this will be enough to keep you busy?"

"Piece of cake. Speaking of which, I don't suppose you have any of that chocolate cake left?"

Clueless, he looked to O'Sullivan for help, and received a don't-ask-me-mate shrug.

"I felt sure there was a Sara Lee in the shopping I did for you, but not to worry." Hand on belly, Julia grinned ruefully. "It's probably best if I don't spoil my appetite, seeing as Chantal's cooking dinner."

"She's a good cook?" Quade couldn't help asking.

"She's good at everything she sets her mind to."

"Except golf."

He hadn't meant to share that observation, but it appeared he had. A stunned silence followed.

"Chantal has taken up golf?" Julia asked on a rising note of disbelief.

He hitched a shoulder. "She's taking lessons."

"From Craig McLeod at the Country Club?"

"Pretty Boy's a golf pro?" O'Sullivan sounded as surprised by this as Julia was about the Chantal/golf connection.

While the other two discussed their former schoolmate, Quade chewed over the nickname. He wasn't sure if he should be laughing or scowling. He didn't want to ask, but he couldn't help himself. "People call him Pretty Boy?"

"Not to his face."

"Which, I hasten to add, really lives up to the promise," Julia chipped in. "How is it you know about Chantal's golf lessons?"

Her question interrupted a mental scenario where Chantal's backswing caught McLeod square in his pretty face. The image cheered Quade far more than it had any right to. "She mentioned it, in passing."

"In passing, huh? Do you two pass often?"

"We're neighbors."

It might have been his imagination, but her ever-present smile seemed to turn speculative. "So, Just Quade, before we get down to garden business, what plans do *you* have for dinner tonight?"

"Hey, sis. Where are you?" Piping from the answering machine, Julia's voice sounded even chirpier than usual, Chantal decided, although that might have only been in comparison to her own unchirpy mood. ''I thought you'd be slaving over a hot stove with us coming to dinner in less than an hour. Which is why I rang. Hope you don't mind but we're bringing your neighbor…although that took some talking. You must have made quite an impression. Not. Anyway, see you soon.''

Chantal sank slowly into a lounge chair. Quade was coming to dinner. Exactly as she'd imagined in all those midnight fantasies. Except—unlike her fantasies—he wouldn't be turning up on her doorstep with a bottle of wine in one arm and a bunch of flowers in the other.

Oh, no, he was being dragged by the bootlaces because Julia had a way with persuasion. With a growl of frustrated despair, Chantal buried her face in her hands. She would kill Julia, truly she would, but first she needed to pull herself together. She peered through a gap in her fingers and groaned. On second thought, she would postpone pulling herself together until she had pulled her house together.

Scooting around the living room, she straightened furniture and tossed pillows onto chairs, arranged the magazines into careful piles and gathered up all her work files from the floor in front of the fire. The dead fire. Cold ashes. Unwelcoming. *Help!*

With a hand splayed against her chest, she could feel her escalating heartbeat. A glance to the mirror above the hearth—hair a windswept mess, no makeup, unflattering brown sweater—did nothing to alleviate her rising panic. She had forty minutes. She needed a plan of action. She needed music, a soothing antidote in times of stress.

Six long strides took her to the sound system and she dropped to her knees. Brows knit, she ran a finger down the CD tower. Where was her favorite stress-buster? Her mind slid instantly to the last time she had needed it...

It was likely *still* sitting in Quade's stereo.

The forty minutes flew, but not as fast as Chantal's hands or feet. In the time between first hearing the rumble of Zane's approaching truck and the sound of Julia calling, "We've let ourselves in, okay?" she changed into her best jeans and her second-favorite rust-colored knit.

Her favorite off-white angora lay inside out on the bed, discarded on an issue of practicality. Pasta sauce would be so much less noticeable sloshed down the front of *this* sweater, and, when she cooked, stuff inevitably ended up sloshed. She constrained her hair with a couple of tortoiseshell clips, dusted her overheated face with powder, then, with significant effort, stopped herself dashing back at the same breakneck speed.

Difficult, but she impressed herself by managing.

Unfortunately she didn't manage to coax her face into a smile. As she walked—*slow down, Chantal, don't stride!*—into the large informal living room, she felt as if her attempt might actually crack her cheeks. When she noticed Quade, alone, bending down to a low bookcase shelf, she gave up her attempt altogether.

Side-lit by a table lamp, he looked—she licked her lips and blew out a hot breath—he looked delicious. She knew the kelly-green sweater would do amazing things to his eyes and when he hunkered lower, his jeans pulled tight and did amazing things to his thighs and buttocks. Oh, my Lord!

Pulse leaping as crazily as the flames in the fireplace, she watched him select her well-worn copy of *To Kill a Mockingbird* then straighten. "How old were you when you first read this?" he asked, still with his back to her.

How had he known she was there? Could he hear the pounding of her heart above the music? Chantal swallowed and prayed her voice would work. "I don't recall. Fourteen, maybe." A little husky, but working, which impressed her all over again.

"And you decided you wanted to be a lawyer?"

"I was never going to be anything else," she said simply.

He turned the book over in his hands, touching the cover in a way that caused her skin to tingle. As if those strong hands stroked her with the same gentle reverence. "I bet there's a big difference between what you're doing now and your childhood dreams," he said, turning to face her. "I bet you dreamed of being a big trial lawyer."

"Didn't we all?"

"Not me. I never did acquire the gift of rhetoric."

"I don't know about that." She arced a brow at him. "Although your particular gift might see you in constant contempt."

"You think I curse too much?"

Tilting her head on the side, she smiled wryly. "Let's just say you've always been a straight-shooter."

"Are you referring to that…difference of opinion…we had at Barker Cowan?"

Difference of opinion? What an interesting interpretation. "As I recall, it was more a hauling over the coals."

"You deserved it."

Chantal felt herself stiffen reflexively. "I was perfectly justified—"

"See? A difference of opinion, just as I called it."

Chin raised combatively, she glared into his green eyes and saw he was fighting a smile. Dang. How could she retain her righteous indignation with that smile hovering, teasing, threatening to turn her to instant mush?

"Water under the bridge," she said with a dismissive shrug, but only because he'd managed to totally deflect her argument. She still knew she was right, she just couldn't remember why. "Where did Julia get to?"

"She went to see if she could help in the kitchen."

"And Zane?"

"He followed."

"What on earth could they be doing all this time?" She frowned crossly, and then her brain kicked in again. "Oh."

His smile spread. "Indeed."

They were probably lip-locked at this very moment. She wanted to roll her eyes and say something smart, but with her gaze fixed on the curve of Quade's mouth all she could think was *lucky, lucky Julia.*

"I brought something—"

"My CD?" Distracted by kissing-envy, she jumped in without thinking, and he stared back at her blankly. Okay, not the CD... "My sheets?"

"I didn't know you'd left a CD and as for your sheets—" He looked right into her eyes. "They're still on my bed."

This was exactly why she'd sent Julia shopping for new sheets. To keep his hot body—his hot *naked* body—from between hers. Chantal swallowed weakly. "I thought you preferred the satin ones."

"Yeah, but yours turned out to be much softer than I imagined."

"High thread count."

"If you say so." His shrug highlighted the breadth of his shoulders. She imagined them bare, in golden-skinned contrast to her stark white linen, and her knees turned to putty. "Don't you want to know what I did bring?"

He inclined his head toward the coffee table and for the first time she noticed the two bottles sitting there.

"Do you like merlot?" he asked in a voice as intoxicating as that soft red brew. But before she could reply, Julia's head appeared through the doorway to the kitchen. She looked flushed and very thoroughly kissed.

"There you are, sis. Do you want me to do anything to help with dinner? Because I'm starving."

Chantal gathered herself. She had guests, a dinner to prepare. A bedazzled head to clear. "You can*not* eat the food before it's served. That would be helpful."

Julia grinned, then popped something into her mouth. It looked awfully like the remains of one of the dinner rolls. "Oops, too late."

The only way she could concentrate on cooking was to chase all chattering you-didn't-mention-what-a-first-grade-hunk-Quade-is distractions from her kitchen with instructions to set the table. Delving deep into the chest freezer for more bread rolls, she sensed a new disruption.

Her first abstracted thought was: *so that's how he knew when I came into the living room—he felt me eyeballing his backside.*

Her second abstracted thought: *if I stay here much longer, generating this amount of body heat, I'll defrost the whole freezer-load of food.*

While she extracted herself from the freezer depths, she rued the fact that her jeans, like everything else in her wardrobe, fit a little too snugly.

"Julia sent me after a corkscrew."

"Top drawer, beside the stove," she instructed.

He fetched it—she heard the drawer slide open then click shut—but she felt the touch of his gaze as she placed the rolls in the microwave. Suddenly her roomy kitchen felt very small, the lack of words between them awkward.

"For some reason I'm one roll short," she said, punching buttons to start the oven. She turned to find him leaning against the bench top, tapping the corkscrew against his thigh. A frown drew his dark brows together.

"Sorry for the lack of notice. Julia said you wouldn't mind."

"Julia's right—I don't mind. And the bread shortage isn't because you're one extra but because *she's* been sampling the goods."

She crossed to the stove, lifted the lid and carefully stirred the simmering soup. It looked good, smelled even better. Thank you, God.

"Knowing Julia," she continued conversationally, "you'd have had little choice on whether you came or not."

"I had choice. That bossy thing you Goodwin girls have going doesn't sway me."

Funny, but she'd never heard *bossy* sound like a compliment before. It was *that* voice, *that* mouth. Irresistible. The word drifted unbidden through her senses but she shook it away. "So, why did you come?"

"Curiosity."

What a curious answer… She turned a little, resting her hip against the stove, so she could see his face. "Curiosity about?"

"Your sister says you're an excellent cook."

And he didn't believe her. Well! Indignation rising, she lifted a ladle full of the thick orange puree and tilted it this way and that in the light.

"Pumpkin?" he asked.

"Roasted pumpkin with green apple and thyme."

"Gourmet," he murmured but she noticed him inhale the aromatic steam. She noticed his eyes haze just a smidge and her stomach dipped with satisfaction. He would change his mind about her cooking skills before the night was over.

"Would you like a taste?" she asked.

"Is it safe?"

Perhaps it was her imagination, but his cool Midori gaze seemed to slide to her mouth and back again. Chantal felt the impact flow through her blood in a prolonged wave of longing.

The touch of his lips wouldn't be safe, not to her sanity, not to her senses, but she didn't care. Oh, how she didn't care!

Gaze locked with hers, he slowly ducked his head to the ladle suspended between them. When he sipped from the edge of the tilted spoon, she felt her own lips open reflexively, felt her tongue touch the very center of her top lip. Felt a soft sigh of appreciation slide between her open lips. Saw something flicker darkly in his eyes. Desire? Resolve?

He leaned closer, beyond the spoon, and another sound escaped her throat, a sound of heightened anticipation. When his tongue touched her top lip, one soft stroke, she allowed her lids to drift shut. She needed to concentrate, to categorize each nuance, the whisper of his exhalation against her cheek, the slight change in angle that brought their lips into perfect alignment, the sensual slide of his tongue. Top lip, bottom lip. Sweet, spicy, hot. So delicious, the rush of flavor, of heat, of desire, but still just a sample, she knew, of what was to come…

Her knees turned weak, her shoulders slumped, her elbows gave way as a rich multitude of sensations coursed through her body. And then the ladle slipped from her fingers, bumped down the front of her jumper and clattered to the floor. Eyes flying open, she jumped back just as Julia barreled through the door. Pulling up short, she took in the scene in one raised-eyebrows look, turned on her heel, and left as quickly as she'd arrived.

Which left Chantal to deal with sloshed soup and one very uncomfortable man. He stood rubbing his forehead and looking as if he couldn't quite believe what he'd just done. *She* couldn't quite believe what he'd just done. She definitely couldn't believe what he was about to do…

He grabbed a dishcloth and started dabbing at her sweater. Down her abdomen, over her belly…and everywhere he touched seared like molten flame. Face flushed, pulse galloping, she drew in a shallow shuddery breath and felt him still. His eyes were lowered but she saw his nostrils flare and a shiver—hot, cold, *yes, please*—raced through her.

But he pushed the cloth into her hand and muttered, "That's got the worst of it," before stepping well clear.

Disappointment thundered hard on the heels of hope. Obviously he didn't want to talk about the kiss, let alone carry on where they'd left off.

Well, fine. She wasn't about to ask. Or beg.

"I guess I'd better get on with this cooking or we won't be eating till midnight," she said, shucking off a disturbingly intense sense of regret. She ducked down to grab a saucepan, dashed to the sink, back to the stove.

"Are you all right?" he asked after a frantic minute's activity.

"I'm fine. Why?"

"You look a bit…flustered."

Really? she thought. *Only flustered?* She could have sworn she looked somewhere between full boil and complete meltdown whereas he looked as cool as ever. Totally unaffected. Her heart did a duck and dive.

"Heat from the cooking." She flapped a hand in front of her face and inspiration struck. "Or perhaps I'm coming down with something. I've been feeling a bit fluish all day."

"You have?"

Well, no, but when he frowned at her she thought he looked concerned. Concerned she was contagious, no doubt, so she kept on talking. "The other day we were playing the back nine and got caught in the rain. By the time we made it to shelter, we were drenched.''

"Golf in the rain? Isn't that a bit much even for you?"

Chantal bridled at his tone of voice. "The shower caught us by surprise."

"The clouds gave you no clue?"

"I didn't care about the clouds," she snapped back. "I needed to catch up on my lessons."

"With Craig I presume?"

"Yes."

He snorted. Then said nothing while she measured pasta and counted to ten to control her temper. She about had it under control when he muttered, as if through a tightly clenched jaw, "It's only a game, Chantal."

"You think I put myself through all this frustration for *a game?*" she asked, whirling around to stare at him.

"Let me guess…golf is a smart career move. You want to impress Godfrey and maybe a client or two?"

Yes, she had taken it on for precisely that reason but it had become a personal challenge, a task to conquer. She wanted to succeed. But she wasn't about to make any apologies or to defend herself. She merely murmured, with just a touch of sarcasm, "How perceptive of you."

"Not particularly." His tone was as cutting as his gaze. "Kristin would play golf in a hurricane for a pat on the head from her boss."

He left her standing there stunned, not by his words but by the bitterness that sharpened the taut planes of his face and glittered in his eyes. By the knowledge that whatever had broken up his engagement had totally torn him up inside.

Five

"**O**h, no, you don't." Julia moved pretty speedily for a well-fed pregnant lady, snagging Chantal's arm before she could follow Quade and Zane and a cartload of crockery into the kitchen. "Yes, they're men, but I think we can trust them to pack a dishwasher."

"They're my guests."

"Technically I'd say more freeloaders than guests. Besides, Quade offered."

"He was being polite. No one offers to do dishes because they want to."

"True, but in this case you're doing them a favor."

Incredulous, Chantal laughed.

"No, really. They've been dying to get rid of us womenfolk so they can talk cars to their hearts' content." Julia tugged at Chantal's sleeve. "Let's go take a weight off. And please, could you try to relax?"

After Cameron Quade had raised her core temperature to boiling with one expert kiss, only to dunk her straight into the ice-cold water of his condemnation? No, she didn't think she could relax any more now than she had during dinner. Not when she kept re-calling the look in his eyes when he mentioned Kristin's name. Not when her own response was a worrisome need to reach out, to soothe the hurt, to make it better. She was pretty sure Cameron Quade wasn't looking to her for emotional healing.

Finally she relented to her sister's insistent arm-jiggling and allowed herself to be led to the lounge setting by the fire. She didn't follow Julia's eloquent suggestion to take a weight off.

"If you're not going to sit, could you at least stop pacing?" Julia said after several seconds. "I'm getting tired watching you."

Chantal planted her feet in front of the hearth, forc-ing herself to still. Unfortunately this allowed her sis-ter to fix her with a now-I-have-you-alone look. *Way safer to instigate the conversation myself,* Chantal de-cided. "What do you mean about the men wanting to talk cars?"

"Apparently Quade has some old sports classic in his shed." A smug smile curved Julia's lips. "Zane says its line and shape are almost as sweet as mine."

"The MG," Chantal said softly, recalling the car's sexy low-slung frame as clearly as if she'd seen it yesterday.

"The what?"

"The old sports car—it's an MG."

Julia shook her head. "You amaze me. How did you know that?"

"I…" Chantal hesitated. Why not share the whole sordid tale? It would definitely distract Julia from the story she really wanted to hear, the one about what she'd stumbled upon in the kitchen earlier. "Do you remember the summer I clerked at Barker Cowan? The firm Quade used to work for?"

"I remember how deadly important it was for you to clerk at the 'right' places. I remember *those* discussions around the dinner table," Julia said dryly.

"Well, it *was* important."

She'd wanted to experience a diversity of practices and to learn from the best in their fields, although in this case there'd been another factor influencing her choice. A twenty-something-year-old hunk of a factor.

She couldn't stand still; she had to pace. "It was the October long weekend. I was home from uni and I heard Quade was visiting with his father, so I drove out there. I wanted to know more about the firm, to see if I wanted to clerk there." A perfectly acceptable reason, she had decided at the time, to meet the intriguing Cameron Quade. "Anyway, his father answered the door and said Cameron was down at the shed, tinkering with the car."

"Ahh. So he was working on this MG way back then?"

Yes and no. Chantal moistened her dry mouth and decided to spill it all. "When I walked in, it wasn't the car he was working on."

Julia's brows rose sharply. "Who was he, um, working on?"

"An associate at Barker Cowan, as it turned out. Quade's father hadn't mentioned he had company, although I was so naive I'd probably still have waltzed right in there."

Almost seven years and she still flinched recalling

that moment of discovery. Still felt the rapid flush of heat that had washed through her, part embarrassment and part fascination.

"They didn't see you, right?"

"Good God, no. I turned and ran." Although not straight away. In fact, she'd been too paralyzed to move for a long enthralled moment.

"How did you know it was an MG?"

Chantal stopped pacing and blew out a hot breath. "I'm observant. Besides, I was looking anywhere but at…them."

"I can't believe you never told me about this." Julia puffed out a disbelieving breath before continuing, "I can't believe you ended up going to work at this Barker place."

"Mother organized it through Godfrey. She thought she was doing me a favor."

And so began the summer-in-hell, as she struggled to shut out those car hood images and her own fantasies born of them. She'd dreamed of being the woman spread across stark red duco. In her dreams she had felt the cool steel under her back and the hot man against her front; she'd experienced the magic of a lover's kiss and heard the low sounds of pleasure in her own throat. From each such dream she'd woken perspiring, disoriented, and still untouched by any lover.

"Wow," Julia breathed softly, as if party to Chantal's secret thoughts. "How did you deal with seeing Quade and what's-her-name every day?"

"I focused on the work." *Or at least I tried to.*

"But could you look them in the face? You know, around the coffee machine or over depositions or whatever law clerks do?"

"You remember me at nineteen." Chantal's attempt at a smile felt leaden. "Take a wild guess."

"Hmm...even before you transformed yourself into Ms. Cool and Competent, even when you were a bookish nerd with no social skills, you never chose avoidance. In fact, under pressure you tended to go the other way." Eyes widening, she slapped a hand to her cheek. "Were you very obnoxious?"

"Insufferably."

"Argumentative?" Julia asked, grimacing as if she dreaded the answer.

"Naturally."

"Oh, dear." Shaking her head, Julia started to laugh and Chantal's own smile grew until it warmed her from the inside out. Oh, but it felt good to share something personal, painfully personal, and to end up laughing about it. Although now she had started it seemed like she had to tell the rest.

"There's more," she said, taking a sobering breath and feeling the warmth of shared laughter and memories begin to chill. "There was this...incident. To cut a long story short, I was trying to impress Quade by impressing his boss and it backfired."

"He wasn't impressed?"

"Understatement."

Julia winced sympathetically.

"I was perfectly justified, though. He had no right to dress me down as he did."

Julia's mouth twitched. "Goes without saying. And you know, this whole story explains a lot."

"About?"

"About why you're like you are with him."

Chantal felt her shoulders stiffen. "How am I?"

"Not yourself, that's for sure. I've never seen you

so frazzled, sis. Not since you came back here a fully-fledged lawyer, at any rate. During dinner you didn't sit still long enough—''

''I've had a lousy day, okay? The crowning glory being you dropping an extra dinner guest on me.''

''Lousy days have never driven you to drink before.''

''I often have a glass of wine with dinner,'' Chantal defended stubbornly. ''You know that.''

''A glass, yes, but tonight you could have dispensed with the glass. It only slowed you down.''

''Very funny.'' Chantal pulled a face. She knew she'd only had two glasses—three at most. Because she'd needed to take an edge off her nervous reaction to Quade beside her at the table. His scent, the brush of his knee, the memory of his lips on hers, the pain in his eyes. The whole confusingly complex issue of her feelings for the man.

''Is it so obvious?'' she asked, stomach churning. Did she really want to know the answer?

''The fact that you like him?'' A telltale blush started to rise in Chantal's throat and her sister clapped her hands with delight. ''You're blushing which means you *do* like him.''

Chantal rolled her eyes. ''I'm not about to engage in a game of *do so, do not.*''

''You are definitely blushing.''

''It's the fire. Plus I've been feeling fluish all day. Not to mention all the hot air you're spurting.''

''Pish!'' Julia's delighted gaze narrowed slightly. ''I've always wondered what kind of man it would take to light your fire.''

''I hardly know him.''

''And this matters, why?''

"He's…" Chantal paused to weigh her words.

"Hot?" Julia teased, wiggling her eyebrows. "Sexy?"

"Does Zane know you feel this way about another man?"

"It's not working, you won't distract me. He's…what?"

"He's not interested," Chantal supplied finally. *Yes, he's hot. Yes, he's sexy. Yes, he kissed me but then he wished it back.*

"How do you know? You're hardly an expert on men."

And wasn't that the truth! Heck, before her distant fascination for Quade matured into her first full-scale crush she'd never spared men a thought. But that summer had exposed a gaping hole in her education, a hole she'd spent the next several semesters at university attempting to fill. Interaction Between The Sexes turned out to be the only subject she ever failed.

"Well?" Julia prompted. "How do you know?"

"I asked him to supper…he wasn't interested."

"Perhaps he wasn't hungry."

"And perhaps he isn't interested. He wasn't exactly busting down doors to come here tonight, was he?"

Julia's expression turned contemplative. "Methinks he protested a little too much."

"Yeah, right," Chantal scoffed while something inside leaped to life.

"Hey, I've been watching you two dancing around each other all night. And I don't know what I interrupted in the kitchen earlier, but I know when I'm interrupting."

"You don't think it's completely one-sided? Oh, heck, what am I thinking?" She laughed, but it was a nervous uncertain sound in perfect harmony with everything churning inside her, with every self-doubt and insecurity. "What does it matter? I have no clue how to go about this, what to do, even if I want to—"

Julia leaned forward and touched her arm, stopping her midinsecurity. "Why is it you relish every challenge work throws your way but you completely wuss out when it comes to men?"

That stopped Chantal for a moment, but only for a moment. Then she answered truthfully. "There's no set procedure, no course I can study."

"Quade would be a master class."

Skillful hands and talented lips, patience and finesse…a premonition of how that class might play out shivered through Chantal. Julia must have seen the reaction and misinterpreted, because her expression softened sympathetically. "Scary, huh?"

"I am not sc—"

"Yeah, yeah, I know. You don't do scared, at least not out loud. You also tend to go after what you want."

"This is different. Quade's…difficult."

Julia's brows rose. "And you think a challenge should be easy?"

"Not easy, just doable. I like to think I have some chance of succeeding."

"It's always about success with you, isn't it?"

"Yes. Yes, it is." Chantal expelled a harsh laugh. "Heck, I spent all those years chasing after you and Mitch, trying to measure up, vying for some scrap of our parents' attention."

"There never was enough to go around, was there?"

"Once I realized how to win their affection...I guess it's become habit."

"Well, don't let it become a habit you can't kick." Her sister's tone grew serious, her gaze strong and steady. "You spend way too much time with your work."

"I love my work. It's the *only* thing I do well and the only place I feel competent, okay?"

"Pish! You do everything well. What about the cooking and the flower arranging and the—"

"I took courses and I practiced and I *made* myself do well. But with my work...it's not an effort. It *is* my fun, okay?" Eager to escape, Chantal rose to her feet. "I'm going to make coffee. Would you like anything?"

For a long moment Julia looked mulishly like she wouldn't be deterred, as if she would keep hammering away at her insecurities, attacking the comfort blanket of her work. But in the end she let it go, diverted by the prospect of after-dinner treats. "Do you have cake? Chocolate, preferably? You always have good stuff in your pantry."

"By that, I gather you mean *bad* stuff."

Julia waved that distinction aside derisively. "Your addiction to junk food is one of your few redeeming qualities. Don't spoil it."

It was a throwaway line, Chantal knew that. She shouldn't have needed to ask... "I have other redeeming features?"

"Well, sure. For a start, there's your complete lack of vanity. You have no idea how stunning you are. Or could be, if you tried a bit harder."

Chantal rolled her eyes.

"Then there's the most important one—you would do anything for your family. I know that. Mitch knows that."

She could have played coy, could have denied it, but Julia had that one right. "Thanks." It was all she could manage through the sudden cloying thickness in her throat.

"You're welcome. Now, how about that cake?"

Shaking her head, Chantal headed for the kitchen door, but a sudden thought brought her up short. "What we've just talked about—everything—could it be under the cone?"

"The cone of silence? Of course." Julia smiled, nostalgically, Chantal thought, as if remembering childhood confidences shared under their own version of *Get Smart*'s cone of silence. "We haven't done that in a long time, have we? Same as we haven't talked, really talked like this, in ages. Let's do it more often, okay?"

Chantal was too choked up to answer so she simply nodded.

"Oh, and one last thing…"

Hand poised on the kitchen door, Chantal waited.

"I figure it's past time you took on something—or someone—that really challenges you, even scares you more than a little. Something that really *is* fun." She held up a hand. "Don't say anything, just promise to think about it, okay?"

"More coffee?" Chantal asked.

Her husky-edged voice and the slow sweep of her dark-eyed gaze cranked Quade's awareness up another notch, but before he had a chance to adjust she was on her feet—*again*—in full hostess role. He felt his jaw clench.

With the dishes done and the coffee made, they had settled in front of the open fire which should have been all homey and relaxed—*would have* been all homey and relaxed—if the furniture pieces weren't so strictly aligned, if a few cushions and magazines were tossed on the floor and if Chantal herself would sit still and relax.

Covering his cup with one hand, he unclenched his jaw enough to speak. "Forget the coffee. Find yourself a comfortable spot, park that delectable rear end, and take the rest of the night off," he said, low enough so as not to reach the ears of Julia and Zane, who sat cozily on the lounge talking wedding plans.

She blinked, long black lashes against smooth pale skin, and then her gaze seemed to gravitate toward his lap. Quade's body was quick to respond. Shifting uncomfortably in one of her big leather easy chairs, he told himself the effect was subliminal. A man's reaction to a suggestive glance, he decided, watching a delicate flush stain her cheeks. He swore silently.

Every time he finished convincing himself how snugly she fit the tough career woman stereotype, every time he resolved to leave her to her Kristin-like ambitions, some piece of paradoxical behavior turned his thinking around. Those shy-girl flushes, her concern over his scratched hands, the self-derision over her golf game. Her tentative response to his kiss, as if she didn't quite know what came next.

Hell, he'd come back to Plenty to sort out his life not to complicate it. And from where he sat—from where his body surged just imagining those tight hip-hugging jeans sliding into his lap—Chantal Goodwin represented one king-size complication.

As for her family…his gaze swung to where the other two sat, still immersed in their own conversation. Sometime during the afternoon O'Sullivan had graduated to Zane and Julia had slipped right under his guard. He'd been after a helping hand with his garden not the hand of friendship.

Watching them together filled him with…hell, he didn't know what it was. Some complex mix of envy and anger and regret over what he no longer had, and a hollow sense of loss for what he could never regain. Resolutely, he shoved those thoughts aside. No more self-pity, no more self-castigation, he reminded himself. He had moved past that mawkishness, not to any place concrete but he was working on it. Huffing out a breath, he forced himself to zone into the conversation.

"Did I tell you Mother rang this morning, wanting to know if we've chosen a time for the rehearsal?" Julia's question was directed at Chantal who had chosen to park her delectable rear end on the floor instead of in the vacant chair, or in his lap.

"Have you decided on a night?" she asked back.

Julia pulled a face. "I don't see why we need to practice at all."

"Easy for you to say," Zane muttered. "You're experienced."

"Best if everyone knows where they have to be, and when," Chantal added.

"Which is just fine if *everyone* could get to a rehearsal!"

"You'll have to ring Mitch and Gavin tomorrow, tie them both down to a definite answer."

Frowning, Quade backed the conversation up a few steps. "You've been married before?"

"Just the once," Julia answered cheerfully. "First time around I was looking for all the wrong things."

Same here. Except he was thinking about his career, about how he'd chosen law for the money and the prestige, and how Kristin had chosen him for the very same reasons. All the wrong reasons. A muscle jumped in his tight jaw, and he felt the touch of Chantal's gaze.

"Perhaps we could talk about something other than weddings," she suggested. To protect his sensibilities? Did she think he needed cosseting?

"Marriage isn't a touchy subject with me," he said shortly.

"It is with Chantal," Julia supplied. "She has very strong opinions on the subject."

"And why wouldn't I? In my job I see too many couples who have vowed to love and cherish tear each other apart over divorce settlements."

She'd spoken evenly, almost with restraint, and Quade couldn't stop himself from playing devil's advocate. "That's the ugly side."

"It's the one I see."

"You don't have to look far to see the other side." His gaze flicked to the happy couple then back again.

"Yes, Julia's about the happiest woman this side of the Great Divide but that doesn't alter history. First time around, she was plain miserable." She glanced apologetically toward her sister before returning her attention to Quade. "And as for our brother Mitch, well, his marriage breakup is damned near killing him."

Quade kept his gaze locked on hers, on eyes that

glowed more fiercely than the flames at her back. Because she ached so deeply for her brother, because she felt so intensely for both her siblings. "And what about you, Chantal?" he asked. "Have you vowed to save yourself from all this heartache?"

"Let's just say marriage isn't on my To Do list," she replied with a cynical half smile. It froze almost immediately. "Oh my God, I didn't think…" She shook her head remorsefully. "I'm sorry."

"Why? Because it's not on my To Do list anymore?" And he showed her a true cynic's twisted smile. "No need to apologize. I've moved on."

An awkward pause followed, the silence broken only by the stark crackle of burning firewood, and then by Julia groaning about bladders not structured for two.

In a sudden rush of activity, Zane helped her to her feet, and everyone else followed suit. Julia dashed off to the bathroom, Chantal started gathering coffee cups, and Zane yawned widely. "Time to call it a night. I've got an early start tomorrow. I'll warm up the truck and get the heater going. Coming, man?"

Before he could answer, Chantal cleared her throat. "He'll be along in a minute," she told Zane.

Too surprised to object, he waited through their thank-yous and goodbyes, until Zane had let himself out the front door. Then he waited while she drew a deep breath and straightened her shoulders. He heard the clink of cups touching, as if she had clutched her load more tightly. From where he stood it seemed like she didn't particularly relish whatever she had to say.

"I'm truly sorry about before," she started softly. "I should have thought before I opened my mouth."

"Is that why you kept me here? Is that all you wanted to say?"

"No." She lifted her chin and looked right at him. "Why did you kiss me?"

Shaking his head, he expelled a short wry-sounding laugh. Of all the questions she could have asked, he hadn't expected that one. "Damned if I know."

His gaze slid back to hers, caught and held. The atmosphere seemed to do the same, to catch and hold and wait in tense anticipation for whatever came next. He decided it might as well be the truth, as much as he knew of it.

"I haven't looked sideways at another woman in four years, not when I was with Kristin, and not since."

She moistened her lips. "How long since you broke up?"

"Six months." He rubbed at his jaw. "Six months and I simply haven't been interested. Yet the instant I saw you in my bedroom..."

"You were interested?" Her voice was barely a whisper.

"Oh, yeah. I can't tell you how many times I've replayed that first encounter. Those satin sheets sliding across the floor. You leaning over the bed. The creaking mattress."

"So..." Her gaze drifted to his lips and it might have been his imagination but she seemed to drift closer, too. When he breathed, his senses swam with her scent. "Where does that leave us?"

Before he could do more than think *anywhere you'd like,* the bathroom door smacked shut. She jumped guiltily. A cup slipped from her grip and thudded to the carpet, and she immediately moved to retrieve it. He stayed her with a hand on her arm. The sound of footsteps signaled Julia's approach and Chantal's question still hung there, suspended in the charged atmosphere, unanswered.

"Do you want there to be an us?" he asked.

"Do *you?*" she countered.

"Ready to go?" Julia asked coming into the room. For the second time she stopped in her tracks, eyebrows raised as she looked from one to the other. Quade didn't care. When Chantal squirmed he tightened his hold, ignoring her soft hiss of disapproval. He waited until she stilled, until she looked back up at him, eyes spitting her annoyance. And he realized he had no clue how to answer her question.

"I don't know," he said, easing his grip on her arm. He smoothed his fingers down the length of her delicate angora sleeve, so at odds with the fiercely held tension in the arm beneath, then stepped away. "Hell, I can't even make up my mind if I like you or not."

Six

At lunchtime the next day, Chantal admitted defeat. She simply couldn't focus on the papers spread before her on the dining-room table, a fact that confounded, annoyed and frustrated her in equal measures.

This was the Warner case, for Pete's sake, an estate wrangle with as many complicated twists and as much high drama as any soap opera...plus a wronged step-daughter who just happened to be a scrappy fighter. Most days Chantal couldn't find enough hours to spend building Emily Warner's case. It represented everything she loved most about her job.

Today wasn't "most days."

For a start it was the day after Cameron Quade showed her ten seconds of pure lip-to-lip bliss. It was also the day after he'd told her he wasn't sure if he even liked her, and the two events had been playing war games in her brain ever since. She pressed her fingers to a throbbing temple. And as if that weren't enough, there remained the small matter of Julia. Already she had phoned, twice, leaving messages to "call me, immediately."

With a heartfelt sigh, she smacked the file shut. There was a slim chance that Julia's urgency concerned wedding plans. Zane may have made those calls and firmed up a rehearsal time, although she had a bad feeling about that. His side of the wedding party had produced more headaches than Quade's mixed messages and several glasses of merlot combined.

The best man was stranded somewhere up north in his fishing boat, return time indefinite. The groomsman had chickenpox running rampant through his young family. Mitch had been asked to understudy if one or the other didn't make it, but no one knew when Mitch planned to show up, including their parents who had moved into his Sydney apartment to help care for their grandson.

Chantal buried her aching head in her hands. She needed to ring her sister. Unlike Zane's support team, she had vowed to be there for Julia. It was a sister thing, it was a bridesmaid thing. None of which made it any easier to pick up the phone. She dreaded Julia's inevitable questions, especially since she didn't have any answers.

What did I interrupt when I came out of the bathroom? What did he mean, he doesn't know if he likes you or not?

And wasn't that the million-dollar question! She shouldn't have stood there with her mouth flapping in the breeze while he walked away. She should have been mad as hell. She should have fired right back at him, some really cutting line like…like…

Well, same here, hotshot!

Except Chantal wasn't into self-delusion. In spite of all that had happened and not happened seven years ago, she liked him, she fancied him, she wanted him. Maybe her feelings were intricately linked with that early fascination, that whole first-teenage-crush factor, but there lurked a capacity for something infinitely more complex.

Did she want there to be an us?

Oh, yes. Absolutely. Indisputably. Unquestionably.

But—she drew herself up out of a slouch and lifted her chin—not unless he admitted to liking her. Not unless she believed he really did like her. Her pride demanded that much.

Pleased with such strong resolve, she blew out a breath, but it tickled the back of her throat and turned into a cough. And wasn't that the ultimate irony? After blaming her heated face on a fictional cold—to Quade and then to Julia—it looked as if she really might be coming down with one.

Checking the clock, she realized she had less than an hour until today's golf lesson and, with a gloomy sense of inevitability, she reached for the phone.

After five minutes of wedding updates and cross-examination—Chantal chose to plead ignorant on all charges—the ever-suspicious Julia caught a hint of the cold in her voice.

"Are you all right?" she asked. "You sound kinda croaky."

Concerned her nurturing sister might hotfoot it out from town bearing chicken soup and tissues, Chantal denied it, even while stymieing a cough. "Really, I'm fine,'' she lied as brightly as she could. ''And I'm on my way out. I'll talk to you later.''

''I hope this is leisure…?''

''It's golf.''

Julia sighed. ''Take it easy, okay? It really is supposed to be a relaxing way to spend a Sunday afternoon.''

Grimacing and trying not to cough, Chantal replaced the receiver, and all the way around the nine holes she played with Craig she really did try to relax. It proved impossible. In fact, the whole golf concept was proving nigh impossible, and that did nothing to improve her mood.

After returning home feeling miserable and sorry for herself, she wallowed in a herbal-scented bath until her skin turned wrinkly. Then she decided to allow herself another rare and luxurious treat…a night off.

Preparations were simple: she donned her comfiest pajamas and fluffy slippers, took the phone off the hook, and selected some soothing R & B for the stereo and something escapist from her bookshelf.

Just before she settled into the nest of pillows she'd created in front of the fire, she considered food.

Ice cream? Popcorn? Chocolate? One by one she rejected the options, and she couldn't lay all the blame on her budding cold. Lately none of her favorite junk food had interested her. As an appetite depressant, Quade was proving remarkably effective. Who knows, if he hung around long enough, she might even lose all the extra pounds she'd managed to accumulate over winter!

When the doorbell rang she was lost on the Hampshire moors, pursued by a brooding stranger with the cold hard eyes of a hunter. At the first chime, she closed her eyes. As the second chime sliced into her story-world mood of sensual menace, she swore softly but succinctly.

The word wasn't dang.

For the next six chimes she seriously considered ignoring her visitor. Except her car would be clearly visible in the open-fronted garage. And being—she checked the clock—after eight on a Sunday night, it could only be family. With the rest of them in Sydney, that meant Julia. Who she couldn't leave standing in the chill night air. No, really, she couldn't, although that didn't mean she had to welcome her with open arms. Perhaps if she described a bride whose red nose clashed horribly with her pink bouquet and whose vows came out as a hoarse croak...

Heartened by that plan, she bounded upright too quickly and needed to steady herself with a hand on the mantelpiece. Big-time woozy head, she thought as she tucked her open book under one arm and carefully stepped over the pile of pillows. And this time she couldn't blame Quade for the dizziness. A dozen more careful steps and she reevaluated that call.

The long narrow panels bordering her front door were glazed in an ornate frosty pattern that distorted size and shape, but not enough that she could ever mistake the long-legged, broad-shouldered silhouette as belonging to Julia.

Her most recent breath held in her lungs, expanding them until her chest hurt. She exhaled the backed up air in a long whoosh and realized she had stopped several yards shy of the door. She wasn't exactly dressed for company—had she even brushed her hair after her bath?—but Cameron Quade didn't strike her as the kind of man who would give up easily. As if to punctuate that thought, he leaned on her doorbell again. Hard.

She *was* home. If he stopped stamping his feet and leaning on the doorbell and rustling the paper sack in his hand, he would hear the soft strains of music drifting from beyond the very solid, very closed door.

So, why didn't she answer said door?

Scowling felt like a perfect response. Hell, he'd left a toasty warm fire, a Clint Eastwood restrospective, and a half-consumed bottle of his father's finest to venture over here. After Julia's concerned phone call he'd had no choice. Ten years in the cutthroat corporate world and he still had a conscience. His mother would be smiling down on that happenstance.

Beyond the decorative glass panels he detected movement and stopped fidgeting. "About bloody time," he muttered as the door swung open.

First thing he noticed was her put-upon expression. Then her crossed arms. Then her...*pink flannel pajamas?*

Yep, his eyes didn't deceive him. She wore pink flannel pajamas with some very lucky sheep gamboling across their hills and dales. And he'd been right about the music. It swirled from the living room at her back, as softly romantic as the flickering firelight and her pink cheeks and her ruffled curls. As his gaze climbed back to meet hers, he realized his sour temper had dissipated. Just from looking at her.

"You're alive," he said, purposely and perversely deepening his scowl. He didn't want to be wooed out of his dark mood. It suited him just fine.

"There was a doubt?"

"Your sister rang me. She was concerned about your phone being off the hook."

"That's because I didn't want to be disturbed," she said pointedly.

Quade chose to disregard her point and pushed past her. Ignoring the audible sound of her indrawn breath, he closed the door behind him. "Thanks. If you'd left me out there any longer I'd have frozen my... lemons...off."

Her eyes—which he noticed, belatedly, were glassy as well as bright and annoyed—seemed to finally take in his offerings. "You brought lemons?"

"And rum." He held up the bottle in his other hand. "Oh, and I remembered your CD."

"Thank you." The tight line of her lips softened. "I suppose Julia told you I'm getting a cold."

"Yeah. She wanted to come out here herself to administer TLC, but Zane was called out on a break-down."

"And she's forbidden from driving alone at night." She sighed. "I guess it's a good thing, him being so protective."

"A very good thing."

She nodded, then lifted her chin. "Okay. You might as well get the I-told-you-so lecture over with."

"For playing golf in the rain?" Hell, he'd practiced that exact speech on his way down here but now she expected it, the idea suddenly lost its appeal. "I told you so," he said mildly, then, "What do you want me to do with these?"

A small smile curved her lips. "You brought them, so I assume you know what to do with them."

"My mother used to make some sort of hot lemon concoction. That's all I know."

Her smiling eyes widened. "Your mother gave you rum?"

"Hell, no. That's my contribution."

"It goes in the hot lemon drink?" She sounded dubious.

Quade shrugged. "Can't hurt."

Suddenly, unexpectedly, she laughed and the spontaneous sound danced all over his senses. "Oh, I think it would hurt."

"How's that?"

"I'm taking cold tablets which are making me woozy enough." She gestured at the rum. "I don't think *that* would go with."

She had a point but before he could agree he started thinking about her turning woozy and him having to pick her up and carry her to her bed, and he turned a little woozy himself. Which only annoyed him. Frowning, he shuffled the awkward bag into the crook of his elbow but it started to slip. They both made a grab for the spilling fruit, and their hands became all mixed up in a strange slow-motion juggling affair.

Their bodies bumped and brushed, hard planes against soft curves. Her laughter hitched on a breathless note, and he drew in air filled with a subtle green scent. They were standing close, and he wasn't thinking about germs. He was thinking about the fact that she wasn't wearing a bra under that soft giving fabric. He hadn't missed that not-so-small point.

"Ta-da!" She held the bag aloft triumphantly. "We didn't drop one."

Quade's fingers curled around the lone lemon in his hand. Lucky *she'd* been concentrating on the job at hand or they'd have been ankle-deep in fruit.

"Thank you for bringing these," she said. "It was really sweet of you."

Sweet? Obviously she didn't know what was going on in his mind. Not to mention his jeans. He shrugged. "I can't take the credit, although I had to improvise. Haven't a clue how to make chicken soup."

"Julia suggested you bring *soup?*" Her dark eyes narrowed. "She had no right!"

"She's your sister. That gives her the right to worry."

"But not to send you over here."

He shrugged. "You fed me last night."

"Oh boy, we're not back to who-owes-who are we, because I had about enough of that the last time." She huffed out a breath. "Okay, I'll accept your offerings because we are neighbors, after all. But then we call it quits. No more payback, no more mention of beholden. Okay?"

"Fine with me."

Their eyes met and held. And in that second something shifted between them, some tacit agreement made, a new bond formed. Neighbors? Quade rejected the notion out of hand. He didn't yet know what he wanted from Chantal Goodwin but it definitely wasn't neighborly sugar borrowing and back-fence chitchat.

"Good." She took the rum, then turned on her heel and headed toward the kitchen.

It would have been the perfect time for Quade to do something similar—to turn on *his* heel and get the hell out of there. But instead he found himself watching the sway of her backside inside those soft pink pajama pants and reliving the brush of her unfettered breasts against his arm as they struggled to contain those lemons.

He exhaled a long hot breath. Hell, he was one sick puppy to be turned on by an obviously unwell woman. In flannel pajamas. He forced himself to look away, down, anywhere else, which is when he saw the book lying on the floor.

Hunkering down to pick it up, he couldn't help but notice the title. Chantal Goodwin read romance. Hot, steamy romance by the look of the cover. He pulled her CD from his jacket pocket and shook his head ruefully. Romance novels and boy bands and the body of a centerfold. Talk about contrasts and contradictions—she was one surprise after another and every new disclosure, each newly uncloaked facet, drew him closer to capitulation.

Did he even want to fight it? Honestly?

Hell, if she hadn't looked so bright-eyed and feverish he wouldn't be standing out here with a book and a CD in his hands. Instead his hands would be filled with soft flannel-covered curves, at least for as long as it took to get those curves naked.

Did that mean he liked her? Because he had never, not ever, wanted to get naked with a woman he didn't like. Yes, he liked her. Probably had from the first time she opened her sassy-talking mouth, or at least from the first time she surprised him to laughter. But he hadn't wanted to like her, hadn't wanted to open himself to that possibility. It was so much easier to classify her by stereotype: ambitious lawyer, Kristin-clone, off limits. And until she tossed this cold, she remained off limits. Pink flannel pajamas firmly buttoned. Centerfold curves covered. Which meant he needed to get his sorry one-track mind out the door and down the road. Once he deposited her belongings.

With a new determination, he strode across the living room but pulled up short. Last night's straitjacket furniture had been shoved aside in a higgledy-piggledy fashion; a golf putter and several balls lay discarded in the middle of the floor; newspaper sections littered the coffee table. Hallelujah. He scanned further, to the fire crackling in the stone hearth, to the pillows spread before it. And it took less than a second for his imagination to paint a picture of her reclining there, sans pajamas, hair wildly mussed and creamy curves warmed by the dancing firelight. Desire, as quick and hot as those flames, licked through his body. He wanted his hands in her fire-bright hair. He wanted to spread her body before the flames. He wanted to make her burn.

''There you are.''

Quade shook his head firmly to clear the unruly heat, then turned slowly to find her in the kitchen doorway.

As her gaze swept the scene before her, her expression turned to dismay. ''You'll have to excuse the mess. I wasn't expecting anyone.''

''Why would I excuse it? I prefer it this way.''

''Oh.''

Obviously not the answer she'd expected. Now she looked nonplussed, more so when she noticed the book in his hand. Flushing prettily, she shifted her weight from one slippered foot to the other. Quade felt the banked heat within shift from lust to something softer, warmer. More dangerous. Damn. He should have left when he had the chance.

"I was reading," she explained, as if the book needed an explanation. "When you arrived."

He tossed book and CD on top of the mess. "Not working?"

Her chin came up a notch. "It's Sunday."

"Last Sunday you were working on your golf."

"Not after dark."

After dark. Two simple words that conjured up all sorts of images, most of them cast in red-gold firelight. *Down puppy,* he scolded himself.

"I've put the kettle on. Would you like tea? Or coffee?"

"I should be going. Don't want to miss *Dirty Harry.*"

She looked interested. "Is it on TV tonight?"

"Yeah." He paused, not sure if he really wanted to know. "Don't tell me you're a *Dirty Harry* fan."

"Go ahead, punk. Make my day."

He didn't know if his overimaginative libido was playing tricks, but she didn't sound like she was quoting a movie line. She sounded…suggestive. The heat in his belly shifted again but he ignored it. He was leaving. Before he did something regrettable. Like making *his* day.

"Normally I'd say it's a classic and not to be missed." He tossed the lemon still in his hand and caught it. "But you need to be squeezing these into mother's magic remedy."

"You're not going to do that for me? What kind of neighbor are you?"

For an unseemly length of time, he lost himself in her smiling eyes. Then he saw the amusement dim, saw her nostrils flare slightly and, God help him, she moistened her lips with the tip of her very pink tongue. But the glassy brightness remained in her eyes and one corner of his mouth kicked up in a wry half smile. "I'm thinking, a pretty sick one."

"Oh my God." Eyes widening with concern, she slapped a hand over her lips but kept on talking through the splayed fingers. "Did I give you this bug? The other night…"

"When I kissed you?"

"Yes."

"Not that kind of sick." He shook his head. "I meant sick as in I'm looking at you in those pajamas and imagining taking them off you."

She must have inhaled sharply because her breasts rose, stretching the material of her pajama top…

He didn't mean to, he tried not to, but his gaze dropped to the top button. When had pink flannel turned into the world's most erotic material? *No, no, no.* Hands curled into fists, he started backing away. Toward the door. He was not thinking naked thoughts again, not even in terms of rubbing her chest with VapoRub. He didn't stop backing up until he reached the door.

Just to be extra sure he wrapped his hand around the doorknob before forcing his gaze back to hers. She was looking at him like *he* was the cot case. She had a point. For that reason alone he made damned sure his voice came out a lot stronger than his watery willpower. "Make yourself the hot drink, dose yourself up on those tablets, and take yourself off to bed. And don't get out again until you're better."

"But I have to—"

"Go to work? Really?" Dark eyes flashed and he knew he'd called it right. The thought ticked him off just enough to keep the words rolling. "Your idea of commitment to work got you sick in the first place, don't let it put you in hospital.''

''I'm not *that* sick. In fact I'm hardly—''

''What about next Saturday? Are you going to be fit for the wedding? Or do you want to give Julia something else to worry about?''

That tempting curve of mouth compressed in a tight line and remained silent. Satisfaction unfurled deep in Quade's gut—twice on the trot he'd managed to get the last word in. As he turned the knob and opened the door he decided to make sure.

''And ring your sister. Let her know you're all right.''

Seven

Ring her sister? For quite some time after Quade backed his way out her front door, Chantal felt like wringing her sister's neck!

Instead she wrung the juice out of too many lemons, all the while muttering to herself about pushy sisters and pushier neighbors. He had some hide coming into her house and throwing his weight around, no matter how splendidly proportioned his weight looked in tight jeans. Blinking that visual distraction aside, she sloshed her juice into a mug. Too much? Probably. She doubled up on honey to compensate.

Did he really think she needed reminding of her obligation to Julia and the wedding? Of course she would take time off work if she felt sick. She wasn't a fool or a martyr or a child…even if her taste in music and nightwear might point toward the latter.

Quade didn't seem to mind your choice of nightwear.

Frowning, she topped her mug up with boiling water. Or perhaps she had misinterpreted. Perhaps he'd wanted her out of her pajamas because they looked so hideous, which is precisely why she wanted to wring Julia's neck. For sending Quade over without any warning. For not having any chance to dress, to brush her hair, to glamify.

Leaning back against the bench she took her first tentative sip of his mother's magic remedy…and almost spat it back. Shuddering with distaste, she scraped her tingling tongue through her teeth. *Aaack.* Still, she mused, it was awfully sweet of him to bring the ingredients over even if he didn't stick around long enough to help her put them together.

Because he didn't trust himself not to touch her.

She shuddered again, this time with a hot/cold stream of sensual memory. No, she hadn't misinterpreted. Cameron Quade, acclaimed hunk, had confirmed that he wanted *her,* Chantal Goodwin, acclaimed man-deterrent!

The notion was dizzying, confidence boosting, and, quite possibly, the world's best cold remedy. Either that or the half mug of thick lemon glug she eventually forced down did the trick, because she woke the next morning feeling considerably more healthy. Her throat didn't hurt, her head didn't throb, but then she opened her curtains to gloomy gray dampness and decided to play safe. She could work from home; she had enough on hand to keep her busy.

Or so she thought before she spent the next forty-eight hours doing as much thumb-twiddling and phone-watching as concentrating on the contracts she was allegedly working on. When her phone only rang six times—work twice, Julia four times—disappointment hung over her with the same brooding presence as the rain clouds outside.

She had been so certain Quade would check up on her, if only to ensure she'd followed orders and stayed home. Perhaps he didn't care one way or the other. Perhaps he had only been responding to Julia's prompting, or acting on some sense of neighborly duty. Perhaps he had caught her cold, but worse, and he was really sick. And perhaps all the cold medication had scrambled her brain.

Wednesday she woke to a gorgeous spring morning, the kind where doubts dry as quickly as last night's dew in the sun's gathering warmth. Chantal caught herself humming as she dressed for work and laughed at herself. If getting out of the house felt this good, imagine how wonderful it would feel to do something really radical…such as ringing Quade to check if he was all right.

Hardly radical. He was her neighbor, after all. With no one looking out for him except an aunt and uncle whose existence centered around a whirlwind of business and social engagements.

Something radical such as…acting like a grown-up instead of a schoolgirl with a crush. She liked the man more than a little, she enjoyed his company, she definitely wanted to finish the kissing, so why wasn't she doing something about it? Why was she waiting around for him to make a move?

Because you don't know any moves.

In a moment of uncharacteristic ruthlessness, she stamped all over that voice of insecurity. Today she

felt up for a challenge. Today she was going to do
something scary, she decided, recklessly discarding
her somber gray sweater and selecting a bright red
shirt. With a dash of bravado she added matching
lipstick and felt her pulse do a little red-lipstick salsa.

After work she would call on him, show him she
was all recovered, let him know she wanted that
"us." And if *that* didn't qualify as scarily radical, she
didn't know what did.

She followed the thumping of rock music to the
shed behind his house and found him working on the
MG...under it, actually. From where she stood she
could see a pair of heavy work boots and a pair of
denim-clad legs that extended far beyond the car's
perimeter. They didn't need labeling for quick iden-
tification.

Probably that should have bothered her. Instead she
found herself moving closer, skin tingling with the
thrill of the illicit and unexpected. He hadn't heard
her. She could look her fill. The impulse proved irresistible and she tracked those long muscular columns of denim slowly and thoroughly. For an inde-
cent amount of time. All the way up to the top of his
thighs.

A metallic clunk resounded from the car's under-
belly, followed closely by a singular curse. Chantal
started backward guiltily. He rolled a further foot
clear of the car exposing his hips and several inches
of scruffy black T-shirt. She was about to clear her
throat, to say something to reveal her presence, when
he must have reached up over his head.

That was the logical explanation for the shirt pulling clear of his low, hip-hugging waistband and ex-

posing several inches of flat hard belly and a feathering of dark hair.

Oh my Lord.

Heat pooled deep in her stomach. Her breath came fast and shallow. Her skin grew hot just thinking about the possibilities of touching him on that bare slice of skin. With her lips.

Another clunk, several more pungent curses, and suddenly he slid all the way out. Hands still raised above his head, eyes fixed on her legs, he paused—but only for the scant second it took her to back up out of his space—then in one smooth fluid motion he was on his feet. Eyes cool, expression unperturbed, he reached for a rag and wiped his hands then turned off the blaring radio.

"Enjoying yourself?"

Chantal licked her dry lips, felt the caught-out heat in her face, but managed to match his conversational tone. "I had a nice view."

"Yeah?" His gaze rolled from the rag in his hands to her legs. "As nice as the one I copped from down there?"

Instinctively her hands flattened against the sides of her skirt—her remarkably proper straight gray skirt. "You couldn't see a thing."

"Hardly fair, is it?"

"I don't know about that. You *are* wearing jeans," she pointed out. "So, in all fairness, *I* didn't see a thing." She smiled. He didn't. He stared at her in a way that made her hold her breath, wondering what would come next, then he threw down the rag and studied his hands. "Been to work, I take it?"

Despite the casual tone of his question, she stiffened defensively. "Yes. I'm on my way home."

"This early?"

"The wedding rehearsal's tonight. In an hour, actually." And this was her chance to explain her presence, the reason for her visit. "When I hadn't seen you or heard from you, I thought I should check that you were all right. That you hadn't caught my cold or anything."

"I'm fine. And you're looking much better."

"Than the last time you saw me?" She thought about her nightwear and red eyes and laughed self-consciously. "That wouldn't be difficult."

This time he looked at her with lazy deliberation, a thorough once-over that made her think he saw beyond the practical skirt and bright but plain shirt to what lay beneath. Her skin warmed instantly, her senses sharpened.

"Nice shirt," he said softly. "And that skirt is a particular favorite of mine."

Because she'd been wearing it that first day? The day he'd looked at her and decided he was interested?

"But I do like you in pink flannel...and nothing else."

Of course. She'd been nattering about lemons and cold medication and her messy living room and he'd been checking out her lack of underwear. She tried— Lord, help her, she tried—but she couldn't rustle up anything but token umbrage. And heat. Lots of swirling, pleasurable, sultry heat. Especially when he started to close the gap between them with steady deliberation.

"Is concern for my health the only reason you came visiting?" he asked, stopping right in front of her. Chantal didn't even know she'd been backing away until she felt something solid at her backside. The car, she noted dimly. His hot, sexy sports car. "Or do you have another agenda?"

Did he expect an answer? With all of her erotic fantasies within touching and kissing and undressing distance? Then he planted his hands on the car hood, either side of her hips, and she felt a thready whimper building in her throat and a low thrum building in her blood.

"You're vibrating," he said.

And you're incredibly intuitive, knowing that.

His hand tugged at her waistband and she reached to help him. If Cameron Quade wanted her out of her skirt, who was she to quibble? He planted a cell phone in her hand, a *vibrating* cell phone, which she recalled, somewhat belatedly, attaching to her belt loop.

It was Julia—wasn't it always?—but at least her sister's introductory soliloquy gave her time to gather her scattered wits. As did the fact Quade had removed himself from her personal space. *Dang.* With a sinking sense of what might have been, she watched him redirect his focus to some piece of automotive paraphernalia on a nearby bench. To think he had almost been tinkering with *her* paraphernalia. She really would have to kill Julia this time.

One word, one name, drew her attention back to the phone.

"Quade isn't answering his phone?" she repeated. His tinkering hands stilled and he turned, met her gaze. *Julia,* she mouthed. "I suppose I could ask if he wants to speak to you."

She enjoyed the beat of a pause as Julia put the

pieces together. "Where are you?" her sister asked suspiciously.

"Right now? In his shed."

"Is he there?"

She waited for some signal, but he was leaning against the bench, expression deadpan.

"Yes. He's here."

She offered him the phone. If he didn't want to speak to her sister, he didn't have to take it. He took it. And when Julia's opening gambit delivered a quick smile to his face and her next line brought easy laughter to his lips, Chantal felt an intense stab of jealousy. *Whoa, there.*

Jealous of her sister? Her about-to-be-married deliriously-in-love sister?

Shaking her head at such irrationality, she glanced at Quade and saw him straighten out of his relaxed slouch against the car. A muscle flexed in his jaw.

"I don't think so," he said stiffly. "Isn't there someone—"

Julia must have interrupted…at length. He rubbed a hand over his face, issued a long defeated sigh. "All right. I'll do it."

Whatever Julia said drew a response that fell somewhere between a snort and a laugh. Then he looked up and met her watchful gaze, his expression so intense she couldn't breathe for a long eye-locked moment. "Lady, I'm holding you to that."

Holding her to what? Chantal's heart skipped a beat as she ran a quick inventory of the things she would like to be held to. His chest. That flat belly she'd caught a peek of earlier. One place she'd done more than peek at… And then she realized he'd been speaking to Julia. But looking right at her. What was that all about?

He finished the conversation with another short bark of laughter and, "See you later." Chantal had a pretty good idea why and when he'd be seeing Julia later and, recalling his initial reaction, she didn't like it.

"I thought you said you weren't doing anything that aggravated you," she said, taking back the phone.

"It's no big deal." He lifted a shoulder with seeming indifference, but she detected a tension in the gesture and in the set of his jaw. "It's just filling in tonight. Apparently Mitch hasn't arrived, Zane's out on a towing job, and Julia didn't know who else to ask."

Filling in at a wedding rehearsal, listening to vows and promises. Her heart dipped in sympathy. Damn Julia for putting him in this situation. And Mitch. "You don't have to do this. You could have said you were busy."

He was still leaning against the side of the car, legs crossed at the ankle, but he looked at her steadily, eyes glittering with some dark and dangerous purpose. "Who says I don't want to?"

"I thought—"

"I'm getting a free dinner, anything I care to drink. *And* a ride in a Mercedes coupe."

Is that what Julia proposed? What he was holding Julia to? It didn't matter that the arrangement was convenient and suited her just fine, it was the principle. This time she didn't have to summons indignation, it barreled on up, hot and ready for action. "Don't *I* have any say in this arrangement?"

"Only if it's quick. You're picking me up in thirty minutes and you might want to take a shower and change. I know I do."

"And what do you propose I change into?"

His eyes narrowed speculatively and the hint of a grin teased his lips. "Anything that's easy to get out of."

He made a sterling stand-in for Mitch at the rehearsal. Silent, tense, poker-faced. During dinner—a casual affair at the local pub bistro—he was uncharacteristically quiet, but then who could get a word in edgeways between Kree and Julia? Not to mention Bill the best man's interminable tales of his adventures up north.

Bill was sitting to Chantal's left and taking up far too much of the booth's bench seat with his sprawled posture and expansive arm gestures. This meant she'd been hemmed closer to Quade, on her other side, than was comfortable. Between Julia's smug glances and her acute awareness of his big hard body and the effort of participating in meaningful conversation, she felt ready to explode.

If Quade hadn't volunteered to chase up another round of drinks, she might well have done so. Reprieve. She blew out a relieved sigh and glanced toward the bar…and immediately tensed up again. Looking much more at ease than he had all evening, Quade leaned against the bar chatting with the pretty blond barmaid. As she watched, as she worried her lip and wondered if he'd been more uptight about the wedding vows or being jammed thigh to thigh with her, he threw back his head and laughed.

Longing rolled through her, so strong it winded her

for a long airless minute. She could only stare, bowled over by the intensity of the need, by the total power this attraction held over her. Then someone moved between them, blocking her view, and she managed to suck in a deep restorative breath. The someone she recognized as Prudence Ford, and she was sliding her considerable curves onto the bar stool right next to Quade.

Across the table Kree noticed, too, elbowing her brother and ordering him to, "Go rescue Quade. There's vultures on the prowl."

Suddenly it struck her that she had forgotten one important piece of information about Cameron Quade. He wasn't merely irresistible to *her;* he attracted women like steel chips to a magnet.

What could he possibly want with her?

Easy question for a smart girl like you, Chantal.

Hadn't he suggested she wear something easy to take off? She glanced down at her button-fly jeans and the shirt she'd buttoned tightly all the way to her throat. It didn't mean she hadn't considered wearing a pull-on skirt and pull-off top. Or that she hadn't left home with half her wardrobe discarded on her bed.

It simply meant she didn't want to appear too…compliant.

If he wanted easy then he could have Prudence Ford. That woman knew what she wanted from a man and went right after it. *Just like you vowed to do this morning, Chantal. Just like you would have done this afternoon, Chantal, in Quade's shed, against Quade's car, on Quade's car…*

What had changed between then and now?

Another no-brainer, if she cared to acknowledge the real thing that had been bugging her all evening.

If she cared to look beyond the hot, elemental desire to the plain, simple truth.

Standing in Julia's rose bower, watching the garden lights paint shadows across Quade's tense features, she had felt something grab hold deep inside. Not a simple pang of empathy for what he might be feeling, but something more personal. A need in herself that transcended desire, a need that spoke to her very core. She heard the breathy catch in Julia's voice as she practiced her vows, and she wanted that moment for herself. She wanted to hear those solemn vows of love and fidelity, of companionship and commitment. She wanted to gaze into lush green eyes and hear the words fall from her own tongue.

She wanted more than sex from Cameron Quade; she wanted it all.

There. She'd admitted it. She sat very still, forcing herself to *breathe in, breathe out, relax and calm,* freeing herself from the worst of the tension so that the warmth of the truth could settle over her in the way self-honesty usually did. It didn't.

Glancing toward the bar, she saw that Zane had completed his rescue mission and both men were returning to the table. Her confused dark gaze met his unreadable one, met and held, and her heart started hammering against her ribs. Her stomach churned.

She couldn't do this. She had to get out of here. Fast.

Pasting on a fake smile and not meeting anyone's eyes, she blabbered something about work tomorrow and having a lot to catch up on after her days off. Then she grabbed her bag and bolted for the door.

She had a good thirty seconds head start, more than enough time for a decent virtuous grievance to mix with Quade's simmering frustration. It was a volatile brew. By the time he saw her standing beside her car, her skin tone changing blue-green-white in cue with The Lion's flashing neon sign, a dozen alternate phrases clamored for first bite.

He was ten yards away and still tossing up between *you figured I'd walk home?* and *start unbuttoning that damned shirt, now!* when he saw her shoulders sag. His long strides slowed. His angry scowl cooled to a frown.

Then he cleared the long-tray truck that had partly blocked his view, and her sleek silver coupe came into sight. It had been keyed. From one end to the other, a deep ugly gouge. Every hot infuriated word fled his brain.

"Ouch," he said softly.

She didn't turn her head, but he heard her draw a fractured breath, saw the flash of anger in her eyes. "Not exactly the word I was thinking. In fact, not even close."

"I guess not." He knew not. "Had the same thing happen to my Beemer once. I'd only had it two weeks."

"I've had mine four." She touched the door, running her fingers gently along the wound. "What did you do?"

"Reported it and had it fixed."

She laughed, a short harsh sound completely at odds with the way her hand caressed her car, completely at odds with the softness of the night. "Then I guess that's what I'll do, too."

Straightening her shoulders, she reached for the

driver's door but he stopped her with a hand on her shoulder. "Give me the keys. I'll drive."

She shook her head. "No one drives this car but me."

"You're shaken up, you're angry, and you drive too fast when you're not. I'd rather not take my chances."

Her eyes flashed dark fire. "It's a nice night for a walk, Quade."

"Is that what you intended when you rushed out of the bar? That I should walk home?"

With his hand still on her shoulder, he felt her tension. "I…I wasn't thinking. I wouldn't have left you there."

"Pleased to hear it. Now give me the keys."

"I'm not angry anymore. And I'm a good driver."

"Subjective. I was in the passenger seat earlier. You drive too fast." She opened her mouth to protest and he didn't let her. "How about when you took on that truck up Quilty's Hill? You couldn't back off. Tell me, Chantal, is everything a contest with you? Do you tackle everything full throttle?"

His subtle emphasis on *everything* was deliberate. So was the way his gaze shifted to her lips, to the soft rise and fall of her breasts as she drew a shaky breath. The way his hand shifted on her shoulder, gentling, one caressing stroke down her upper arm and back to her shoulder. He felt her slight tremor, his own tightening response.

Then he took the keys from her lax hand and slipped between her and the driver's door. "And before you start thinking up reasons why I shouldn't drive, I don't speed, I do pay courtesies to other drivers and I sat on the one glass of wine all night."

Eight

After ten minutes, Chantal couldn't stand the silence any longer. She could have put some music on—God knows, she had enough to choose from—but she had already provided one opportunity for smirking without him seeing her entire boy band collection.

Besides, she didn't want him to think she was brooding over the who-drives issue. That would be petty, given she *had* been angry and shaken, and not only over the car vandalism. When she took off out of The Lion she hadn't outpaced the doubt demons— they had all come along for the ride. Better to talk than to brood, she concluded. Better for the sake of learning more about Quade, and better for the sake of quieting those demons and calming her jumpy nerves and distracting her jumpy imagination. *That* kept leaping ahead to the end of the drive.

Did he still want her out of these clothes?

Oh, dear Lord, she really had to stop thinking about that...

"I hope you don't mind me asking—"

"That phrase only ever precedes a question I *do* mind being asked," he interrupted, but she heard wry humor in his voice.

Good, she thought. *Humor is good.*

He made a carry-on gesture with one hand, a strong, capable hand with long, elegant fingers. He used them a lot when he talked and a lot when they were close. Recalling his hand on her shoulder, her arm, brought on a familiar rush of warmth. Imagining them on her bare skin caused a fiercer lick of desire, and then she felt him watching her, watching her watching his hand.

Caught, her face heated and she looked away, clearing her throat and remembering what she had meant to ask. "I've been wondering about your MG. Will you have it going soon?"

"Maybe." He smiled that sexy little smile, the one that just hinted at dimples. "Hope you're not thinking turnabout is fair play, because you are not getting behind the wheel of that baby. No way."

"Because I drive too fast?"

"Yes."

She didn't bother taking offence because she sensed there was more to come, *important* more to come. It was in the slight narrowing of his gaze, in the drumming of his fingers on the wheel.

"It's my father's car, really. He did all the early work, spent years chasing after parts. Ever heard the fourth rule of restoration?"

She shook her head. "Not that I recall."

"The bloke who has the part you desperately need got rid of it yesterday."

"Sounds like a cousin to Murphy's Law."

"Twice removed." Their eyes met and held for a moment, smiling, enjoying the subtle irony until he needed to look back at the road. "Dad lost his enthusiasm after Mum died and didn't ever get back to finishing it. It's giving me something to do while I'm waiting on Julia's garden plans. I decided to finish the job, for Dad. Kind of a…"

His voice trailed off and Chantal finished for him. *A memorial.* Wow. Overwhelmed by the notion, she didn't speak for several minutes, not until she could trust her voice.

"Is that why you're restoring the garden? Is that for your mother?"

His drumming fingers stilled. He glanced her way, surprise and something warmer in his expression. The something warmer took a firm hold on Chantal's heart, made her feel like she was smiling right there in her chest. "I guess I want things the same as they used to be, or close to. I don't know what that says about me…probably that I'm not much good at doing nothing."

"Or that you loved your parents and miss them."

He lifted a shoulder and shifted in his seat. Uncomfortably? Self-consciously? The band of warmth around Chantal's heart squeezed a little tighter. She was in big trouble here, she knew it, but she liked the feeling too much to fight it. Way too much.

"Any other plans for the way things were?" she asked.

"There's the land. It's been neglected, wasted. I've been thinking about what to do with it."

"You could start a free-range egg enterprise. You already have the stock."

He laughed. "If I could only find where they're hiding the eggs."

"Have you considered grapes?"

"They're on my short list. Why?" She saw a slight shift in his posture and felt a sharp shift in his interest.

"They do well around here. Climate and soil are ideal and there's boutique wineries springing up everywhere which add to the marketing options."

"Downside?"

"You have to know what you're doing."

"You sound like you do."

"Yeah, I *sound* like I do." She smiled wryly, thinking about how little she knew about other things, such as the getting-her-clothes-off thing. "I've done some work for the local Wine Producers Co-op, that's all."

"Are grapes profitable?"

"I couldn't say. James would know." When he lifted a brow in a *who's James?* look, she expounded. "James Harrier. He's a consultant who specializes in vines and orchards."

She offered to introduce them at the wedding, which changed the course of the conversation to Saturday's guest list and the fun job of seating such a motley assortment where they were likely to do the least damage during the reception dinner. Midway through the easy exchange they arrived in his yard, and he turned off the engine. Chantal had been aware of all that, but she kept batting the conversational ball back, knowing that once it went out of play she would have to deal with *what happens now?*

Now had arrived.

Closeted in the darkness, in the stillness, the atmosphere felt intensely intimate. She closed her eyes and breathed an intricate mix of man and machine, male and Mercedes. A night bird hoo-hooed and she heard the subtle creak of leather as he shifted in his seat, but he hadn't turned her way. His eyes weren't on her face, her body. She would have known.

Without opening her eyes, without so much as a peek, she could picture exactly how he looked, wrists crooked over the top of the steering wheel, a slight frown drawing his dark brows together as he searched the darkness of his garden for the owl. The image filled her mind, filled her senses.

"I haven't done this in a lot of years," he said softly.

"Sat in a car and talked?" Is that what he meant? She opened her eyes and turned to see him. *Exactly as she'd pictured.* "Did you used to do that a lot?"

"Not so much of the talking." Slowly his head rolled her way, and there was something about the smooth control of the movement, something about the white flash of his smile that mesmerized her. She could picture that exact motion in bed, dark hair against pale pillow, and the smile that seduced. "How about you?"

She swallowed. "Not me."

"You've never been parking?"

"No."

In a move as practiced and seductive as that smile, he turned his shoulders to rest an arm along the back of her seat. When his fingertips brushed her hair she ached to dip her head into the almost-caress. "Never necked?"

"No." She moistened her lips and watched his

eyes track the movement, felt those long, elegant fingers curl into her hair.

"No time like the present," he murmured, leaning forward slowly—much too slowly—and pressing his lips to her forehead in a kiss so gentle she barely felt it. But when he trailed those heavenly lips all the way to her temple, he left behind a delicate thread of desire that seeped all the way into her soul.

He eased away and her soul sighed with disappointment. "Have we started yet?" she asked.

Smiling, he touched her bottom lip with his thumb. "Just about."

That thumb continued to tease her lips, the bottom and then the top, turning her weak with desire. To be kissed, to be touched in other places. Hot, breathless, she imagined that lazy stroke tracing the line of her throat, cruising over the swell of her breasts, pressing against her tightly aroused nipples.

With an impatient growl she grabbed at him, sinking her hands into the soft knit of his sweater, dragging him those last few inches until his lips were on hers, her mouth under his. A satisfied sound escaped her throat as she opened her mouth, inviting him, accepting him, and the kiss exploded. From restrained exploration to consuming passion in one little sound, in one beat of her heart, in one long unrestrained stroke of his tongue.

Inspired, she followed him, learned from him, dueled with him. When he retreated she took the lead, sinking into the hot cavern of his mouth, feeling the smooth edge of his teeth, sampling every flavor. Pleasure sang in her veins, pleasure and a rush of feminine power she had never experienced before.

When she paused for breath, the hands cupping her

face slid to her shoulders and his lips slid to her throat. The nuzzling warmth of his lips, the gentle bite on her earlobe, made her hum low in her throat.

"If this is necking," she breathed, "then I'm sorry I missed out."

He laughed, a soft harsh sound, velvet in the darkness. "If you wore straitjacket shirts like this, I'm not surprised you missed out."

"I don't think I can blame my clothes." Her voice sounded thick and throaty, but then his hands were on her shirt, swiftly and expertly popping buttons.

"No?"

The backs of his fingers touched bare flesh, and she sucked in a shallow breath. "You remember me as a teenager. I was a natural born man-deterrent."

His hands stilled, she prayed because he'd finished with the buttons, not because she'd sounded too derisive or, worse, self-pitying.

"I remember you being a pain in the ass. I guess that's a deterrent."

Relief washed through her, so intense and heady she laughed out loud. "Yeah, well, I overplayed every hand trying to get your attention. The completely inept virgin with a king-size crush, that was me."

The ensuing silence reverberated through Chantal's body. Relief turned to cold dread. The big V word, proven atmosphere chiller, and she had just tossed it out there. *Dumb move, Chantal, very dumb.* She couldn't look at him, couldn't do anything but shake her head and cringe deep inside as he drew back into his own space, as she waited for his response.

None was forthcoming. No jokey rejoinders, no stunned expression of disbelief. Chantal felt so twitchy, so tightly wired, she thought she would snap. Pasting some semblance of breeziness on her face, she waved a hand dismissively. With the other she, belatedly, drew the open sides of her shirt together. "And I guess that was way more information than the occasion demanded."

She felt his gaze on her face, heard him inhale, and the whistle of breath sounded unnaturally loud in the oppressive atmosphere. "Are you still…?"

"A virgin? Technically, no."

"You want to elaborate on that?"

No, she didn't *want* to elaborate but seeing as she had dug herself into this hole, she might as well bury herself. "There's not a lot to tell. One regrettably ordinary experience a long while ago and that's my sexual CV. Short and not so sweet. Big surprise, huh?"

He huffed out a breath. "You might say that…although that in itself is no surprise. You've been surprising me and confusing me on a regular basis from the minute I arrived home."

His admission twined itself through Chantal's intense sense of letdown, halting the downward spiral. It almost sounded like… She studied him closely in the darkness but could read nothing in his expression. "Is this a good thing?" she asked.

"Yes. No." He laughed shortly. "I came home to sort out my life. I don't want confusion, I don't need complications."

"Perhaps you should have thought of that before you started undoing buttons." Defiantly she met his gaze, daring him to take issue. But when his gaze dropped, a liquid slide down her bare throat, her breasts tightened reflexively. She clutched the sides of her shirt together.

"Sex doesn't have to be complicated," he said as his gaze rose to meet hers. "Not if both players know the score."

And wasn't that the rub? He knew exactly what he wanted and she...she had a mind overflowing with insecurities and a heart overflowing with foolish hopes. She also had her pride. Swallowing, she lifted her chin. "You think, just because I'm inexperienced, I don't know what this is about?"

"You tell me, Chantal. Look me in the eye and tell me this is only about getting naked. Tell me you're not hanging onto some teenage infatuation that's all tied up in hearts and flowers and walks down the aisle."

"You know my opinion on marriage," she said stiffly. "I thought it was pretty close to yours."

"That's not what I asked. Why have you been celibate for so long? What have you been holding out for?"

She could tell him the truth. *I haven't bothered because no one had made me feel it was worth my while. No one has ever made me feel the things you do.* Or she could bluff.

Chin high, she forced her gaze to his, to the sharp glitter of his eyes in the darkness. "Your ego's severely inflated if you think I was holding out for you, especially since I thought I'd never see you again."

"Still not an answer."

Damn him. "You want a yes or no answer? Okay, yes. I do want to get naked with you. Is that what you wanted to hear?"

"All I want to hear is the truth, Chantal."

"And how will you know when you're getting it?

As you've pointed out more than once, I'm a lawyer, one you can't even decide if you like.''

"Oh, I like you all right." His voice was low and rough, his gaze dark and dangerous. Nerves started jitterbugging in Chantal's stomach. "This afternoon in my shed, I liked the hell out of the way you looked at me. Tonight at dinner, every time your thigh brushed against mine, I liked you a little better. And just now, with my tongue in your mouth, I was about ready to explode with liking you.''

Oh. Her nerves stopped dancing and settled as a sick heavy weight in the pit of her stomach. All those things, purely physical. He didn't like her, he wanted her. Naked. For sex. A one-night stand, or maybe not even a whole night. Wham-bam, see you later ma'am. She knew all about the last.

Could she accept that and nothing more? Remembering all she had felt earlier in Julia's garden? Knowing she was more than halfway in love with him? Worrying her bottom lip, she stared out into the night, but he saved her from answering. At least for now.

"It's your call, sweetheart, and your time frame. Once you've stopped biting that lip, you know where to find me.''

Ever since he'd come home, Quade's conscience had ridden him hard. Some days he figured it was his mother's influence ensuring he lived up to her standards. Other times it was guilt driven, remnants of the months spent chiding himself for not seeing what was going on before his own eyes, in his own home, in his own bedroom. All because he'd been too wrapped up in his career.

Conscience, a need to do the right thing, obligation—whatever the reason, he found himself dressed in a dinner suit and walking through the flower-covered arches into Zane and Julia's garden on Saturday afternoon. Zane had asked him to come early, to maybe play groomsman, if Mitch didn't show. Mitch had shown. Expression distant, eyes flat, he looked as though he'd rather be swimming with sharks.

Quade knew how he felt.

Edgy, hollow, conflicted. All the things *he* had felt during the rehearsal would be ten times worse this afternoon, and that was without the extra complication of the bride's little sister. As good as a virgin. With a seven-year-old crush on him. He blew out a hot breath. Those revelations still unsettled him, made his feet itch with the need to bolt. Now would be the perfect time, before the sprinkling of guests who'd already arrived for the nuptials noticed him.

Except bolting felt too much like cowardice, as if he couldn't handle whatever she might dish up to him next. Quade shook his head and expelled a self-mocking laugh. What could she possibly come up with to top Wednesday's gobsmackers?

Three minutes later she rushed out the back door and answered his question. Holy hell. He could only stare. *That* was a bridesmaid's dress? Wasn't there some rule about taking the attention away from the bride? He couldn't imagine there'd be an eye—a male one, at any rate—fixed anywhere but on those curves encased in lace the color of her kiss. Rich, luscious, rose-pink.

With her focus fixed on her brother, she didn't see him right off. Thank heavens for small mercies. He needed recovery time, tongue-recoil time, eyes-back-in-head time. Still, he couldn't stop staring as she delivered a quick message to Mitch, fussing with his tie in a way that made his own feel like a neck noose. An affectionate smile curving her lips, she turned and started back toward whence she had come.

He knew the instant she saw him. Less than five yards away her hurrying strides faltered and her smile faded. She blinked, one slow-motion slide of her lashes, and then she was there, right in front of him, lifting her chin and pushing back her shoulders and drawing all his attention to the way she filled the bodice of the killer dress.

Did it come with built-in underwear? Because he sure couldn't see—and he *was* looking closely—how she could fit anything between the stretchy lace fabric and her skin. From the low dip of the neckline to the top of her shapely knees it caressed every contour.

When she tugged at the neckline, he realized how long he'd been staring, and where he'd been staring. Not good. He knew that for a fact when he looked up into her furious eyes. It seemed like a good time to take a teasing approach. "Is that dress legal?"

"It shouldn't be," she replied darkly, and he realized her crossness wasn't directed at him but at the dress.

Releasing muscles he didn't recall tensing, he grinned. "Do I take it this wasn't your choice?"

"Kree and Julia outvoted me."

He made a mental note to buy them both a drink or ten.

Then someone called her name from the back of the house and she wrinkled her nose. "Duty calls."

"Chantal."

Halfway to leaving, she paused, looking back at

him over one smooth bare shoulder. "It's a killer dress. The only way I can imagine you looking better is out of it."

Her lips parted on a soft surprised "Oh," and his body quickened. How many times the past two nights had he recalled the feel of those plush lips under his, imagined their moist openmouthed kisses on his body? He rubbed a hand over his jaw, a hand that stopped stock still as his gaze fastened on her retreating rearview, on the way the killer dress cupped the round curves of her buttocks.

With a low groan, he bowed his head in supplication. It was going to be a long, torturous evening.

Nine

Six hours later he was still riveted by that dress...or by the woman wearing it, he acknowledged ruefully, as he led the other bridesmaid through a series of fancy steps on the dance floor. Kree wore the same dress but on her it was just a dress, not an instrument of torment.

At that moment Chantal swung by, laughing up at her sixth partner in the half hour since the band struck up the bridal waltz. Quade clenched his teeth. So, okay, he hated the fact he'd been counting. He didn't begrudge her the turn with her father or her brother or the best man, but he begrudged the hell out of every other man with his hands on her body.

"You could always cut in," Kree suggested.

Yeah, and he could always swallow his pride and go drag her outside, into his car, and all the way home to his bed. Except he'd told her she had to come to him, in her own time, once she had nothing but sex burning in the depths of those espresso dark eyes.

She came by again, hips moving seductively in time to the music, and he felt a snarl building in his throat. When her partner slid his hand from a proper shoulder height to mid-back, the snarl slid through his teeth.

Kree held up her hands and stepped out of his hold. "James is a good customer. Don't hurt him too badly."

"One inch lower and he loses his hand."

Eyes intent on the other couple, he pushed through the press of dancers, and when he heard her throaty laughter, when he saw her fingers tapping a beat on the man's shoulder, he hoped Kree's good customer *had* lowered his hand. Just so he could inflict bodily harm.

Such uncivilized possessiveness was alien but undeniable. Before he could tap the man's shoulder he had to unclench his fists; before he could say, "Excuse me, she's mine," he needed to release the rigid set of his jaw. Surprise flickered across her face as he took her into his arms, and he liked the fact *he'd* jolted *her* for a change. Even more, he liked the way she felt in his arms.

Intense satisfaction chased all the violence from his body. When she lifted her head to talk, he splayed his hand wider against her silken back and tucked her closer to his body. More times than not, when they talked, they argued. Tonight he didn't want to take that chance. For ten minutes everything narrowed to the feel of the woman in his arms, to the certainty that she would be his. Tonight.

He deflected two attempted cut-ins, maneuvered

them past two attempted conversations, and would have happily kept doing more of the same if the music hadn't stopped. The MC took the microphone to inform the guests that Mr. and Mrs. O'Sullivan were about to leave, and while Quade allowed Chantal to slip out of the traditional dance hold, he kept a firm hold of her hand. She didn't seem to mind, at least until Julia sought her out, and then she tugged free to fall into her sister's embrace.

While they talked and wiped tears from each other's faces, a weird feeling settled over him, a foreboding that only intensified when Julia stepped to the center of the crowd and raised her bouquet high. With dramatic flair she paused to scan the faces before sending it sailing in a high arc. He felt positively sick as he watched the flowers spiral through the air directly toward the woman at his side.

When the jostling intensified, he stepped hastily out of the fray. When he heard a high-pitched shriek of delight, he glanced up to see a tall redhead waving the spoils of victory above her head. And with a jolt of surprise he realized Chantal was still by his side, that despite her competitive nature, despite the bouquet being hers for the taking, she had stepped aside. All his misgivings faded.

"You want to dance?" he asked.

Gaze steady and resolute, she looked him right in the eye. "I'd rather go home."

Quade's pulse kicked hard. "Are you sure?"

"I know what I'm doing, Quade. I know what I want. Do you?"

He nodded, a short curt movement of his head, and grabbed her hand. He wanted her and he was sick of not having her. But when he tugged on her hand, she resisted, and he turned impatiently. "What?"

"The other night I scared you off with the virgin thing. I want to be sure that won't happen again, that you won't run screaming for the hills because I'm not what you expected."

"I don't doubt there'll be screaming." His gaze fastened on her lips and his body burned with sudden intense need. "But that'll be you."

Quade's instructions for the drive home were short. "No chitchat, no revelations, no thinking."

How dictatorial, Chantal thought, objections taking shape in her brain. But then he took her hand and rested it on his thigh and that took care of the objections and the thinking in one fell swoop. Total mental vacuum until she moved her hand, spreading her fingers over the finely woven fabric of his trousers and feeling the instant grab of tension in the hard muscle beneath.

Then her vacant mind filled with vivid sensual images. The cool caress of satin against her naked skin. The hot gleam of his eyes as he lowered himself to the bed. Those long lean muscles flexing as he lifted himself over her body. Uninhibited cries of pleasure.

Champagne bubbles fizzed through her veins with dizzying, intoxicating speed. No doubt he *could* make her scream. He could, quite probably, make her do anything his heart desired.

Except it's not his heart doing the desiring, Chantal.

Before she could prevent it, her own heart performed the swan dive it had perfected over the past few days, plunging to a new low whenever she thought about the impossibility of her feelings for Cameron Quade, soaring high with Julia's series of pep talks.

"It's the male mantra, sis. No intimacy, no promises, no commitment. The thing is, they don't *know* what they want, apart from sex. They need showing. They need loving."

"And what if he doesn't want me for anything, apart from sex?"

"Do you want to find that out? Or are you going to hem and haw until it's too late and he's gone."

"You don't think he'll stay?"

"Not unless he has something to stay for."

Julia was right. Once he finished putting Merindee back together, he would be gone. He might call himself an ex-lawyer but he was a man used to doing, a man used to challenges. A man worth putting all her insecurities and self-doubts on the line for, because, deep in her soul, she sensed he was The One for her. For even the slim possibility of love, he was worth the chance of heartache.

His leg shifted infinitesimally, but it was enough to jolt her back to the present, enough to send a tingle of awareness skittering through her nerve endings, enough to cause her fingers to tighten reflexively on his thigh. Were all his muscles so taut, hard, hot? Instantly she was assailed with visions—taut, hard, hot visions—of sliding her hand higher. Moistening her lips, she edged her fingers a bold centimeter only to find them instantly imprisoned.

"Not a good idea, sweetheart. Not if you want to make it home."

The impact of those words—and the implication behind them—pulsed through her blood. If she tested him, would he pull over to the side of the road? Would he push her back in the seat and take her there, with all the hot urgency she saw in his eyes?

Oh dear Lord.

Heat, white and incandescent, suffused her, tempted her, teased her. And then she thought about afterward, about the inevitable awkwardness, and about him dropping her off at her own doorstep, his needs assuaged. No. That wasn't how she wanted this night to end, not by a long shot.

Settling back in her seat, she vowed to behave herself, at least until they made it to a bedroom.

His bedroom. She was pleased by his choice, pleased and so nervous she felt perilously close to nausea, which explained why she'd excused herself and bolted for the bathroom.

Getting this far had been relatively easy. For the last half of the trip his hand had covered hers, and the slow stroke of his thumb over her wrist steadily escalated her level of awareness. When he'd turned into his drive he must have felt her jumpy reaction, because he lifted her hand and pressed a kiss into her palm, a kiss that calmed as much as it aroused.

Then he took her by the hand and led her into his house, all the way to his bedroom. Eyes closed, she concentrated on the little things that suddenly seemed so difficult, important little things such as walking and breathing. And when she heard the pad of her bare feet on the hardwood floor—such a smooth, cool contrast to the jagged, hot edges of her senses—she laughed out loud.

"What's so funny?" he asked, and she heard the frown in his voice.

"My shoes must be still in your car. I don't even remember taking them off."

"It's a start," he said shortly, pulling her through the door into his bedroom. "One less thing I have to take off you."

If he'd started taking the rest off her then and there, she would have been fine. But a muscle jumped in his jaw and he'd looked so tense, so hard and untouchable, she freaked. And bolted.

Splashing water on her face cooled and calmed her. It also smeared the eye makeup Kree had applied with a liberal hand. Obviously not waterproof. Fixing the damage took several more minutes and, thankfully, distracted her.

"Stop being a coward," she instructed her pallid reflection. "You've come this far, now get back out there."

Nerves still danced about in her stomach, but she kept her head high as she padded back to his room. On the threshold she came to an abrupt halt.

Bare from the waist up, he sat on the edge of the turned-down bed removing his shoes. Soft warm light poured from a bedside lamp, turning the satin sheets to a gleaming midnight pool. As he bent and pulled at the second shoe the light fell across the smooth, clean lines of his back, playing on the flex of muscle, shadowing the dips and hollows.

The longing to touch was so strong, the anticipation so keen, she couldn't stifle the sound that rose in her throat. He looked up, saw her standing there, went still.

"You need help with that dress?" he asked in a low, controlled voice.

She licked her dry lips. "Yes."

"Good." Again, that muscle jumped in his cheek. "Come over here."

Heart beating so hard she could hear each individual thud, she started toward him. She saw the flare of his nostrils, the slide of his Adam's apple as he swallowed, the unwavering intensity of his eyes on her, and everything else faded. He wanted her. That's all that mattered.

He took one of her hands and tugged her closer, right into the space between his spread knees, and before she could think more than *nice move,* he hooked his other arm around her hips and pressed his face to her belly. It was such an unexpected embrace, so incredibly sensual, that Chantal thought she might shatter with the intensity of her pleasure.

Closing her eyes, she laced her fingers through his hair and sucked in a surprised breath at its softness. She had never equated softness with this man.

"Nervous?" he asked.

"Not any more."

Through the unsubstantial dress she felt the touch of his lips, the hint of a smile, and her toes curled against the hardwood floor.

"I love this dress." His hands skimmed her hips, slid down the back of her thighs, came to rest on her stockinged legs. "But it has to go."

In one practiced motion he peeled it from her body.

"Much better," he murmured and when his lips touched bare skin, Chantal's knees all but gave way…would have given way but for the hands curled around her hips and holding her steady, holding her captive to the touch of his lips, the stroke of his tongue, and the soft sounds of approval he murmured low in his throat.

Suddenly he rolled backward pulling her with him. The move should have been smooth except he caught her unprepared and she fell clumsily, laughing in nervous reaction as he tumbled her onto the bed beside him.

"Sorry." With an apologetic grimace she removed her elbow from his stomach.

"I'm not complaining." He had come to rest with his large hands cupping her bare buttocks. "Another surprise."

Chantal felt the heat of a flush warming her throat. "I had to wear a thong on account of that dress."

"It drove me crazy wondering what you had on under it."

The slow sexy circle of his hands was driving *her* crazy. "Now you know," she whispered breathily.

"Now I know."

She expected the teasing to continue, expected him to transfer his attention to the strapless bra that barely covered her breasts, but those tormenting hands stilled as he looked deeply into her eyes and the mood shifted to something more solemn. As he eased closer, need shuddered through her, an aching need to press herself against him, soft to hard, curves to flat lean planes, but his hands moved to her hips, holding her at bay.

"Slowly," he murmured as he lowered his lips to hers. "We have all night."

He started out as if he intended that one kiss to last all night: a languid sharing of breath, lazy strokes of his tongue, a slow meandering journey of her mouth. Chantal tasted champagne and chocolate dessert, pleasure and passion, and when he drew her bottom lip into his mouth she looked right into his eyes and the kiss became as involved as their myriad hues of green and amber, as deep as the strength and tenderness she felt.

Palms tingling, she explored his back, sliding over the smooth planes, touching each nub of his spine, slowing in surprise at the softer skin beneath his arms. Every touch he mirrored—the brushing of fingertips, open-palmed caresses, sometimes giving, other times greedy. A frisson of fear immobilized her when he unsnapped her bra, when she felt the slough of his breath against her bared breasts, but with one awed word her nerves fell calm.

They learned each other's bodies in slow increments, encouraged by murmured words of praise and pleasure. With hands and mouth he discovered secret places—behind her ear, inside her wrists, the dip of her spine—that set her body adrift on a sea of sensual delight. How could he know to linger over such places? How could he know such a perfect touch? How could he not know that her breasts screamed for equal attention?

He knew.

He knew so well that at his first touch, a gently exquisite pressure to one tight nipple, she thought she might weep. When he cupped the fullness of each breast in his hands, when she felt the pressure of those work-roughened palms and his low rough sound of need, her nails dug into the flesh of his back. And when he took those breasts to his mouth, when she felt the moist stroke of his tongue and the gentle scrape of his teeth and the insistent tug of his lips, she cried out, a sharp needy call for more.

So much, too much, not enough.

He left her breasts to slide lower, hooking his fingers into the elastic of her skimpy pants and peeling them from her body. A restless fire licked through her blood. Then his hands were on her legs, rolling away each stocking before sliding up her thighs to spread her, to find her hot and wet and wanting.

Craving.

And, oh, those hands. They knew how to torment and to tantalize, how to turn her into a panting, quivering mass of need. But it wasn't enough. She wanted her hands on him. She wanted his body on hers, in hers. Naked. But he rolled out of reach of her questing hands and onto his feet in one fluid movement. Light and shadow rippled across his skin as he shed the rest of his clothes, as he unselfconsciously revealed a body that turned her weak with wanting and renewed nerves.

He was extremely big, he was extremely aroused, and he was going about the whole find-and-fit-protection process with a practiced ease that reminded her of their extremely divergent levels of experience. But before she could finish thinking *what am I doing here and what am I going to do with all that?* he was back at her side, kissing her, reassuring her, touching her. Finding supersensitive flesh with those magical fingers and circling, pressing, lingering. Blowing all her fears out the back of her head as a delicious pressure coiled low in her belly, as a restless pulse pounded through her blood.

"Please," she cried, catching at his hand, searching out his gaze and holding it steady with hers, forcing her voice to a strong, purposeful level. "I want you. Inside me. Before you touch me one more time."

Heat blazed in his eyes as he pulled her body under his, as he leaned down and pressed a slow, intoxicating kiss to her open mouth. He eased away a fraction and smiled. "I thought you'd never ask."

And while she was still absorbing the irresistible impact of that smile, she felt him between her legs, apology tightening his face and his voice as he eased into her body.

"Bear with me…" He stilled, whistled out a breath between his teeth. "You're so snug." He pressed forward again, restraint taut on his lips, his brow, in the tendons standing out on his neck. "So damned…tight."

Chantal couldn't bear the suspense, the restraint, the slowness any longer. "And perhaps you're just too damned big."

"Oh, man." He shook his head, once, one side to the other. Then he laughed, a strained guttural sound that cut short in the middle as he gazed down into her eyes. "You're really something."

"I am?"

Eyes fixed on hers he eased partway out and she felt a mild moment of panic. Digging her fingers into his back, she held him there, poised at the brink of her body.

"Do you happen to know what that something is?" she asked.

Slowly he pressed into her, a little deeper this time. Sweat broke out on his forehead when he stopped, waiting for her body to adjust. "I'm working on it."

"Not nearly quickly enough."

"I'm trying—" he spoke through gritted teeth "—to be considerate."

"And I totally appreciate the effort."

Smiling sweetly, she lifted her hips in silent invitation but still he held himself there, unmoving, unrelenting. A tremor quivered through his body, through the long sweat-dampened muscles of his back, through the bulging arms that held him clear of her body, through the passion-hazed turmoil in his eyes. And in that moment Chantal felt an overwhelming sense of rightness along with an incomprehensible rush of tenderness.

She lifted a trembling hand to cup his face, touched the pad of her thumb to his lips and whispered, "Go ahead. Make my day."

He swore. Succinctly. Fiercely. And then he let himself go, plunging into her body with an intensity that rocked her to her toes, once, twice, three times, penetrating so deeply, so completely, that she knew she would never be the same again.

Knew she never wanted to be the same again.

"This isn't the way I wanted it to be."

The guttural depth of his voice, the burning intensity in his eyes, the heavy pulse of his body inside hers, all combined to fill Chantal with a primitive power, an elemental strength. Then he bent down and dragged her earlobe between his teeth and she felt as weak and helpless as a newborn kitten.

"I wanted slow and steady," he growled near her ear, retreating then filling her again with one smooth languid stroke. "Control."

He repeated the exercise as he repeated the words. Smooth. Steady. Control. It was exquisite. It was mind numbing. It was sheer, unadulterated torture. Chantal whimpered low in her throat as the pressure built to an unbearable intensity.

Then he reached between them, seeking, stroking, one expert thumb and one flashpoint of wildly spinning sensation that traveled so quickly and grabbed so ferociously she could barely breath. Wave after wave of delight shuddered through her body and she cried out long and loud as his strokes gathered momentum, no longer languid and smooth and controlled, just an ever escalating force that hammered at her senses until he buried himself with a shout that sounded something like triumph and something like desperation, a shout of release that echoed through the room and reverberated through her soul.

Ten

She was watching him. Quade knew it the instant he came awake, yet the notion didn't feel as intrusive as it should have done. Or perhaps he was simply too spent, too sated, to register any feelings.

"How long have you been awake?" he asked, eyes still closed against the morning sun's white brilliance.

"A while." The sheets rustled softly as she shifted position. "Do you always sleep so soundly?"

"No." *Never. At least not in the last several months.* Yet he had slept like the dead, on the flat of his back, limbs heedlessly sprawled, with a strange woman in his bed and beneath several of those sprawled limbs. *Strange?* Only because her presence felt too familiar—*that* constituted strange.

He lay there a moment longer, waiting for the *what-am-I-doing-here?* misgivings to rouse him from his perfectly relaxed state. When they didn't he rolled onto his side, opening his eyes a mere slit to find her less than a foot away, solemn eyes looking right into his.

The effect jolted him to full consciousness in one heartbeat. Like the first shot of morning caffeine, he thought, still mesmerized by those deep espresso eyes...or by the expression in them. Grave, yes, but intensely focused, as if he were the only thing worth her regard. Chest tight—not with the expected dread, but *good* tight—he lifted a hand and touched her cheek, touched skin so pale and fine it seemed almost translucent in the bright light.

"Good morning." Her voice rasped with more than an edge of huskiness. From overuse during those long night hours before sleep claimed them?

The thought made him smile. "Yeah, it is. Especially since you're still here."

"I did think about leaving, but—" She shrugged. "It seemed like too much trouble."

Because she could barely move? Damn. Remorse washed through him. He had tried for restraint, for consideration, but she tackled lovemaking like everything else. Full on, take no prisoners, last man standing.

Heat chased hard on the heels of remorse, but he tamped it with thoughts of her inexperience. All but a virgin. "You must be feeling a bit..."

"Exhausted? Awed? Wonderful?"

"I was going to say sore."

"That too, but in the nicest possible way. Muscles I haven't used and all that." Self-reproach must have shown on his face because she suddenly smiled and touched a gentle hand to his frown. "Hey, no need to feel bad. I'm tough."

"You're a marshmallow." He kissed the soft sweetness of her lips before she could voice an objection. And because he felt like it. "Which, before you take issue, isn't necessarily a bad thing."

"You think?"

He kissed her again.

"And now you're trying to distract me," she murmured, clearly distracted.

Quade laced his fingers into her wildly tumbled hair and reminded himself how this conversation started. With self-reproach for the reason her hair arrived at that state—through excessive wild tumbling. He shouldn't be kissing her. Shouldn't be thinking about starting all over again the way he should have started. Soft and gentle and tender. Long quiet lovemaking that whiled away the hours and left a body blissful and boneless.

With a mental grimace, he removed his hand from her hair and scrubbed it over his face. Boneless was not an apt word choice, not given his current ever hardening state. *He* needed distracting.

"You up for breakfast?"

"What do you have in mind?" she asked lazily, propping herself up on one elbow in a way that enticed the sheet to mould her curves more closely.

"The usual. Coffee. Toast." *You. On toast.*

"French toast? With lashings of maple syrup?"

"Not unless you know somewhere that does home delivery."

Laughing, she shook her head and a tiny pink flower drifted to rest on his pillow. Eyes narrowed, he leaned closer and plucked another from her curls.

"Kree sprinkled those through our hair for the

wedding. Apparently when I took them out in the bathroom last night, I missed a couple.''

''Is that what took you so long?''

When she paused a second, hesitant, Quade instinctively held his breath. He wasn't sure he was up for any more surprises. ''Actually I suffered a mild panic attack.''

No surprise there. As soon as he'd pulled her into his bedroom he'd seen the anxiety and uncertainty in her eyes, but he'd let her go, left her to take her time, even though… ''Back here I was having my own panic attack, not so mild.''

''Really?''

''I thought you might do a runner. Out the window and across the paddocks.''

''Would you have followed me? Would you have chased me across the paddocks?''

Awareness arced between them—he saw it in the teasing smile, in the slight flare of her nostrils—and like wildfire the scene filled his senses. Pumping legs and panting breath, the pale flash of her dress flitting in and out of view, the excitement as the distance between them closed, as his hands found her in the darkness. The clash of bodies, the sensation of falling, rolling over and over in the lush green grass. The knowledge of having her under the moon and the stars. Under him.

''Careful,'' he murmured, cautioning himself and cautioning her from responding to the images that burned in his eyes, to the heat he saw reflected in hers. ''Let's just back this up a few degrees.''

''Okay.'' She exhaled a hot breath that whispered over his bare arm. ''Back to where you panicked about me leaving—''

"You first. What frightened you?"

"Insecurities." Her gaze dropped from his and she laughed softly, in that self-derisive way she had. "Or insecurity. I'm never sure if that should be plural or singular, although last night, in your bathroom, it felt like a whole seething mass of the suckers for a minute or two."

The need to reach out, to comfort her, was powerful. Irresistible. He touched a finger to her shoulder, stroked it the long beautiful length of her bare arm. "You care to tell me what a stunning, sexy, sharp woman has to be insecure about?"

"Not if it makes me sound like a neurotic nutcase."

He smiled but his gaze remained serious. "You don't see yourself the way I described, do you?"

"I'm sharp. I'm a woman. And you seem to have the knack of making me feel sexy."

"And beautiful?"

She sighed. "Look, I know the sight of me doesn't scare children, but when I was growing up I was always the shy, chubby one. The brainiac. The one with her nose stuck in a book…and I'm not talking about the Bobbsey Twins."

"Steinbeck? Tolstoy? Dostoevsky?"

"If they were on the syllabus," she said matter-of-factly. "Schoolwork happened to be the one thing I did well at, so I immersed myself in it. It became a habit."

"Study?"

"Success." Eyes lowered, she paused. Moistened her lips. "I started avoiding things where I thought I might fail. Sport, parties, boys."

"And after one…" *What had she called it? For-*

gettable? Regrettable? "One experience, you started avoiding men?"

"Let's assume it was a spectacular *un*success and leave it at that, okay?"

Yeah, he could do that. He could press a kiss to her wry smile and make some teasing comment and go start on breakfast. Or he could act on the compulsion barreling around inside him, the need to expunge the bad memories from her eyes, to replace them with spectacular present experiences. What the hell…

With lightning speed, he rolled her onto her back and pinned her to the bed. "So, how did last night rate on your success-o-meter?"

"Off the scale."

A simple response, three little words, but her lack of guile, the absence of premeditation, the clear honesty in her eyes, blew Quade away. He felt like puffing his chest out, thumping it Tarzan-style, swinging from the ceiling. And he couldn't help repeating her words. "Off the scale, huh?" Couldn't stop grinning like some big loon who *would* beat his chest and swing from light fittings.

"I heard you'd be a master class," she said, smiling right back at him.

"You heard? From whom?"

"My lips are sealed."

"I have ways of unsealing them." He nuzzled her neck until she squirmed against his hold, the laughter gurgling against her lips. "You know I can make you talk. And moan. And beg."

When he slid lower he took the sheet with him, playing it over the lush swell of her breasts until the nipples hardened and darkened, until he heard the hot rush of breath past her lips. Ducking his head he wet one, then the other, with one gentle slide of his tongue then he rocked back to inspect the results.

Glorious. The contrast of milk-pale flesh against midnight-dark satin. The gleam of their kiss-moistened tips, the flush of arousal pink in her skin, her lips plump and soft and begging to be taken. He obliged, losing himself in the deep dark complexity of the kiss, then, as he lifted his head, in the deep dark complexity of her eyes.

"Now you've gone and done it," she murmured.

"Not hardly." Not yet, but soon.

"You kiss me like that and, poof, my mind clears. I can't even remember what you're trying to coax out of me."

"Does it matter?"

"Probably not, but don't let that stop you." Her sultry come-hither smile was about the sexiest thing Quade had ever seen. The fact that it came dressed in nothing but pale skin and framed in dark satin didn't do it any harm either. "I'm rather enjoying the process."

"Settle in because this particular process takes a while."

A wicked anticipation danced in her eyes. "I don't have anywhere else to be."

"No golf lessons to run off to?" He touched the soft curve of her belly with the backs of his fingers.

"Yes." The answer whistled through her teeth as he dragged his fingers lower. "But you're making me forget again."

"Should I feel flattered?"

"Only if it doesn't augment your ego. That's had quite enough stroking this weekend."

Quade snorted. "No such thing as enough stroking. Not where a man's…ego…is concerned."

She rolled her eyes and warm laughter streamed through him. It struck him how much he was enjoying her, not just the feel of her under his hands, under his body, but the banter. The teasing. The laughter that no longer felt strange on his face.

"If you ask nicely I'll give you a few pointers later."

"Are we talking golf?" All wide-eyed innocence. "Because I do need a few pointers. It's my big debut on Friday."

"You don't sound very concerned." Not for a confessed success junkie who, last time he looked, had trouble even connecting with the ball.

"When Godfrey set the time last week I just about lost my lunch, but you're providing one heck of a displacement activity."

Well, hell. Quade's hand stilled. A displacement activity. Is that all this was to her? Frowning, he looked into her eyes and saw the teasing laughter dim. What was wrong with him? Five days before he'd been ready to run screaming for the hills—her words, pretty accurate—when she'd revealed her long-term crush on him. He'd feared she would place too much importance on this affair, that she was looking for more than short-term pleasure. And now he was getting bent out of shape about *her* calling it a displacement activity.

"Is something wrong?" she asked. "You've gone awfully quiet."

Shoving his qualms aside, he smiled slowly and found her again. "Just trying to remember what comes next."

"Or who…" she murmured on a serrated sigh of pleasure. *Short-term* pleasure, Quade reminded himself as he watched her eyes widen with delight. That's all this was about, for both of them.

Over the next four days they shared plenty of pleasure and Quade gave her many pointers. Some were even about golf. "And wasn't *that* a waste of time," he groused out loud, just for a change.

He'd been stewing in silence for—he glared at the clock on his shed wall—five hours now, and it was becoming old. So was pacing the walls of his shed, cursing at every tool that slipped from his fingers, and blaming the clock. Where the hell was she? Throwing aside his buffing cloth, he expelled a frustrated sigh and gave up all pretence of work.

One phone call, that's all he needed. *Hi, I'm fine. I haven't wrapped my missile of a car around a tree. Talk to you later.* How much trouble was that? Too much, obviously. At last count he'd left six messages, three on her cell phone, one on her home phone, one on her work phone, and, when those cold spears of accident dread jabbed through him, one on her parents' phone.

What more could he do except stew and grouse? Julia and Zane were honeymooning and Godfrey didn't have a clue. He knew that firsthand. He'd willingly subjected himself to a whole afternoon in his uncle's company, nine holes of well-oiled maneuvers and manipulations, more aimed at getting him on board at M.A.B. than at winning a round of golf, and all for her benefit.

Because at breakfast that morning she'd knocked over the milk jug *and* burned the toast. Oh, she'd covered with jokes about clumsiness, but he'd known it was nerves, edginess, because of the afternoon's golf appointment. And as soon as she'd waltzed out the door, all breezy smiles and fake bravado, he'd picked up the phone and weaseled an invitation to join them. He'd wanted to be there for her, to provide moral and coaching support, because it meant so much to her.

And what had she done? She hadn't even turned up.

Godfrey had shrugged his concerns aside. "She couldn't make it this afternoon. Left a message with my secretary. Some fire to put out and she had to rush off somewhere. Work first with Chantal, always. That's why she's such a valuable member of our firm."

Hardly news to Quade, except this last week... *No.* Jaw clenched he shoved that dangerous thought aside. This week she'd been coasting—straight nine to five, few after-hours calls. Slow weeks happened along from time to time and, fortuitously, he'd gotten to share this one with her.

Didn't mean she rushed home to be with him. Didn't mean she chose his company above extra night hours. Didn't mean a thing in the big scheme of things.

When she hadn't returned his first message by seven, his irritation over an ill-spent afternoon had grown claws of worry, anxiety, unease. The golf had seemed so important. Impressing Godfrey the be-all and end-all. Hell, she'd even practiced in the rain to fit herself for this afternoon. She wouldn't have just blown it off...would she? *I started avoiding things where I thought I might fail.* No, not Chantal. She wasn't a quitter. Not any more.

So, what had dragged her off in such a rush? What had kept her occupied all this time?

The phone rang while he was in the shower and he didn't even stop to grab a towel. When he heard her voice, nothing but a simple *hello,* relief stole his breath, his strength, his cool.

"Where the hell are you?" he ground between clenched teeth. "Why didn't you turn up for golf this afternoon?"

She paused, just long enough for him to picture the hint of a frown furrowing the pale skin of her forehead. "How did you know that?"

Her quiet question, his racing pulse, the water pooling around his feet, the tick of the old-fashioned clock—every damn thing grated against the fractured edges of his temper. "Because I was there, damn it. Where were you?"

"I'm in Sydney. It's a long story—"

"Then let's just stick to the short version."

"Fine." One second to the next, her voice had chilled twenty degrees. *That* grated as well. "Mitch had a child-care crisis. I'm helping him out."

"You flew to Sydney to *baby-sit?*"

"I flew to Sydney because my brother needed me."

"Sounds like your brother needs to get his act together."

"Really?" she asked, the sarcasm so heavy he could feel it dripping through the phone line. "That's funny because, of all people, I thought you might understand."

"What? Your need to skip out on something you were afraid you'd fail at?"

Silence followed, so thick he felt its presence like a physical thing, like a cold, solid wall of dread. What was he doing here? Scrubbing a hand over his face, he struggled to form some words of apology. Some explanation for the irrational clutch of fear that had carried him along, unthinking, on a reactive wave.

"Actually, I didn't mean you skipping out on your career. I meant you might understand what Mitch has been going through ever since his wife decided marriage and rearing a child was inconvenient to her career."

Her words hit him sidelong with the force of a sledgehammer. *How the hell did she know about Kristin, about her decision?* "What are you talking about?" he asked slowly.

"About Mitch, about broken hearts, about pain that rips you apart inside." She'd been talking about Mitch's wife, her choices, not Kristin. He felt the tension in his jaw give a fraction. "Look, I only rang to let you know my whereabouts because I thought you wanted to know. For some dumb reason I imagined I heard concern in your messages."

"You did."

"Oh."

He wanted to say more, to explain why he'd been on that damned golf course in the first place, but not over the phone. He'd handled this whole thing poorly—okay, disastrously—from the get-go, and he intended making it up to her grandly. Not over the phone, not with her hundreds of miles away. In person. Very much in person.

"When are you coming home?" he asked, feeling

in control for the first time all day. It was a sensation he welcomed with open arms.

"I'm here for the weekend, flying back Monday morning. I'll be going straight to work."

"Will you call in here after work, on your way home?" Eyes closed, he waited for her answer. Told himself it didn't matter because if she didn't call on him, he'd be down there in a flash, bashing on her door, demanding she hear him out.

"Okay."

"Okay," he repeated, feeling like a man who'd just earned a reprieve, a guilty man who didn't deserve one. "I'll see you then."

Three hours until she was due—*if* she finished work on time, *if* she didn't have hours to make up after leaving early Friday, *if* she didn't decide to make him sweat it out in penance—and he was as edgy as the feral chickens that skittered around his shed. Every time he rolled out from under the car he seemed to startle one into wild wing-flapping retreat. The way he'd been tossing tools around today, he didn't blame the birds.

With a wry shake of his head, he propelled himself back beneath the jacked-up vehicle. It was a way to pass the time. Plus he'd found extra incentive to get the car finished—sometime during the past week he'd learned that Chantal had a thing for it. Not an historical interest, not a mechanical curiosity, not even an aesthetic attraction for the low-slung, red classic.

She had a fantasy. A hot, sweaty, no-holds-barred sexual fantasy involving this car. In what context he didn't know, but he was up for finding out.

With a grin on his face, he returned some of his

attention to the job in hand, the rest to a sultry stream of car fantasies. When he heard the low thrum of an engine ten or so minutes later, he thought the fantasy thing was getting a little too real and shook his head clear.

The engine cut out and a car door slammed. Quade's heart slammed against his ribs. This was no figment of his imagination, although he couldn't help conjuring up a few reasons for her early arrival. As edgy as he, she couldn't wait for the end of the day. She had to see him now. She had to have him now.

As he rolled out from beneath the car, anticipation filled his body with fierce intensity. The explanations and apologies better not get too involved. She better be wearing a skirt. Because car finished or not, he was up for finding out all her car fantasies right now. Fully up.

By the time she came through the door he was on his feet and wiping the grime from his hands. Before he'd finished one finger, he could tell she was in no mood for fantasies…unless they involved extreme violence. Great big galloping qualms trampled all through him, but he smiled regardless. "Would it help if I explained that phone call?"

Eyes flashing dark fire, she came to a halt in front of him. "It would help if you *explained* what you were doing on that golf course with Godfrey on Friday."

Eleven

"Helping you out."

Chantal had trained hard at the school of cool and collected, but every lesson exploded in a blistering red mist when Quade shrugged and calmly offered that answer. Rage shimmered through her as she whipped the rag from his hands and threw it to the floor.

"By offering advice to Godfrey? By recommending he send clients to big-city firms? Is that how you were helping me out?" She didn't wait for his answer, barely gave him a chance to narrow his gaze before she lit into him again. "Because from where I'm standing it looks more like you're helping out one of your old buddies. Andrew McKinley. Name ring a bell?"

His head lifted a fraction, as if she had rocked him and that felt good. Incredibly, vindictively good.

"Well, of course you've heard the name. After all, you recommended him!"

"Godfrey asked my advice on a hypothetical situation, I gave it. You want to tell me why that's a problem?"

"Damn right I do. That was *my* client. *My* case!" Not a hypothetical, but Emily Warner. To her mortification tears blurred her vision and she had to look away, to gather herself, before she could continue. "You had no right to interfere."

"Now hang on a minute—"

"I will not hang on to anything a minute unless it's your neck!"

He stared at her a moment, a muscle working in his cheek. "Don't you think you should take this up with your boss?"

"I did. But my boss happens to have this hotshot international attorney—sorry, *ex*-attorney—for a nephew and when *he* gives advice, it's gospel."

"I called it as I saw it," he replied all cool, unperturbed logic.

Chantal felt her cool and logic slip another notch. "During a casual chat on a golf course? For crying out loud, you didn't even have all the facts!"

"I had enough to discern it's a complicated case, one worthy of an estate specialist. I offered that opinion, and I stand by it."

"You don't think I'm up to it, do you?" Eyes narrowed, she glared up at him. "Same old, same old."

"If you're referring to what happened at Barker Cowan, then you're way off beam. You were a second year student—"

"Who you didn't trust to do a simple job."

"Don't you think it's time you let that go?"

Until Quade came back into her life, she thought she had. But somehow he managed to dredge up every buried insecurity, every old doubt about her ability, even when the voice of logic told her to take another look. Exhaling heavily, she looked away, down, studied an oil stain on the concrete floor.

"It's only a case, Chantal," he said very softly.

Her head whipped up. "It's *only* the most important thing in my life. I've been working my butt off for weeks on this, night and day and weekends. It's the case I've been waiting for. The one that will make a difference."

"For your career prospects."

Not a question. A statement of fact, as cold and hard as the look in his eyes. He folded his arms across his chest and Chantal felt a sudden urge to shake her head. *No, no, no, no. That's not what I meant, at all. I have handled this all wrong. Don't shut me out.*

"Shouldn't this be about what's best for your client?" he asked.

"Yes. You're right." Absolutely right.

"Pleased we agree on something."

Silence settled, awkward and uncomfortable. So much had been said poorly, so much left unsaid, and Chantal searched for an opening, a chink in his impenetrable expression. "What else did you and Godfrey discuss?"

"Is that any of your business?"

The coolness in his eyes should have been a signal. *Don't go there, Chantal. Don't pursue this.* But she couldn't help herself. "If it's about my workplace, then, yes, it is my business."

"No, and here's some free advice." The set of his jaw hard and unyielding, he leaned forward as if to lend weight to his words. "Don't ever presume that I will discuss any business with you, your workplace or mine, just because we are sleeping together."

Staggered—by his icy tone, his uncompromising expression, but mostly by the message—she took a step back. He was cautioning her against using their relationship, against using *pillow talk?* To what ends? To gain some kind of privileged information?

A short burst of laughter rose inside her. The idea was ludicrous. She'd been scratching for a conversation starter and he'd turned it into…into a character judgment. And how little he thought of her. As the notion took hold, hurt swamped her, so powerful it forced her back another step.

"Don't worry your conscience over that happening." Her voice sounded as tight and brittle as she felt. As if one more knock would shatter her like fine china on the concrete floor. "We won't be sleeping together any more."

"Quitting, Chantal?"

Chin high, she glared back at him. "You're the expert, Quade. What do you think?"

"Meaning?"

"You seem to have managed your share of quitting lately. Your job, your engagement. Your whole life, pretty much."

The calm line of his mouth thinned. Well, good. Finally she had managed to make some impact. "You don't know anything about that."

"Oh, and I wonder why? Could it be because you haven't told me one damned thing about it? Because all you were prepared to share with me was your body?"

"I never promised you anything else."

But during the last idyllic week she had allowed her heart to hope, to dream of a future beyond the bedroom. She had even convinced herself that Friday night's phone call was born of concern for her well-being, and her soaring hopes had delivered her home on a cloud of blissful anticipation.

To Godfrey's bombshell. To *this* eye-opener.

The man she imagined herself in love with had no confidence in her capability as a lawyer and no respect for her ethical integrity.

Head high, she forced herself to hold it together, to contain the angsty pain that screamed for release. To twist her mouth into a tight little smile and respond to that final slap of reality. He had offered her nothing but his body.

"No, you didn't."

Pride kept her walking out of that shed, head high despite the tears misting her vision, praying that her movements didn't look as wooden and jerky as they felt. That same pride kept her going over the next weeks, filling the long days and nights with any tedious, mind-sapping work she could find. It kept her from spilling her heartache to Julia, and it kept her driving past Quade's driveway with her head held high, kept her from succumbing to the powerful urge to pull the wheel right and not stop until she was in his arms.

Pride did all that, but self-honesty forced her to accept one truth—he had been right about Andrew McKinley. To build the strongest possible case, to ensure the best chance of winning, Emily needed a man like Quade's estate specialist buddy on her team. Unfortunately Emily didn't see it quite the same way.

Even after they traveled to Sydney for a meeting, she stubbornly insisted they could do without an arrogant city wig.

Two weeks later they had reached an impasse. Chantal expelled a frustrated breath and buried her head in her hands just as a knock sounded on her office door.

"Everything all right?" Godfrey asked from the doorway.

"Nothing I can't handle."

"I don't doubt that for a minute, but sometimes it helps to talk it through."

"Do you have a free hour or ten?" she asked with a mocking smile.

"If you don't mind walking while you're talking then, yes, I do."

Friday afternoon, golf afternoon. Chantal sat back in her chair and chewed her lip. For the past three weeks and four days Quade's *quitting* allegation had plagued her conscience. When Mitch's phone call came—that solid-gold excuse to bail out of the golf engagement—she'd been one second away from calling Quade, begging him to come and hold her hand. She'd proven herself as a first-rate nine-carat coward, one step removed from a quitter.

This afternoon, right now, she could make it up to herself. She could do this golf thing. She *would* do it.

Slapping her palms down on the desk, she pushed to her feet. "I'm up for some walking and talking. Thank you, Godfrey."

I hope neither of us regrets it.

Thirty minutes later the first arrow of regret pierced her right through the heart. Quade. In the Country

Club car park. Hauling a golf bag from the trunk of his car.

Her instant response—an actual physical jolt that stiffened her limbs and tensed her muscles—brought her car to an abrupt halt. And she sat there hunched over the wheel, heart beating erratically, while her eyes ate him up. The long line of his back, the sun-brightened gleam of his hair, the square line of his jaw, the dark shadow of a frown as he lifted his head.

His whole body stilled, paused as if he sensed her watching, and in that second she swore her heart stopped beating. Then he swung around, a swift movement that brought his gaze directly to hers. She could not look away. The pull of that vivid green gaze was so forceful she could feel herself trapped in it, sucked forward by it, as if into a vortex.

Dimly she heard the honk of a horn and, with immense difficulty, she shook herself out of a moment as intense as any she had ever experienced. The horn sounded again, more urgently, and she realized that she was blocking the road. With an apologetic wave, she released her foot from the brake pedal and steered into a park, a regular spot, not one situated in the middle of the road.

By the time she turned off the engine and looked around Godfrey blocked her view, but she could see he was shaking Quade's hand and that two golf buggies sat side by side behind their parked cars. Tension curled in her stomach as—somewhat belatedly—the significance struck. No coincidence but a prearranged meeting. There were no other cars she recognized, no one else preparing to hit off.

Just Godfrey and Quade and she as the third.

* * *

Avoiding awkward conversation was as easy as hooking every drive into the rough, as simple as pretending utter concentration on every approach shot and putt. But after four holes Chantal despised her cowardly tactics. Wasn't this afternoon about proving something to herself? Hiding behind trees was not the way to go about bolstering her self-respect. Playing no-speaks with her neighbor, ditto.

The next time Godfrey strode away to take his shot, she set her shoulders, stiffened her spine and made an effort. "Zane tells me you've almost finished the MG."

"Almost." He was gazing off into the distance, as if he couldn't stand to look at her. Swallowing the bitter hurt of that thought, she forced herself to try again. Three chances. Three innocuous conversation starters. If he couldn't do better than one-word answers, the message would be clear.

"And the garden's coming along? Julia thinks it's going to look magnificent in a couple of years."

"It will be." Three words. Wonderful.

They both watched as Godfrey's approach shot popped up, bounced all the way across the green and plopped into a deep sand bunker on the far side. Talk about symbolic. Her heart had just executed the exact same deep fall.

"Have you decided what you're going to do with your acres? Because I didn't ever introduce you to the vineyard consultant. I promised to do that, at the wedding."

Perhaps her last-ditch attempt at conversation had sounded as frantic as she felt, because he finally looked at her. Right at her. Her heart raced as she gazed back into those tired, shadowed eyes. *Tired? Shadowed?* She swallowed and tried not to conjecture why.

"I managed to meet up with Harrier," he said slowly.

"You did?"

"Yeah. His number's in the book."

Of course it was. But she'd been incapable of such simple deduction. The way he'd been looking at her, the way her crazy heart and body and soul responded with a wild cry of hope. Oh dear Lord.

"He mentioned how I cut in on him at the wedding. When he was dancing with you." Their gazes met. Memories of that night blazed between them in a bolt of vivid blue heat, before he looked away. His mouth twisted wryly. "Lucky for me he doesn't hold a grudge."

When he strolled away to take his shot—Godfrey's ball had just burst from the bunker in a spray of sand and come to rest by the flag—she released a long whoosh of breath. Her pulse still hadn't settled, and as he hunkered down to line up his putt, she allowed herself a brief, silent *whoop* of cautious optimism. Then she noticed the way his chinos pulled across the muscles of his thighs, and unadulterated heat obliterated her tempered warm optimism.

Through the heat haze she watched him sink his putt. Three putts later she'd done the same, a decent result for her, and when Godfrey finished they walked to the next tee and started all over. Two holes later she found herself alone with Quade again, as they walked toward their second shots. Godfrey's drive had landed on the opposite side of the fairway.

"I didn't realize you still played," she said, just for something to say.

"Haven't in a long while. Until…" He stopped suddenly, waited for her to do the same, to turn and face him. "Godfrey's invited me to play every Friday since I came back. I figured I'd spend all afternoon fielding offers to work with him, so I kept knocking him back."

Heart knocking against her ribs, she met his gaze. "Until the day I went to Sydney."

"Yeah. Except I invited myself that day. I wanted to be there for you."

The sincerity of that quiet admission knocked the stuffing right out of Chantal.

"I wanted to tell you the day you came home. I didn't and I've regretted it ever since."

That's what he'd meant by helping her…and she hadn't even bothered to ask. "I wish I had known," she said, her voice barely a whisper.

"Would it have made any difference?"

Remembering her all-fire rage that day… "Probably not."

He nodded. Then, turned and started walking again. Somehow she coaxed her legs into doing the same.

"I guess we both have regrets from that day." She felt his interest, a stillness in his gaze as it rested on the side of her face, but she couldn't look up. All her focus concentrated on placing one foot in front of the other and not screwing up her apology. "In the heat of the moment I said things I wish I hadn't. Especially about quitting your job." *And your engagement.* "I'm sorry. Truly, deeply sorry."

Their walking slowed until they barely moved, until they stopped, although neither turned. And in that long silence the air felt so taut Chantal swore she heard it sing, high-pitched with the strain.

It was her phone.

As she automatically reached for it, he circled her wrist in an iron-hard grip. "Don't answer it."

"Okay."

He released his breath in what sounded like relief. "I didn't quit. I was fired."

Wow. Cautiously she turned toward him and the movement drew his attention to his tight hold on her wrist. Frowning, he eased his grip to a gentling caress, as if he intended to smooth away any marks left by his fingers. A myriad of sensations swirled through Chantal. The fierce longing to wipe that frown away. To kiss it away. Warmth as tenderhearted as the marshmallow he'd proclaimed her, yet cloaked in a fierce possessiveness. To fight every fight for him, to right every wrong.

"Why would they fire you?" she asked, hackles rising. "Have they no brains?"

"They had their reasons."

Breath held, she silently implored him to share those reasons. Whether he chose to or not seemed immensely significant, a sign of his willingness to include her in more of his life. And just when she didn't believe she could stand the suspense any longer, her phone rang again, a shrill intrusion that she reached to shut off.

"Go ahead," he said shortly. "It might be important."

"Not as important as why you were…"

Her voice trailed off when she identified the caller. Zane's mobile, which he rarely used. He'd started carrying one in case Julia needed him urgently. Her heart constricted with a sudden irrational fear. Three weeks to go, but…

"Is it Julia?" she breathed into the phone. "What's happened?"

She heard three words—pain, bleeding, hospital—before everything faded in a paroxysm of fear.

Twelve

One look at her stricken face, and Quade had asked two questions: "Where to?" and "How fast?"

At Cliffton Base Hospital they learned that Julia was being prepped for a Caesarian delivery and despite all the reassurance—it's precautionary due to the placental bleeding, thirty-seven weeks isn't too early, the baby's being monitored and is fine—Chantal's face had turned an ashen shade of pale.

She clutched the coffee he'd just fetched between hands that shook more than a little. "You don't have to stay," she said. "Kree will be here any minute. And my parents. They should be on the five-forty plane."

"I'm not going anywhere."

She didn't argue—not that it would have made any difference. He was staying. He didn't want to analyze why, didn't want to think about the ramifications, he just knew he wasn't leaving her. Not while her hands still trembled so badly she couldn't put down her cup without slopping coffee on the side table. Not when her eyes pooled with tears as she fumbled about in her bag. When she started to mop ineffectually at the spill with a wad of tissues, Quade reached for her hand.

"Leave it," he said more gruffly than he'd intended.

She stilled, tensing beneath his touch, and he turned her hand over to link fingers, palm to palm. For a long while he said nothing, simply sitting and letting her absorb strength and comfort from his touch. Gradually he felt an easing in her tension, an acceptance of the solace he offered, and when she gently squeezed his fingers the instant explosion of emotion poleaxed him.

For another long while he didn't speak, couldn't speak past the tight constriction that spread from his gut through his chest to take a stranglehold on his throat.

"Thank you," she said quietly.

He didn't bother with *you're welcome,* same as she hadn't added *it means a lot to me.* Both were givens.

After another minute, she spoke again. "You can't have a good association with hospitals."

"Does anyone?"

"Not everyone has your history."

Her quiet observation and the degree of perception behind it stunned him all over again. So did his sudden compulsion to invite her into a past he'd always kept under lock and key. Even from Kristin…but then she hadn't been interested in his past. Only in what his present could do for her future.

"We must have visited Mum, I don't know, at least fifty times when she was in Sydney. *Undergoing treatment,* they called it, and I remember wondering how the word 'treat' could be associated with what she was going through."

Gently, barely perceptibly, she increased the pressure of her palm against his. Comforting him, encouraging him. Offering the same kind of strength as he had offered her.

"The sensory things get me the most. The smell, the rattle of those carts they use, the way the nurses' shoes squeak on the floors. They trigger this reflex reaction...I guess it's fear."

"Of the very worst kind."

He knew she wasn't thinking only of his mother's death, but of her sister and her unborn baby. Her fear that all would not be well with them. This time he returned the pressure of her fingers twined in his, tightening his grip until their forearms came into contact, elbow to wrist, along the aligned arms of their chairs.

"Thank you." No more than a husky whisper of sound but he knew she was thanking him for sharing as well as for the comfort.

Countless times over the past weeks he had replayed her words from that day in his shed, the day she walked out on him. *You haven't told me one damned thing about it. All you were prepared to share with me was your body.* Until today he'd clutched stubbornly at some warped sense of righteousness, because he'd never promised anything else, because he hadn't believed he wanted anything else.

But the instant he saw her again, the truth had hit like a sucker punch. Recovering from that initial blow had taken some time; so had accepting the truth. He wanted more. He didn't know how much, but it had started back on the golf course with his *I was fired* admission. Then, in the aftermath of Zane's phone call, his need to look after her, to be there for her, crushed any lingering doubts.

Now he had shared a glimpse of himself but there was so much left unsaid. Yet he felt no urgency, no cause for panic. Sitting hand in hand, offering her comfort and drawing some back, he felt a sense of harmony, as if suddenly all the fragmented pieces of his life had fallen back into place.

Glancing around the maternity ward, taking in the worried tightness between her brows, he knew this wasn't the time or place for the whole of his story but he would offer part as a sign of intention. The rest would wait.

"They fired me because another firm secured confidential information." Before she could voice the protest he saw in her eyes—and that instant defense warmed him gut-deep—he shook his head. "They were justified. It came from me."

"I don't understand. How?"

"Kristin's boss enticed her to extract information. Pillow talk." He released a disgusted breath. "I didn't even realize what was going on."

"That's treachery. She was your fiancée." Outrage brought color to her pale cheeks, fire to her dark eyes.

"First and foremost, she was an attorney."

"And this is why you broke up." A quiet statement of fact, not a question, and Quade knew he needed to explain the full circumstances later but, for now, this would do.

"Yeah, and why I fired into you so unjustly."

"I'm not Kristin."

"I know that." He'd known it for a long time; he just hadn't been ready to admit it.

"I'm sorry." A wry smile quirked her mouth. "Not about you breaking up with that evil woman, but about losing your job. About losing the life you had."

For the first time he felt no bitterness, no sense of loss. "They did me a favor."

"Really?"

"I took up law for the wrong reasons. After Mum died, when Dad could barely look after himself, Godfrey found out about the scholarship to Melbourne Grammar. It didn't cover everything, not by a long shot, and for the next ten years he paid the bills Dad couldn't handle, right through school and university.

"I had to prove I was worth all that money. Law seemed the perfect choice—prestige and money—plus what better way to prove myself than doing better in my benefactor's career?"

"You won't ever go back to law?"

"No." He was absolutely certain, at total peace with that decision.

"What will you do?"

"I'm going to put vines in. I've been looking at a viticulture course, thinking about external study."

Smiling—hell, he'd missed that slice of sunshine—she turned a little in her seat, enough that he could see the teasing twinkle in her eyes. "Farmer Quade, huh?"

"I'll see how it fits." But already the notion was sitting as comfortably as the feel of her by his side, as warmly as the effect of that smile. Eyes fixed on her mouth, he started to lean toward her...

"Chantal. There you are. I thought I'd never get

here. Has twenty miles *ever* taken so long?'' Kree fell upon them in a rush of words and hugs and demands. ''Tell me I'm panicking for nothing. Zane left a message with Tina and it was *so* not helpful. Tell me she heard it wrong. Tell me it's all good.''

Quade let Chantal explain, settling back in his chair as they reassured each other. A half hour later the rest of the Goodwins rushed into the room—both parents, Mitch and his son—and before the tumult of their arrival settled, Zane arrived wearing hospital scrubs and a dazed expression. The noisy rabble sobered instantly, and in the long beat of silence Quade noted the gleam of tears in Zane's pale eyes, and then an inkling of a smile. Still dazed, but a smile nonetheless.

''A girl.'' His deep voice hitched with emotion and he scrubbed a hand across his eyes before he could continue. ''We have a baby girl.''

He was instantly enclosed in a huddle of high emotion, questions falling upon questions without any pause for answers. Finally he pulled clear and held up his hands. ''I need to get back there. I just wanted to let you all know they're both fine. Everything's fine.''

''When can we see her? Them?''

''Is she dark like Jules?''

''The baby's all right, isn't she?''

As the questions streamed around him, Quade felt the first pangs of disquiet. Until this moment he'd been too focused on Chantal's worry to even consider the baby's arrival. A real infant, newly pulled from her mother's womb. *Uh-uh.* He took several automatic steps backward. *He was not ready for this.* And with so many family members, Chantal no longer needed his shoulder. Superfluous. He would leave them to savor their intense relief, their joy, the euphoria of the moment. Birth. Such a stark contrast to his hospital experiences. Such a stark reminder of his only remaining regret from Kristin and Dallas.

As he headed for the car park, he felt the sharp prick of tears in the back of his throat.

For a glimmer of a moment Chantal caught the look in Quade's eyes. Fear? No, more than that. Pain. Was he remembering his mother? The loss of his family?

She tried to catch his eye, but he seemed too tightly focused on his own inner thoughts, his expression remote. Never had she felt such a bittersweet ache of need, never had she wanted to reach out more, but before she could act Mitch caught her up in a wild whooping hug that swung her off her feet.

Around and around she spun, while Joshua bounced and yelled encouragement and Mother shushed their exuberance with loud disapproval. Back on her feet, her head spun with giddiness and when she finally regained her bearings, she turned around, once, twice, searching each corner of the large waiting room. Her stomach hollowed out. He was gone.

Disappointment settled quickly and heavily but lifted with equal alacrity. Nothing could dampen her elation nor her conviction that this afternoon marked a sea change in their relationship.

Relationship.

Her heart gladdened as she silently repeated the word. He had stayed and he had shared so much more than his body—he had shared the stuff of his heart.

With a resolute smile, she vowed that before this night was over she would share the essence of hers.

Call it telepathy or call it love-blinkered confidence, Quade knew she was coming. He didn't bother fixing dinner or turning on the television and although he opened a bottle of red, it sat untouched on the coffee table as he paced the floor with an impatience he had never experienced before.

He swore he heard the sound of her engine before she turned off the main road. Impossible but tonight his senses felt so finely tuned he believed it. He opened the door before she knocked, but she showed no sign of surprise.

"We have to talk," she said with steadfast purpose. "Really talk."

Quade knew that. But talk involved mouths and once his gaze shifted from the dark intensity of her eyes to her soft pink lips, he decided the talking could wait.

He couldn't.

"We will," he promised, pulling her inside and shouldering the door shut in one blink of her long lashes. In the next he had her pushed up against the slab of wood with her hands trapped above her head. *Now* she looked surprised. Satisfaction gathered low in his gut. So did a month's load of frustrated abstinence. "After."

She started to smile and he was there before it formed, sinking into her with a hunger that drove her hard against the door. His hands slid the length of her arms, fingertips to armpits, releasing them to capture her breasts with the same urgent compulsion.

She matched his mood immediately. Hands hard in

his hair, holding him to her mouth, she arched her back and pressed the fullness of her breasts into his hands, driving him wild with the need to possess.

Here, now, take no prisoners.

A torrent of heat flooded his groin as his hands slid to her buttocks, lifting her from the floor and hard against him. Without pause, she hooked her legs high and rocked her hips in perfect synchronicity with his. Perfect but for excess clothing.

Wrenching his mouth from hers—two hands didn't seem sufficient, teeth might come in handy—he started to right that wrong. He pulled her shirt from her waistband and started on the buttons but she was quicker. Hands already at his waist, releasing his belt buckle, unzipping, freeing him with a sharp cry of triumph.

Quade sucked in a long tortured groan at the incredible softness of her hand, moving on him with mind-numbing tenderness, stroking him until the heat and need roared in his ears.

He had to be inside her. Now. Yesterday. Last week. Forever.

"Condom." He hissed in a breath as she rolled her thumb over the head of his erection. "Jeans pocket."

His hands were otherwise occupied, under her skirt, ripping down her pants, touching her moist center without preliminaries. Or enough preliminaries judging by her instant response. Her breathing grew harsh, her pleas raw and earthy, and he had to stop, to plant his hands on her hips and remind her about her interrupted task.

"Protection. *Now*."

"I can't," she breathed with equal desperation, "seem to get it."

Teeth gritted, he endured her fumbling ministrations, the exquisite pleasure-pain of her hand on him, stretching and rolling until he was sure his head would explode. Either one of them, both of them, it didn't matter. And when she was done, he rasped out something that might have been a curse or a blessing or a promise as he plunged into her.

Holy hell. How he had missed this. The hot caress of her body, drawing him in, to plunge again and again. The silken heat of her skin beneath his hands, the taste of her mouth, her throat, her breasts. The sounds of their breathing, harsh and ragged in the thick silence; the dark words they whispered, encouraging the fervent need to possess and be possessed.

It should have felt like lust, pure and elemental, but in those last seconds, as his climax gathered power and his senses clamored with the need for release, he gazed into her eyes and knew he loved her with the same unstoppable power as their joining, with the same savage intensity as the thunder that roared through his body as he came.

It took long minutes to collect himself from the ceiling, to gradually sink back into the shattered remains of his body. To realize where they were. Standing, slumped against his front door. More than half-dressed. His arms seemed barely capable of supporting him as he eased back from her body, out of her body, and in that instant he understood the significance of her stillness. The slightly puzzled look on her face.

The condom had broken.

Thirteen

Knees weak and trembling, Chantal sank to the rim of his bath and buried her face in her hands. Unfortunately that didn't obliterate either his surgically bright bathroom light or the memory of what had just happened in his hallway.

In the aftermath of that wild coupling, he seemed to freeze as if too stunned for words, and, when he had finally spoken, Chantal wished he'd kept that one succinct four-letter oath to himself. And that she had kept her eyes averted. Then she wouldn't have seen the unguarded flash of anguish in his eyes, wouldn't have been reminded of that moment in the hospital when he'd backed away from her family's joy over a new baby.

Fear had glazed his eyes. Fear of the consequences of that torn condom, sheer terror at the thought of being permanently tied to her through an unplanned pregnancy. The knowledge banded around her chest, driving the zillion shards of her splintered heart deeper into her flesh.

What a stupid loveblind fool she had been. He didn't love her. How could she have misconstrued so badly?

Tonight hadn't been about building a relationship of any kind. It was about sexual chemistry and raw desire and a man missing out for too long. It was about doing it, hard and rough, against that man's front door. And the consequences had to be faced.

Mustering her pride, she pushed to her feet. So, okay, she could take charge here. She could supply the response a man in this situation wanted to hear, and perhaps she could even toss in a cool, accepting shrug. She could do all that and maybe even walk out the door with her head held high. If not, she would die trying.

The living area seemed gloomily dim after the brightness of the bathroom, and that pretty much described the mood as well as the lighting. Quade stood in front of the unlit fireplace, his posture as stiff and unyielding as the columns of brick at his back. His face looked even more forbidding.

A lesser woman might have turned tail and fled, but, after one faltering step, Chantal pushed back her shoulders and kept on going. It didn't matter if it felt as though she were wading through treacle, all that mattered was getting through the next five minutes so she *could* turn tail and flee.

"Now we really *do* need to talk," she said with fake breeziness. "And it would be easier if you weren't glowering at me."

Hands on hips, he stared back at her. "You think I should be smiling? You think *you* should be smiling? Have you forgotten what just happened out here? Hell, Chantal, you might be pregnant."

"I don't think even yours would swim that fast."

"Now isn't the time for cute," he ground out. "Think about this."

"I have."

"Obviously not hard enough. I assume you wouldn't want a baby?"

Obviously *he* didn't, but what about her? How would she feel to be carrying Quade's baby, to be building a bond through their joint love of a child? How would she feel to see her man reduced to unashamed tears by the birth of his child? Hope bloomed, shy and tentative, in the remains of her shattered heart.

"It's not something I've considered," she said carefully. "At the moment I'm flat out keeping up with my job and my family."

"And if you are pregnant?"

The harsh intensity of his eyes sent a chill through her whole body, freezing out that first fragile inkling of warmth. And that just made her mad.

She didn't want to feel cold and hollow; she wanted to feel warm and whole again. In that moment it didn't matter that he didn't love her. He knew how to touch her, how to make her come alive, how to make her feel a thousand times stronger, a million times happier, than anything else in her life. She wouldn't let him cut her out of that. She would not allow that.

"Damn, Quade, I don't have to be pregnant. Isn't this what the morning after pill is for?"

His head rocked back as if he'd been slapped, and for a split second Chantal thought she had made a terrible mistake. But before that thought had half-formed his expression turned stony.

"You'll see your doctor in the morning?" he asked in a cold, flat voice.

Yes. No. Please, give me some sign. A muscle flicked in his tight, shadowed jaw, and she couldn't stand it any longer. Couldn't keep up the pretence any longer. She had to get out of there.

"Chantal."

She stopped before she reached the door but didn't turn around.

"Let me know if you change your mind."

"Well?" Kree asked, lowering her scissors. The question could have been for Chantal herself, or for the other stylist at the next station.

Tina lowered her blow-dryer and inspected Chantal's head through seriously narrowed eyes. "Sexy, yet stylish."

"Precisely." Kree smiled with satisfaction. "Now, don't go letting it get so out of hand again, okay?"

Chantal agreed. It was easiest, and sometime in the past seven weeks that had become her motto. Whatever's easiest. Whatever got every concerned family member off her back. Whatever got her through the next long day and even longer night.

Kree finished brushing away the loose hair and whipped off the cape with a flourish. When a frown creased her mobile face, Chantal felt a lecture coming on. Rising from the chair, she checked her watch and winced. "I'm running late, again. What do I owe you?"

"Don't keep running till you drop, okay?"

"You sound so much like Julia, it's scary."

Laughing, Kree reached for a bottle from the shelf behind her and plonked it on the counter. "You want to try this product? Your hair seems awfully dry."

She'd said much the same before she started cutting. As she ran her fingers through its length she'd tutted about the coarse texture and Chantal's stomach had pitched. Lately she'd been reading up on expected changes during pregnancy and breastfeeding. Hair texture wasn't supposed to change until much later.

"You want?" Kree prompted.

"Okay." *I doubt it will help, but whatever's easiest.*

Kree punched cash register buttons, and, from somewhere to her right, Chantal heard a soft whistle of appreciation.

"Cool car." Tina was peering out the window into the main street. "Know anyone who drives an old red sports car?"

This time Chantal's stomach did more than pitch. It rolled like something on the high seas. Dimly she heard other voices, conjecture over who might own such a vehicle, while the certainty turned her inside out.

Quade was back. After six weeks on some work experience jaunt at a Hunter Valley vineyard. At least that's what she'd extrapolated about his whereabouts from the various tidbits she'd heard from Godfrey or Zane or Julia. No one knew very much but they all knew more than she.

Six weeks of no see, no hear, no contact. No

chance to tell him that her only trip to the doctor had been to confirm the home pregnancy kit result.

"Hello? Earth calling Chantal?"

She snatched the credit card Kree was waving in front of her nose and dropped it into her purse, then she forced her legs to take her out the door, forced her eyes to locate her car, forced her hands to open the door. Twice she fumbled her keys before she got them into the ignition, but once the engine kicked over she drew several deep calming breaths and allowed the solid feel of the wheel in her hands and the smooth hum of the engine to gradually center her.

This is a good thing. Once I tell Quade, I can share with Julia. I won't have to pretend I can't hold Bridie through horror of her sicking on my clothes. I can hold her without fear of my response signposting my secret. I can relax and laugh and cry and shake with trepidation over this incredible, amazing, terrifying event. This tiny life growing inside me.

The shadow of a smile skittered across her lips as she reversed out of the car park. A complicated mix of apprehension and relief and anticipation rolled through her as she drove down Plenty's main street. Her glance flicked left and right, pulse rocketing any time she glimpsed a red car. Whether in town or at home, she would find him now. She would end this now.

On the outskirts of town she started to accelerate, picking up speed as the houses gave way to farming land. She didn't even see the truck until it was too late. A flash of movement coming out of a lane to her right, too fast to stop, too big to avoid.

The last thing she heard before it hit was her own cry of distress at not finding Quade, at never having

the chance to tell him about their baby. To tell him
she loved him.

"Ready to go, man."

Zane patted the hood of the MG he'd just returned
from a last test and grinned, the relaxed easy grin of
a thoroughly contented man. Quade tried not to resent
that, even as he tried to think of another reason to
delay his departure. The thought of walking through
the front door—*that* front door—and into his empty
house filled him with a panicky kind of dread.

"You got time for a drink?" he asked, hoping the
question sounded casual rather than desperate.

"Yeah." Zane's grin returned. "I can tell you all
about Bridie."

*Yeah, and then you can go right ahead and stick a
dagger in my gut.* He shifted uncomfortably. "On
second thoughts, I'd better be getting home."

Laughing, Zane punched his arm. "Come on, man,
I was only joshing. We can talk about your baby instead."

Dagger. Not in his gut, but right through his heart.
Reflexively he took a step back, but Zane was in-
specting the MG. *That's* what he'd meant by baby.

"Hey, Zane." Bill stuck his head out of the work-
shop door. "Tow call. An accident out near Harmer's.
You want me to take it?"

"Yeah. Please."

Zane sighed. "Looks like we'll have to take a rain
check, unless you want to go pick up a six-pack and
bring it back here."

"Sounds like a plan."

The phone rang before they'd finished their first
beer. Still laughing at the story he'd been telling,

Zane picked it up. "Bill. What's up?" His smile died, instantly supplanted by tension. His gaze jumped to meet Quade's across the office desk.

"Who?" he asked before Zane had the receiver down. Already on his feet. Already knowing in his gut.

"Chantal."

Fear sliced through him, as sharp and quick as a steel blade. "How bad?"

"According to the other driver, not too, but Bill says her car's totaled. They've taken her to Cliffton Base."

Quade was already moving but Zane stopped him before he cleared the office door. "I'll drive."

He started to object, needing to be in control, needing to be there, with her, now. But then memories of *their* fight over who drove assailed him, and he felt the fine trembling in his hands, in his legs. In his heart.

He nodded once. "Just drive fast, okay."

Chantal heard the commotion, the sound of raised voices, demands and objections, about five seconds before Quade burst through the door into the examination cubicle where they'd parked her. For another five seconds he stood there staring at her, head to foot and back again, as if checking that she was all present and correct.

Dimly, she heard the clearing of a throat and realized a sister had followed him in—obviously the one he'd been remonstrating with outside. "Now, you've seen her," she said with studied patience, "how about you do as you promised and wait outside?"

Quade's gaze didn't leave hers. "I'm not going anywhere."

Chantal felt her heart skip a long beat, then start to pound. She wanted to smile, to reassure him she was fine, to tell him never to leave her again, but she couldn't manage anything for the thickness of tears in her throat.

"What is she doing here?" he asked, finally turning to fix the sister with that fierce glare. "Where's the doctor?"

"Dr. Lui has examined her. She's under observation."

"Because?"

"Because of the bump on her head." The sister smiled reassuringly. "She's fine, the baby's fine. In a few hours you'll be able to take them home."

The door swung shut noiselessly behind her and Chantal closed her eyes. She couldn't bear to see the confusion on his face, couldn't stand the thought of watching it turn to anger. Perhaps he would leave now, as noiselessly as the sister.

When she felt the first tears leaking from the corners of her eyes, she squeezed her lids more tightly shut hoping to contain them, concentrating so hard on staunching them she didn't hear his approach, didn't know he had hunkered down at her side until she felt the touch of his hand, wiping away her tears with a hand that shook. Then kissing them away.

With a long sniffling breath, she managed to ease the flood but not to stop it completely. Through the moist blur she could see his dark scowl, the shadows beneath his eyes, the tightness at the corners of his mouth. She kept her gaze fixed there, away from his eyes, avoiding what she didn't want to know.

"Thank God you're all right. When I heard about your accident…" He trailed off, shaking his head, and she couldn't bear it any longer. Her gaze slid to his, found it and couldn't let go. The sharp intensity of fear, the soft glitter of tears. Oh dear God. *Fear for her; tears for her.* An ache started in her chest, so deep and bittersweet with hope, she could barely breathe. And she had to explain. She had to tell him everything…

"I have to tell you…"

"I saw your car and…"

They both spoke at the same time, both stopped at the same time. Both drew a breath. Chantal's hitched in the middle when he picked up her hands and touched them to his lips.

"I've never been so afraid."

"Me, too. They said the restraints and the air bags stopped me being…" A shudder run through her. The memory, the sound, her fear. "I thought I wouldn't have the chance to tell you."

"About the baby?"

"Yes."

It was no more than a hiss of sound yet it seemed to slither through her, filling her with a new trepidation, an old apprehension. When she tried to pull her hands away, his grip tightened and that lent her strength. Determination.

"I was going to tell you. Today. I heard you were back and I was on my way home…" Her voice shook and she needed to stop. Tears built again, annoying her, frustrating her. She hated this fragility, hated this shakiness.

"That morning..." He paused, studying their joined hands. "Did you go to the doctor?"

"No."

"Too busy?"

She started to shake her head but stopped, flinching. She'd forgotten about the bump. "No. I couldn't. I didn't want to."

His grip on her hands tightened painfully and she looked away, didn't want to see his anger.

"Look, I know you don't want this—"

"What?"

Startled by his loud exclamation, she stared at him openmouthed.

"What makes you think I don't want a baby?"

"Here, the day Bridie was born, as soon as Zane mentioned the 'b' word, you left with the hounds of hell at your heels."

He rocked back, the look on his face almost comically bewildered. "You thought that was because I have an aversion to babies?"

"What else was I to think?"

"Is that why you reacted as you did, said what you did, after the condom business?" His grip on her hands was almost painful. "Were you saying what you thought I *wanted* to hear?"

She nodded, gingerly in deference to her head, and heard him laugh. It sounded like a rough husky mixture of relief and self-derision. It sounded like a glimpse of heaven.

"Talk about misconstruing." He shook his head. "When I saw Zane, the look in his eyes... Hell, there's nothing I want more than babies. Children. Laughter. My home as it should be, like it was when I was a child."

He huffed out a breath full of emotion, anguish hope.

"When I learned what Kristin had done, when I found out that I'd not even had a choice about that child..."

"Kristin was pregnant?"

"Yes, but I didn't know. She didn't ever tell me. She just went and had an abortion and carried on as if she'd been to have a tooth out or something."

Oh dear Lord. This woman was some piece of work. If Chantal weren't trussed up on a hospital stretcher with a head that threatened to explode every time she moved it more than an inch, she would chase her down and do some serious damage.

"I found out after the blowup at work. When I confronted her about that, she tossed in the pregnancy story as well. A going-away present."

"Do you still love her?" Immediately the words left her mouth, she wished them back. "Forget I asked that. Don't answer."

"I don't love her. I don't know if I ever did." The simplicity of that statement blew her away. That and the look in his eyes as he lifted her hands and turned them over, as he pressed a kiss into each palm. "I don't remember ever feeling the way I do about you."

Good answer. No, great *answer.* "How is that?" she asked huskily, needing to hear the words.

"Like I never want to let you go. Like I can't think of living any way but with you by my side. As my friend, my lover, my wife." He kissed the tender skin on the inside of her wrist. "I love you, Chantal and I know this isn't the most romantic place and, hell, I'm not so good with romantic gestures."

Chantal thought he was doing just fine. Especially when he did the down-on-one-knee bit.

"Will you marry me?"

When the stupid choking tears started again, she couldn't do any more than sob out her answer. "Yes." And again in case he didn't hear the first time. "Yes. Yes. Yes." And when he gently kissed her, on her forehead, her cheeks, and finally her lips, she thought her heart would burst with love.

"Will you take me home?"

He laughed, a soft rough-edged sound that hummed over her senses with the same gentleness as his lips. "I'll go see."

"Wait." Her demand pulled him up short of the door. "Come back here."

"Bossy." But he was smiling as he came back to her. "You must be feeling better."

"You have a way with your kisses."

"The healing touch?"

"Apparently." She paused, studying him soberly. The man she loved, the man who would be her husband. Her lifelong lover. "There's something I haven't told you, yet."

"I don't know if I can take any more of your revelations."

"Oh, I think you want to hear this one."

He arced a brow.

"I love you, Cameron Quade. With all my heart. There's nothing I want to do more than be your wife and fill your home with babies."

He smiled as he ducked his head a little, and she thought she caught the glint of tears in his eyes. "Will they all be as bossy as you?" he asked.

"Most probably."

"Good." He nodded with satisfaction and turned on his heel. "I wouldn't have it any other way."

* * * * *

Melanie Milburne says: "I am married to a surgeon, Steve, and have two gorgeous sons, Paul and Phil. I live in Hobart, Tasmania, where I enjoy an active life as a long-distance runner and a nationally ranked top ten Master's swimmer. I also have a Master's Degree in Education, but my children totally turned me off the idea of teaching! When not running or swimming I write and, when I'm not doing all of the above, I'm reading. And if someone could invent a way for me to read during a four-kilometre swim I'd be even happier!"

CHAPTER ONE

IT WAS the screaming siren that annoyed Amy the most. Not to mention the flashing lights, which were totally unnecessary given there wasn't another car in sight and hadn't been for more than an hour on that part of the Western Australian Batavia Coast.

She pulled over to the side of the road and drummed her fingers on the steering-wheel as she watched the officer unfold himself from the police vehicle behind.

He sauntered over with long lazy strides as if he had all the time in the world, which he probably did, she thought with a cynical curl of her lip. He was no doubt below his day's booking quota and had singled her out to nudge it up before he finished his shift.

Amy activated her electric window as he approached and gave him the overly sweet smile that had rarely let her down in the whole twenty-seven years of her life. 'Hi, Officer, was I doing something wrong?' she asked.

'Do you realise what speed you were travelling at, miss?' he asked in a deep voice that contained a heavy dose of reproof.

Hmm, Amy thought. So he's not one to be impressed by a bright white smile. She took off her sunglasses and, using the second weapon in her feminine arsenal, blinked up at him in lash-fluttering innocence with her slate-blue eyes. '*Was* I speeding? I was sure I was well under the limit.'

'I clocked you on my radar doing seventeen kilometres per hour over the legal limit,' he said in the same reproachful tone. 'That's three demerit points and a hefty fine.'

Amy felt a tiny tremor of panic rumble deep inside her. She only had three points left on her licence as it was. If she was to have it revoked out here where there was no public transport worth speaking of, her three-month stint at the isolated medical clinic at Marraburra was going to prove difficult, if not impossible.

OK, this means I will have to rely on weapon number three, she thought as she got out of the car, smoothing down her tight-fitting short denim skirt as she did so.

'May I see your licence?' he asked, still looking at her face and nowhere near her long tanned legs, which produced another twinge of feminine pique inside her.

Amy suppressed a tiny irritated sigh and turning back to her car leaned in and rummaged in her handbag. She dug her licence out from between her stash of credit cards and handed it to him, her fingers coming briefly into contact with his. She felt a sudden jolt of energy pass from his body to hers and snatched her hand back quickly. Jeepers, surely she wasn't getting *that* desperate, she thought with a wry inward grimace. Sure, she hadn't had a man touch her other than a patient since Simon Wyndam had left her more than eighteen months ago, but that didn't mean she had to go all weak at the knees at brushing against a perfect stranger. Although, sneaking a quick glance at him as he examined her licence, she did have to admit he was a rather gorgeous-looking stranger, even if he happened to be a cop.

He was much taller than she had at first realised, and although he was still wearing his hat she could see he had dark brown hair and olive skin that had clearly seen plenty of sun.

The landscape of his face hinted at the man beneath the surface—there was a suggestion of inflexibility in his lean, chiselled jaw and his mouth looked like it rationed its smiles rather sparingly.

'So you're from New South Wales,' he said, removing his sunglasses to meet her eyes.

Amy felt another shock wave go through her when she looked up into the darkest brown eyes she had ever seen. They were fringed with impossibly long sooty eyelashes that partially shielded his gaze from the glare of the late afternoon sun. 'Um…er…yes…' she faltered as her heart did a little flip-flop in her chest.

'Did you drive all the way across the Nullarbor in this?' he asked, giving her cherry-red sports car what could only be described as a scathing glance.

Amy felt her hackles rising. 'No,' she said a little stiffly. 'I had it shipped on the train and drove up here from Perth.'

'Are you aware of the Western Australian maximum speed limit, Miss Tanner?' he asked.

Amy put up her chin. 'It's *Dr* Tanner,' she said with a hint of professional pride.

His top lip lifted slightly in what suspiciously looked like a smirk. 'Well, then, *Dr* Tanner,' he drawled with insulting exactitude, 'I suggest you slow down or you might find yourself without a licence or even worse—without a life.'

'I wasn't speeding,' she bit out, her patience finally running out. 'I had my car set on cruise-control the whole time.'

'Then perhaps you need to have your speedometer recalibrated, Dr Tanner.'

She sent him an icy glare. 'How typical of a cop to blame someone else's equipment when it very well could be yours that's faulty,' she said. 'Have *you* had yours checked to see if it's working as it should?'

His dark eyes gleamed with a spark of sardonic amusement. 'I can assure you, Dr Tanner, there's absolutely nothing wrong with any of my equipment.'

For some inexplicable reason Amy's eyes dipped to his middle where his gun belt was hanging with all its impressive attachments on his lean waist. She felt her cheeks flare with colour and forced her gaze upwards to meet his black-brown eyes.

'Are you going to book me?' she asked, resorting to one last attempt at her eyelash-fluttering routine which had got her out of more tight spots than she could remember.

He appeared to give the matter some thought, his tongue moving inside his cheek as he looked down at her. Amy tried not to squirm under his scrutiny, but as each pulsing second passed she felt as if his eyes were seeing things she would much prefer to keep hidden.

'I'm going to give you a warning this time,' he said at last. 'But you need to remember these are unfamiliar roads to you, with long stretches between towns. You're not only putting your own life at risk but those of others. Medical help is not around the next bend either—it's a four-hour road trip to Geraldton, or a flight with the Royal Flying Doctor Service.'

Amy had to bite back her stinging retort. Who did he think he was, giving her a roadside lecture on road safety awareness? She had done enough trauma training to know the risks. And apart from those few little suburban speeding tickets on her record, which had more to do with revenue-raising by the district police force than lack of care on her part, she was a perfectly capable and safe driver.

'Thank you,' she said, with a measure of forced gratitude. 'I'll try to be more careful in future.'

He put his sunglasses back on. 'Where are you heading to?' he asked.

'Marraburra,' she answered.

'Are you touring or visiting someone?'

'I'm…going there to work,' she said, hoping he hadn't noticed her slight hesitation. 'I'm doing a three-month locum at the medical clinic.'

'So you're filling in for Jacqui Ridley, are you?'

'Yes,' she said. 'She's taken maternity leave.'

A small silence swirled in the hot dusty air for a moment. Amy couldn't help wondering if he was deliberately allowing it to continue to force her to reveal her real reason for taking such an out-of-the-way and short-term post. It was a cop tactic she was well used to, but there was no way she was going to tell him she was here to visit the place where her cousin Lindsay had recently committed suicide.

'Jacqui's husband is one of the other police officers in town,' he finally said, replacing his sunglasses. 'There are four of us stationed at Marraburra.'

Amy said the first thing that came into her head. 'That seems rather a lot of cops for such a remote area.'

'Maybe, but, then, it seems to me rather a long way to come for just three months,' he countered neatly. 'You'll hardly have time to unpack before you leave again.'

Amy wondered what motivation was lurking behind the casually delivered comment. There was something about the cop's demeanour that, in spite of the dark impenetrable screen of his sunglasses, suggested he was watching her closely. But, then, she reminded herself, a lot of cops saw everyone as a potential criminal—he was probably no different.

'Perhaps, but I've not long come back from England,' she said. 'I was at a loose end so I thought I'd take this post until I decide what I want to do.'

'Seems reasonable,' he said, but Amy couldn't help feeling his tone suggested he thought otherwise.

'Well,' she said, stretching her mouth into a tight smile. 'I'd better let you get back to what you're supposed to be doing.'

'This is what I'm supposed to be doing,' he said. 'But I'm just about to knock off.'

'So I was the last hope of the day, was I?' she asked, and then added before she could stop herself, 'One last ticket to impress the boss.'

'Actually,' he said, removing his sunglasses once more to meet her up-tilted gaze, 'I *am* the boss. The only person I have to impress out here is me.'

Amy felt the wind taken right out of her self-righteous sails. He didn't look old enough to be the senior officer in town—he was maybe thirty-three or -four, according to her rough reckoning. But then she saw the stripes on his shirt which indicated he held the rank of sergeant.

A man in his reproductive prime. Her mother's voice echoed in her ears. She hastily shoved the thought aside. Her mother was desperate for grandchildren. Whenever she could, she purposely wound up Amy's biological clock. Not that Amy needed any help in that department; she could feel it ticking like a time bomb herself every time she thought of her ex-boyfriend Simon and his new wife and baby son.

'Well, no doubt I'll see you around some time,' she said, affecting an airy tone.

'No doubt.'

She shifted from foot to foot and gave him another on-off smile. 'Er… Could I have my licence back?' she asked.

He handed it to her, his fingers meeting hers again. 'It's not such a great photo,' he said indicating the wide-eyed mug shot on her licence.

Amy wasn't sure what to make of his comment. She hadn't thought it *that* bad. She'd had her chestnut hair specially highlighted and had even put on some make-up, but she had to admit the prior weekend on call had probably taken its toll regardless. She stuffed it back in her purse without responding and got back behind the wheel.

'Take care when driving at dusk,' he added. 'The kangaroos are as big as horses out here. If you hit one in a car this size you're going to come off second best.'

'Thank you for the safety lecture, Sergeant,' she said tersely. 'But I do know how to drive. I might have spent the last year overseas but I am well aware of the dangers on Australian roads.'

'The biggest danger out here is excessive speed. Keep an eye on it, Dr Tanner,' he said, and, tapping her car on the roof with his hand, walked back to his car.

Amy watched in her rear-vision mirror as his long legs ate up the short distance, his broad shoulders having to almost hunch together to get back into the car as he slid back behind the wheel.

She was familiar enough with cops, city or country, to know he wouldn't pull out until she did so. She flicked on her indicator and, checking for traffic—she used the term loosely by Sydney and London standards—pulled out and drove at a snail's pace, with him on her heels the whole way into the tiny remote settlement of Marraburra.

The township was even smaller than she had been expecting and in spite of her personal mission she felt her heart begin to sink. It was going to be a long three months. What on earth did people do out here to keep themselves occupied? she wondered as she drove past the small general store, a café-cum fish and chip shop, the rundown-looking hotel with a pub attached where she had booked in to stay, and a single service station. There was a shoebox-sized post office and a tiny pharmacy which was located next to the medical clinic.

She turned into the clinic parking area and watched as the

police car continued on, three blocks down the street to where the police station was situated.

The late afternoon heat was fierce as she got out of the car, and she could hardly wait to get into the cool air-conditioned clinic.

A middle-aged woman looked up from the reception desk as Amy came in. 'Can I help you?' she asked.

'Hi. I'm Amy Tanner, the new GP filling in for Dr Ridley. I've just arrived in town,' Amy said with a friendly smile.

'Oh, Dr Tanner—it's so nice to meet you, Amy.' The woman got to her feet and, proffering her hand over the counter, gave her a firm handshake. 'I'm Helen Scott, the receptionist for the clinic. We've been looking forward to you arriving.'

'Thank you,' Amy said. 'It's great to be here at last. It was a long drive.'

Helen gave her a knowing smile. 'It's a long drive to anywhere out here. You get used to it. You've been in London for the past year, Allan Peddington, our other GP, was telling me. This will be a right change from that, I imagine.'

'I'm looking forward to the challenge of working in a remote area,' Amy said. 'And I've never been to Western Australia before so it will be a bit of an adventure.'

'We've organised a little welcome thing for you down at the pub tonight,' Helen said. 'You can meet some of the locals. The hotel's where you're staying, isn't it?'

Amy couldn't help wondering if her plan to stay at the hotel had been the right decision. She had reasoned when she'd booked in that it was only going to be for three months, and while she hadn't been expecting the Ritz, the Dolphin View had looked a lot less attractive as she'd driven past just now than the Marraburra website had portrayed.

'Yes,' she said distantly. 'I thought it would be close to the clinic.'

'Well, it's certainly close to everything, but that might not be what you want after a hard day's work,' Helen said, confirming Amy's suspicions. 'If it doesn't work out I know someone who has a spare room for rent at his house near the beach at Marraburra Point. He had a boarder move out a couple of weeks ago. It's about a fifteen-minute drive from here but well worth the view. '

'I'll keep that in mind,' Amy said, privately hoping she wouldn't have to resort to sharing a house with a perfect stranger after what had happened to her in London. The all-night parties and constant stream of women trailing in and out to visit her flatmate Dylan Janssen had nearly driven her crazy.

'Allan's been called away on a family matter but he'll see you tonight at the pub with the rest of us, say, about seven?' Helen said.

'Seven. Great,' Amy said, dreaming of lying flat in bed after her long drive. 'Do you mind if I have a quick look around the clinic? So I'm a bit more prepared.'

'Sure,' Helen said, and got to her feet with a smile. 'But there's not a lot to see. It won't take long.'

Amy followed the older woman as she showed her through the small two-doctor practice. Apart from basic resuscitation equipment, portable X-ray machine and the standard equipment trolley with its array of bandages and dressings, and one bed for stabilising patients prior to transfer, there was nothing in the way of the high-tech medical gear she'd grown used to working with in a large teaching hospital. But then she reminded herself she wasn't here to further her career. She was here to find out what had led her cousin to take her own life.

'Allan will explain the details about patient transfer to you tomorrow,' Helen said. 'But as you've already seen, this is a remote area. We have a volunteer ambulance, the guys are trained to St John's Ambulance standard. A paramedic ambulance has to come up from Geraldton, or we have to call in the Flying Doctor Service.'

'I understand,' Amy said. 'So what about nursing support? How many do you have attached to the clinic?'

'Well, we only have two nurses at the moment,' she said. 'We could do with more but it's hard to fill country posts nowadays—no one wants to give up the high life in the city.'

Amy knew all about the difficulty of attracting good staff to isolated areas. The long hours and lack of back-up always took their toll in the end. She had even toyed with the idea herself, quite fancying the idea of getting to know one's patients more intimately than the time constraints of working in a large busy city practice allowed, but she knew her mother would have a blue fit if she lived so far away. As it was, Grace Tanner had flown to London three times in the year Amy had spent there.

'What about community support for the elderly or mentally ill?' she asked.

A shadow passed briefly over the older woman's features. 'We do what we can but it's pretty ad hoc,' she admitted, returning to her chair behind the counter. 'If people don't ask for help it's hard to give it to them.' She paused for a moment before adding, 'We had a suicide a few months back. In a community as small as this, everyone feels guilty.'

'Who committed suicide?' Amy asked, hoping she sounded just casually interested.

Helen's sun-lined forehead became even more furrowed. 'A woman in her early thirties,' she said. 'She was an artist, not a professional one—she sort of just dabbled, if you know what I mean. She was a bit of a loner, kept to herself most of the time. She lived in a tiny shack out near the dunes at Caveside Cove a bit further round from Marraburra Point.'

'Was there any indication she was contemplating ending her life?' Amy asked.

Helen's grey gaze flickered again with the shadow Amy had

een earlier. 'I don't usually talk about this but my younger brother committed suicide when he was nineteen,' she said. 'It was such a shock. No one suspected a thing. He'd broken up with his girlfriend but no one thought it would cause him to take his life. In Lindsay Redgrove's case, however, at least there was a history of depression and mental illness.'

'I'm so sorry about your brother,' Amy said gently, thinking of what her uncle and aunt had gone through. 'It must have been truly devastating for you and your parents.'

'They never got over it,' Helen said with haunting sadness. 'None of us have really, even after all these years. That's why I feel so damned guilty about Lindsay. I can't help feeling I could have done something to stop her. There are a few of us around here who feel like that.'

'Was she close to anyone in particular?' Amy asked.

'One or two of the locals got to know her a bit,' Helen said. 'And I always stopped to chat to her whenever she came into town or the clinic. But as I said, she pretty much kept to herself. She didn't make friends easily. I think it had something to do with her background. I heard she'd been institutionalised when she was younger. She didn't trust people much.'

Amy was cautious about asking too many pertinent questions. 'So she was pretty eccentric, then?'

'Yes, she was a quirky sort of person—childlike in a sort of a way, innocent and a bit naïve at times. Some people around here thought she was mad. But from what I saw, as long as she took her medication she was fine.'

Even though Amy knew the circumstances of her cousin's death she thought it was appropriate to continue her line of questioning. 'How did she take her life?'

'An overdose of the medication she was on.'

'Did she leave a note?'

'No, but the coroner's report along with the investigating

officer's said the same—it was suicide, nothing more…
Helen said.

Amy frowned at the receptionist's left-hanging-in-the-air tone.
'But you have some reservations about that verdict?' she asked.

Helen gave her a smile touched with sadness. 'When my
brother took his life so suddenly and unexpectedly I was determined someone must have done it, you know—murdered
him. He didn't leave a note either. But Lindsay's parents
seemed resigned to the fact that at some stage she was going
to end it all. Apparently she'd tried a few times in her teens
before she was diagnosed with a mental disorder, and a couple
of times afterwards. I can't help thinking they felt it was almost
a relief to put it all behind them. They came and took some of
her paintings and a few personal belongings but her shack is
still out there, as if she's going to walk back in any minute.'
She gave a little shudder and added, 'I took a small wreath I'd
made out there just after she died but the place gave me the
creeps the whole time I was there.'

'Why is that?' Amy asked.

Helen gave her upper arms a rub with her hands, as if
warding off a chill. 'It's never been a particularly popular
beach—too far from any conveniences—and to make it worse
a couple of teenagers were killed about twenty years ago when
a rockfall occurred in one of the caves they were camping in.
The surf out there is rough and there's usually a big undertow
so the locals more or less keep to the main beach at
Marraburra.' She gave Amy a sheepish look and confessed, 'I
know this is going to sound really dumb but a lot of people
around here think the place is haunted. I don't know why
Lindsay wanted to live way out there in the first place. I certainly wouldn't.'

'Perhaps she enjoyed the solitude. A lot of creative types
enjoy being alone to reflect on their work,' Amy said.

Helen smiled. 'You know, it's a real shame you didn't come here when Lindsay Redgrove was still alive. I have the feeling you would have got on with her famously. You seem to have the right attitude to mental illness. Let me tell you a lot of people around here aren't as understanding.'

Amy hoped her guilt at not revealing her true connection to Lindsay wasn't showing on her face. 'Thank you,' she said, and added wryly, 'I'm glad *you* think so.'

Helen's brows rose slightly. 'Have you had trouble with someone already?'

'I was pulled over by a cop coming in to town,' she said. 'I was bang on the speed limit but he wouldn't listen. Told me my speedometer was faulty.'

'Did he give you a ticket?'

'No, he gave me a warning and a bit of a lecture.'

Helen's expression softened. 'That would be Sergeant Ford. You should consider yourself lucky. He's got a real thing about speeding, but he's all right when you get to know him.'

'I'm not planning on getting to know him,' Amy said determinedly. 'My father was a cop. He made my mother's and my life hell until he left when I was nine.'

'I suppose there are good and bad cops just like there are good and bad doctors,' Helen offered.

'I guess you're right,' Amy said, suddenly regretting her uncharacteristic disclosure. She hardly ever spoke of her father to anyone. She hadn't seen him in years—the last she'd heard he'd left the force and was living in an alcoholic haze with his fourth wife.

'You'd better go and check in at the hotel,' Helen said. 'Don't dress up for tonight. Everyone's pretty casual around here, even the cops.'

Yeah, right, Amy thought cynically as the dark, serious features of the highway patrol officer came to mind when she

CHAPTER TWO

THE pub was stuffy and crowded and smelt of beer and perspiration as Amy walked in to check into her room. Every head swivelled to look at her, the sudden silence making her feel like a piece of meat in a piranha tank—every eye was assessing her and she couldn't help noticing that every one of them was male.

The bartender gave the bar a quick wipe with a cloth as he directed a roving eye over her chest before meeting her eyes. 'So you must be the new doctor.'

'Yes,' Amy said, amazed at the speed of the town's grapevine. 'Amy Tanner.'

'Bill Huxley,' he said and stretched out a massive paw of a hand to grip hers. 'Your room's ready upstairs, number three. I'll get the key for you.'

Amy surreptitiously massaged her crushed fingers as he lumbered away for the key.

'I wonder if there's anyone who could help me upstairs with my things?' she asked as he returned and handed the key over the bar.

A snicker of laughter came from behind her and a slurred voice called out. 'There aren't any bell boys here, girlie. But buy me a drink and I'll ashist you to your room.'

Amy turned to see a man in his mid to late forties leering at

her, a beer in one hand and several more empty ones on the table
where he was sitting. She drew in a tight breath and sent him
a polite smile. 'Thanks for the offer,' she said, 'but actually
think I can manage.'

'Put a lid on it, Carl,' Bill Huxley said, and addressing
Amy added, 'Don't mind him, he's had one too many like the
rest of them in here. I'll get your stuff up to your room a
soon as I can.'

'Thank you, Bill,' she said and made her way to the rickety
staircase which led to the upper floor. She came to the door with
a number three hanging lopsidedly on it, and as she opened i
she was surprised the window on the opposite wall wasn'
broken by the doorknob, the space inside was so limited. The
room itself looked clean enough. The narrow single bed was
made up with a faded orange chenille bedspread which made
her think longingly of her queen-size orthopaedic-approved
mattress, fluffy down pillows and superfine Egyptian cotton
quilt and sheet set on the other side of the continent.

The floorboards creaked noisily as she took the two steps
across to the small window, the heat from the afternoon sun
hitting her in the face like a slap as she pulled the worn curtains
aside. She fanned her burning face with her hands and blew ou
a breath, her shoulders sagging as the three months stretching
ahead of her suddenly became even more daunting.

She turned and out of the corner of her eye saw a dark black
shape scuttle across the floor and disappear beneath the bed
Fear clogged her throat and her heart began to hammer errati
cally as she imagined those eight hairy legs making a pathway
across her pillow some time during the night. She forced herself
to breathe through her panic, taking deep controlled breaths tha
were supposed to help her confront and deal with her phobia
as the very expensive cognitive behaviour therapist she had seen
in London had promised.

There was a knock at the door and she edged her way along the wall well away from the bed to answer it, her eyes going wide when she saw the police officer she'd met earlier standing there with her luggage in his hands.

'Oh...' she said, flushing furiously.

'Bill asked me to bring these up,' he said. 'Where do you want them?'

'Um...' She stepped back to let him in and said hesitantly, 'Anywhere's...er...fine.'

He placed her two bulging suitcases and doctor's bag on the floor next to the bed and straightened. Suddenly the room seemed a whole lot smaller, and not just because of her over-sized luggage. It felt as if someone had sucked most of the air out of the room, leaving only a tiny ration that made her feel as if every breath she took in was somehow connected to him.

He was out of uniform now, dressed in jeans and a close-fitting white T-shirt that showed off his toned body to perfection. In fact, he had muscles in places she hadn't even seen in *Grant's Atlas of Anatomy*.

'I'm Angus, by the way,' he said, offering her his hand. 'Angus Ford.'

Amy slipped her hand into the dry solid warmth of his, the brush of his slightly calloused fingers sending a current of electricity through her all over again.

'How are you settling in?' he asked, releasing her hand.

'Um...fine...' she said, trying not to glance past him nervously.

He gave the room a sweeping glance before returning his eyes to hers. 'It can get quite noisy here. If you can't handle it let me know and I'll organise alternative accommodation. I have a spare room for rent at my place if you're interested.'

So *he* was the one with the spare room. Spiders or no spiders, there was no way she going to share a house with him! He'd probably book her for sleeping in or leaving a cup unwashed or something.

'I'm sure this will be perfectly fine,' she said with a tiny hitch of her chin.

He held her look for a little longer than was necessary. 'I suggest you lock your door at night,' he said. 'The natives can get a little restless out there.'

'I'm a big girl, Sergeant Ford,' she said, straightening her shoulders. 'I can look after myself.'

It was absolutely typical, Amy thought, that that wretched spider chose exactly that moment to make its next curtain call. She watched in frozen horror as it made its way up the curtain from behind her bed. Even though she desperately tried to contain her reaction, her legs began shaking and her palms became sticky from the rush of adrenalin flooding her system.

'Is everything all right?' Angus asked, frowning at her expression.

'Er…' Amy began to flap her hands in panic, her months of therapy completely obliterated when the spider paused on the wall as if deciding which direction to take next. 'Th-there's a big hairy spider behind you… *Oh, no!*' she screeched as it dropped from the wall to land in a grotesque configuration on her pillow. 'Get it off! *Get it off!* Oh, my God, get that thing out of here!'

Angus calmly picked up the pillow and carried it to the window where he released the spider before turning back to face her with an amused expression on his darkly handsome face.

Amy glared at him before he could speak. 'Don't you dare, *dare* laugh at me,' she said through tight lips.

His lips twitched but didn't make the full distance into a smile. They didn't need to, she noted with resentment. His dark brown eyes were more than doing the job for them.

'Don't tell me a big girl like you is scared of a tiny spider,' he said with a faint trace of mockery in his tone.

'All right, I won't tell you,' she responded tartly. 'And it wasn't tiny—it was huge.'

'It was completely harmless,' he said. 'We get them all the time during the dry season.'

Amy gave a visible shiver and hated that he saw it. 'I don't care what season they like, as long as they stay out of my room and out of my bed,' she said.

'My offer of a room still stands if you find the company here a little offputting.'

'Thanks but, no, thanks,' she said, pleased that her terse response had hit the mark. She saw the way his eyes hardened slightly as if he wasn't used to having women say no to him, and privately congratulated herself.

But as if to test her resolve a ruckus suddenly erupted downstairs, the shouts and swearing and overturned chairs echoing like thunder through the floorboards.

Angus stepped towards the door. 'I'd better sort this out. Let me know if you change your mind.'

'I won't be changing my—' she said, but he'd already gone.

Amy winced as she heard another chair hit the floor and then listened as Angus's deep authoritative voice sounded out. 'Come on, Carl, give it a break. Time to go home, mate, and sleep it off.'

'You can flaming well go to hell,' she heard Carl shout, throwing in a few choice expletives for good measure. 'I want another drink now!'

There was the sound of another scuffle and a glass breaking, as well as a few grunts as a punch or two landed on someone.

Amy couldn't stop herself from rushing from her room to see if help was needed. She raced downstairs to see Angus Ford restraining Carl with one hand, the muscles of his arm bulging as he led him to the door by the scruff of the neck. Angus's other hand was dabbing a handkerchief at his left eyebrow, which was bleeding profusely.

'You'd better get the doc here to see to that eye of yours, Sarge,' Bill said as he tried to right what was left of one of the chairs.

'I'll be fine,' Angus ground out, and tightened his hold on the struggling Carl.

Amy watched helplessly as Angus hauled the drunken man outside, bundling him down the street towards the police station.

'He won't even remember that tomorrow,' Bill said, coming to stand next to her in the doorway.

She turned to look at him. 'Carl, you mean?'

He nodded grimly. 'He shouldn't drink on the medication he's on, but what can you do? He lost his wife and two little daughters in a road accident a couple of years back. He drinks to forget.'

'How terribly sad,' she said. 'What medication is he on?'

Bill's lip curled. 'Antidepressant of some kind. Waste of money if you ask me. Nothing's going to bring Julie and his little girls back. Nothing.'

Amy frowned as she looked at the two men in the distance— Angus tall and in control, and the broken, stumbling, drunken man beside him. She'd had no idea such a small town could contain such drama and sadness.

'You'd better go down and see to Angus's eye,' Bill said. 'Allan Peddington won't be back from Geraldton yet. Looks to me like it needs stitching up.'

Amy frowned as the hotel owner went back inside. Then, blowing out a little sigh, she went upstairs to collect her doctor's bag, came back down and walked the short distance to the police station.

The police station was actually a small house which had been modified to serve its new purpose. On a pole by the front gate was a white sign with POLICE painted in blue letters on both sides. It looked as if someone had used it for target practice as it was pockmarked with four or five rusty bullet holes. The front verandah had been filled in, and there were metal grilles on the windows. Amy opened the front door, and entered the front office, which was adorned with the usual array of missing-person posters and police notices pinned to corkboards on the walls, and a tall counter, behind which sat Angus Ford, pressing his now bloodstained handkerchief to his eye. From some-where in the rear of the house emanated muffled bursts of slurred expletives interspersed with the occasional sob.

He looked up as she approached the front desk, his dark brown gaze containing a hint of annoyance. 'What can I do for you, Dr Tanner?' he asked as he got to his feet. 'Or have you changed your mind about my offer?'

'No,' Amy said. 'I'm here because that eye looks like it needs medical attention.'

'I'll see Allan Peddington when he gets back from out of town,' he said, and turned back to the papers on the desk.

Amy stood in a seething silence. How dared he dismiss her as if she were a schoolgirl?

'Do you have something against female doctors or is it just women in general?' she asked with a glittering look.

His head came up and his gaze pinned hers. 'On the ex-tremely rare occasions when I have been unwell, or in need of medical attention, I have been Allan Peddington's patient. I see no point in switching now, irrespective of your sex or your skill.'

'Dr Peddington is not present and in my expert medical opinion you need to have at least two or three stitches in that cut, and soon, otherwise it will leave a nasty scar if the edges aren't pulled together properly,' she informed him in her best stern doctor's voice.

There was another brittle silence; even the noise from Carl in the lock-up out back had stopped.

'Will you at least let me take a closer look at it?' she asked.

She heard the slow release of his breath as he moved across

to open the waist-high barrier that separated the office from the front. 'All right,' he said. 'But make it snappy. I've got to run Carl home once he cools down.'

'Is there anywhere you can lie down?' Amy asked.

'Not unless I bunk down with Carl, so whatever you have to do, do it here,' he said with increasing impatience as he rolled his chair back and sat down.

Amy opened her doctor's bag, took out a sterile pad and applied it to quell the trickle of blood running down his face.

'Sorry if this hurts,' she said, annoyed that her voice sounded scratchy instead of in control and doctor-like. She suddenly realised she was practically standing between his open thighs, their hard muscular presence so close she felt a tiny flicker of nervousness, or was it excitement?

Don't be stupid, she remonstrated with herself. He's a cop, remember? You don't do cops or control freaks and he's both.

She checked the bleeding after a moment, trying not to notice the citrus grace notes of his aftershave as they drifted towards her nostrils. 'It needs three stitches,' she said. Looking down at his blood-spattered T-shirt, she added, 'Perhaps you'd better take your T-shirt off. Have you got something else you can put on?'

'I've got a police shirt in the cupboard out back,' he said as he hauled his T-shirt over his head and tossed it to one side.

Amy had trouble keeping her eyes from widening as she took in his pectoralis majors and his six-pack of rectus abdominus muscles, deciding she would never be able to look at *Grant's Atlas* in quite the same way again.

She distracted herself by concentrating on drawing up 10 ml of 1 per cent xylocaine with adrenalin. 'This is going to sting for a minute,' she warned him, and injected the local anaesthetic into the edges of the wound after swabbing it with antiseptic. But unlike every other patient into whom she had injected local anaesthetic, Sergeant Angus Ford didn't even flinch.

She opened a small suture pack from her bag and onto it opened a 4/0 nylon, some sterile gauze squares and a squirt of cetrimide, then donned a pair of sterile gloves. After swabbing the wound and putting a couple of gauze squares onto his eye to soak up the diminishing trickle of blood, she inserted three sutures, bringing the edges of the cut together and stopping the bleeding.

'There,' she said. 'That's better. I'll put a sticking plaster on it now and you can change it each day. I'll need to remove the sutures in five or six days. Are you up to date with your tetanus cover, do you know?'

'Yes.' Then after a small pause he added, 'Thanks. You can send me the bill.'

She shifted her eyes from the dark brown intensity of his. 'There's no charge,' she said as she stripped off her gloves and began clearing away the mess.

'I wonder if I had booked you, as I intended doing, would you have said the same?' he mused as he got to his feet. 'Or perhaps I redeemed myself by removing your eight-legged roommate.'

She turned back to face him. 'It's not too late to slap a speeding fine on me if that's what you want to do, Sergeant Ford. Is that how you get your kicks out here? Charging innocent people with made-up offences to pass the time?'

The slight, almost undetectable tightening of his mouth was the only clue that he was irritated by her jibe. 'How many road accidents have you attended, Dr Tanner?' he asked.

Amy disguised a small swallow. 'Not many...'

'How many?'

'Er...none...' She felt her face grow hot.

'You city doctors are all the same,' he bit out, this time not bothering to conceal his anger. 'By the time the casualties get to you they've been patched up by the ambos or concealed in a body bag. You don't have a clue what it's like to be the first on the scene, identifying bodies, some of them your own friends, locating body parts and who knows what else. You need to think about *that* the next time you get behind the wheel of your fancy little high-performance sports car, *Dr* Tanner.'

Amy stood her ground but only as a matter of personal pride. She knew her experience at the coal face was limited; she had done the Early Management of Severe Trauma course and passed it easily, admittedly with mock-up patients and scenarios, but that didn't mean she wouldn't be able to handle a real-life emergency and she resented him for implying it.

'You really do have a problem with women, don't you, Sergeant?' she said. 'Tell me something, are you married?'

His dark brows snapped together. 'What sort of question is that?'

'If you are, I pity your wife,' she said. 'I bet you'd slap a ticket on her for smiling without your permission. I've met cops like you before—total control freaks who like to push their weight around just for the heck of it.'

'I'm not married,' he said. 'Not that it's any of your business. But while we're on the subject of personal questions, I've got a couple of my own.'

She drew herself up to her full height but he still seemed to tower over her. 'Go on, fire away,' she said.

'What brings a young woman out into the middle of nowhere for only three months?'

'I told you—I'm doing the locum for Jacqui Ridley.'

'And after that?'

'I haven't decided.'

'So there's no boyfriend or husband to go back home to?' he asked.

'No.' As soon as Amy had said it she wished she hadn't. It made her sound desperate and dateless, a woman rapidly approaching thirty with no man in her life.

'This is a rough place, Dr Tanner,' he said. 'It might not look like it on the surface but let me tell you it's not a picnic out here. If you think the spiders are terrifying, wait until you meet some of the locals.'

'Then why are you here?' she asked. 'What made you come to such a dead-end place?'

A shutter seemed to come down over his face. 'It suits me for now,' he answered.

'Well, this suits me for now, too,' she retorted. 'Now, if you'll excuse me, I have to get ready for the town's welcome for me tonight.' She gave him an arch look, and added, 'I don't suppose you'll be coming?'

'I already have something else planned.'

'Fine, then,' she said, surprised at the little nick of disappointment that pierced her. She picked up her bag and, brushing past him, left before she was tempted to ask him what he had planned. It was none of her business. She didn't want to know.

Well…perhaps only a tiny *weeny* bit…

CHAPTER THREE

HELEN was the first to greet Amy as she came downstairs on the dot of seven. 'I'm sorry to tell you that Allan Peddington can't make it,' she said. 'He's been held up in Geraldton. His daughter lives there and she's had some sort of personal crisis. Boyfriend issues, I think.'

'That's OK,' Amy said with a rueful grimace. 'Believe me, I know all about that sort of thing.'

'Come over and meet the rest of the gang,' Helen said, and led her to a cluster of tables. 'Everybody, this is Amy Tanner, the temporary GP filling in for Jacqui.'

'Hi, Amy.' A woman of a similar age to Helen extended her hand. 'I'm Teresa Clarke, one of the nurses, and this is Kathy Leeman, the other one.'

The introductions were made, although Amy had trouble re-membering all their names. But in the end it didn't matter as everyone seemed intent on having a few drinks and kicking back to relax from a hot summer's day.

After a couple of glasses of wine Teresa changed places so she could sit next to Amy. 'Helen told me you got pulled over by our sexy sergeant,' she said, bringing her glass up to her lips, her china blue eyes sparkling.

Amy rolled her eyes and reached for her glass of rather

dubious red. 'Yes, he did, but fortunately he let me off with a warning.'

'You were lucky. He's not usually so lenient,' Teresa said. 'He's got a real thing about speeding. We've all learned the hard way to keep under the limit. He makes few allowances. Even for friends, not that he gets too close to people. I guess because his plan is to eventually move back to Perth.'

'He doesn't strike me as the friendly type,' Amy commented.

'Angus is certainly a bit reserved,' Teresa said. 'Aloof, if you know what I mean. But, then, some women find that very attractive.'

'Well, I don't.' Amy mentally kicked herself for responding so quickly and emphatically.

Teresa gave her a knowing look that instantly reminded her of her mother. 'So what made you decide to come all the way out here for three months?' she asked.

Amy shifted her gaze, uncomfortable with concealing the truth about why she had travelled so far. 'I spent the last year in London and felt like I needed to have some breathing space before I decide what to do next. A stint out in the bush seemed like a good idea.'

'This is about as far away as you can get from a big city,' Teresa said. 'I'm used to it now but I hated it at first.'

'So why did you come here?'

'My husband is a fitter and turner on a fishing boat,' she said. 'I suppose you know how rich these shores are in terms of fishing. He's away a lot on the boat, but now the kids are grown up it suits me to work at the clinic to fill in the time.'

'How many kids do you have?'

'Three boys,' Teresa answered with a proud smile. 'They all live in Perth but we see them every couple of months. But what about you? Who have you left pining for you on the other side of the country?'

Amy's mouth twisted. 'No one apart from my mother,' she said. 'I had a boyfriend a year or so back but he moved on. He's married with a little baby now.'

Teresa winced in empathy. 'That must have hurt.'

'It did but I'm more or less over it now.'

'The change will do you good,' Teresa said wisely. 'You never know, you might like it so much you could end up staying longer. It wouldn't be the first time it's happened.'

Amy looked into the contents of her glass. 'I guess I'll take it one day at a time.'

'Oh, look who's turned up,' Teresa said. 'You must have made an impression after all.'

Amy looked up to lock gazes with Sergeant Angus Ford. She just as quickly looked away again but she could feel the creep of colour seep into her cheeks all the same. She picked up her glass and drained the contents, hoping her head wouldn't punish her for it in the morning.

She watched covertly as Angus approached Bill at the bar, exchanging a few words and accepting what looked like a soda water before he came over to where Teresa made a space for him right next to her.

'What did you do to your eye?' Teresa asked.

'I ran into a drunken door,' he answered dryly.

'How's Carl?' Helen leaned across the table to ask. 'I heard he was on a bit of a bender this afternoon.' Her eyes went to his brow momentarily. 'Looks like he was pretty tanked if you copped that from him.'

'He was, but he's sleeping it off at home now,' he answered. 'I'll go and check on him in the morning.'

'How's your wound feeling?' Amy asked.

His dark brown gaze met hers, a glint of challenge lurking there. 'As you see, I haven't bled to death as yet.'

'You should take care for the next few days,' she said, her

mouth pursing slightly. 'The slightest knock can make head wounds bleed a lot.'

'I've got it under control.'

Amy wasn't quite sure how it happened but suddenly it seemed as if everyone else had moved away, leaving her alone with him. She felt the awkward silence nudge her for inspiration but for the life of her couldn't think of a single thing to fill it.

'Would you like another drink?' Angus asked.

Amy was caught off guard. Her eyes flicked to her empty glass and back to his, but before she could say a word he had got to his feet and spoken to Bill. He came back with a glass of something that looked a whole lot smoother than what she'd been drinking and set it down in front of her.

'I figured since you're staying upstairs you won't drink and drive,' he said.

'Thank you,' she said, and stiffening in affront added, 'But just for the record, I don't drink and drive.'

He ignored her comment to inform her, 'Bill keeps the good stuff out the back. You don't look like the cask type.'

She picked up the glass and sent him a pointed look. 'I thought you had something already planned for this evening.'

He inspected the slice of lemon in his glass before meeting her eyes, his dark gaze all of a sudden very direct and cop-like. 'Why didn't you tell me you were Lindsay Redgrove's cousin?' he asked. 'In fact, why have you not told anyone?'

Amy felt the colour drain from her face. Her fingers holding her glass gave a betraying tremble and her stomach felt as if it had been sucked of all its contents, the sudden hollowness making her feel faint. 'I can't imagine how you came by that information,' she said by way of stalling.

He leaned back in his chair in an indolent manner. 'I'm a cop. I make it my business to know everything about everyone who drifts into town.'

'So you're the control freak I first assumed,' she said. 'I knew it the minute I met you. Exerting public power is important to people like you because you lack it in your personal life.'

He lifted one shoulder in a shrug that indicated it didn't bother him in the least what she thought of him. 'It seems rather a coincidence that you've taken this temporary post,' he said. 'Weren't you satisfied with the coroner's verdict on your cousin's death?'

Amy was wary about revealing her concerns to anyone, and in particular to one of the police officers who had investigated the death of her cousin. She hadn't even gone as far as admitting them to herself. Lindsay had been a suicide threat ever since her first attempt at the age of seventeen, but as the senior officer in town it seemed Angus Ford would be the last person she would be able to confide in. He would have overseen the CIB and forensics investigation and sent his report to the coroner.

'I hadn't seen Lindsay for three years or so,' she said. 'She wrote to me once or twice and told me she loved it here. I wanted to visit the place where she had found the most happiness and I guess to pay my last respects.'

'You didn't go to her memorial service.'

Amy wasn't sure if he had stated a fact, asked a question or delivered a criticism. 'No,' she said. 'I was unable to get back from London in time.'

He leaned back in his chair, the ice cubes in his glass rattling together slightly. 'It was a nice ceremony,' he said. 'She would have liked it.'

Her eyes flared with surprise. '*You* went to my cousin's funeral?'

He gave a brief nod. 'I had to fly to Sydney on another matter so it was a chance to kill two birds…' His mouth twisted ruefully, 'Sorry—wrong choice of words. It was a chance to pay my respects.'

'How well did you know Lindsay?' she asked.

'As well as anyone else around here did,' he answered. 'She was a loner, didn't seem to need people around her. She was mostly aloof and unreachable unless she wanted to connect with someone, but even then it was always only a temporary thing.'

'Like you?' Amy found herself asking, recalling Helen's words about him, which he had practically used verbatim.

His black-brown unspeaking gaze prolonged the silence, making the tension in the air crackle between them.

'You're rather quick to make character assessments, aren't you, Dr Tanner?' he said with a derisive twist to his mouth. 'You only met me…what is it now…three or four hours ago and you think you've got me all figured out.'

'I know enough about body language to be able to read the "Keep Away" sign you have permanently etched on your face,' she retorted.

The right side of his mouth tipped up even more mockingly. '"Keep Away" sign, huh?'

'Yes.' She straightened her spine and sent him a fixed glare. 'You don't trust people, particularly women.'

'I'm a cop,' he said, running his eyes over her in an assessing manner. 'It's my job to be suspicious.'

'Not everyone is a criminal.'

'Perhaps not. But everyone is a potential one, don't you agree?' he said.

'No, of course I don't agree,' she said. 'I know plenty of people who've never done a single thing wrong.'

He pushed his drink to one side and, leaning his forearms on the table separating them, looked deep into her eyes. 'What about you, Dr Tanner?' he asked in a low velvety tone that sent an unexpected trickling hot river of sensation racing up her spine. 'Are you trying to tell me you've never done a single thing wrong in the whole of your life?'

Amy could feel the brush of his knees against hers beneath the table, the intimate contact sending shooting sparks of heat between her thighs. She looked into that fathoms-deep gaze and felt her stomach give a little quiver of unruly desire. It was unlike anything that had ever happened to her before. She had never felt such a powerful physical attraction for anyone so instantly, and what made it all the more bewildering was he was exactly the type of man she had effectively avoided for most of her life. She didn't even like him and he clearly felt the same towards her if the derisive glint in his eyes was to be taken at face value.

'I'm the first to admit I'm not perfect,' she said. 'But I try to be a good citizen, as indeed I believe the majority of people do.'

'Most people, given the opportunity to stretch the boundaries, do so, particularly if they think there's a chance they're going to get away with it,' he said.

'So what about you, Sergeant Ford?' she asked. 'What laws have *you* been tempted to break recently?'

His smouldering gaze travelled slowly, *very* slowly from her eyes to her mouth, and down to the hint of cleavage her close-fitting white top revealed, before doing the return journey with the same lazy indolence. Amy felt as if she may as well have been sitting there stark naked. Her breasts tightened, their peaks thrusting against the stretch fabric of her top, her skin feathering all over with acute awareness of his undisguised male appraisal.

He leant back in his chair, his eyes tethering hers once more. 'I generally try to stay out of trouble,' he said. 'But very occasionally I'm tempted to step over one of my personal boundaries.'

'What sort of boundaries do you mean?' she asked. 'Putting your foot down when no one's looking, parking in a loading zone?'

'No, nothing like that,' he answered. 'More intimate ones.'

Amy sent her tongue out to moisten her suddenly parch-ment-dry lips. 'Like what? Having a one-night stand or some-thing?' she asked.

His eyes glinted with something that made her toes instantly curl. 'Is that a proposition, Dr Tanner?' he asked.

She felt her face flare with scorching heat. 'No, of course not!' she said. 'What sort of person do you think I am? I don't even like you.'

'Liking someone has very little to do with sexual attraction,' he said with another one of his stomach-flipping looks.

Amy couldn't recall a time when she had felt more flustered and out of her depth. 'Just where do you get off, Sergeant?' she asked with caustic bite. 'If you think I'm the least bit interested in becoming involved with an arrogant control freak such as yourself then you really need to have some emergency liposuc-tion done on your overweight ego.'

His sudden laugh nearly made her fall off her chair. It was so unexpected and so very masculine she felt her heart kick in response to the deep, rich sound of it. His lingering smile—the first one she'd seen on his face—totally transformed his features. His eyes crinkled up at the corners, and his cleanly shaven jaw relaxed, giving him a playful air that was devastatingly attractive.

'It's been quite a while since a woman's been able to make me laugh,' he said, still smiling. 'Congratulations.'

She felt an answering smile tug at her mouth but wouldn't allow it purchase and sent him a reproachful glare instead. 'I feel insulted that you assumed I'd jump into bed with you just because you're relatively good-looking.'

Angus couldn't help grinning at her frowning look. She was certainly a cute little thing with her flashing dark blue eyes and pouting mouth. He felt the tightening in his groin when one of her knees bumped his underneath the table, and smiled to himself when he felt her move away as if he had burnt her.

'Only relatively good-looking, huh?' he asked, stretching his legs beneath the table again.

She rolled her eyes at him and shifted even further backwards in her chair. 'I'm not going to force-feed your ego, I'm sure it gets enough nourishment from all the other women in town.'

He didn't answer but sat watching her as she lifted her glass to her lips. Amy felt self-conscious under his scrutiny, her cheeks still felt hot and her skin suddenly felt too tight for her body. She was shocked at her reaction to him. Her body seemed to have a mind of its own when it was anywhere near his. She could feel the thrum of her pulse beneath her skin, her stomach giving little sharp kicks every time his legs brushed against hers.

Was he doing it deliberately? she wondered. She sneaked a glance at him as she reached for her drink but his face had gone all cop-like again, although there was a hint of a smile lurking about his sensual mouth. She wondered what it would feel like to have that mouth on hers, to feel the probe of his tongue, the rasp of his unshaven jaw on her…

Amy was jerked away from her traitorous thoughts when Bill Huxley came over and removed Angus's empty soda-water glass. 'How about a light beer, Sarge?' he asked. 'Surely you've earned it after this afternoon's drama.'

'No, thanks, Bill,' he said. 'I'm on the light stuff tonight.'

'Are you on call?' Amy asked once Bill had left to gather empty glasses from the other tables.

'No, one of the constables is on tonight. I just have to see to something out at the Cove before I head home.'

'Do you mean Caveside Cove?'

He gave a brief nod.

'Helen was telling me that's where my cousin lived,' she said. 'I had always sent her letters via the post office but I thought I might go out and have a look around some time.'

The unreadable mask settled back down on his features like

a curtain coming down on a stage. 'There's nothing out there,' he said. 'It's little more than a lean-to full of spiders and junk. You wouldn't last a minute if this afternoon's arachnophobia routine was any indication.'

'Well, all the same I want to see where Lindsay spent her time,' she said, doing her best to ignore his jibe. 'And her last day…'

'I would advise against it, Dr Tanner. It won't bring her back, and visiting the scene of where a suicide took place can be very distressing, even for distant relatives.'

Amy frowned at him in indignation. 'I'm not a distant relative! She was my only cousin.'

'Whom you never once visited in the whole time she was here,' he said with more than a hint of reproach.

'I was training to be a doctor, for goodness' sake,' she protested. 'And it's a very long way to come. Besides I couldn't afford the time.'

'You can't have been that close to her,' he said. 'She never once mentioned you.'

Amy's resentment rose inside her, bubbling hot. 'She was a very private person, that's why,' she said. 'You said it yourself.'

'Even very private people occasionally mention the most important people in their life.'

'Oh, really?' She arched one brow at him. 'Let's test that little theory of yours, shall we? How about you, Sergeant Ford? You're a private and aloof person—who are the most important people in your life?'

He held her challenging look for several pulsing seconds, making Amy wonder if he was even going to bother to answer.

'My parents, who live in Perth, are important to me,' he finally said.

'Any brothers or sisters?' she asked.

'No, I'm an only child.'

'Is there a woman in your life?' she asked.

There was a tiny, almost undetectable pause.

'Not at present.'

'So that's it?' She frowned at him. 'Your parents and no one else?'

'I have a dog.'

She let out a cynical laugh. 'Yeah, well, I guess that makes sense.'

'What do you mean by that?' he asked, his eyes narrowing slightly.

Amy felt her skin prickle at his tone. 'What sort of dog have you got?' she asked. 'I bet it's not a teacup Chihuahua. '

His top lip lifted slightly. 'He's a German shepherd.'

'That figures as well,' she said. 'You can always tell a person by their dog.'

'What kind of comment is that, Dr Tanner?' He laughed mockingly. 'Perhaps you have something against dogs?'

'I have no problem with dogs,' she returned. 'It's the owners I take issue with. I've seen too many dog attacks on small children to be under any illusions about controlling a large dog. They're instinctive animals and should never be trusted.'

'Are you talking about men or dogs?' Angus countered, stretching his legs again.

Her chair squeaked along the floor as she inched back a fraction. 'You think I have some sort of hang-up about men, don't you?' she said with a withering look.

He laid one arm along the back of the neighbouring chair, the action making his biceps bulge as he met her flashing eyes. 'You have all the signs of a woman recently spurned,' he said.

Amy felt her face glow with betraying colour. 'That's not true,' she spluttered. *Well, it was sort of true,* she had to admit, although not to him. Eighteen months was fairly recent, wasn't it?

His expression indicated he didn't believe her for a second.

She threw him an accusing glare. 'I suppose you've had me

investigated or something, have you? Interviewed a few past boyfriends, got an update on my social life? Is that how you found out I was Lindsay's cousin? Did you run a background check on me?'

'No,' he said. 'I remember your aunt mentioning your name. She also showed me a photo—one that put your licence photo to shame.'

'Oh…' Amy felt herself backing down. She toyed with her drink, wondering if she should just finish it and move on, but something about his summation of her so far intrigued her. How on earth had he guessed about Simon if he hadn't done some sort of check? Was she really giving off such easy-to-read signals? she wondered. Her mother had told her repeatedly to put Simon's betrayal behind her but she had been too busy to even think about dating again.

In fact, up until now she hadn't even been the slightest bit tempted…

'I suppose you know I'm sailing a bit close to the wind on my licence,' she inserted into the silence.

'I did happen to notice that,' he said. 'But don't expect any favours from me out here, Dr Tanner. You might need to drive for your job, but one strike and you're out.'

She tightened her mouth. 'You'd do it, wouldn't you?'

'I'm here to uphold the law and if you're breaking it then naturally we're going to clash.'

Her lip curled contemptuously. 'You remind me of someone I once knew,' she said. 'He never missed a chance to point out a misdemeanour, real or imagined.'

'I take it that would be your father?' he asked.

She stared at him in shock. Had he a sixth sense or what? 'Don't tell me,' she said when she had regained her composure. 'I show the classic signs of a daughter with father issues, right?'

'It seems to me you have issues with men—period.'

Amy decided to swing the conversation back to safer ground. 'You said you were only close to your parents and your dog, but what about your work colleagues?' she asked. 'I would have thought you'd get rather close to them working side by side each day, at times under very trying circumstances.'

'That's to some degree true but it's not always wise to get too attached. It can interfere with how you view their work if you have too close an attachment to them.'

She screwed up her mouth at him. 'You really have cynicism down to an art, don't you?'

'I'm a realist, Dr Tanner,' he said. 'I've seen too much to be under any illusions about human nature.'

'What do your parents do for a living?' she asked, suddenly keen to find out more about what had contributed to his skewed world view.

'My father was a cop like me but is now retired, and my mother manages a child-care centre. She says it's her way of compensating for the lack of grandchildren.'

'You don't want kids at some point?'

'At some point, yes, but first I have to find a woman who can cope with the long hours I work without nagging me all the time to consider a career change.' He sent her a small rueful smile. 'Not an easy task, I can assure you.'

Amy sensed there was a world of information in his comment about his previous relationships with women. In spite of her negative experiences with her father, she knew being a cop was a tough call and contributed to a lot of stress and relationship breakdowns.

'My father was a cop, too,' she said. 'But, then, I suppose you've already guessed that.'

'I had noticed you don't seem to like cops all that much.'

'Yeah, well, I don't like my father all that much so that more or less explains it, I guess,' she said.

'What about your mother?'

'She's great,' Amy said with a glimmer of a smile. 'A bit overprotective and full-on at times, but we're really close. She's a vet. I used to help her in the practice when I was a kid.'

'So how come you chose medicine instead?'

She sent him a quick there-one-second-gone-the-next smile. 'Dealing with animals was too frustrating for me. They can't tell you their symptoms so you're always left guessing. I much prefer to deal with humans who can at least tell me what they're feeling.'

'Dogs can do that, too,' he said. 'I know every one of Fergus's moods.'

'So that's his name,' she said. 'It's not very Germanic, is it?'

'No, but it's the name of a loyal friend I once had,' he said. 'I thought it was appropriate.'

She looked at him with a questioning glance. *'Had?'*

He rose from his chair in a single movement, his tall shadow falling over her like a warning. 'I'd better get going,' he said. 'I have some things to see to. No doubt I'll see you around.'

Amy's brow furrowed as he strode out of the pub, his long purposeful strides taking him and his closely guarded secrets out of her reach.

CHAPTER FOUR

AMY'S first morning at the clinic started with meeting the other GP in the practice, Allan Peddington, a man in his late sixties who looked like he had done too many nights on call.

'I'm sorry I wasn't here to meet you yesterday,' he said, briefly shaking her hand. 'I had a family emergency down in Geraldton.'

'That's fine,' she said, smiling at him reassuringly. 'I hope everything's OK with your family now.'

Allan's tired eyes spoke volumes. 'Yes, more or less, I think,' he said. 'But you never know with kids, they seem right one minute and the next they're running off the rails. My daughter Claire is not coping too well after a break-up with her live-in partner. They were supposed to be getting married in a few months. It's such a disappointment for her.'

'I'm so sorry,' she said. 'It must be very hard for you, and your wife as well.'

'My wife died a few years ago,' he said in a flat emotion-less tone that didn't fool Amy for a second. 'There's just Claire and me now.'

'I'm sorry,' she said. 'I didn't realise.'

He gave her a forced smile. 'Well, we'd better get on with the day. Helen told me she showed you around yesterday. It's a one in two on call but if you have anything special planned any time, just let me know and I'll fill in for you.'

'And likewise,' Amy offered, although for the life of her couldn't imagine what would crop up for her to do in the evenings in a place as small as this.

Her first patient was a young man in his early twenties who had been welding the day before, and presented with a foreign object in his right eye.

'It hurts like hell, my eye's watering and it feels like there's sand under my eyelid,' Josh Taylor complained as he got up on the table and lay back as Amy had directed. 'I should have done something about it yesterday but I had to get the job done for the boss.'

She inspected the eye under a bright light. 'It looks like you've got a metal fragment lodged on the surface of your cornea,' she said. 'I'll put some anaesthetic drops in your eye and remove it for you, but next time you really shouldn't wait when something like this happens. You could have developed an ulcer, which is much harder to treat.'

'I know, but I've only been working in this job a short time and I didn't want the boss to think I was slacking off,' he said.

After Amy reassured herself that Josh was not using powerful enough equipment to have caused an intraocular foreign body, which would have required a trip to Geraldton and an ocular X-ray, she put three drops of proxymetacaine into his eye and waited for a couple of minutes, chatting to him about his work. She found out he worked for one of the fishermen in town as a general deckhand and that he had family further north in Broome.

'OK, now keep very still,' she said. 'I know it can seem a bit weird looking at a needle coming towards your eye but you won't feel a thing.'

She took a 22-gauge needle and, donning a pair of magnifying glasses and steadying her arm on a rest, she approached the cornea from the side. She could see the irritating metal fragment and with great care pried off the object with the tip of the needle. Then she applied some chloromycetin ointment and a double pad to the eye.

'You'll need to leave the pad in place for the rest of the day and night to protect your eye. Once the anaesthetic drops wear off you'll probably feel as if something is still in there, but that's because you've scratched the surface of the cornea. It will feel better in a day or so. I'd like to see you tomorrow to make sure it's healing well.'

'Thanks, Dr Tanner,' he said with a grateful smile. 'Hey, you know something? You look too young to be a doctor.'

She gave him an exaggerated smile and opened the door. 'You're seeing me with one eye, Josh,' she said. 'I might look old enough to be your mother when you come back tomorrow.'

There was a five-minute break in the appointment book so Amy dashed out to the general store to buy a snack for morning tea. She had forgone breakfast at the hotel, deciding that the bacon and eggs and sausages on the menu weren't going to do her thighs any favours.

She came out of the store, her head down against the glare of the hot bright sunshine, and cannoned straight into a blue-uniformed, rock-hard chest.

'Oops…' she said as strong male arms steadied her. 'Sorry, I wasn't watching where I was going.'

'In a hurry again, Dr Tanner?' Angus asked with a tilt of his mouth.

Amy rolled her lips together in disapproval at his little jibe. 'I missed breakfast,' she said. 'I've only got five minutes between patients.'

His hands fell away from her upper arms, but Amy could still feel her flesh tingling. Her stomach did a funny little somersault as his gaze went to her mouth before returning to her eyes.

'How's your first day on the job?' he asked.

'Fine,' she said with a little toss of her head. 'Nothing I can't handle.'

'So far,' he drawled.

Amy gave him a brittle look and made to brush past him, but he counteracted it with a hand on her arm. She looked down at his strong tanned fingers against the lighter tone of her slim wrist, a feathery sensation running up her spine as she brought her gaze upwards to meet his. 'Am I under arrest, Sergeant Ford?' she asked in a pert tone.

'Is there any reason why you should be under arrest, Dr Tanner?' he asked as he released her.

'I haven't done anything wrong,' she said with a hitch of her chin.

He rocked back on his heels as he looked down at her. 'So far.'

She gave him one last blistering look and stomped across the road back to the clinic, clutching her apple and tub of low-fat yogurt.

Angus squinted against the bright sunlight as he watched her, a slow smile spreading across his face.

'Is that the new doctor?' Jonathon Upton asked as he got out of his dusty utility in front of the store.

'G'day, Jonno,' Angus said, flicking a quick glance his way before returning to the little figure who'd had to wait in the middle of the street for a car to pass. 'Yep, that's her all right.'

Jonno whistled through his teeth as he followed the line of Angus's dark brown gaze. 'Damn nice figure,' he said. 'What's she like as a person?'

Angus wrenched his gaze away from the other side of the street. He put his sunglasses on and gave the farmer a tight-lipped, on-off smile. 'She drives too fast,' he said, and walked back to the police station.

'So how was your first morning?' Helen asked as Amy came out after seeing another patient.

'Not bad,' she said handing her a pile of files. 'It's a bit of change from working in a city hospital, of course, but to tell you the truth, it's a bit of a relief to be away from all that pressure.'

'Oh, it can get pretty pressured out here at times,' Helen said, pulling out the filing cabinet drawer. 'You just wait until there's a major accident on the highway or something. You can get called out at any time of the night to attend. And Friday and Saturday nights can get a bit lively. The young ones are bored and drink too much and get into all sorts of trouble.'

'I suppose kids will kick up their heels wherever they live,' Amy said thinking of her own teenage years.

'It's hard, though, in isolated areas,' Helen said. 'I've heard stories of kids petrol-sniffing in some communities further north, which just adds to the on-going problem of alcohol abuse. We haven't had anything like that out here yet, but I have a friend who lives in Perth whose daughter nearly died after taking ecstasy. The party drug scene in some places is really scary. I certainly hope it doesn't get like that out here. We don't have the infrastructure in these country areas to deal with drug abuse. It'll be left to the families to deal with, there's no drug counselling or rehab facilities out here.'

'What about educational programmes at the local schools?' Amy suggested. 'That might prevent the problem from starting in the first place.'

'We don't have a senior high school here, only kindergarten to year ten. Sergeant Ford's done a couple of lectures but you know what kids are like—particularly boys—with people in positions of authority, especially those in uniform. He decided to try another tactic instead. He coaches a soccer team on Tuesday afternoons. One or two of the tough kids have started coming along. Mixing with the others seems to be helping. There's been a lot less petty crime since.'

'That does sound like a good tactic,' Amy said, privately impressed with Angus's initiative in spite of her annoyance towards him.

'You should go down after your clinic finishes this afternoon and watch them,' Helen suggested. 'They play on the oval a few blocks down from the pub. It will be a way to get to know some of the lads, most of whom will no doubt turn out to be your patients at one time or the other.'

'I might just do that,' Amy said. 'Soccer's one of my favourite games.'

'You never know, Sergeant Ford might even let you have a kick or two,' Helen said with a twinkling smile. 'I saw the two of you chatting like old friends last night. Could there be a hint of romance in the air?'

'You must be joking,' Amy said, perhaps a little too quickly to be convincing. 'He's *so* not my type, for one thing…'

'And the other thing?' Helen prompted.

'I'm only here for three months,' she said, more to remind herself than the receptionist. 'I'm not interested in temporary relationships. I'm not that sort of woman.'

'All the same, it wouldn't hurt to have a little fun while you're out here,' Helen advised. 'It can be a lonely place without some company in the evenings.'

'I have plenty of company at the hotel,' Amy said, recalling how she'd spent most of the night twitching with fear in case her hairy roommate returned, not to mention the noise from the pub downstairs before it finally closed for the night.

Helen gave a little snort as she reached for the next patient's file just as the front door of the clinic opened. 'You might not be so positive come Friday or Saturday night. That place can really jump and let me tell you—it ain't pretty.'

Amy didn't answer but turned to greet the next patient. 'Mrs Horsham?'

Gillian Horsham followed her and took the chair Amy offered her in her consulting room, her eyes slightly downcast as she twisted her thin hands together in her lap.

'What can I do for you, Mrs Horsham?' Amy asked.

'I keep getting headaches,' Gillian said.

Amy felt like rolling her eyes in frustration. How many middle-aged women were there in the world with headaches? she wondered. It was every GP's nightmare. She glanced down at the thick file of notes, her eyes widening at how many tests had already been carried out with no specific diagnosis. It had quite clearly been both Allan Peddington's and Jacqui Ridley's nightmare as well.

'Describe to me what your headache feels like,' Amy said. 'Is it a slow build-up, or a rapid onset, do you get blurred vision or nausea?'

'No…just a headache…'

'Is it centred over one or both of your eyes or somewhere else?' Amy asked.

'I don't know…it's just there…' She pointed vaguely to her head.

Amy reached for the blood-pressure machine. 'I'll start with your blood pressure first as that can sometimes cause head-aches,' she said. 'Are you currently on any medication?'

'No,' Gillian said, wincing slightly as Amy pumped up the cuff over the thin cotton of the sleeve of her blouse on her upper arm.

'Is that hurting?' she asked.

'No, I guess I did too much in the garden yesterday.'

Amy frowned as she measured the woman's blood pressure: 120 over 70, as expected—normal. After a thorough physical examination, which excluded papilloedema, cranial nerve deficits or other neurological signs, Amy was left without a physical diagnosis.

'I can't find any signs of disease on examination. You've had some basic bloods done in the past, but I'll run a couple of more specific blood tests on you to check thyroid and parathyroid function,' she said, and reached for the blood-collection trolley. She searched for a vein in Gillian's arm and, finding one, drew up sufficient blood before placing a circular sticking plaster on the puncture site. 'Don't lift anything heavy with that arm for an hour or so,' Amy instructed her. 'The results should be back in a few days so make another appointment on your way out.'

'Thank you, Doctor,' Gillian said, and got to her feet. 'I know the other doctors think it's all in my mind but I do feel unwell a lot of the time. I have for years.'

'I'll do my best to find out what's causing your headaches,' Amy promised as she walked with her back out to Reception.

Helen waited until the woman had left before turning to Amy. 'She's a weird one, that,' she said. 'I suppose she came in with a headache or something equally vague?'

Amy frowned. 'Yes, she did, actually. Why, is that commonplace with her?'

'It drove Jacqui crazy,' Helen said. 'She ran every test known to medical science on that woman and came up with nothing. Allan did, too. Gillian Horsham is basically a bored housewife. She sits in front of her computer all day searching the internet for new symptoms. She knows more about rare diseases than a university professor. She's lonely. Her only daughter lives in America. She comes in for attention, regular as clockwork, at least once a month, sometimes more.'

Amy handed Helen the blood specimen for pathology with

a slightly embarrassed look. 'I guess I have a lot to learn about the locals,' she said.

Helen patted her hand. 'You'll soon get the hang of it.'

CHAPTER FIVE

AMY hadn't really intended going down to the oval, but the
hotel bar was crowded and the noise deafening when she went
up to her room, so she put on her trainers, shorts and a T-shirt
and told herself she was going for a walk to blow away the
cobwebs. She gave a little shiver and amended quickly—the
dust of the day.

The heat was as intense as ever, the sun burning through the
light cotton of her top as she walked past the police station
towards the oval.

She could hear the sound of young male voices calling out
to each other and the deeper voice of Angus Ford as he issued
instructions. She stood in the shade of the dilapidated grandstand and watched as the boys went through some kicking
drills. She couldn't help noticing how athletic Angus looked in
his shorts and lightweight muscle top. His upper body was obviously used to some sort of regular and strenuous workout if
his well-formed muscles were any indication, and his legs too
looked as if they were well used to being pushed to the limits
of endurance.

He looked magnificent.

A loud wolf-whistle suddenly cut through the air. 'Hey,
Jake, Matt, have a look at that!' one young boy called out.

Angus turned his head and that same slight hint of annoyance she'd seen the night before showed briefly in his dark eyes as they met hers. He turned away again and addressed the young men under his tutelage. 'Just keep on with that training drill for a couple of minutes. I won't be long.'

'Is she your new girlfriend, Sarge?' the boy who had delivered the wolf-whistle asked with a cheeky grin.

'You've *got* to be joking,' Angus said, and came over to where Amy was now silently seething.

She gave him an arch look. *'You've got to be joking?'* She mimicked his deep, scathing tone.

'I thought that might get a rise out of you,' he said. 'What can I do for you, Dr Tanner?'

'I didn't come here to see *you*,' she said with a little toss of her head. 'I came to see the boys playing.'

'They can probably do without the distraction,' he said as his eyes dipped to where her breasts pushed against her top.

She folded her arms across her chest but all it did was give him an even better view of her cleavage. 'If I'm not welcome, I'll leave,' she bit out.

'I didn't mean to imply that.'

'Oh, yes, you did,' she said. 'But while I'm here, there is something I want to ask you.'

'My head wound, as you see, is fine.'

'It's not about your wound,' she said. 'I have something else I wish to discuss with you.'

He stood with his arms folded, rocking back on his heels slightly as he looked down at her. 'Let me guess, you've been speeding and want to confess.'

She sent him a frosty look. 'Must you be so…so annoying?'

'Just doing my job, Dr Tanner.'

She drew in a tight breath and asked, 'Have you told anyone else in town that I am Lindsay's cousin?'

'No.'

She frowned. 'Why not?'

'I kind of figured you didn't want anyone to know,' he said. 'If you had, you would have mentioned it from the first.'

Amy compressed her lips for a moment. 'You're right,' she said, blowing out a little breath. 'I don't really want people to know.'

'Your reasons being?'

'I wasn't sure how well liked she was,' she answered, thinking on her feet as she continued, 'Mental illness is still not properly understood in the community and probably less so in one as isolated as this one. I didn't want to have to deal with any prejudice.'

'So you don't want to be associated with her, is that right?' There was an element of censure in his tone. 'Too embarrassing for you to have a not-quite-normal relative, eh, *Dr* Tanner?'

Amy ground her teeth and held her hands stiffly by her sides. 'That's not what I said.'

'Isn't it?' His dark brown eyes challenged hers.

'No.'

'So what *are* you saying, Dr Tanner?'

'I told you last night. I wanted to visit Lindsay's home and community,' she said.

'But you don't want anyone to know who you are.'

'I don't think it's relevant,' she said. 'Besides, grief is a very private and personal thing.'

'Undoubtedly, but you don't strike me as particularly grief-stricken,' he said.

'And I suppose you're an expert on analysing the depth of grief people show, are you, Sergeant?' she said with increasing temper. 'Running it through your own little grief meter to see if it's genuine or not? Well, let me tell you that there are different ways of showing grief. Not everybody does it with copious amounts of tears at the mere mention of the loved one's name.'

'That's certainly true, but I can't help thinking you're not telling me the whole story behind your pilgrimage to Marraburra,' he said.

'I don't have to explain myself to you,' she flashed back.

Angus opened his mouth to respond but there was a sound of a hard thud and a rough swear word, closely followed by a groan of agony on the oval behind him. He turned to see Matt Healey stumbling, as white as a sheet, clutching his left shoulder.

'Matt? What happened?' he asked, rushing over.

'It's my shoulder,' Matt groaned. 'I ran into Jake and something went crack.'

Amy was close behind Angus and offered to help. 'Matt, let me have a look,' she said. 'Where does it hurt?'

'It hurts like hell…' Matt said, biting his lip in an effort to keep control in front of his mates.

Amy gently examined the shoulder, seeing through the singlet top the typical flattening of the front contour of the joint due to dislocation. Feeling the area confirmed her diagnosis. Fortunately his sensation over the shoulder was normal, indicating he hadn't damaged any sensory nerves.

'Matt I'm afraid you've dislocated your shoulder,' she said. 'We'll have to get it back in place but it's going to be too painful to do it here. It'll be much better if we can get you back to the medical clinic and give you some sedation. But we'll need to contact your parents first.'

Matt exchanged a quick glance with Angus before looking at Amy again. 'I live with my dad but he's out on a boat. I'm not sure if his mobile will be on.'

'What about your mother? Can she be contacted?' Amy asked.

'I'll contact Matt's mother,' Angus said. Turning to the rest of the team, he went on, 'Sorry guys, we'll have to finish there for today. I'll try and make some time later in the week, perhaps Thursday. I'll let Jake know.'

'Good luck, Matt,' the boys chorused.

A tall dark-haired, dark-skinned boy came over to Matt, his expression sheepish. 'Sorry, Matt,' he mumbled. 'I didn't mean to hurt you, mate.'

Matt's smile was more of a grimace. 'It's all right, Jake. You did me a favour. I won't have to do the English test tomorrow.'

Amy turned to Angus. 'Have you got your car nearby? I know it's not far to the clinic but that shoulder will be killing him and the sooner it's put back in the better.'

'I'll jog over and get it—won't be a minute,' Angus said, and rushed off.

'Come over here into the shade,' Amy said, leading the boy towards the shadow of the grandstand.

'Sorry, Doc,' Matt said with another twisted grimace. 'You'd probably finished for the day.'

'It's no problem, Matt,' she said with a smile. 'It's just a shame you had such a freak accident. It can take a while for a dislocated shoulder to heal. You'll have to take things easy for a while.'

'You mean I won't be able to train?'

She shook her head. 'Not for a couple of weeks. Maybe you can run, but just not use the shoulder. The good news is in most cases the shoulder returns to normal.'

Amy looked up to see Angus pull into the kerb closest to the grandstand and she led Matt towards the car.

'Better sit in the front, Matt,' Angus said, holding the door open. 'I've phoned your mother and she's on her way down now.'

'Thanks, Sarge. I hope she wasn't too upset,' Matt said.

Angus gave him a man-to-man smile. 'You know what mothers are like—it's their job to be upset.'

It was a short journey to the clinic and Amy led them inside to the main treatment room, where Teresa was the nurse on duty.

'So what have you been doing to yourself, Mattie?' she asked.

'Popped my shoulder,' he said with a rueful look. 'The doctor's going to put it back in.'

'Has Matt's mother arrived yet?' Amy asked.

'*Matthew!*' A distraught female voice suddenly echoed through the building and Matt rolled his eyes.

'Looks like it,' Teresa said with a knowing wink towards the blushing boy. 'I'll bring her in.'

Rowena Healey was crying as she came in and would have crushed her son in a hug except for Amy anticipating it and blocking her. 'It's all right, Mrs Healey,' she said reassuringly. 'Matt's got a dislocated shoulder and I need your permission to administer an IV sedative to relax him while I reposition it. Could you sign the consent form Teresa has? Then we'll get it done.'

'Oh, my poor baby...' Rowena sobbed as she signed the form with a trembling hand.

'*Mu-um,*' Matt groaned in embarrassment.

Amy looked at Angus. 'Could you help Matt onto the bed, please?'

'Sure.'

Once Matt was lying on the bed Amy prepared his hand for an IV canula, with Teresa standing nearby in case of any problems with airway. She injected some midazolam, which almost immediately took effect and relaxed the teenager.

'Sergeant Ford, could you put your arms under Matt's shoulders like this to stop him from sliding from the bed?' she asked, demonstrating the position.

'Like this?' Angus asked.

'Exactly like that,' Amy said, and for the benefit of the witnesses added pleasantly, 'You must have done this before.'

'Yeah,' he answered, holding her gaze for a fraction longer than was needed.

Amy bent Matt's elbow to ninety degrees and, pulling downwards on the arm, rotated the shoulder joint to the front. With a clunk the joint popped back into place.

'I'll put his shoulder into a collar and cuff,' Amy said to Matt's mother, who was hovering anxiously. 'And if you could make sure he has some paracetomol four-hourly for pain, and keep him resting, I'll see him tomorrow in the clinic.'

'Can I take him home now?' Rowena asked.

'Wait here half an hour till the sedation wears off a bit,' Amy said. 'He's still groggy but that will be a good thing for a few minutes. Let's sit him up in one of the armchairs in the waiting area.'

'I'll help you out with him,' Angus said to the boy's mother.

Amy stood back as Angus escorted the boy out with his mother, supporting him gently but firmly to get him settled into a comfortable chair.

Teresa tidied up the treatment bay, commenting over her shoulder, 'He's done a wonder with that kid, you know.'

Amy pretended an interest in the suture and bandage trolley, her tone offhand as she answered, 'Oh?'

'Yeah,' the nurse said. 'Matt was up on three shoplifting charges all before the age of thirteen, not to mention under-age drinking when he was fourteen and driving an unlicensed vehicle without a licence at fifteen. But look at him now. He's not long turned sixteen and he's one of the nicest kids around here.'

Amy turned to look at the nurse. 'So how do you attribute that to Sergeant Ford's influence?' she asked.

'Angus spends time with the lads around here,' Teresa said. 'In fact, he spends more time with some of those boys than their own fathers—or at least the few that are still around, that is.' She straightened the bed and added, 'Angus is a good role model for them. He's the best thing that ever happened to this place, I can tell you. The other cops are good enough, don't get me wrong, but Angus has a real heart for youth in isolated areas.'

'He sounds like an angel in cop's clothing,' Amy said with a cynical tilt to her mouth. 'I wonder where he hides his halo.'

'You're very welcome to search me and find out,' Angus said from just behind her.

Amy flushed to the roots of her hair as she swung around, her eyes meeting the sardonic gleam of his. 'I didn't hear you come back in…' she said.

'Obviously.'

'Er…' Teresa cleared her throat. 'I'm about to close up shop now. Allan's on call tonight and so am I if there's any trouble. I'll head off as soon as Matt and his mum are ready to go.'

Amy turned to face the nurse. 'Thanks, Teresa, for helping out. I'll see you tomorrow.'

'Have a good night, both of you,' Teresa said with a twinkle in her eye.

Amy walked out, her face still feeling unbearably hot. She heard Angus following a few paces behind her.

'Do you want a lift back to the hotel?' he asked as they came out from the air-conditioned interior of the clinic.

'I think I can manage to survive the hundred-and-fifty-metre journey without collapsing from dehydration or heatstroke,' she said with a defiant little toss of her head.

A small smile began to play at the edges of his mouth. 'You look like you're overheating right now,' he observed.

She gave him a withering look and made to stalk past but he caught her wrist to stall her. She felt that same quick snap of electricity shoot through her flesh as his long fingers curled around the slender bones of her wrist like a steel handcuff. Her eyes went to his, hers flashing with anger.

'What is it this time, Sergeant? Am I walking too fast for your liking?'

His hand released hers but she could still feel his touch as if he had branded her. Her stomach gave a tiny shuffling movement as his eyes flicked to her mouth before coming back to tether her gaze.

'I was going to suggest you come out to Caveside Cove with me to look at your cousin's shack,' he said. 'That's if you've got nothing better to do right now.'

Amy looked up at him, a hint of suspicion in her expression. 'I thought you said there was nothing out there. "Spiders and junk" were your exact words, if I remember correctly.'

'That's right, but I thought you might like some company, particularly if any spiders get too close and personal,' he said. 'It's not an easy place to find, it's isolated out there, and, besides, I happen to have the only key.'

'I don't need a bodyguard,' she said, still bristling with pride. 'And I'm perfectly able to read a road map.'

'But you don't have a four-wheel-drive vehicle,' he said. 'It's a rough road and if you get into trouble it's a long walk back to town.'

'Oh…' She chewed at her lip for a moment, a small frown forming. 'But…but how did my cousin manage? I didn't think she had a car of any sort—as far as I know, she never learned to drive.'

'She didn't,' he answered. 'She rode her bike to the main road and if anyone she knew was going past she'd leave the bike in the bushes and get a lift the rest of the way, and do the same on the way back.'

Amy was tempted to take him up on his offer but couldn't help wondering why he was offering it the first place. But then the thought of getting her brand new car bogged down in sand or the suspension damaged by deep potholes was enough incentive to push her pride to one side and accept.

'All right,' she said. 'I would like to go and see where she lived if it's not too much trouble for you.'

'No trouble at all,' he said, and led the way to his four-wheel-drive police vehicle. 'Besides, the pub's a pig of a place to be at this time of day.'

'Tell me about it,' she said scathingly as he opened the car door for her.

His eyes met hers. 'If you want to move out I still have that room I was telling you about.'

'Thanks, but so far I'm managing,' she said as she got into the car.

He got behind the wheel and reached the outskirts of town before he spoke again. 'That was a good job you did on Matt Healey.'

'Thank you.'

'He's had a rough time,' he said. 'His mother, as you probably guessed, is the nervous type and his father is away a lot.'

'He's a fisherman, right?'

He nodded. 'Yeah. Off the coast is the continental shelf so there's an abundance of fish. The big boats go out for a couple of weeks at a time so it can be a lonely existence for the women and children left at home, given that there's not much to do in terms of entertainment.'

'How long have you been coaching the boys?' she asked.

'For about a year and a bit now.'

'How long have you been here at Marraburra?'

'Two and a half years,' he said.

She turned to look at him. 'So what brought you way up here?'

He kept his eyes on the road but Amy noticed his hands on the steering-wheel had tightened just enough for the knuckles to go pale beneath his tan.

'I decided it was time for a change,' he said evenly. 'I'd been working on a big case in Perth and after several months it began to take its toll. I was living and breathing work, forgetting to have a life. I'm sure you're familiar with the syndrome.'

'Yes, I am,' she agreed wholeheartedly. 'All work and no

play makes for a very burnt-out person. I have to constantly be on guard against it. I guess it's that type-A personality most driven, professional people are lumbered with.'

'So you would describe yourself as driven?' he asked.

'Well…' Amy thought about her reasons for coming all this way. 'Yes, I guess you could say that. I like to see things through to the end. I hate quitting halfway through something.'

'Yeah, well, I guess I'm a bit like that, too.'

'Someone, I think it was one of the nurses, said you weren't planning on staying here indefinitely,' she said. 'What will you do, go back to Perth?'

'Probably,' he said. 'But at the moment I'm taking it one day at a time. When it feels like the right time to go back I will.'

Amy wondered what was keeping him here in Marraburra. The town hardly seemed big enough to warrant four police officers, and even though he had said he had wanted a break from his work in Perth, surely he would have put some sort of time frame on it?

'Do you mind if I make a quick detour to pick up someone?' he asked after a tiny pause.

'No, no, of course not,' Amy answered, not quite understanding why she should be feeling disappointed. It wasn't that she wanted to be alone with him. She didn't even like him. If he wanted to dilute her company then that was perfectly fine with her.

She told herself it was because she wanted to visit Lindsay's shack in solitude.

Yes, that was it.

It couldn't possibly be anything else.

CHAPTER SIX

ANGUS turned into a road marked Marraburra Point and drove up a steep hill to where a large open-plan house overlooked the sparkling blue ocean. The height of the cliffs was breathtaking, and the salty tang of the air rising up from the crawling sea below made Amy long for a swim after the blistering heat of the day.

'Wow!' she said. 'This is a fabulous place your friend has here.'

'Yes, it is,' he said, as he brought the car to a halt in front of the glass and stone residence. 'I'm house-sitting it for the owner, who's living overseas at the moment.'

She swivelled to look at him. 'So who are we picking up?' she asked.

He got out and, putting two fingers into his mouth, whistled once, the sound piercing in spite of the pounding of the surf down below.

Amy watched as a glossy-coated German shepherd appeared as if from nowhere to come to his master, his snout nuzzling against Angus's hand affectionately, the dog's tail wagging in greeting.

'Hi, there, boy,' Angus said ruffling the dog's ears. 'Want to come down to the beach?'

Fergus barked as if he had understood every word and Angus

smiled and gave him another quick pat. 'Fergus, this is Dr Tanner. Friend, Fergus, friend.'

Amy stood very still as the dog came over and gave her hand a sniff. 'Hi, there, Fergus…'

'Don't be nervous,' Angus said. 'If he didn't like you he would have shown it by now.'

Unlike his owner, Amy couldn't help thinking as she gave the dog a scratch under the chin. 'Pleased to meet you, Fergus,' she said.

Angus opened the lock-up compartment at the back of the vehicle and with a quick non-verbal command Fergus jumped in and sat down as if he had done it many times.

Amy swung an ironic glance Angus's way as they resumed their seats. 'So how come Fergus has to travel like a criminal in the back?' she asked.

He answered as he turned the car back towards the exit. 'Unrestrained dogs in vehicles are like missiles if you have to brake suddenly, especially a large dog. It's safer for him and for us if he stays back there.'

Amy couldn't help feeling her mother would approve of Angus's attitude. How many times had Grace Tanner said the very same thing?

'He's a beautiful dog,' she inserted into the silence. 'And obviously adores you.'

His eyes met hers briefly. 'Thanks.'

Amy looked around with interest as Angus turned into a road further along the coast marked Caveside Cove. Banksia, grevillea and melaleuca lined each side of the road and in the distance she could hear the roar of the surf.

The road was as he'd said: rough. She jerked from side to side in her seat in spite of the police vehicle's sophisticated suspension and she inwardly sighed with relief when he finally drew the car to a halt.

'It's a bit of a walk,' he said as she joined him on the track leading to the beach. 'Your cousin's shack is tucked in behind the dunes.'

'It's certainly very private,' Amy said as she fell into step beside him. 'Helen Scott was telling me it's not very popular with the locals. She told me there was a tragic rockfall in the caves some years ago.'

'Yes,' he said, stopping briefly to pick up a piece of drift wood and throwing it for Fergus to fetch. 'The caves have been blocked off ever since. But even without that there's usually a strong undertow here and submerged rocks. If you want a swim it's best to go to Marraburra Bay, closer to town.'

'What about the beach below your place, Marraburra Point?

His eyes met hers in a quick sideways glance, his expression hard to read. 'It's not for the inexperienced either,' he said

They continued walking until they came to a rustic-looking one-room shack.

'I'll unlock it for you but do you want me to check for spiders first?' he asked.

Amy searched his face for a moment. She suspected he was still amused by her revulsion for spiders but his tone this time held no trace of mockery. She captured her bottom lip for a fraction of a second before answering softly, 'That would be great.'

She waited for him outside, lifting her face to the fresh air and breathing deeply, relishing in the total peace of the place. No wonder her cousin had loved it so much. The red ochre of the cliffs in the distance and the icing-sugar softness of the sand and the wild untamed sound of the sea all added to the sense of isolation and privacy.

The sound of Angus's footsteps brought her head around and she unconsciously rubbed at her arms. 'Did you find any?'

'I've removed a few tenants but as long as you can cope with cobwebs, it should be all clear for half an hour or so,' he said

She gave a little shiver as she approached the door. 'Cobwebs are OK as long as they stay out of my hair.'

His eyes met hers as he held the door open for her. 'You really are scared, aren't you?'

'I've had some treatment for it,' she confessed. 'But, as you can see, it wasn't entirely successful. My Harley Street psychologist would be terribly disappointed in me.'

His gaze shifted away from hers. 'Yeah, well, they don't always have all the answers so I wouldn't let it worry you.'

There was something in his comment that alerted her to the possibility that he had spent time with a counsellor himself, but she didn't feel comfortable asking him for details. He had his 'keep out' sign on his face again, but when she met his eyes once more she couldn't help thinking they looked too old for his face, as if they'd seen things they hadn't wanted to see and now couldn't erase.

She stepped into the room and tried to keep her eyes from darting nervously about, but it was almost impossible not to be on edge in the badly lit, dusty room. In spite of the heat burning its way into the shack she felt a little icy shiver pass over her flesh as the door creaked to a close behind her.

'Would you like to be alone for a while?' Angus asked.

'*No!*' Amy said, quickly swinging around to face him. 'Er…I mean it's fine…you know…you being here. It's fine… really…' *Please, don't go,* she added silently.

He didn't answer but she could feel the penetration of his dark contemplative gaze even when she turned her back to look around the room.

Her cousin's narrow bed had been made, its smooth neat cover seeming rather incongruous to Amy, considering Lindsay had never been known for tidiness. For most of Amy's childhood and adolescence she had heard her aunt lamenting the fact that her daughter seemed incapable of keeping order either on

her person or with any of her possessions. On the few occasio
she had visited her cousin's inner-city flat, Amy had private
wondered how anyone could live in such squalor. Empty take
away food containers and unwashed dishes had seemed to lin
every surface, along with paint tins and tubes and brushes i
amongst her cousin's half-finished artwork. When she ha
offered to help her tidy up, Lindsay had become extremel
agitated until Amy had assured her she wouldn't touch a thing

Amy went to the bed and, reaching out a hand, ran it dow
the cover. 'Is this where she was found?' Her voice sounded thi
in the silence.

'Yes.'

She turned to look at him, her voice wobbling slightly ove
the words. 'S-someone must have made her bed.'

'Yes.'

A small sigh escaped her lips. 'I don't think she knew ho
to do it…' A bubble of emotion popped up from deep insid
her and she tried to swallow it back down. 'She was the messie
person I've ever met… She didn't even brush her hair or he
teeth unless someone reminded her…'

Amy would have been able to control the second bubble i
it hadn't been for Fergus. He padded across from his master'
side and gently nudged her hand with his long snout, a so
crooning sound coming from deep inside his throat. She gulpe
back a sob but another one came to take its place. Sh
rummaged for a tissue but before she could locate one Angu
stepped forward and offered her his handkerchief.

She met his gaze through tear-washed eyes as she took th
folded square, the brief brush of his fingers yet again joltin
her with a charge of his body's heat and energy.

'I'm sorry…' she began in embarrassment. 'I thought I ha
dealt with all this six months ago.'

He took one of her hands in the dry warmth of his, th

slightly roughened pads of his fingers alerting her all over again to his essential maleness. 'You should let it out,' he said. 'It won't do any good buried deep inside.'

She eased her hand out of his and, wiping her eyes, gave him a somewhat twisted smile. 'Doctors aren't supposed to cry, or at least not in front of people.'

'Is that what they teach you in medical school?' he asked.

'No not really,' she said. 'Things have changed from the old days. We're allowed to be human as long as it doesn't affect clinical judgement.'

'Lindsay was your cousin, not your patient,' he reminded her.

'Yes...' Amy said, absently fondling the dog's ears.

'He likes you,' Angus said into the long silence.

She raised her eyes back to his. 'I like him, too,' she said softly.

Three beats of silence passed.

'He looks mean but he's a real softie when you get to know him,' he said.

Amy wondered if he was talking about the dog or obliquely referring to himself. She hunted his face, her eyes still locked on his as the air around them tightened with the tension of their mutual unwilling attraction. She could see it in his eyes, the flicker of male interest as his gaze dipped to her mouth and lingered there. Her tongue came out before she could control it and added a glisten of moisture to the dusty dryness of her lips. The silence was like a throb in the air. A resonant, heavy throb she could feel deep and low in every secret place in her body.

Thump, thump, thump.

She could see the very same pulse beating in his neck, the tanned skin of his throat a temptation she could barely withstand. She could almost taste the salt of his skin in her mouth, her tongue coming out again to sweep across the sensitive surface of her lips.

He suddenly took a step backwards. 'We should get going,'

he said in a brusque tone. 'I'll leave you to have a final look around. I'll wait for you outside.'

Amy did her best to ignore the sharp prick of disappointment that deflated her feminine ego to an all-time low. She gave herself a mental kick for being so stupid as to even think he was attracted to her. It was clear he wasn't. She'd been fooling herself, no doubt in an effort to restore her confidence when it came to men.

'At least his dog likes me,' she muttered under her breath, as she took a last look around.

She didn't stay long. She was conscious of the lengthening shadows that seemed all the more menacing now that she was alone. The room felt cold, too, as if a cold sea breeze had found its way beneath the door, curling around her ankles and moving up her body until she began to shiver.

'Why did you do it, Lindsay?' she asked the empty room in a soft whisper. 'Why on earth did you do it?'

There was no answer but the rough unstained floorboards creaked almost painfully as Amy made her way across them to leave…

Angus threw a stick for Fergus with such force it took the dog a few minutes to locate it. He came back with it in his mouth, dropped it at Angus's feet and barked.

'Quiet, Fergus,' Angus said, frowning.

The dog looked instantly crestfallen, his tail stopped wagging and he lowered himself to the ground.

Angus let out a sigh and bent down to ruffle the dog's ears. 'Sorry, boy,' he said gruffly. 'I'm taking it out on you, aren't I?'

He straightened when he heard the sound of Amy approaching, his groin tightening all over again at the sight of her. She had a youthful, totally feminine freshness about her that was a heady reminder of what he had denied himself for too long. It had been so long ago he couldn't quite remember the last time he had held a woman in his arms or even who it had been. But getting involved with the visiting doctor was asking for the sort of trouble he could do without just now. Dr Amy Tanner had suspicion written all over her beautiful face. Why else had she come all this way if not to ask questions he didn't want asked?

'All done?' he asked her, as she came towards him.

She nodded and, releasing a sigh, cast her gaze towards the far end of the beach where the crumbling cliff met the ocean. 'Is that where the caves are?' she asked.

'Yes, but it's not advisable to go too close,' he said. 'The rockface is a bit unstable after recent rain.' He opened the car for her and added, 'I'll go and lock up. Won't be a minute.'

She watched in the side mirror as he returned and put the dog in the back, the warm affection he held for Fergus clearly evident in the way his dark brown eyes softened as he stroked the dog's ears before he closed the door.

Careful, Amy warned herself sternly. Yes, he may be seriously gorgeous and he loves dogs, but he's still a cop.

She turned to face him as he slid in behind the wheel. 'Thank you for bringing me out here,' she said. 'I'm not sure I would have coped very well on my own.'

He gunned the engine and began to back out of the rough driveway, his outstretched arm along the seat close to the back of her neck. 'How long have you had arachnophobia?' he asked.

She bit her lip and looked down at her hands. 'For as long as I can remember.'

Angus swung his gaze her way, his brief look taking in the vulnerable downward turn of her mouth and the slightly hunched set of her slim shoulders. He turned his attention back to the ridged road but he couldn't help wondering what had started that irrational pattern of fear. He knew from experience that a traumatic episode was often cited in the onset of post-traumatic syndrome and a phobia was more or less an extension of that.

'I suppose you think it's totally pathetic that a woman of twenty-seven and a doctor to boot should be scared of spiders,' she said after another moment or two of silence.

'As far as I recall, I didn't express that view.'

'You didn't have to. I could see it on your face yesterday at the hotel.'

'I was momentarily surprised, that's all.'

'You were laughing at me.'

'I can assure you I was not.'

'I think I should warn you that if you have any intention of spreading the news of my phobia around town, I will be very angry with you,' she said.

'Your secret is safe with me.'

She gave a little snort that he took to be disbelief. 'It will ruin my credibility if it got out. I've worked hard to keep it under control.'

'Which clearly hasn't worked.'

'Is that a criticism?'

'No, it was an observation,' he answered.

'But you still think it's pathetic, don't you?'

'I think it's a shame you are controlled by an irrational fear but, no, I don't think it's pathetic. Lots of people have phobias.'

'You're just saying that.'

He blew out a breath of frustration. 'All right, have it your way. I think it's pathetic. Happy now? Is that what you wanted me to say?'

Amy could feel herself backing down. 'I'm sorry,' she mumbled. 'I'm just a little sensitive about it. I don't like people to know how weak I am.'

'It's not a weakness to confront your fears,' he said. 'You've just spent fifteen minutes in a spider-infested environment. That's not weakness—that's courage.'

Amy was surprised at how much his compliment affected her.

His comment was so far removed from those of her father's she was tempted to tell him so, but before she could get the words out his radio started to crackle and a voice sounded out from the dashboard, informing Angus of an accident on a back road.

'The volunteer ambulance is about thirty minutes away,' the voice said. 'Dr Peddington is not answering his phone or pager but the clinic nurse said you had the new doctor with you—is that correct?'

'Yes, that's right,' Angus said taking the next turn. 'We'll be there in ten minutes, tops.'

Amy looked at him after he'd signed off. 'Have we got time to pick up my doctor's bag?'

He gave a quick nod. 'We have to go back through town anyway.'

'What happened, do you know?' she asked in an effort to prepare herself as they approached town a few minutes later.

'One of the locals has rolled his car evidently,' he said. 'That back road is notorious for loose gravel. It sounds nasty, from what Nick Winters was saying.' He sent her a quick glance before adding, 'Have you had any experience with roadside trauma recovery?'

Amy felt herself bristling all over again. What did he think she was, some sort of novice? 'I have both the Australian EMST and UK equivalent trauma qualifications,' she said.

'Just checking,' he said as he pulled up in front of the hotel. 'Is your bag in your car or upstairs?'

'Upstairs,' she said, and jumped out. 'I'll be as quick as I can.'

Angus watched her bolt inside, his fingers drumming against the steering-wheel impatiently. He would have preferred Allan Peddington on a callout like this. Allan was rock steady in a crisis, always in control, which had a calming affect on everyone else around him. Amy Tanner, with her wild curly chestnut hair, pouting mouth and coltish figure, looked like she'd just finished

high school. It didn't seem possible she could handle seriou
trauma and certainly not on a dusty roadside.

She came bounding back with her bag and tossed it on the
back seat before getting back in beside him. 'Right. Let's go.

He drove out of town and took a turn down a back road tha
led them to the wreckage of an old-model Holden lying on it
roof. A man was standing next to a body lying on the side o
the road about twenty metres from the car.

'Thank God you're here!' the white-faced man said as he
came towards them. 'Is the ambulance on its way?'

'Should be here in ten to fifteen minutes, Nick,' Angus said a
he retrieved Amy's bag for her and carried it towards the victim

'It's young Bobby Williams,' Nick informed Angus soberly
'He's in a bad way.'

Amy began to examine the injured man. 'He's unconsciou
and not responding to pain or voice,' she said, more to hersel
than to anyone else in an effort to maintain professional calm
She knew this was going to test her skills. She had limited ex
perience with roadside retrieval and, as the man called Nick ha
said, the victim looked as if he was seriously injured. She coul
feel the adrenalin surging through her system and had to figh
to control the slight tremble of her hands.

'His left femur is at an angle and obviously fractured, an
he has abrasions all over the front of his chest where he's sli
along the gravel.' She took a breath to steady herself and aske
Angus, 'Can you help me to steady his neck? His airway's ob
structed—I'll need to clear it.'

Amy donned gloves and goggles and began removing debri
from the boy's mouth. Without instruction Angus held the hea
steady while she tried chin lift and jaw thrust, but there was n
air movement. A Guedell's airway did not improve the situation

'I'm going to have to intubate him,' she said, suppressing
another wave of panic.

Angus moved around to the victim's side, and with a gloved hand on each side expertly stabilised the boy's neck while Amy retrieved the laryngoscope and an endotracheal tube from the kit. It was a bit of a struggle because of blood in the back of the throat, which Amy had no means to aspirate, but somehow she managed to intubate him regardless. While she tied in the tube and started bagging on air using the Air-Viva set from her kit, Angus automatically sized and fitted a hard cervical collar. Once fitted, this allowed him to take over ventilation while Amy continued assessment.

'You seem to know what you're doing,' she remarked as she put her stethoscope to the victim's chest to check breathing. 'You must have done this before as well.'

'Once or twice too often,' Angus confessed with a grim set to his features. God, he hated accidents like this. He felt so useless and out of control. He had to force his mind away from that day with Dan.

That day with Dan.

He gave an inward grimace. It sounded like the title of a movie, not the life of his best mate draining away beneath his hands...

'There's no air entry on the right side,' Amy said, and, feeling the trachea, added, 'The trachea's shifted to the left.' She percussed the chest to find it was dull on the right side and even more so on the left.

'The neck veins were distended when I put on the cervical collar,' Angus said, forcing the images of Dan's grief-stricken wife and children out of his head.

'I'm pretty sure he's got a right pneumothorax but the chest isn't that resonant,' Amy said. 'It could be a haemothorax. If we put in a chest drain without IV access, we could kill him with blood loss.'

'He's very difficult to ventilate,' Angus said, as a vision of the Bobby's parents slipped into his mind. His stomach clenched with dread as he added, 'If we don't do something soon, he's going to die anyway.'

Amy took a 12-gauge canula and, after swabbing the skin with alcohol, inserted it into the right second intercostal space. A small amount of air and a trickle of blood came out. 'It's definitely not a tension pneumothorax,' she said. 'I think he's bled into the right chest. He needs a chest drain and IV resus.' She looked up in rising panic. 'When is that ambulance coming?'

'Shouldn't be too long now,' Angus said with enviable calm. 'Can you get an IV line in?'

'Yes, I've got a couple of bags of saline—that might tide him over for a short period,' she added, taking the pulse and fitting a BP cuff. 'Pulse is 140 and BP is only 80 systolic.'

She inserted a 14-gauge canula, but with a lot of difficulty as the victim's veins were not distending with the tourniquet. She started a saline bag running full bore, and then got another line into the other arm and started the second bag of saline.

The wail of the ambulance sounded in the distance and Amy exchanged a brief glance of relief with Angus. She took over ventilation and asked him to straighten the patient's leg but there was no pain response. Amy noted the patient's GCS at 8 or 9.

The ambulance arrived but the two volunteers were clearly not very experienced. Amy felt her heart sink when she saw the way they hovered about, waiting for direction.

'Right,' she said, pointing to the woman in her mid-fifties who had introduced herself as Joan. 'Can you get me a chest drain set from the ambulance?'

Jim, the other, elderly ambo, set about procuring a Donway splint from one of the ambulance cupboards.

Amy was able to insert a right chest drain without local anesthesia. About 200 ml of blood immediately drained out into the underwater bottle, then nothing else. She joined up a litre of colloid to each IV line and asked Angus, 'Are the neck veins still distended?'

Angus loosened the collar and answered, 'Yes, more than before.'

She listened to the heart with the stethoscope but the heart sounded very muffled and hard to hear.

Jim by this stage had fitted and pumped up the Donway, and now set about connecting an ECG, while Joan rechecked the victim's obs.

'BP 70 systolic, Dr Tanner, pulse 140,' she reported.

'Thanks, Joan.' Amy sat back on her heels and looked at Angus, not even bothering to disguise her fear. 'I think he has a haemopericardium. That would make sense from the mechanism of injury—a sudden deceleration as he was thrown out of the car. The standard thing to do is put in a pericardial needle. I've never done that before, and the reports say it might not be that effective anyway. And it could kill him if I puncture his heart or a coronary vessel.'

'Looks to me like he's running out of chances anyway,' Angus said. 'Even if we do manage to stabilise him, he still has a long journey ahead of him to Geraldton. I've called for the flying doctor on the police radio but they couldn't give me an accurate ETA. They're in the air north of Geraldton now on a routine transfer. They're turning back and deciding whether they have to drop off their transfer patient first. I've told them how urgent things here are.'

Amy gave him a grim look and reached for a long needle and attached a three-way tap and syringe. Swabbing the upper abdomen with alcohol, she inserted the needle just to the left of the xiphisternum, aiming for the tip of the left scapula.

'The ECG's showing funny rhythms, Dr Tanner,' Jim informed her.

Amy looked at the monitor and saw the runs of VF. 'Crunch

time,' she said, and further advanced the needle, aspirating as she went. Suddenly she was able to withdraw dark blood and, using the three-way tap, took out 40 ml more blood.

'BP's come up to 110 systolic—something seems to be working,' Jim said.

Angus responded to a call coming in on his phone. Then he clipped it back on his belt. 'The plane is landing in ten minutes, they've kept their transfer patient on board. We'll meet them at the airstrip. They'll take him straight down to Geraldton. But you'd better go with him. This guy's not out of the woods yet.'

'But—'

'I'll organise someone to bring you back to Marraburra,' he said.

'Thanks,' she said, and supervised the loading of the accident victim into the back of the ambulance. She suppressed an inward sigh and gathered up her things in preparation for the journey, deciding that this probably wasn't the best time to tell Sergeant Angus Ford that, along with spiders, she wasn't too keen on small aircraft either.

CHAPTER SEVEN

AMY was totally exhausted by the time the patient had been assessed by the Geraldton A and E team. She had been convinced for the entire journey that at any minute the plane would come crashing down. To her shame she'd even had to use a sick bag a couple of times when they'd hit a patch of turbulence. In her misery she had begun to mentally compose the next day's newspaper headlines: YOUNG FEMALE GP KILLED IN MERCY DASH WITH ACCIDENT VICTIM.

She brought her head up when she realised someone was speaking to her in A and E.

'You did a great job,' Derek Payton, the A and E doctor on duty, said as the patient was being transferred to the operating Theatre. 'I heard it's only your second day on the coast.'

'Yes,' she said with a tired smile. 'And here I was thinking things would be pretty quiet way out here.'

'Yeah, well, not always,' he said. 'Is someone coming to pick you up?'

'The local sergeant was organising a lift for me.'

'Help yourself to coffee and a sandwich in the doctors' room on the third floor while you wait.' He looked at his watch and added, 'You've been here almost three hours so it shouldn't be much longer. I'll give you a buzz when your lift arrives.'

'Thanks,' she said and made her way to the elevator.

The doctors' room was thankfully vacant, which meant Amy could sink into one of the armchairs, kick off her shoes, lay her head back and close her eyes. She was way beyond appetite and although the aroma of coffee in the air was tempting, she felt too tired to get up and pour herself a cup.

She woke what felt like only seconds later when someone touched her on the arm. She blinked and Angus's handsome features came into focus. She rubbed at her gritty eyes and dragged herself upright from her slumped position, her cheeks feeling warm all of a sudden.

'I must have fallen asleep,' she said as she got to her feet and straightened her crumpled clothes.

'You probably needed it,' he said. 'Are you ready to leave?'

She met his eyes with a questioning look. 'I thought you were organising someone to pick me up?'

'I did—me.'

She gnawed at her bottom lip as she began to hunt for her missing shoe.

'Is this what you're looking for?' He held out her shoe.

'Yes…' She took it from him and stuffed her foot back into it. 'But I could have waited till morning. You didn't have to drive all the way down here just for me.'

'I had to bring Bobby's parents down in any case,' he said. 'His father is in a wheelchair and his mother isn't a confident driver. Besides they were both pretty upset about their son's accident, especially as alcohol was involved.'

'All the same, you must be tired,' she said, trying to squash her disappointment that he hadn't made the trip just for her after all. 'It seems a month since Matt Healy's shoulder and yet it was only hours ago.'

'I'm used to long hours,' he said, and shouldered open the door. 'Come on. You can have another power nap in the car.'

Amy determined she would stay awake for the whole journey but somehow as soon as they were on their way her eyelids began to drop as if weighted with house bricks and her head began to slip sideways…

She woke as the car came to halt outside the hotel. The lights were all off and the place looked deserted and even more rundown without the glare of fluorescent illumination.

'Have you got a key to the side entrance?' Angus asked.

'Um…' She bit her lip when she realised it was on her car keyring, which was upstairs in her room. 'Not on me right now.'

He gave her a musing look. 'I don't quite fancy waking Bill Huxley at this hour. Perhaps you'd better come home with me for what's left of the night.'

'Do you really think that's necessary?' she asked. 'I mean, surely Bill won't mind opening the door for me just this once.'

'You can take your chances with Bill, who probably sank a few after closing time and is now sleeping them off, or you can take a chance on me. Take it or leave it. But to reassure you, I'm sober as a judge and dog tired so if you're anticipating any trouble from me, forget it.'

'I wasn't for a moment implying that you—'

'Yes, you were,' he interjected. 'You keep looking at me as if I'm going to drag you off to my cave and ravish you.'

'I do not!'

'Yes, you do,' he said, 'which makes me wonder what type of guys you've been hanging out with in London.'

'No one like you, I can assure you,' she tossed back.

'I kind of assumed that,' he returned.

She glared at him. 'What do you mean by that?'

He ignored her question by asking one of his own. 'So what's it to be, Dr Tanner? Catching a couple of hours on the steps of the Dolphin View or a comfortable bed at my place?'

'Well…' She sent him a sheepish look. 'When you put it like *that*…'

His lips moved upwards in what could almost be described as a smile as he put the car back into gear. 'My place it is.'

Unlike the hotel they had just left, his house was all the more attractive in the soft glow of moonlight. The blue-black blanket of stars above combined with the soporific pulse of the ocean crawling below made Amy wish she hadn't been so adamant about her choice of accommodation. The thought of a bathroom all to herself and a bed that didn't squeak was suddenly all too tempting.

And no spiders!

Angus led her inside where Fergus greeted her like an old friend, the soft whimper he gave her as he nudged her hand thrilling her that he had accepted her so readily.

'Cool it, Fergus,' Angus scolded. 'You're making a fool of yourself.'

'No, he's not,' Amy insisted. 'Besides, don't you know women love a man who's prepared to wear his heart on his sleeve?'

'Not any of the women I know,' he said as he tossed his keys to the counter before removing his gun and phone from his belt and laying them beside them.

Amy tilted her head at him. 'So how many women do you actually know, Sergeant Ford?'

He unclipped his pager and laid it next to his gun, his eyes steady on hers. 'Are you by any chance flirting with me, Dr Tanner?' he asked.

'No, of course not!'

He raised his brows at her vehement denial, the line of his mouth faintly mocking.

'Please, don't concern yourself,' she said, folding her arms. 'You're *so* not my type.'

'I brought you here to offer you a bed, not a relationship,' he said. 'However, if you're looking for someone to entertain you while you're in town, I'm sure I could summon up the enthusiasm to do so.'

She sent him a flinty look. 'I'm perfectly happy at the hotel and I am definitely *not* looking for a relationship, and certainly not a temporary one and definitely not with you.'

'Every unattached woman is looking for a relationship.'

'Not this one,' she said, turning up her nose. 'I'm still getting over the last one.'

'How long ago was that?'

'Eighteen months.'

'Time to get back on the horse, so to speak.'

She tightened her mouth without responding.

'So what happened?' he asked as he led the way to the kitchen.

Amy followed and at his invitation pulled out a breakfast bar stool to sit on. 'To this day I'm not really sure…'

Angus turned to look at her, noting her small frown and the cute way her teeth sank into the fullness of her bottom lip. 'It's like that sometimes,' he offered, thinking of his own relationship disasters.

She released her lip and he watched as the tip of her tongue came out and smoothed over the small indentation her teeth had made.

'I guess I read the signals all wrong or something,' she said. 'You know…saw things that weren't there in an effort to reassure myself things were on track.'

'He was a doctor?'

'Yes, an anaesthetist. He's married with a baby now.'

'Ouch.'

Amy felt a rueful smile tug at her mouth. 'Very definitely ouch.'

He pushed himself away from the bench to open the fridge.

'Do you want a cold drink? Orange juice or milk?' he asked over his shoulder.

'Um…no, thanks,' she answered, trying not to stare at his firm buttocks as he leaned into the fridge.

He took out a carton of milk and, closing the door of the fridge, leaned his hips back against the nearest bench and drained the contents.

Amy felt a fluttery pulse inside her stomach when he lowered the empty carton to the bench. 'Er…' She tapped her finger against her upper lip. 'You have a milk moustache.'

He wiped his mouth with the back of his hand. 'Gone?'

'All gone,' she said, and blushed like a schoolgirl.

He held her gaze for a tiny beat before he pushed himself away from the bench. 'Come on, I'll show you to your room.'

Amy followed him on legs that weren't quite steady, mentally chiding herself for being so foolish as to be affected by such an everyday thing as a man drinking out of a milk carton. *Sheesh!* She had to get some control. What on earth would her mother say if she told her she was attracted to a cop?

She was concentrating so hard on putting one foot in front of the other she didn't realise Angus had stopped halfway down the hall. She cannoned into him as he turned, his hands going to her upper arms to steady her.

'Whoa there,' he said, still holding her.

'Oops… I mean sorry. I didn't realise you'd stopped.'

His mouth tilted in a half smile. 'For a moment there I thought you were going to fall flat on your face, like this morning,' he said.

Actually, I think I'm falling in love, Amy surprised herself by admitting silently. She held her breath, not game to draw in a new one with his chest so close to hers. 'Um…you can let me go now,' she managed to croak out, her colour still high.

His hands loosened their grip and gradually fell away to drop by his sides. 'There's a bathrobe on the back of the door and fresh towels in the main bathroom two doors down,' he said, his voice sounding faintly rusty.

'Thank you…'

'What time do you need to be at the clinic in the morning?'

'Eight-thirty or so.'

'Fine,' he said. 'I'll run you in.'

'Um…you don't happen to have a spare toothbrush, do you?' she asked. Pausing for a moment, she found herself confessing, 'I was sick in the plane.'

He stood looking at her.

'What's that look for?' she asked, starting to squirm under his scrutiny. 'Lot's of people get airsick.'

He shook his head at her and moved past. 'There's a spare toothbrush in the cupboard beneath the basin. Goodnight.'

Amy spun around to glare at him as he strode away to his room. 'Lots and lots of people,' she reiterated. 'I bet even *you* would be sick, given the right circumstances.'

'Goodnight, Dr Tanner,' he said in a bored tone.

'Goodnight, Sergeant Ford,' she said crisply. 'And just in case you're interested, I was only sick twice. Believe me, that's sort of a record. I'm usually much worse.'

He didn't answer but she was sure he was still rolling his eyes as he disappeared into his bedroom.

Amy woke during the next hour or so to hear a soft scratching noise outside her door. Her eyes sprang open and she stiffened in the bed as she imagined a giant spider trying to make its way under the door. She began to talk herself through the panic, taking deep breaths as she reached for the bedside lamp, the soft glow instantly calming her fears as the scratching sound this time was accompanied by a low-pitched doggy whine.

She tossed the covers aside and, picking up the towel she'd

used earlier after her quick but totally refreshing shower, she covered her nakedness and opened the door. 'Fergus,' she said, looking down at the soulful brown eyes gazing up at her. 'What's wrong? Can't you sleep?'

The dog gave another whine and began moving down the hall, stopping now and again to look back at her as if to ask her to follow him.

'Hey, boy,' she whispered as she tiptoed past Angus's room. 'Do you need to go outside? Is that what's wrong?'

The dog finally came to a stop in front of the front door and gave another whine deep in his throat.

'OK, I'll let you out, but don't be long,' she said as she opened the door. 'I really need my beauty sleep and I'm about five hours short as it is.'

Fergus slunk off to the side of the house, the soft pad of his paws drowned out by the pounding of the surf below. Amy lifted her face to look at the brilliant night sky, her nostrils flaring to take in the fresh salty air.

A bird shuffled in a nearby shrub, its soft chirping signalling that dawn wasn't far away.

Amy stepped away from the open door to inspect the eastern sky, which the bulk of the house hid from view. The first light of the sun was streaking the sky with fingers of gold that were stretching outwards and upwards as if to collect all the shining stars and keep them hidden until the next night.

There was a soft thud behind her and she spun around to find the front door had closed on a breath of a breeze. She made her way back to the door, her heart sinking when she discovered it had locked on closing.

'Typical security-conscious cop,' she muttered under her breath as she jiggled the doorknob, to no avail.

She blew out a breath of frustration and, clutching her slipping towel, whispered to Fergus. 'Here, boy, come on. I want you with me when I wake up your master. He's not going to be happy to be woken after less than two hours' sleep.'

Fergus was nowhere to be seen or heard. Amy strained her ears for the sound of his paws on the gravelly area in front of the house but it was as quiet as the grave.

She called out again, slightly louder this time, but her voice came back to her in a ghostly echo that lifted the skin on her bare arms.

'And here I was thinking you were well trained,' she grumbled softly as she stepped gingerly over the rough gravel in her bare feet, one hand clutching her towel to her breasts. 'Come on, Fergus, you big mutt. Get your backside inside or I'll tell your master what a wicked truant you really are. Some police dog you turned out to be. You can't even obey the simplest orders.'

She rounded another corner of the house and opened her mouth to call out again when a tall dark figure stepped out of the shadows of the shrubbery on her right. Fear choked back her scream as every other survival instinct came to the fore. She fought viciously against the hands reaching for her, kicking and wriggling until she landed on the gravel on her back with her assailant on top of her. She bucked and arched in spite of the rough stones digging into her back and shoulders. In fact, if she hadn't been so absolutely terrified she would have even been a little proud of herself, given she'd never progressed past a white belt in tae kwon do.

Somehow she managed to open her mouth beneath the pressure of the palm against her and sank her teeth into it, but all it produced in her assailant was a cut-off expletive.

She wasn't quite sure how she did it but somehow she managed to catch him off guard and land a hard punch to his face before she rolled away, but it cost her the covering of the towel. She scrambled to her feet and began to run, shrieking at the top of her voice, 'Fergus! Angus! *Help!*'

She had only taken three stumbling steps when Angus's deep voice halted her. 'It's all right. It's me.'

She swung around to glare at him, her chest still heaving in fear. *'You!'*

He stepped out of the shadows and in the spreading light of dawn she saw his eyebrow wound had split open and was bleeding again.

She crossed her arms over her chest. 'Would you, please, hand me my towel?' she bit out in between ragged breaths as her heart rate struggled to return to normal.

'What were you doing outside, for God's sake?' he asked with a heavy frown. 'I could have hurt you.'

She lifted her chin at him. 'You *did* hurt me.' She gave him an icy glare. 'My back and shoulders are rubbed raw. What the hell were you doing? Why didn't you call out, instead of jumping on me and throwing me to the ground like that?'

'I thought you were an intruder and I did *not* throw you to the ground,' he said, a thin thread of anger entering his tone as he wiped the blood away from his face. 'You were struggling like a wildcat and took us both down.'

Amy would have put her hands on her hips but she needed them to offer what little modesty she could achieve in the brightening light of the morning. 'Will you, *please,* hand me my towel?' she asked again.

He turned around and, finding the towel, scooped it up off the ground and handed it to her without a word.

Amy took it with one hand, her breath tripping in her chest when she saw the way his eyes moved lazily over her. 'Do you mind?' She flashed her eyes at him in indignation.

His eyes came back to hers but not before he had seen practically all there was to see, she noted with burning resentment.

'You didn't answer my question,' he said. 'What were you doing outside?'

She secured the towel and, sending him another reproachful glare, informed him coldly, 'It was Fergus's fault. He woke me and begged to be let out. The door swung shut behind me.'

'Has he come back?'

'How would I know?' she asked. 'I've been too busy fighting off my would-be assailant.'

'Sorry about that,' he said. 'I thought I heard voices. I came outside to check.'

'I was talking to Fergus. That's probably what you heard.'

'I thought it was a male voice.'

'Oh…'

'You'd better go inside and clean up,' he said leading the way back to the door and unlocking it for her. 'I'll just do a quick check of the boatshed and see where Fergus has got to.'

'Your head looks like it needs to be re-stitched,' she said as the light from the house shone on his face. She bit her lip and mumbled self-consciously, 'I didn't mean to hit you that hard. Sorry.'

'Who taught you how to punch like that?' he asked with a twisted smile.

'Believe me, you really wouldn't want to know,' she said, and disappeared inside.

CHAPTER EIGHT

ANGUS searched the property before taking the cliff path to the beach, but if anyone had been there they had moved on. He looked out to sea and saw the faint light of a fishing boat in the distance but the vessel was too far away to have been responsible for the voices he'd heard, even though, at this time of day, sound carried over the water.

He met Fergus as he turned back for the path. The dog's coat was sandy and damp, as if he had been in the sea.

'You picked a bad time for a swim, mate,' he said, reaching to tickle his ears. 'You're supposed to be keeping an eye on things around here. You're getting soft, old boy. One pretty face and trim figure and you go to pieces.'

Fergus licked his hand and whined softly.

'Yeah, right,' Angus said wryly, heading back towards the house. 'Believe me, mate, I'm trying to take my own advice. I'm really trying, but she's quite a package even if she does have a lead foot.'

He heard Amy in the bathroom on his way past. He stopped and gave the door a gentle knock. 'You all right in there?'

The door swung open to reveal her dressed in a bathrobe. 'Look at my back!' she railed at him, swinging round and lowering the robe to show him her back and shoulders. 'I look like I've been dragged across a bed of nails.'

Angus couldn't help wincing in empathy. Her soft skin was pockmarked with gravel rash, some spots dark where the tiny stones had dug in and stayed put.

'I'll get some tweezers and get that gravel out for you,' he offered.

She pulled the bathrobe back up and turned back to face him as she tied it securely. 'I'd better do your head first,' she said. 'It's still seeping blood.'

He took a facecloth from the rack and pressed it to the wound above his eye, grimacing when he removed it and saw the red stain. 'It'll be fine in a minute.'

She blew out a breath of frustration. 'You can quit it with that I'm-a-bulletproof-macho-man routine,' she said. 'Your eyebrow needs re-stitching otherwise it won't heal the way it should, and then no doubt I'll get the blame for scarring you for life.'

Brown eyes challenged blue for several pulsing seconds.

'All right,' he said. 'You go first.'

'I'll get my bag,' she said, and brushed past him.

She came back a short time later with her bag and set it on the bench that housed the basin.

'You're probably going to have a real shiner by morning,' she said as she bathed the area with betadine.

'I hate to point it out, but it *is* morning.'

Amy felt the rumble of his deep voice as she brushed closer to place the first suture, and her hand wobbled. 'Keep still,' she said.

'I didn't move a muscle.'

'Stop talking, then,' she said. 'I can't concentrate.'

'If you can't concentrate, maybe I should get Allan Peddington to do it.'

'Shut up and let me get on with it.'

'You were much quicker last time,' he said.

'I've been awake most of the night and I've been attacked

and rolled like a rug across a gravel path, so if I'm a little bit off par, don't blame me.'

'If you had woken me when Fergus came to your door none of this would have happened,' he said as she put in th final stitch.

'So it's all my fault now, is it?' she asked, stripping off he gloves and tossing them in the bin. 'Your dog came to me and I assumed it would be all right to let him out. Besides, you' had a long drive. I was trying to be helpful, if you must know but apparently you don't agree.'

He got to his feet which made the bathroom seem way too small. 'Turn around,' he commanded.

She almost put her neck out, looking up at him. 'Maybe I' let Allan Peddington fix me. At least he'll know what he's doing.

A tiny nerve flickered at the side of his mouth. 'Turn around Dr Tanner.'

Amy felt her tummy give a tiny tremor of excitement at th brooding dark intensity in his eyes as they held hers. 'No,' she said

His hands came down on her shoulders and turned her s swiftly her breath came out in a startled whoosh. He was standing so close she could feel the brace of his thighs behind her, thei steely presence sending her heart on a roller-coaster ride.

'Pull the bathrobe down or I'll do it for you,' he said.

After a moment's hesitation she wriggled it down past he shoulders and muttered, 'No wonder you're not married o attached. No woman would ever put up with your cavemar attitude.'

'I'm not married or attached because I don't have time fo female histrionics,' he returned as he began to bathe her uppe back with a solution of betadine.

'*Ouch!*' She winced. 'That hurts!'

'I rest my case,' he drawled.

She gritted her teeth when he started using the tweezers, he hands gripping the edge of the bench in an effort to stop herself from squealing in pain.

I'll show him, she silently fumed. I'm not going to make a sound.

'Right,' he said after a few agonising, eye-watering minutes. 'That's the upper back done. Anywhere else?'

Amy decided against telling him her buttocks had taken their fare share of gravel from the path. 'No,' she said as she turned.

His eyes locked down on hers.

The air tightened around them, each second beginning to throb with a current of erotic promise. Amy felt the magnetic pull of his body; his naked chest, so close her fingertips ached to explore his muscular contours to see if they were as hard and sculpted as they looked.

She sent her tongue out to moisten her lips, her stomach free-falling when she saw his eyes darken as they followed the movement. His throat rose and fell on a swallow, as if he was fighting the temptation to close the tiny distance that separated them.

Her eyes went to his mouth, her breath stumbling to a halt as she saw the way its normally hard contours softened slightly as he came closer, his warm breath caressing her upturned face as his eyelashes fanned down over his eyes.

He paused just above her parted lips, as if he was still struggling with himself, but before he could change his mind, Amy closed the space between them and sealed his mouth with the full softness of hers.

It was like an explosion.

Flames of need flashed and sparked as their mouths fused, the white-hot scorch of hard male on soft female lips, the burning stroke and glide of tongues duelling as the kiss drifted into even more dangerous sensual territory.

Amy whimpered in delight when he took over the kiss with

a commanding force that was somewhere between pleasure and pain. The bruising quality of his mouth grinding against hers spoke of physical needs left unmet for far too long. There was anger in his kiss, anger and frustration and red-hot desire. She felt it ridge his lower body as his blood surged through his veins, the thickness of him against her sending her senses spinning.

His tongue probed and thrust against hers, calling it into a dance of heated sexual purpose. Excitement zinged along her nerve endings, her skin tightening all over in anticipation of his touch on other parts of her body. Her belly quivered and shook with desire, her inner thighs already anointed with the dewy moistness of her arousal. Her breasts swelled and ached, their hardened points rubbing up against him as he crushed her to him, his mouth still wreaking its sensual havoc on hers.

He dragged his mouth off hers after another few breathless moments, his eyes glittering with rampant need, his chest rising and falling as he fought to regain control. 'Now, that was a really stupid thing to for you to do,' he said.

Her eyes widened in affront. 'What did *I* do?'

'You started it by kissing me first.'

'I did not!'

'Yes, you did,' he said. 'I admit I was tempted, but I wasn't going to go through with it.'

'Oh really?' Her expression was sceptical.

He held her challenging look with ease. 'I'm as human as the next man,' he said. 'When a woman throws herself at me, like you did, it takes a moment or two to tame the instinctive response.'

'I did *not* throw myself at you!'

'Don't get me wrong, Dr Tanner. You're a good-looking woman but anything that happens between us is not going to work out in the long term.'

She gave him a scathing look. 'If you think for one moment I'd be interested in any length of term with someone like you then you've got yourself an even bigger ego problem than I originally thought. You're exactly the sort of man I have avoided all my dating life.'

'Good to know where we both stand on this,' he said. 'I didn't want you to get the wrong idea about one kiss.'

She scooped up her doctor's bag and stormed out of the bathroom with her head held high. 'It wasn't such a great kiss anyway,' she tossed over her shoulder.

Angus didn't answer but when he turned and caught sight of himself in the mirror he found his fingers had somehow crept up to his mouth where the softness of hers had pressed against his...

Amy sat in a stiff silence as Angus drove her to town an hour or so later. She felt his gaze swing in her direction once or twice but stalwartly refused to acknowledge it. She hated that he had painted her as some sort of female desperado in search of a temporary mate. Her skin still prickled with irritation at his summation of her character. Who was he to cast the first stone anyway? He was locked out here in the wilderness with nothing but a dog for company on the long lonely nights. At least she had tried to have some sort of life with Simon, even if it hadn't worked out the way she had hoped.

She mumbled a quick thanks as he pulled up outside the hotel so she could get changed before starting at the clinic.

'I forgot to tell you what a good job you did yesterday with Bobby Williams,' he said through his open window as she began to stalk away. 'I wasn't sure you'd be able to manage such severe injuries.'

She turned back to look at him, a tiny pout hovering around her mouth. 'I hope that wasn't too painful, Sergeant,' she said. 'Giving me a compliment, I mean.'

'I thought I gave you the biggest compliment earlier this morning,' he returned with an unreadable look.

'Oh, yes, indeed you did,' she answered. 'You told me how resistible I am. Thanks a bunch.'

'You should be thankful I didn't take advantage of your…er…generosity,' he said.

Amy came back to stand in front of his window and, leaning down, eyeballed him determinedly. 'I forgot to tell *you* something yesterday,' she said echoing his earlier words.

'Go right ahead,' Angus said, doing his best to keep his eyes trained on hers instead of the tempting shadow of her cleavage currently on show.

'The nicest thing about you is your dog,' she said. 'As far as I can see, it's the only thing you've got going for you.'

His lips twitched. 'Is that so, Dr Tanner? I'm sure he'll be delighted to hear it.'

'And another thing,' she went on, with her blue eyes flashing at him furiously. 'You could have stopped that kiss before it started so it's no good laying the blame solely at my door.'

He gave her a nod of assent. 'Point taken.'

A little frown began to tease her brow. 'So you admit it was just as much your fault?'

'It was just a kiss, Dr Tanner, and like you said—not a particularly good one.' He put the car into gear and gave the engine a couple of revs before adding coolly, 'Have a nice day.'

Amy watched as he drove off, taking her chance of the last word with him. She huffed out a breath of pique and trudged into the hotel.

'Morning, Dr Tanner,' Bill called out from behind the bar. 'I left the side door open for you last night but I see you spent the night with Angus.'

Amy felt her face heating. 'Um…I didn't realise you had left it open,' she said. 'Sergeant Ford told me it would be locked. He thought it best not to wake you. We got back rather late from Geraldton.'

'I heard about young Bobby's accident. He's been asking for that for months, you know. He's got in with the wrong crowd. I hope he makes it, for the sake of his parents if not for himself.'

'He's doing OK, or so the surgeon said when I phoned this morning,' she said. 'He's going to have a long period of rehabilitation but hopefully it will give him time to see the error of his ways.'

'It's a nice place Angus is looking after out there at the Point, isn't it?' Bill said as he gave the bench another wipe.

'Yes…it's very nice.'

He smiled a knowing smile. 'You know you wouldn't be putting my nose out of joint if you moved out there with him. It's not much of a room for you upstairs and sharing a bathroom with the other guests can't be too pleasant, not to mention the dining room, which is probably nothing like those posh London restaurants you're used to.'

'It's fine, really.'

'Yeah, well, I thought I should warn you old Maurie Morrison is back in town,' he said. 'He's a bit of a drifter who blows in and out now and again. He's in room four. I hope he doesn't disturb you. He's a nice enough bloke. A bit lonely since his wife died so if you haven't got time to chat, make sure you let him know. He can talk the leg off an iron pot and he takes ages in the bathroom.'

'I'm sure he won't be any bother to me,' Amy reassured him pleasantly.

'Will you be in for dinner tonight? The kitchen opens at six and closes at seven-thirty. Betty's a bit of a stickler for punctuality but if you're late don't worry. I can always rustle up some leftovers for you.'

Amy tried not to think of her beautifully appointed kitchen in her apartment in Sydney and her massive pile of gourmet cookbooks. 'Leftovers will be fine,' she said.

Bill gave her a grin. 'You have yourself a nice day, now Dr Tanner.'

She gave him a weak smile. 'I sure will.'

And she would have if it hadn't been for her second-last patient

Mona Tennant was a woman in her late sixties who obviously didn't require the diagnostic skills of a doctor. She came in with a full list of medications she insisted be prescribed for her without a prior examination or history taken.

'I'm sorry, Mrs Tennant.' Amy tried for the third time to reason with her. 'I can't prescribe narcotic medication for pain unless I know the source of pain. I see from your notes that Dr Ridley ordered a MRI scan of your lower back some month ago. Did you have one taken? I can't see any evidence of the report in your file.'

'Of course I didn't have it done,' the elderly woman said. 'Why would I waste all that time and money travelling all the way to Geraldton for a procedure that will tell me nothing I don't already know? I have a bad back. I've had it for years. Now, if you're not going to give me my pills, I'll go and see Dr Peddington instead.'

'Mrs Tennant, it's not that I don't want to help you but it would make things easier if I knew exactly what it was I was actually treating. Back pain can be debilitating and needs proper management. But sometimes, instead of drugs, some simple exercises or physiotherapy can be just as good if not more effective.'

'Well, forget about the painkillers and write me up for some nerve pills,' Mrs Tennant said. 'But make them stronger this time. The dosage Dr Ridley gave me last time didn't do a thing.'

Amy glanced back down at the notes. 'But, Mrs Tennant, ten milligrams of Valium is considered a reasonably high dose. Five milligrams is usually enough to settle feelings of anxiety or sleeplessness.'

The old woman pursed her lips for a moment. 'What about the antibiotics, then? I need them in case I get a cold.'

Amy only just resisted the urge to roll her eyes. 'Taking anti-biotics when you don't need them can make you resistant to them when you do. Most colds are viral—they only need antibiotics if an infection moves onto the chest or into the nasal passages.'

Mrs Tennant got to her feet and threw Amy a look of disdain. 'Just as well you're only going to be here three months, young lady,' she said. 'Most of us would end up dead and buried if you stayed any longer for lack of proper medical care.'

'Mrs Tennant, I—'

'I know when I need medication. I haven't been on this earth almost seventy years without learning a thing or two about my own body.'

'I'm sure you're very good at—'

'And another thing,' she huffed and puffed before Amy could finish her sentence. 'Everyone knows why you're really here. You're not interested in the locals at all. All you're interested in is stirring the pot over Lindsay Redgrove's suicide.'

Amy's mouth fell open.

'Don't bother denying it,' the woman went on. 'You were seen with Sergeant Ford out at her shack yesterday at Caveside Cove. The whole town is talking about it.'

'I had a very good reason for wanting to visit Lindsay's shack.'

'Oh, really?' Mrs Tennant looked sceptical. 'Now, what would that be, I wonder?'

'I'm her cousin, that's why.' As soon as Amy had said the words she wished she hadn't.

Mrs Tennant frowned. 'Her cousin? You don't look anything like her in build or looks.'

'No, I know, but that doesn't mean we weren't related. I wanted to visit the place she loved.'

'Then why not be up front about it instead of going about it so furtively? You won't win any friends out here with such underhand tactics, let me tell you.'

'I didn't and don't see that it's anyone's business but my own

The elderly woman peered at her over her glasses. 'If yo
cared about your cousin, you would have come and visited he
before she got so desperate as to take her own her life.'

Amy had to swallow against her rising guilt. 'I was plannin
to as soon as I finished my term in London.'

'Yes, well, you were too late,' Mrs Tennant said unnecessaril

'I realise that.'

'I hope you are going to leave her in peace. She did wha
she did and it should be left at that.'

'I don't want to cause any trouble,' Amy explained. 'I jus
wanted to pay my respects.'

Mrs Tennant's brows beetled above her bird-like eyes. '
would have taken less than a day to do that. Why come her
for three months?'

It was a good question but Amy wasn't prepared to answe
it, or at least not honestly. 'I'm between jobs,' she said instead
'It seemed a good chance to visit this side of the country.'

'So what do you think of Sergeant Ford?'

Amy was momentarily thrown by the question and looke
blankly at the older woman.

'Are you going to move in with him?' Mrs Tennant asked.

'No.'

'You sound rather definite.'

'I am.'

'He needs some company out there.'

'I'm sure he'll find someone.'

'The hotel can't be that comfortable,' Mrs Tennant said
'Why would you want to stay there when you can stay at th
sergeant's place for free?'

'I'm sure it's a lovely spot but—'

'You stayed there last night,' the elderly woman interrupte
her. 'Everyone knows you did.'

Amy felt the heat storm into her cheeks again. 'We were late getting back to town. The hotel was locked up and…and Sergeant Ford offered me a place to stay for what was left of the night.'

'So how was it?'

'How was what?'

'Spending the night at his place.'

Amy was feeling as if her doctor status had taken a sudden nose dive. 'It was fine. Now, if you'll excuse me, I have one last patient to see.'

'The Healy boy, right?' Mrs Tennant said with another purse of her lips. 'That mother of his needs a kick up the backside if you ask me. Talk about neurotic. Mind you, the boy's been a bit of a handful but Sergeant Ford has taken him under his wing.'

'Yes, I've heard what a good job he does with the local youth.'

'He's a good man is our sergeant but in need of a good woman,' Mrs Tennant said.

'I'm sure he's more than able to find one for himself,' Amy offered pertly.

'He's got scars, you know.'

'Oh, really?'

'Not physical ones,' Mrs Tennant explained. 'Deeper than that, if you know what I mean.'

Amy didn't but decided against showing too much interest. She glanced meaningfully at her watch and sent the older woman a tight smile. 'I'm sorry I wasn't able to help you today. Perhaps you'd like to book another appointment and I can conduct a more thorough investigation into your current ailments.'

'I'll think about it,' Mrs Tennant said, and, snatching up her oversized handbag, bustled out.

The door had only just closed on her exit when Allan opened it after a brief knock.

'I'm sorry to bother you, Amy…'

Amy frowned at his greyish pallor and quickly got to her feet. 'What's wrong, Allan? Are you feeling unwell?'

He gave her a sheepish look and sank to the chair in front of her desk. 'I'm sorry to do this to you, Amy, but I think I'm going to have to take a few days off. I've been pushing myself too hard for too long. Will you be able to manage for a week or so on your own? I can try and organise a locum for back-up, but you probably know how long it takes to get someone to fill these remote positions. It could take a month or more.'

'Don't worry about it, Allan,' she said. 'I can manage. But how about I check you over? How long have you been feeling unwell?'

'It's nothing serious, probably stress-related if anything. I thought I might go and stay with my daughter for a few days, maybe even head down to the Margaret River region with her for a break. Heaven knows, we both could do with it.'

'That sounds like an excellent idea,' Amy said. 'And, please, don't worry about things here. I'm sure I'll cope.'

'I'm sure you will. You did an excellent job on Bobby Williams,' Allan said. 'I couldn't have done better.'

'Thank you, but I didn't do it alone,' she said. 'Sergeant Ford was there with me.'

'He's a good cop,' Allan said as he got up to leave. 'Sharp as a tack. Nothing gets past him.'

Amy couldn't quite remove the dryness from her tone. 'So I've heard.'

'You know you really should think about moving out there with him,' he said. 'The hotel's not the place for a decent young woman like you.'

'What is it about everyone in this town insisting I live with Sergeant Ford?' she asked with an edge of frustration. 'Is this some sort of dastardly conspiracy to find him a wife?'

'You could do a lot worse than Angus,' Allan said. 'And think of how wonderful it would be if you decided to stay for longer than three months. I could finally think about retiring.'

'Sorry to disappoint you, but I don't see that happening,' she said. 'I'm not sure I can handle the intrusion into my personal life, for one thing.'

'Ah, you're referring to dear old Mona, I dare say,' he said. 'Don't take too much notice of her. She likes to have a gossip now and again. She probably only came in to see you to give you the once-over.'

Amy decided to come clean. 'Allan, I have a confession to make. I should have told you when I answered the advertisement, but I didn't want anyone to know...'

'You're Lindsay Redgrove's cousin, aren't you?' Allan said before she could continue.

'You already knew?'

He nodded. 'I spoke at length to her parents while they were here. They mentioned they had a niece who was a doctor. I have a good memory for names so when I saw yours on the application I put two and two together.'

'I'm sorry... I should have told you earlier.'

'I understand your reluctance in revealing your connection to Lindsay, that's why I didn't say anything to you and I haven't told anyone else. She was a difficult person at times.'

'Was she your patient?'

'No, Jacqui looked after her mostly.'

'Do you think it will be a problem, people finding out I'm her cousin?' Amy asked. 'I was caught off guard with Mrs Tennant and let it slip out.'

'I'd like to say that no one will hold it against you but this is a small town and it has its share of bigots,' he said. 'But from what I've seen so far, you're a highly competent and caring doctor. That's really all that matters, isn't it?'

'Thank you,' she said with a grateful smile.

He reached for the door. 'But I would seriously think again about moving in with Angus,' he said. 'You could go a long way to find a man as nice as him.'

'I *have* come a long way,' Amy said a little defensively. 'But it wasn't to find a man, even one as saintly as Sergeant Ford is reputed to be.'

'No harm in keeping your options open,' he said, and with another fatherly smile closed the door as he left.

CHAPTER NINE

Amy buried her head under the pillow for the tenth time that night as the snores from room number four reverberated through the thin walls.

She had met Maurie Morrison over dinner in the dining room, having only just scraped in on time after being held up at the clinic with a last-minute patient with an allergic reaction to a beesting. Betty, the cook, had given her a disapproving frown and placed an overloaded plate in front of her, the greasy food swimming in a congealing pool of gravy doing nothing to encourage her already diminishing appetite.

Maurie had talked non-stop about anything and everything until Amy's eyes had begun to glaze over. She had politely excused herself and gone to her room to escape into a book, but on her last visit to the bathroom before bed, she'd had to stand outside for endless minutes, practically cross-legged, until Maurie had finally come out with a sheepish grin, before shuffling back to his room, his slippers flapping on his feet.

Amy had finally got to bed, closed her eyes and drifted off to sleep, only to be woken a couple of hours later by a racket that would have got a seismologist leaping to his feet in alarm, she was sure.

She glanced at the clock after another sleepless hour and

groaned. How was she supposed to be single-handedly respon
sible for the town's health with no sleep? She hadn't even had
a chance to recover from the stress and drama of the night before

She let another half-hour pass before she decided that rather
than toss and turn any longer she would get up and do some
thing physical. The sky was starting to lighten so she put on her
trainers and a pair of shorts and top and, scooping up her car
keys, tiptoed downstairs.

Without consciously intending to head that way, she suddenly
found herself approaching the turn-off to Caveside Cove. She
turned into the road and, leaving her car in the shade of a tree
took the rough pathway the rest of the way down to the beach

The ocean was rolling in with a two-metre swell, the salt
spray filling the fresh morning air with fine beads of moisture
The sun on the cliffs had turned them almost pink and the sand
beneath her feet was littered with thousands of shells.

She cast her eyes back to the sea and watched in fascination
as a dorsal fin broke the surface of the water just beyond the
breakers. Within moments another one appeared and then the
glistening arc of a dolphin's back surfaced. The rest of the pod
was close behind, their bodies undulating with the smooth
grace of nature at its perfect best.

After a while they swam out of sight and Amy's eyes moved
to where her cousin's shack was situated in the dunes halfway
along the beach, and before she knew it her legs were carrying
her towards it.

Even in the flattering light of the golden glow of early
morning the shack didn't look like a place anyone in their right
mind would want to live in indefinitely.

But, then, Lindsay hadn't been in her right mind, Amy
reminded herself somewhat painfully. She cast her memory
back to the days when she had looked up to her older cousin
before Lindsay's mental health had taken such a sudden unex

pected turn. Being five years older, Lindsay had often babysat Amy when her mother had had some engagement to go to. Amy had loved the funny little pictures her cousin had drawn to entertain her and she had nothing but pleasant memories of their times together during that time.

However, it had all changed seemingly overnight when Lindsay had been in her final year of high school. She had fallen in with a rough crowd and begun to experiment with drugs, cannabis mostly. Within weeks she had started to buckle under the pressure of looming exams, spending sleepless nights in agitation and eventually missing day after day of school. She'd run away from home on more than one occasion, and her first suicide attempt had thrown Amy's aunt and uncle into an emotional tailspin they had never quite recovered from.

Amy could still recall the shock of seeing her cousin lying so ghostly white in that hospital bed, her thin wrists bandaged where she had slashed them.

Over the next few years Lindsay had been under almost constant psychiatric monitoring, a host of drugs prescribed in an attempt to bring her out of her psychosis, but in the end nothing had really seemed to work as effectively as the move to Marraburra. It had been as if the shift away from her troubled past to the quiet coastal town on the other side of the country had been just what she'd needed to find inner peace.

Amy pushed her sadness over her cousin's tragic life aside as she tried the door of the shack, even though she knew Angus had locked it the day before.

'You really shouldn't come out here alone,' a voice said from behind her.

She felt her heart leap upwards as she swung around to see Angus standing there. 'You scared the living daylights out of me!' Her voice came out high-pitched and wobbly. 'Couldn't you have called out or something?'

'I mean it, Dr Tanner. This is an isolated, unpatrolled beach, as I told you previously. You'd be better to stick to the one closer to town if you want an early morning run or swim.'

Amy stuck up her chin. 'I can look after myself.'

His hand came up and briefly touched his eyebrow where a shadow of a bruise was showing beneath his tan. 'Yes, I am in no doubt of that, but I still recommend you keep to the more populated areas.'

She inspected his lightweight running gear before returning her eyes to his. 'You don't seem to suffer the same reservations when choosing where to exercise,' she pointed out.

'Fergus is with me,' he said.

Amy knew he was probably right about being out there all alone. She had seen enough attacks on young women to know there was danger in being too blasé about personal safety, even in supposedly quiet country towns. But something about his demeanour made her wonder if he had his own private reasons for keeping her away from Caveside Cove, and especially away from her cousin's shack.

His dark brown gaze held hers for a pulsing moment. 'I'll walk with you back to your car,' he said.

She stood her ground. 'I'm not planning on leaving just yet.'

A brief flash of irritation passed over his features. 'Fine,' he said. 'I'll wait for you.'

'What's going on, Sergeant Ford?' she asked, her eyes narrowed at him in suspicion. 'Why don't you want me to hang around here?'

Angus could have kicked himself for being so transparent. The last thing he wanted to do was make any alarms bells ring in her head. 'You can come here any time you like,' he said evenly. 'But for your own safety it would be best if you didn't come alone.'

'My cousin lived out here all alone for a couple of years without a problem,' she said.

'Your cousin eventually committed suicide.'

Her brows rose slightly. 'Are you suggesting the loneliness got to her?'

'It would get to anyone after a while.'

She angled her head at him. 'And yet you live all by yourself on top of that cliff around at the Point, don't you, Sergeant? Tell me something, does it get to you? Do you feel yourself going stir crazy with boredom and loneliness?'

He was going crazy, lying awake at night thinking of how her soft mouth had felt beneath his, Angus thought wryly. Not to mention the sight of her gorgeous naked body which he hadn't been able to erase from his mind. 'No, it doesn't,' he said. 'And I'm not usually alone.'

'Oh, yes, you've got Fergus,' she said as the dog came up to her and snuffled her hand.

'Yes.'

Amy returned her gaze to his watchful one. 'I'd better get going. Allan's having a few days off and leaving me in charge.'

Angus frowned. 'Is he unwell?'

'I'm not exactly sure. He didn't go into details. He just said he felt a little stressed and wanted to take a break with his daughter.'

'Will you be able to manage on your own?' he asked.

'It's a small country town, Sergeant Ford,' she said, sending him a haughty look. 'I'm sure I'll manage to keep everyone alive until he gets back, in spite of what some of the locals think.'

'I heard the town's matriarch, Mona Tennant, came to see you,' he said with a ghost of a smile.

She rolled her eyes. 'Mona is right. She moaned the whole time she was there.'

'She's used to getting her way,' Angus said, and then after a little pause added, 'I think I should warn you not to tell her about your connection with Lindsay. Mona is likely to spread it around pretty widely.'

Amy gave a frown of annoyance. 'Too late,' she said. 'I wouldn't have said anything but she half guessed it anyway. She said we were seen out here on Monday and she knew we'd spent the night together.'

'And that bothered you?'

Her cheeks took on a rosy hue. 'Why should it bother me?'

He gave a tiny shrug, his eyes still locked on hers. 'You tell me.'

Amy fidgeted under his scrutiny. 'I don't like the thought of people gossiping about me.'

'Small towns like this are known for their gossip loops,' he said. 'You either get used to it or circumvent it.'

'Is that why you don't have a woman in your life?'

His eyes hardened a fraction. 'I told you my reasons.'

'Yes, you did, but I still find it hard to believe a full-blooded man like you would be content to go for months at a stretch without female company,' she said. 'The way you kissed me the other night seemed to suggest you're currently feeling the effects of the drought.'

There was a moment of tense silence broken only by the deep pulse of the ocean in the background.

'Are you offering to alleviate the boredom for me, Dr Tanner?'

Amy felt her stomach clench against the sudden kick of desire his smoothly drawled words triggered. His dark gaze smouldered as he stepped closer, his hands coming down on the tops of her shoulders as he brought her up against him in preparation for his descending mouth.

His kiss was just earth-shattering as the last time, the movement of his lips and tongue driving every rational thought out of her brain. Sexual energy fired like a surging current from his body to hers, leaving her boneless in his crushing hold.

She kissed him back with passion-charged heat, her tongue

dancing around the determined thrust of his, her breasts jammed up against him, her pelvis burning where he pressed against her.

He shifted position which afforded her a chance to suck greedily on his bottom lip, the action drawing a deep guttural groan from his throat. She pushed her tongue back into his mouth as one of his hands found her breast, the warmth of his palm exploring her boldly and possessively through the thin cotton of her T-shirt.

His unshaven jaw scored her soft skin when he deepened the kiss even further, but she was beyond caring. She had never felt such overwhelming desire. Her love-making with Simon seemed so pathetically tame in comparison. She had never clawed at Simon so wantonly, never felt the scrape of teeth against her own as each kiss became more urgent, never felt her body burn and turn to liquid with such intense longing.

She sucked in a sharp almost painful breath as Angus lifted her T-shirt and moved his mouth from hers to suckle on her breast, the exquisite sensation of his lips and tongue on her naked flesh sending arrows of need to every secret part of her.

He went to her other breast and subjected it to the same passionate onslaught until she was practically swaying in his arms. Her hands looked for an anchor and looped around his neck, pulling his head back down for his mouth to meet hers.

In the end it was Fergus who brought the kiss to an end. His sharp bark from further down the beach brought Angus's head up, his eyes narrowing against the early slant of the sun as he stepped away from her.

'Excuse me,' he said, his expression becoming all cop-like and closed again.

Amy stood on unsteady legs as she watched him walk to where Fergus was standing at the base of the crumbling cliff at

the far end of the beach, her heart coming to a chugging stop
when she what the dog had spotted in amongst the fallen debris.

A pair of legs, the feet clad in trainers, was protruding from
behind the screen of the rocks.

Angus straightened from the body and called out to her as
he reached for his mobile. 'Come quickly. He's alive. I'll call
the ambulance.'

Amy ran down the beach to join him, and he moved out of
her way as she kneeled next to the supine body of a man in his
late thirties. He was breathing, but only just, his airway almost
obstructed by his tongue, his colour cyanotic and his eyes closed.

'Help me turn him onto his side,' Amy instructed, the priorities of trauma resuscitation assembling in her mind, even
though her heart sank at how limited she was with no equipment at hand.

Angus assisted her in rolling the body into the coma
position, Amy supporting the head and neck and providing
jaw-thrust whilst Angus did most of the physical work. The ma-
noeuvre instantly improved the airway as the stertorous breath
sounds became quiet, the body breathing now in a regular
rhythm as long as Amy supported the jaw.

'He's got a boggy haematoma over the occiput,' she said, not
realising she was speaking aloud until she caught sight of
Angus's raised brow. 'The back of his head,' she clarified.

'Right, I had noticed that,' he said.

'Can you see any other injuries? I can't let go of the airway.'

Angus began to undo the short dark-coloured cotton shirt on
the body. 'No signs of any obvious chest trauma,' he said, and
proceeded to the abdomen and back and then lower and upper
limbs. 'There are abrasions all over his arms and legs and his
back, and his ankle looks as if it's broken.'

'Do you think he's fallen from the cliff?' Amy asked as she
glanced at the man's contorted ankle.

'Looks like it,' he said, looking at the man's face, a small frown bringing his brows together.

'Do you know who it is?' she asked.

He shook his head. 'Never seen him before.'

'Maybe he's a tourist…you know, out for a hike and lost his footing.'

'Maybe,' Angus answered absently as he glanced back up at the cliff face.

Amy followed the line of his gaze. 'It's a long way to fall.'

'Yeah,' he said, looking down the beach for any sign of the ambulance arriving.

A stray thought wandered into Amy's head. 'What if he was pushed?'

His eyes came back to hers. 'You've been watching too many cop shows, Dr Tanner.'

She found his tone a little condescending and pursed her mouth at him. 'So you don't think there's anything suspicious about this?' she asked.

'A full and proper investigation will be carried out in due course. Let's hope he lives long enough to tell us what he was doing up there in the first place. For all we know, he might have jumped.'

Amy's eyes clashed momentarily with his. 'Yet another suicide, Sergeant Ford? Isn't that rather a coincidence?'

'What are you suggesting, Dr Tanner?'

She raised her chin a fraction. 'You were the one to report my cousin's death as suicide, weren't you?'

His gaze hardened as it collided with hers. 'And your point is?'

'What if you got it wrong?' she asked. 'What if she didn't commit suicide at all? What if someone murdered her and made it look like a suicide?'

'You're letting your emotions rule your head,' he said. 'It's understandable because she was your cousin, but let me assure you the proper channels of investigation were followed at all times, as they will be in this case as well.'

'I don't believe Lindsay took her own life and I'm not going to rest until I find out who killed her.'

'Then you'll be wasting your time because the results of my investigation and the decision of the coroner were one and the same. It was suicide and the sooner you accept it the better.'

'There has hardly been a police investigation that I can tell,' she threw back. 'It seems to me a verdict of suicide was reached before a proper investigation was carried out.'

'You are welcome to see the records on the investigation.'

Amy wondered if he was calling her bluff. She hunted his face but it was hard to tell what he was thinking behind the screen of his dark, unreadable eyes.

The rest of their conversation was interrupted by the arrival of the volunteer ambulance officers who drove as close as they could to the cliff base before removing the spinal board from the back of the four wheel drive vehicle.

'The Flying Doctor's been called up to Monkey Mia for a mild case of hypothermia—some guy stayed down too long on a dive,' Joan said. 'The doctor accompanying the patient said they'll stop in to pick up this guy on the way back. It'll be quicker than the paramedics anyway.'

As they were transferring the man into the ambulance a police vehicle arrived and a man of similar age to Angus came over to speak to them.

'Anyone we know?' James Ridley asked Angus after brief introductions were made.

'No,' Angus said. 'But it looks like he might have been there overnight. He was lucky the tide didn't take him out to sea.'

'He was fortunate you and Dr Tanner found him when you did,' James said with a speculative glance in Amy's direction. 'So what brought you way out here so early in the morning?'

Amy felt her colour rise. 'I was out…er…walking and ran into Sergeant Ford.'

James's gaze swung back to his colleague, his hazel eyes twinkling. 'I'd better get back to town. I'll let you see Dr Tanner back to her car.' He turned back to address Amy. 'Nice to meet you, Dr Tanner. My wife is really keen to meet you. I'll have a word with her and see if we can organise something soon.'

'That would be very nice,' she said, smiling weakly.

Angus walked her back to her car once James had left. 'I was expecting you to tell Senior Constable Ridley what we were doing prior to finding the body,' he said with a glint of devilment in his eyes. 'Why didn't you?'

She stopped to look up at him in shock. 'You surely don't think I would reveal something like that!'

He gave her a smouldering look as he opened her car door for her. 'So you prefer to keep what goes on between us private, do you?'

'There is *nothing* going on between us,' Amy said sternly. 'It was just a kiss and not a part—'

His fingertip came over her lips to silence her, the ironic glint in his eyes sending her senses into a tailspin. 'Don't say it, Dr Tanner, otherwise I might be tempted to make you eat those words of yours the next time.'

He lifted his finger from her mouth and, stepping back from her, whistled to Fergus.

'There's *not* going to be a next time,' she bit out determinedly, but he had already begun walking back the way he'd come.

CHAPTER TEN

NEWS of the injured man's body on the beach was all over town by the time Amy got to the clinic.

'What a ghastly shock for you!' Helen said. 'Just as well Sergeant Ford was with you at the time.'

'Er…yes…'

Helen gave her a probing look. 'So what *were* you doing out there with him at that time of the morning?' she asked.

Amy wished she had some way of turning off her tendency to blush at the mere mention of Angus's name. 'I went for a walk and…er…ran into him there.'

'I expect you went out there to visit your cousin's shack.' There was a hint of pique in the receptionist's tone.

'I'm sorry I didn't tell you the first day,' Amy said. 'I didn't want to make it public knowledge.'

'Yes, well, Mona is like a gossip hotline so your secret is well and truly out now.'

Amy caught her lip for a moment. 'I hope it's not going to be a negative thing, you know, people knowing Lindsay and I were related. Allan Peddington said it shouldn't make a difference but I'm not so sure.'

'I shouldn't think it will be a problem,' Helen reassured her. 'Lindsay was a bit of an oddball admittedly, but that doesn't mean people will expect you to be the same.'

Amy decided to take the bull by the horns. 'You mentioned that first day that no one expected her to take her life. Do you think there's any possibility that she didn't commit suicide?'

Helen's face visibly paled. 'You mean someone could have…murdered her?'

Amy nodded.

'But the police and the coroner—'

'They could have got it wrong,' Amy said. 'You hinted at it yourself the other day.'

'No,' Helen insisted. 'I just said Lindsay's parents seemed resigned to the fact she was going to do it some day.'

'But that's exactly my point,' Amy argued. 'How easy would it be to pass off murder as a suicide in someone who had been suicidal in the past?'

Helen's expression became guarded. 'I don't think you should spread that opinion around too freely. The police work hard enough out here as it is, without someone from outside questioning every detail of a case that was open and shut from the start.' She straightened her spine and added stiffly, 'The first patients are here. I think we should get on with treating the living instead of speculating about the dead.'

Amy let out a slow breath as she picked up the first patient's file.

It was going to be a long and tiring day.

Just as she was preparing to leave for the afternoon she heard a commotion in Reception, raised voices and furniture being knocked over.

Her door burst open and Helen's worried face appeared. 'Quick, Amy,' she said. 'We've got an emergency. I've called the police and they're on their way.'

Amy rushed out to find a harried father trying to control his teenage son, who was kicking and shouting and swearing volubly, his eyes wild and glazed.

'Help him!' the father cried in panic as he half carried, half dragged the lad into the examination room. 'I think he's taken something. He's gone crazy.'

Amy tried to keep her own panic under control as she tried to avoid the boy's flailing arms and legs.

'Get away! Don't touch me!' the boy screamed at the top of his voice, and fought viciously against his father's iron hold.

Amy felt her stomach clench as the boy's hand came up and punched his father full in the face, the crunch of fist on the man's nose making her own eyes water as the blood began to spurt. The blow loosened the man's hold on his son and the boy rushed for the door but came up against Angus and James, who together managed to restrain him.

'Come on, Hamish,' Angus said in a calm voice. 'It's all right, mate.'

'Let me go!' the boy wailed, his eyes frantic with fear. 'They're eating me alive! Oh, God! There are hundreds of them!'

'Can you hold him down on the treatment table?' Amy directed. 'He's obviously hallucinating.' She turned to the father who was holding his nose with a wad of tissues Helen had handed him. 'Do you have any idea of what your son has taken?'

The father was openly weeping now, and shook his head helplessly. James let out a grunt of pain as Hamish's knee caught him in the groin and he momentarily dropped his hold.

'It looks like crystal meth,' Angus said, putting his whole weight across the boy to hold him down while his colleague got his breath back.

'That's what I was thinking, too,' Amy said. 'Can you hold him while I get an IV in?'

He nodded and then winced as Hamish tried to bite his arm. 'Cool it, Hamish. Dr Tanner is here to help you.'

Amy struggled to insert an IV with the boy bucking and rolling. Somehow she got it in and administered 5 mg midazolam but there was virtually no affect. Hamish kept swearing and in spite of the two police officers doing their level best to restrain him, he appeared to have almost superhuman strength. He almost got out from under them and in his attempt to secure his hold Angus shifted position, allowing the boy's arms to suddenly flail upwards, jerking Angus's elbow back against Amy's cheek.

'Sorry,' he gritted out as he tightened his hold, sending a quick concerned glance over his shoulder, his face pinched and strained. 'Did I hurt you?'

'I'm all right but I need to give him more,' she said, and titrated another 5 mg, which began to take effect almost immediately. Hamish's jerking limbs began to relax and within minutes he was sleeping.

'Is he going to be all right?' the father asked, still holding his bleeding nose.

Amy led him to a vacant chair and helped him to sit down. 'Your son will need to be kept under observation,' she said. 'We don't have the facilities here so I'd like to send him to Geraldton. Crystal meth, or "ice" is a highly toxic drug with a whole host of frightening side effects, some of which you just witnessed—psychosis, extreme violence and hallucinations.'

'I don't know where he got it,' the father said, glancing nervously towards the police officers. 'I swear to God I don't.'

'I'd better see to that nose of yours,' Amy said, and lifted off the blood-soaked pad. The bleeding had stopped but when Amy moved the nasal bones from side to side, there was obvious crepitus, indicating a fracture. 'I'll need to put a plaster bridge across your nose to stabilise it,' she said. 'Helen, can you go get the plaster trolley?'

'I've called the Flying Doctor,' Helen said as she came back in with the trolley. 'The road ambulance will be here to transfer him to the airfield in ten minutes.'

'Thanks, Helen,' Amy said, inwardly quailing at the thought of another stomach-churning journey in that tiny aircraft. She met Angus's dark brown gaze and felt her cheeks flare with colour. She'd been lucky that morning with a doctor already on board offering to escort the cliff-fall man to Geraldton, but now it looked as if she was going to have to face her winged demons again.

'It might be best if someone else goes with Hamish,' Angus said. 'With Allan Peddington away, it leaves the town vulnerable in case of an emergency.'

Amy could have kissed him right there in front of everyone.

'He'll be all right, won't he?' the father asked. 'I mean, nothing could go wrong now, could it?'

'The midazolam will probably keep him sedated until he gets to Geraldton,' Amy said, 'But I'll leave the canula in and send another ampoule of midazolam with him in case he needs further sedation *en route*. The physicians in Geraldton will keep him monitored overnight—he should come through relatively unscathed. But I would recommend some sessions with a drug counsellor. There have been cases where just a single drug use like this has triggered schizophrenia.'

'He's never done this before,' the father said. 'Will he be charged?'

'We'll sort that out later, Rob,' Angus said. 'He's only fifteen so any action taken will be through diversionary conferencing and counselling. But for now you'd better prepare to go with Hamish. Do you want me to call Janelle for you?'

'She's going to kill me for this,' Rob said. 'Trust it to happen when he's with me on a custody visit.'

Angus put his hand on Rob's shoulder. 'Try not to blame yourself, mate. You did the right thing in getting him here quickly. It could have been much worse.'

Amy applied a plaster of Paris strip across Rob Norton's nose while they waited for the ambulance, and once it was on its way, with both father and son on board, James came over to speak to her.

'I spoke to Jacqui, Dr Tanner. She suggested you come around for a barbecue tonight. You, too, Angus,' he said turning back to his colleague. 'That way you can drive so Amy doesn't get lost.'

'I'm sure I can find my own way there if Sergeant Ford is busy this evening,' Amy put in quickly.

'It's fine,' Angus said, sending her one of his inscrutable looks. 'I've got nothing planned. What time do you want us out there?'

'How about seven?' James said. 'Then at least you'll get to see Daisy before she goes to sleep for the night.'

'Seven's fine,' Angus answered for her.

'See you both, then,' James said, lifting his hand in a wave.

Amy turned to leave but Angus stalled her with a hand on her arm. 'It looks to me like you need some ice on that cheek,' he said.

She gave a little shudder. '*Please,* don't mention that word.'

His finger gently brushed the purpling bruise on her cheekbone just below her eye. 'Does it hurt?' he asked.

Not when you do that, Amy thought. 'Not much,' she said. 'It wasn't your fault. I should have got out of the way.'

'I'm sorry you got caught in the crossfire. He was hard to control. They always are.'

'You've had a bit of experience with this, haven't you?'

A shutter came down over his eyes. 'It's part of the job. Yours, too, I imagine. We've both seen things we'd prefer not to have seen.'

'Yes…' she said, stifling a little yawn.

'Am I keeping you awake, Dr Tanner?' he asked.

'I haven't slept more than two hours in a stretch since I arrived,' she confessed. 'That's why I was out so early this morning. I had no idea the old man in the next room could snore at seven on the Richter scale.'

'Yeah, well, I had someone keeping me awake, too,' he said, his eyes going to the soft curve of her mouth.

'Oh?' she said, moistening her lips with the tip of her tongue. 'Who was it?'

'Are you searching for a compliment, Dr Tanner?' he asked with a glint in his dark eyes.

'Are you going to give me one?' she asked.

He didn't answer immediately, but Amy felt his darker-than-night gaze move over her lazily, as if he was slowly removing every article of clothing from her to look at her, making every hair of her skin lift in feverish anticipation.

'Don't you think it's time we dropped the formalities?' he said and gave her his hand. 'Hi, I'm Angus.'

She bit back a giggle as she shook his hand. 'Hi, Angus, I'm Amy.'

'Nice to meet you, Amy.'

'Me, too,' she said, and blushed then rambled on gauchely, 'I mean, you, too. It's nice to meet *you*, not me…well, you know what I mean.'

He smiled a slow smile that made his eyes darken even further. 'I know exactly what you mean.' He put his police hat back on and tipped it at her. 'See you tonight. I'll pick you up at six-forty.'

Amy let out a prickly breath as she watched him stride towards his car. *So what if he's a cop?* she began mentally rehearsing her explanation to her mother. He's the first and only man I've been attracted to since Simon. So what if it's only going to last three months? I'm a modern single girl. It doesn't mean I have to fall in love with him.

I'm not going to be *that* stupid.

She pulled her shoulders back with determination.

No way.

CHAPTER ELEVEN

'OFF out this evening?' Bill asked as Amy came downstairs at six-thirty on the dot.

'Yes, to James and Jacqui Ridley's house.'

'Sounds like a good idea after that drama out at the Cove this morning,' he said. 'Do you need directions? It's a bit hard to find. I can draw you a map if you like.'

Amy felt a slow burn crawl over her cheeks. 'Um…it's all right,' she said. 'I'm getting a lift with someone.'

Bill's eyes began to twinkle. 'That would be Sergeant Ford, right?'

'Yes, but there's nothing—'

'It's about time that lad took his mind off work for a change,' Bill cut her off as he gave the counter a quick wipe. 'I don't think he's been on a date since he called off his engagement when he came out here a couple of years ago.'

'He was engaged?' The question popped out before Amy could stop it.

'Yeah, to a woman back in Perth.'

'So what happened?'

Bill opened his mouth to speak when the door of the pub opened behind Amy. He looked past her and smiled. 'G'day, Sarge. I hear you're taking Dr Tanner out on a date.'

Amy felt like sinking under the bar.

'Is that what she told you?' Angus asked.

She swung around, her colour still high. 'No, of course I didn't tell him that.'

His eyes ran over her pink cotton skirt and white halter top, pausing for a moment on the thrust of her breasts. 'Are you ready?' he asked.

'Yes,' she said, and, snatching up her purse and the chocolates and wine she'd bought earlier, walked stiffly out to the car.

Angus held the passenger door open for her. 'Don't take any notice of Bill,' he said. 'He likes to think of himself as a bit of a matchmaker.'

'He told me you used to be engaged,' she said once they were on their way. 'Funny that you didn't mention that the other night when I told you about my ex-fiancé.'

'I didn't think it was relevant.'

She turned to look at him. 'Why did you break it off?'

His eyes were fixed on the road ahead. 'I changed my mind.'

'Simple as that?'

'Yeah.'

'How did she take it?' she asked.

He lifted one shoulder in a shrug. 'Pretty well as it turned out. She found someone else within a matter of weeks.'

'Were you upset?'

'Why should I be?'

She frowned at him. 'I don't know. Even though you were the one to break it off, I imagine it would have still hurt a bit that she replaced you so quickly.'

'As far as I was concerned, she was a free agent. It was none of my business any more what she did or who she did it with.'

'You're very good at switching off your emotions when you want to, aren't you?' she asked. 'Did you love her?'

'Define what you mean by the word "love".'

Amy gave a choked sound of cynicism. 'Now, that's just absolutely typical. What is it about men that they refuse to acknowledge how deeply a woman affects them?'

'Were you in love with your ex?' he said.

'What sort of question is that? Of course I was in love with him.'

'Are you still in love with him?'

She hesitated over her answer. 'Um….no.'

'It can't have been the real thing if it died just because one person called a halt to the relationship,' he said. 'Don't you agree?'

Amy wasn't sure how to answer. She had thought she had been in love with Simon, truly in love, but she could barely recall what he even looked like now. And as for his kisses and caresses…well, they had been eradicated from her memory by the heat and fire of Angus's.

'What about time being a great healer and all that?' she asked.

'I'm not a great believer in that particular adage. I think people only say it because they can't think of anything else to say.'

'But don't you think it's a waste of time pining over a lost love when you could be out finding someone much more suitable?' she asked.

'Is that what you are doing?' he asked. 'Looking for someone else?'

'Not consciously,' she said. 'Although I guess you could say I'm keeping my options open.'

He sent her a quick sideways glance, his dark brown eyes gleaming. 'So you haven't quite ruled out a short-term fling with me.'

She angled her head at him. 'I thought you said you weren't in the market for a relationship.'

'I said I wasn't in the market for anything long term, but that's not to say I wouldn't be interested in working on lifting your assessment of my kisses to something other than "not particularly good".'

'Are you flirting with me, Sergeant Ford?' she asked.

His mouth stretched into a half-smile as he took the next turn that led to a house overlooking another beach further along the coast. 'Let's just say I'm keeping my options open.'

James came out to meet them, carrying his tiny daughter in his arms. 'Bang on time,' he said, handing the baby to Angus who had already reached out for her.

Amy felt a funny sensation flow through her as she watched Angus cradle the tiny pink bundle close to his broad chest, his finger tipping up the little dimpled chin as he greeted her. 'How are you doing, Daisy? Have you got a smile for your godfather?'

'If she does, it's probably just wind,' said a pragmatic female voice from behind Amy.

Amy turned and saw a woman a couple of years older than herself come towards her with a smile. 'Hi, you must be Amy. I'm Jacqui. Welcome to Marraburra.'

'Hi, Jacqui,' she said. 'This is very good of you, organising a barbecue at such short notice.'

'Not at all.' Jacqui smiled. 'I've been dying to meet you but I'm afraid I haven't made it into town to do so yet. I don't know where the day goes. I swore I would never be one of those new mums who spend the whole day in their dressing-gowns, but Daisy clearly hasn't read the same baby-care manuals as I have.'

Amy laughed at the woman's self-effacing humour. 'I've heard it said that the only people who say they slept like a baby haven't had one.'

Jacqui rolled her eyes expressively. 'Tell me about it. And here I was thinking one in two on call was bad. The other night Daisy kept me up longer than any patient I've ever had.'

'She's beautiful,' Amy said, looking at the gurgling infant, who was tugging with a dimpled hand at the front of Angus's shirt.

'Well, we think so, don't we, darling?' Jacqui said as she nuggled under her husband's outstretched arm.

James's smile for his wife, Amy decided, would be enough to restore anyone's dented belief in true love. It was clear they adored each other and the bond of their child only added to it.

'I heard you both had a pretty gruelling start to the day.' Jacqui addressed both Amy and Angus. 'Has the man's identity been established yet?'

Angus shook his head as he repositioned the baby in his arms. 'Not as yet. No one's reported him missing and he wasn't carrying any ID.'

'Do you think it could be one of the drug mules?' Jacqui asked.

'Drug mules?' Amy asked with a frown.

James exchanged a glance with Angus and after a tiny pause Jacqui took Amy by the arm and led her to the kitchen. 'Come and have a chat with me in the kitchen while the boys talk shop.'

Amy followed but not before sending Angus a quizzical look which, she noted, he pointedly ignored. She followed Jacqui into the large kitchen and at her hostess's direction perched on one of the bar stools surrounding the island bench.

'I guess you haven't heard,' Jacqui said as she took the plastic film off a bowl of salad.

'Heard what?'

'This part of the coast is well known for South-East Asian drug drop-offs,' Jacqui said. 'Heroin mostly. The drugs are off-loaded out at sea and collected by fishing boats and then taken to Perth for redistribution. It's becoming a huge problem over here. So much of the coast is unguarded. Angus and James and the other constables do what they can, but it's not enough to stop such a big operation.'

'So they think the man we found this morning is someho\
connected?' Amy asked.

'Could be, but until they find out who he is, who knows
Besides, he might not recover. James was saying he had a prett
nasty head injury.'

'Yes, he hasn't regained consciousness, as far as I know.'

'James was telling me young Hamish Norton was in earlie
out of his head on crystal meth. That would have been prett
scary. We've never had anything like that to deal with before

'It was awful,' Amy said unable to suppress a small shudde
'I've seen it before in London. Perfectly normal kids turn int
violent animals. But this was the first time I'd had to deal wit
it medically on my own, although James and Angus were there
as you know.'

Jacqui's green eyes went to the bruise on Amy's cheek. '\
that how you got that?' she asked.

'Yes. Angus was trying to hold him down but Hamish wa
all legs and arms.'

'Not a great first week for you,' Jacqui said, 'especially wit
Allan taking time off. It makes me feel guilty for taking ma
ternity leave.'

'I'm fine, really,' Amy assured her. 'And you shouldn't b
feeling guilty for wanting to spend time with your new baby
It's a very special time in your life.'

'Yes, and I'm almost dreading returning to full-time work
Jacqui said, and then with an impish look added, 'I don't suppos
we could tempt you into staying longer than three months?'

Amy felt a wave of guilty colour wash over her. 'I'm sur
you'll find out sooner or later that the only reason I came her
was to see the place my cousin Lindsay Redgrove lived and died

Jacqui's eyes widened. 'So it is true. I heard a rumour tha
you were Lindsay's cousin but I decided to wait to hear
from you first.' Her expression clouded as she added, 'Sh

was my patient, you know. It was such a shock when she took her life. I'd only seen her the week before and she seemed on top of things.'

'Did she have any relapses into psychosis during the time she lived here?' Amy asked.

'Now and again she'd go off the rails a bit,' Jacqui answered. 'She had her ups and downs but she was really good about taking her medication, almost obsessive about it really, as if she was frightened of going back to the dark days of her adolescence. I believe it was a very frightening time for her as well as for her parents. She told me a little about it, the regrets she had about her drug use and so on.'

'It was a frightening horrible time,' Amy said. 'She went from a normal well-adjusted girl to a paranoid stranger almost overnight.'

'They've obviously had it tough, as do any parents struggling to cope with a child with mental illness,' Jacqui said.

'Yes, it was hard on everyone. My mother felt guilty that it was her sister's daughter and not hers who had the problem. I felt it, too. There I was off at university, doing a medical degree, while my only cousin was spending most of her young adult years in and out of psychiatric wards.'

'Survivor guilt is a very common reaction,' Jacqui said. 'But you mustn't blame yourself for making something of your life.'

'No, I guess not.'

'So, has coming here helped?' Jacqui asked. 'Has it answered any questions about her for you?'

'On the contrary, it's thrown up a whole lot more,' Amy confessed.

'What do you mean?'

Amy took a small breath and announced, 'I'm not one hundred per cent convinced Lindsay committed suicide.'

Jacqui stared at her with wide green eyes. 'But Angus and

James did the preliminary report and the coroner agreed it was a straight case of suicide.'

'I know but I can't help feeling there's something not quite right about it all. She was happy here and settled for the first time in over a decade. I can't believe she would throw it all away without showing some sign first, but everyone I've spoken to says the same thing—she seemed perfectly OK even up to a couple of days before.'

'Yes, but you and I both know how quickly things can change in someone struggling with fluctuating serotonin levels,' Jacqui pointed out.

'But you said Lindsay was very good at medicating herself, which would have kept such fluctuations under control.'

'Look, Amy,' Jacqui said with a concerned expression, 'it's understandable you'd be shocked and upset about your cousin's death, but things could get awkward out here for you if you start questioning the verdict. This is a very small community. Can you imagine the impact on the locals if your suspicions became known? You're virtually accusing one of them of being a murderer.'

'I'm well aware of the delicate nature of this, but I feel I owe it to Lindsay to make sure something hasn't been overlooked somewhere.'

'I guess I'd feel the same if it was my cousin,' Jacqui finally conceded, and then, changing the subject, asked, 'So how's it going, staying at the hotel? I bet it's a bit of an eye-opener, what with Carl's bender the other day.'

'Eye-opener is right,' Amy said with a wry grimace. 'I haven't slept more than an hour at a time the whole time I've been here and I thought being a resident was bad.'

'What about boarding with Angus? He's got a spare room now that the engineer from Broome has gone back. It would be much more comfortable for you and certainly less noisy.'

'I wish I had a dollar for every time someone has suggested I move in with him,' she said a little sourly.

'So why don't you?'

The sound of the men coming into the kitchen interrupted the conversation at that point, and Amy turned when Angus asked her if she would like to hold the baby.

'I'd love to,' she said, and reached for the gurgling infant.

In transferring the squirming baby from his arms to hers, one of Angus's hands brushed against Amy's breast. Her eyes met his briefly, the electric pulse of his touch showing in the delicate colour in her cheeks.

'Sorry,' he said.

'It's all right,' she said, and, securing the bundle in her arms, looked down at the baby instead of Angus's all-seeing gaze. 'Isn't she gorgeous?'

'She certainly is,' Angus said, even though his eyes weren't on Daisy at that point.

'How about a drink?' James asked into the small silence. 'Amy? A glass of wine or something soft?'

'No alcohol for me, I'm afraid,' Amy said. 'I'm currently the only doctor in town.'

'None for me either,' Angus said. 'I gave Don and Tim the night off.'

'You work too hard,' Jacqui admonished him fondly. 'When are you going to take some time off and relax?'

'I'll get around to it some time.'

'I was telling Amy she should take your spare room for the time she's here,' Jacqui said. 'The company would do you both good.'

'I'm fine at the hotel,' Amy said quickly.

'Look at those shadows underneath her eyes, Angus,' Jacqui said. 'What that girl needs is a decent night's sleep. Can't you think of a way to convince her to change her mind?'

'Dr Tanner is determined to tough it out with the spiders and snorers at the Dolphin View,' he said with a glinting glance in her direction. 'Aren't you, Dr Tanner?'

Amy sent him a blistering glare. 'You said you wouldn't tell anyone.'

'Tell anyone what?' Jacqui asked, as she took Daisy from Amy's arms as the infant startled to grizzle.

'I have a bit of a phobia,' Amy said, still glaring at Angus. 'Which Sergeant Ford seems to think is highly amusing.'

'Oh, Angus,' Jacqui laughed. 'You monstrous brute. Leave the poor girl alone. I don't like spiders myself. Don't pay any attention to him, Amy.'

'Food's ready,' James announced, as he came in from the barbecue area branding a pair of tongs and a tray of succulent meat and fish. 'And what's this I hear about spiders?'

'I'll tell you later,' Jacqui said with a hushing motion.

Amy got to her feet and, sending Angus another blistering look, brushed past to where James had begun to set out the meal.

CHAPTER TWELVE

AMY waited until they were on their way back to town from the Ridleys' house to vent her spleen. 'I should have known you'd spill the beans,' she said. 'No doubt it will be all over town by morning.'

'Jacqui and James wouldn't dream of telling anyone so you needn't worry on their account.'

She threw him a caustic look. 'Is there anyone else you've told?'

'No.'

She gave a cynical snort. 'I suppose the next thing you'll be doing is planting a spider somewhere just to entertain yourself with my reaction.'

'That would be a very cruel thing to do,' he said, and after a little pause added, 'I'm sorry I let it slip. It won't happen again.'

She shifted her mouth from side to side, wondering whether she should believe him.

'Has that happened to you in the past?' he asked into the silence. 'Has someone exploited you by entertaining themselves with your fear?'

Amy swung her gaze in his direction, yet again surprised by his percipience. 'Do they teach sixth sense at the police academy these days, or is that a talent you've picked up along the way?' she asked.

He sent her a half-smile. 'You provide all the clues, Amy. There's nothing intuitive about it really, just a process of adding one and one together and coming up with two.'

She looked out of the window as the shadow of the scrub passed by. 'My father hated all forms of weakness,' she said in a thread-like voice. 'He wanted a son and was quite open about his disappointment when my mother produced a daughter instead. He always acted as if she had done it deliberately, you know, to thwart his wishes, even though every one knows it is the father's Y chromosome that determines the sex of a baby.'

Angus let her continue without interruption, somehow sensing she needed to get some things off her chest.

'I was about four or five when I had a bad experience with a spider,' she said. 'I woke up to find one on my pillow. It totally freaked me out. I made the mistake of showing my fear to my father…'

Angus felt his stomach clench for what she must have suffered, but still he remained silent.

'He decided I needed to be toughened up,' she went on. 'My mother did everything she could to stop him but he was very clever at leaving his so-called desensitising sessions for whenever she wasn't around.'

'You poor little kid.' The words left his mouth before he could pull them back.

'It was a relief when my parents finally divorced,' she said. 'Of course, my father never forgave me for refusing to go on access visits.'

Angus pulled into the side of the road and turned off the engine, his eyes meeting hers in the moonlit darkness. 'No wonder you hate cops so much.'

She gave him a watery smile. 'I guess they're not all like my father.'

His hand reached for the side of her face, cupping her cheek with his palm and long fingers. 'No, they're not.'

Amy felt the slow burn of his gaze into hers, her stomach unfolding as he leaned closer, his hint-of-mint breath whispering over her face as she closed her eyes for the touchdown of his mouth on hers.

His kiss was soft and sensual and leisurely, stirring her into a melting pool of longing as her arms reached for him, looping around his neck to hold him close. His tongue invited hers to dance with his, the sexy tango lighting spot fires all over her skin. Her thighs trembled with the pulse of need building deep inside her, and her breasts became heavy and aching for his touch.

He dragged his mouth from hers to kiss the side of her neck, his tongue tasting the lingering scent of her perfume before going lower to the shadow of cleavage her halter top revealed.

She felt the brush of his mouth against the upper curve of her breasts and instantly wanted more, her nipples tightening almost painfully in anticipation of the rasp of his tongue and sexy scrape of his teeth against them.

'I want you so badly,' he said into the throbbing silence. 'I can't seem to stop it, no matter what I do to distract myself.'

'I know…' Her breath came out on a prickly sigh. 'I want you, too.'

He pulled back to look at her in the moonlit darkness. 'Come back to my place,' he said. 'Let's enjoy this while we can.'

Out of the depths of her being a periscope of morality reared its unwelcome head and reminded Amy of the heartbreak of a no-strings relationship. Hadn't she learned enough about herself to know there was nothing about her that was without strings? She wanted strings. She wanted permanent strings.

She bit her lip and edged away, unable to hold his gaze. 'I'm sorry, Angus,' she said, staring down at her hands. 'I didn't mean to give you the wrong impression. You'll probably find this hard to believe but I'm not normally so…so…unrestrained.'

'It's OK, I understand,' he said. 'I've been acting a little out of character myself.'

'I don't blame you for being angry with me… I shouldn't have allowed things to go this far.'

'I'm not angry with you.'

She blinked up at him. 'Not even a little bit?'

He brushed the back of his knuckles over the smooth curve of her cheek. 'Not at all,' he said. 'Unlike some men I've locked up in the past, I don't have a problem with the word "no".'

'All the same, I bet you haven't heard it too many times.'

'Now and again,' he said as he leaned back across to restart the car. 'But in every case it wasn't a big deal.'

Amy couldn't help feeling she was being relegated to the same category—no big deal. She sat back in her seat and did what she could to bolster her dented ego, reminding herself that he had never offered her anything but a short-term fling, so there was no sense in feeling affronted by his easy acceptance of her refusal to commit herself physically.

It wasn't as if she was in love with him or anything, she lectured herself severely. She was attracted to him but what woman wouldn't be? Especially seeing the way he'd held little Daisy so gently. It was enough to turn any female to mush. And his mouth was one of those mouths you couldn't stop staring at, the fullness of his bottom lip so sensual it made her insides quiver just thinking about the way it had connected with hers so intimately. And then there were those impossibly dark eyes that burned with the naked flame of desire or hardened to cold diamond chips in anger.

His hands were just as unforgettable. Strong and tanned and dusted with masculine hair that made her smooth skin tingle at the slightest touch. His body was a wall of muscle, toned and powerful, making her legs weaken at the thought of how it would feel to have him possess her…

Amy gave herself a mental slap for being so pathetic as to daydream about a man who had no interest in her other than as a temporary diversion.

'Oh, no, not again,' Angus said as the hotel came into view.

Amy looked up to see Carl stumbling from the front door of the pub, the sound of his swearing clearly audible even from inside the car.

'What are you going to do?' she asked as she got out of the car with him.

He held up the breathalyser machine he had in his hand. 'I'm going to make sure he doesn't get behind the wheel of his car.'

Amy watched as he strode over to the beat-up car the man was trying to unlock, his attempts being hampered by his unsteady legs and lack of hand-eye coordination.

'Don't do it, Carl,' Angus said. 'I don't want to have to charge you with driving under the influence.'

The man swayed on his feet as he turned to face him. 'G'day Sarge,' he slurred. 'Can't seem to get my car unlocked. Wanna give me a hand?'

'You're not really thinking of driving tonight, are you?' Angus asked.

'Why not?' Carl gave him a belligerent look. 'It's my car.'

'How much have you had to drink?'

'Not mush.'

'How much?'

'Go on, give me a break, Sarge,' Carl growled. 'I wanna go home and you can't stop me.'

'Don't bet on it, Carl. How about you blow into the machine and then we'll come to a decision on whether or not you're fit to drive?'

Amy watched as Angus held the breathalyser for Carl, the

look on Angus's face clearly indicating the man was over the legal limit.

'Sorry, mate,' Angus said. 'I can't let you drive when you're blowing one point one. You can pick up your car tomorrow. I'll run you home.'

Carl glanced at Amy, still standing a few feet away from the car. 'So who's your new girlfriend, Sarge?' he asked, and then squinting, added, 'Isn't that the chick that was in the pub the other day?'

'Yes, but she's not my girlfriend,' Angus answered.

'Who is she?'

'She's the new locum doctor filling in for Jacqui Ridley.'

'Nice-looking, though, isn't she?' Carl said.

Angus bundled him into the back seat. 'You're drunk, Carl,' he said dryly. 'Just about anyone would look attractive to you in this state.'

Amy sent him a fulminating glare over the top of the car. 'Goodnight, Sergeant Ford,' she clipped out coldly.

A corner of his mouth tipped upwards, his dark brown eyes glinting. 'Goodnight, Dr Tanner.'

She turned on her heel and stalked into the hotel before she was tempted to say anything else.

The next week went past without Amy seeing Angus and it wasn't until Jacqui came in to see her with Daisy for a check-up that she heard he had gone to Perth for a few days on a police matter.

'Didn't he tell you?' Jacqui said as she began to dress the baby again.

'No but it's not as if we—'

'Don't bother denying it.' Jacqui cut her off with a knowing grin. 'Everyone can see it a mile off. You're both seriously attracted to each other. There are bets going back and forth on how long it will take for you to give in.'

'Oh, for God's sake!' Amy said, folding her arms crossly. 'I don't even like the man.'

Jacqui's smile widened. 'You sound just like I did when I first met my James. He pulled me over and gave me a ticket for failing to indicate. I was so angry about that it took me months to realise how nice he really was. We got called out to an accident late one night and I saw him with new eyes. He was so caring and considerate of the young child who had been injured. I invited him around to dinner a few nights later and we ended up in bed together.' She pressed a soft kiss to Daisy's forehead and added, 'That's how we got you, isn't it, my precious?'

'*You mean you fell pregnant on the first date?*' Amy gasped.

Jacqui's smile was sheepish. 'I may be a doctor but I'm still human. Besides, condoms have a failure rate, right?'

'Er…right…'

'You could do a lot worse, you know,' Jacqui said as she tucked the baby back into the pram. 'He needs someone like you. His ex-fiancée was totally wrong for him. She wanted him to leave the police force and get a nine-to-five job, but Angus is a cop through and through. He loves his job, in spite of the long hours and associated stress.' She straightened from the pram and added, 'Cops are like doctors when you think about it. We have to deal with the most awful stuff at times and yet carry on as if nothing's wrong.'

'I guess you're right,' Amy said. 'It's just that my father was a cop so I'm a bit prejudiced. He wasn't…I mean *isn't* a very nice person.'

'I wonder sometimes how any of them maintain normal lives,' Jacqui said. 'James is pretty level-headed, as is Angus, but they both carry a lot of baggage, Angus particularly.' She paused for a moment before continuing, 'I probably shouldn't tell you without checking with him first, but he lost his partner in a high-speed chase a couple of years ago. They were tailing a well-known drug dealer but a rogue car came out of nowhere and cut them off. Angus had to be dragged away from Daniel Fergusson's body in the end. He'd staunched the bleeding as best he could but it was too late. Dan bled out before the paramedics could get there.'

Amy felt her stomach clench. 'He said he'd named Fergus after a loyal friend... I had no idea...'

'Not only that,' Jacqui went on gravely, 'Angus was the first one on the scene of Carl's wife's accident. Julie and the girls were killed instantly when a young woman in a high-performance sports car hit them head on. The woman's father was a hotshot lawyer in Perth and got her off a dangerous driving charge. Angus was the one who had to tell Carl his family had been killed.'

Amy felt the sharp knife of guilt pierce her for assuming Angus was yet another power-hungry cop. No wonder he had taken such an instant dislike to her that first day, especially with her don't-mess-with-me-I'm-a-doctor attitude.

'I wish I'd known earlier...' She bit her lip. 'I've done nothing but insult him the whole time I've been in town. I've been far nicer to his dog than to him.'

'He really loves that dog, doesn't he?' Jacqui said with a little smile.

'Yes, he does. I love him, too.'

'Fergus or Angus?' Jacqui asked with a twinkle in her eyes.

Amy tried to look stern but it didn't quite work. 'I guess they both have their good points,' she finally conceded. 'But so far the dog's way out in front.'

Jacqui grinned delightedly. 'You're perfect for him. Just perfect.'

'My mother will have a coronary if I tell her I'm thinking about getting involved with a cop.'

'I bet your mother will change her mind as soon as she meets him. Why don't you ask her to come and visit you?'

Amy pointed to the mobile phone on her desk, her tone wry as she said, 'I just got a text from her. She's already on her way.'

CHAPTER THIRTEEN

'BUT darling,' Grace Tanner said as she looked around the tiny room at the hotel she had been assigned. 'This is just *ghastly*. Isn't there something better than this?'

'You can have mine if you like,' Amy offered. 'I think it's a tiny bit bigger than this one.'

'I can't believe you're putting up with this,' Grace said. 'Surely there's somewhere else you can stay.'

Amy decided against telling her mother of the alternative. 'It's fine, Mum. It's only for another ten weeks.'

Grace ran a finger over the top of the dresser and frowned at the dust that came off. 'Sweetie, I'm worried about you,' she said as she turned to face her. 'What if there are…?' She paused delicately over the word and then whispered, '*Spiders?*'

'I'm OK with spiders,' Amy assured her with feigned confidence. 'I told you, I got completely desensitised in London.'

Grace folded her arms and gave her a motherly all-seeing look. 'You surely don't expect me to believe *that*.'

'All right,' Amy confessed with a little sigh, 'I'm not completely cured, but the only spider I've seen was handled very well…by someone…'

Grace's brows rose in speculation. 'So who was this someone? Someone…*special?*'

Amy took a deep breath and mentally prepared herself for the fall out. 'He's one of the local cops.'

'*A cop?*'

'I knew you'd say that.'

'Well, what else did you expect me to say?'

'He's not like Dad.'

'He's a cop, Amy,' Grace said, tightening her mouth. 'They're *all* like your father. They have issues.'

Amy rolled her eyes. 'Issues smissues. Well, guess what— doctors have *issues*. In fact, I bet even vets have issues.'

'Maybe, but their *issues* don't ruin people's lives,' Grace said. 'Come on, darling, surely you're not considering *a cop?*'

'You make it sound like some sort of nasty disease.'

'It is,' Grace said with conviction. 'You're doing the whole rewriting-the-past thing. I read about it in a magazine. It's a recipe for disaster. Women go looking for a chance to rewrite what went wrong in their lives and they end up marrying a version of their father.'

'I'm not going to *marry* the guy, Mum.'

Her mother gave her a probing look. 'But you're interested in him, aren't you?'

Amy blew out a frustrated breath. 'Is that a crime?'

'Bordering on one, yes, and it'll turn into one if you let it get out of hand. What's he offering?'

'A house with a spectacular view, a bathroom of my own, no spiders and *no* snoring next door.'

'*Snoring?*' Grace frowned. 'You mean someone *snores* next door?'

'The last reading was seven on the Richter scale.'

'Oh, my God,' Grace said. 'Maybe there are worse things than cops as boyfriends.'

'He's not my boyfriend,' Amy said. 'In fact, I wouldn't even go as far as saying we're friends.'

'So what's he got going for him?'

'He's got a beautiful dog,' Amy said. 'A German shepherd, and he loves me.'

'The dog or the cop?'

'The dog, of course!'

Grace tapped her bottom lip thoughtfully. 'I guess a quick fling would be all right.'

'I can't believe you said that!'

'It's been more than eighteen months since that wimpy Simon let you down,' Grace said. 'What you need is a bit of fun to set you right.'

'With a cop?'

'Yes, well, occasionally we have to scrape the bottom of the barrel, but as long as you don't promise him for ever, you should come out on top.'

'*Mu-um.*'

Grace gave her a guileless look. 'What?'

'I'm *not* going to go off and have fun with Angus Ford.'

'So that's his name, is it?'

'He's a control freak.'

'Has he booked you yet?'

'He came very close.'

'What stopped him?'

'I'm not sure,' Amy said.

'It was probably your legs,' Grace said, 'or your cleavage.'

'*Mu-um!*'

'If you've got it, flaunt it, darling. And you've definitely got it. At least you take after me in that regard and not your father.'

'Maybe Dad had some issues…you know, being a cop and all. It's not an easy job. They have to deal with such awful tragedy, their lives are in constant danger. I've been thinking about it a lot lately.'

This time it was Grace who rolled her eyes. 'If you're tuning up the violin, forget it. Your father was damaged when I met him and I stupidly thought I'd be the one to make a difference in his life. Some people are beyond help, darling. It's like some of the animals I treat. Some are too traumatised to recover. There's nothing you can do.'

'So you think Dad was like that?'

Grace let out a sigh as she reached for Amy's hands. 'Listen, sweetie. I loved your father. I loved him desperately, but he came with baggage. That baggage was like a third person in our relationship. I don't want you to go through what I went through. Go and find some boring accountant to fall in love with. Sleep with this guy if you want to get it out of your system, but in future stay away from cops. Believe me, they're not worth it.'

Amy bit her lip and confessed, 'But I think I'm falling in love with him.'

Grace threw her hands in the air. 'I knew it! I just knew it was a mistake, coming here, and so did your aunt and uncle. Lindsay did what she did and nothing anyone could do or say was going to stop her. I know you feel guilty about her life but that's the way it goes. She was who she was and you are who you are. You have to let it go, Amy. She was a suicide statistic waiting to happen. Coming here hasn't changed that, now, has it?'

'Yes, it has,' Amy said. 'I think there's more to her death than what we've been told.'

Grace frowned again. 'What are you saying?'

'She was happy here, Mum. You know she was. She was happy in a way she had rarely been before. And she didn't leave a note.'

'That doesn't mean anything, darling. When she tried to kill herself the other times she didn't leave a note either.'

'I know but I still feel uneasy…'

'What does this cop you're falling in love with think about your suspicions?'

'He's not happy about me contradicting his verdict, that's for sure.'

'What does he look like?'

'He's tall,' Amy said, lifting her hand as high above her head as she could get it. 'And he's got olive colouring and the most amazing brown eyes. They go almost black when he's angry.'

Grace's brows moved upwards. 'So you've got him angry already, have you?'

'Yes, well, we didn't exactly hit it off the first day.'

'So when can I meet him?'

'He's out of town at present,' Amy said. 'I'm not sure when he's due back.'

'Come on, then,' Grace said, picking up her handbag. 'Take me to the nearest café. I'm dying for a skinny soy decaf *lattè*.'

'Er…Mum…' Amy gave her mother an I-hate-to-be-the-one-to-tell-you-this grimace. 'There is no café in Marraburra.'

'No café?'

'There's a fish and chip shop but the coffee is instant, the tea is dusty and I'm absolutely sure I haven't seen any soy milk anywhere in town.'

Grace let out a sigh of defeat. 'All right,' she said. 'Let's go downstairs to the pub and have a glass of something bubbly.' She gave her daughter a hopeful look and added, 'I don't suppose they have Bollinger or Moët?'

Amy shook her head. 'No but you can make up for it by drinking my share. I'm on call while the other doctor is away.'

'What! You mean you're running the medical clinic for the whole town on your own?' Grace said as she threaded her arm through her daughter's on the way down the stairs.

'That's about the situation at the moment, yes, but after a

ectic start last week it's been pretty quiet since. I even had time
o catch up on some journals.' Amy had barely finished
peaking when her mobile phone rang.

'Sorry to call you after hours,' Teresa said. 'But I've got a
oung mother here with a three-year-old with a foreign object
p his nose.'

'I'll be right there.' She hung up the phone and turned to her
nother. 'Sorry, Mum, but something's come up, gone up
ctually, at the clinic. I shouldn't be any longer than ten or
ifteen minutes.'

'Don't worry,' Grace said, and pushed open the door of the
ar. 'I'll wait for you here. You never know.' She gave a little
vink. 'I might even pick up a man for myself.'

'*Mu-um!*' Amy groaned.

he was halfway across the road to the clinic when she heard
he screech of brakes and a cloud of dust rose in front of her as
Angus brought his police vehicle to a halt on the side of the road.

'Oops,' she mouthed at him, wincing at his reproving frown
nd waggling finger.

He got out of the car and came to stand in front of her on
he gravelled edge. 'Didn't your mother ever teach you to look
oth ways before crossing a street?' he asked.

'Er…funny you should mention my mother,' Amy said,
ointing to the pub. 'She's in there right now, insisting on
ollinger. I hope Bill can handle her.'

'I'll go and introduce myself, or do you think I should get
ut of uniform first?'

Amy gave him a twisted smile. 'Take Fergus with you,' she
aid. 'Then at least you're in with a chance.'

He grinned as she walked the few short steps to the clinic.
See you around, Dr Tanner,' he called out after her.

She turned to look back at him, her cheeks a delicate shade of pink. 'See you, Sergeant Ford,' she answered, before disappearing inside.

'Hi, I'm Dr Tanner,' Amy introduced herself to an extremely thin, harried-looking young mother trying to control a hyperactive little boy with no success. The waiting room looked as if whirlwind had recently passed through it, the few well-thumbed magazines now strewn over the floor interspersed with the collection of toys scattered from one end of the room to the other.

'Stop that, Nathan,' the mother growled, and wrenched her son up from the floor by one arm. 'Do you want a smack?'

The little boy gave his mother a pugnacious look and poked his tongue out. Amy watched in horror as the young woman walloped him with an open palm on his little legs, leaving red handprint.

'Oh, please, don't do that,' Amy said, and came over to where the child was howling like a banshee.

'He's a brat,' Shontelle Kenton said with a scowl. 'I can do nothing with him half the time. He's ruined my life. I wish he'd never been born.'

Amy did her best to disguise her shock at the woman's blunt statement, everything in her revolting at such harsh treatment towards a small child. But looking at the mother, she realised Shontelle was barely an adult herself—she couldn't have been more than eighteen, if that.

'Hi, Nathan,' she said, bending down to the hiccuping little boy. 'My name is Amy.'

'He won't talk,' Shontelle said. 'He hardly ever talks.'

Amy straightened and faced the sour-faced mother. 'I think it would be best if we take Nathan into the examination room and have a close look at his nose. Teresa said you'd seen him poke a plastic bead in his right nostril, right?'

'Yeah,' Shontelle said with a filthy look towards her son. 'He did it this morning and now it's runny and he's been sneezing. It's driving me nuts.'

'We'll give him a small dose of Phenergan to calm him down,' Amy explained. 'Once it takes effect I'll be able to inspect the nostrils and hopefully retrieve the bead.'

Nathan took the medication without demur, happily distracted by Amy's stethoscope. After about fifteen minutes, chatting while they waited for the sedation to take affect, Amy found out Shontelle was a single mother, having been deserted by Nathan's father when she'd been just fifteen and pregnant.

'It must be hard for you, living out here,' Amy said as she inspected the child's right nostril with a nasal speculum and light. 'Do you have parents or family living nearby?'

'My dad owns a couple of fishing boats,' the girl said. 'He's away a bit, off the coast. My mother left when I was thirteen. Haven't seen her since.'

'Do you ever get a break from Nathan?' Amy asked as she located a green bead lodged a centimetre into the right nostril. 'Perhaps a female friend to mind him for you occasionally?'

The girl let out a sigh. 'I used to have a couple of friends but they've moved on now. I know this guy down at the boatyard, Josh. He sometimes plays with Nathan but it's not regular.'

Amy sprayed the child's nostril with 4 per cent Xylocaine spray and then, gently inserting a wire loop behind the bead, she extracted it. 'There, all done,' she said, and smiled at the drowsy little boy, who sat blinking up at her with huge caramel-brown eyes.

'Can we go now?' Shontelle asked.

'Sure, but I'd like to see you both tomorrow in the clinic,' Amy said. 'Has Nathan had any routine checks done lately—sight, hearing, weight?'

'I can't afford to go to the doctor all the time,' she said with another surly look.

'Who has been looking after you both up till now? Dr Peddington or Dr Ridley?'

'I saw Dr Peddington about a year ago when Nathan had an ear infection. I haven't been back since.'

Amy took them through to the reception area and made an appointment for the following afternoon. Writing it on a card she handed it to the young mother. 'My mobile number is on that so if you are worried about Nathan, call me. It doesn't matter what time of day or night.'

'Thanks…' Shontelle gave her self-conscious look. 'I wasn't sure what to expect when I heard you were the mad lady's cousin. But you're nice. Real nice.'

'So you knew Lindsay?' Amy asked, trying not to feel too offended by the girl's comments in regard to her cousin.

'Not really. I saw her now and again when she came into town. She talked to herself a lot, which was a bit weird. But who wouldn't start talking to themselves around here? I feel like doing it myself when I'm stuck with a screaming kid all day.'

'Come and see me tomorrow. I'll check Nathan's nose again and have a look at his general health, and we'll have a chat about some parenting techniques that might help you handle him a little better,' Amy said. 'Don't be too hard on yourself, Shontelle. You've had a rough start to parenting, being so young and with so little support. You can turn it all around, it's not too late. Nathan is sweet little boy who loves his mummy very much. He's just trying to get your attention because he feels a bit insecure right now.'

Tears shone in the young girl's eyes as she looked down at her little son. 'I don't really wish he hadn't been born,' she said scrubbing at her face with the back of her hand. 'I just sometimes wish I had my mum around to help me, you know?'

Amy nodded as she patted the girl's thin shoulder. 'I under

...and, Shontelle. You're doing the best you can do, that's all that matters for now.'

'Do you really think I can change my life?' the girl asked as she clutched her little son's hand. 'You know…become a better mother?'

'Of course you can. You're not a bad person, Shontelle, and Nathan is not a bad child. You can come to me any time for help. I really mean that.'

Shontelle gave her a shaky smile. 'Thanks…'

Amy went back to the pub to find her mother sitting at a table, chatting with Angus.

Grace looked up and beamed at her proudly. 'You're not going to believe this, darling, but I've solved our little accommodation problem,' she said. 'We're moving in with Sergeant Ford right away. I've already packed our things. Isn't that kind of him to offer to give us two rooms rent-free?'

Amy lifted her brows as she met Angus's glinting dark brown gaze. 'I can see this matter has been taken out of my hands,' she said in a clipped tone. 'Rent-free, huh?'

'No strings, Dr Tanner,' Angus said with a hint of a smile. 'You can stay as long as you like.'

'I'm only going to be here for another couple of days,' Grace said to him. 'But Amy will be here for at least another ten weeks. Are you sure it's not going to put you out too much to have her under your feet for all that time?'

Amy glowered at her mother.

'Not at all,' Angus said as he got to his feet. 'I'll take the bags out to my car while you settle up with Bill.'

Amy waited until she and her mother were alone to give her a pointed look. 'So what happened to stay-away-from-cops-they're-nothing-but-trouble routine?' she asked.

Grace gave her a benign smile as she hoisted her handbag

over her shoulder. 'Come on, darling, he's absolutely *gorgeou*... I can see why you fancy yourself in love with him. I'm halfwa... there myself and I've only just met him. Besides that, he'... nothing like your father.'

Amy's expression was sceptical. 'You can tell that fron... one meeting?'

'He spoke of Lindsay with a great deal of respect,' Grac... said. 'And he likes dogs. That's always a huge plus in a man.'

'I think you should know I have spent the best part of tw... weeks resisting his offer of accommodation,' Amy said. 'I'v... created enough gossip in this town without putting more fue... on the fire by moving in with him.'

Grace looped her arm through her daughter's. 'Don't worr... darling,' she said with an impish smile. 'I'll be the perfec... chaperone. You just wait and see.'

CHAPTER FOURTEEN

'WHERE'S your mother?' Angus asked as he came into the kitchen the following morning.

'She took Fergus out for a walk,' Amy said. 'I hope you don't mind.'

He leant into the fridge to take out the orange juice. 'Why should I mind?'

Amy bit her lip before answering, 'She might be three hours.'

He turned to look at her. 'No kidding?'

'She's a fitness fanatic. Her idea of a walk in the park is to circumnavigate the entire continent.'

He smiled lopsidedly and asked, 'So how did you sleep last night?'

'I got at least seven hours straight,' she said. 'It was heaven.'

A small silence settled into the space between them.

Amy examined her hands for a moment before meeting his eyes again, her gaze narrowing as she looked at his eyebrow. 'You've had the stitches removed,' she said.

His hand came up and traced the red line of his scar. 'Yeah, I did it myself.'

'I hope you used sterile instruments.'

'I did.'

The clock on the wall ticked the next few seconds...one... two...three...four...

'Angus…' She moistened her mouth and continued, 'I want to apologise for being so antagonistic towards you ever since I came to town.'

'It's fine,' he said. 'Your mother told me a little bit about your father. He sounds like a real charmer.'

'Yes, well, he certainly knew how to press the right buttons,' she said. 'But I realise now it was wrong to paint you with the same brush. I'm sorry.'

'Apology accepted.'

'Jacqui told me about your partner Daniel Fergusson.'

His expression tightened. 'I see.'

'She also told me about Carl's family, how you were the first on the scene. That must have been particularly harrowing so soon after the loss of your friend and colleague.'

'Yes, well, that's life in the force. You win some, you lose some.' He put his glass down on the bench as if it were a punctuation mark on the subject.

'Angus…'

'I've got to go,' he said. Sending her a keep-away look, he added, 'You're staying in this house as a guest, not a therapist. I would appreciate it if you would remember that in future.'

Amy opened her mouth to defend herself but he had already snatched up his keys and gone.

Amy went out to Reception after her last patient and looked over Helen's shoulder at the appointment book. 'Did Shontelle Kenton cancel her appointment with Nathan? I was expecting her an hour ago.'

'Her father called earlier,' Helen said. 'He said she'd changed her mind about coming to see you.'

Amy frowned. 'Her father called? Why didn't she cancel it herself?'

'Look, Amy, Barry Kenton's had a hard time with that girl,'

Helen said. 'She's been a bit of a handful ever since her mother left. Barry does what he can to help her but she's a moody little miss. And that brat of hers is going to be trouble later on, if you ask me. He's virtually uncontrollable, as you saw yesterday.'

'He's just a little kid, Helen,' Amy protested. 'And she's only a kid herself. Besides, there's no such thing as a bad child, just a child in a bad place. Shontelle hasn't had the help she needs to cope with the demands of child care, but she could be taught.'

'You're wasting your time on that one,' Helen warned. 'Besides, why bother? You won't be here long enough to make a difference.'

'I don't believe that,' Amy said. 'The right person at the right time can make the most amazing difference in someone's life.'

'You should save your Girl Guide deed for the day for someone who will actually appreciate it,' Helen said as she pushed herself away from the desk. 'I'm off for the day. I hope things are quiet tonight for you. How's your mum settling in? I heard you've both bunked down with Angus, and about time, too.'

'Yes, well, I sort of got railroaded into it, but at least I slept well.'

'You'll need another good night's sleep because you've got a pretty full day tomorrow,' Helen said, pointing to the heavily pencilled appointment book. 'Even Carl Haines has booked in to see you.'

'Oh?'

'He'll just want a repeat prescription for his antidepressants and a cry on your shoulder, poor man.' She took her bag out of the bottom drawer of the desk and added, 'You know, I don't think he would still be with us if it hadn't been for Angus. Your cousin, too, when it comes down to it. Her death hit him pretty hard.'

Amy's brows came together. 'Carl was upset by Lindsay's death?'

Helen nodded. 'Lindsay painted some pictures of his wife

and kids for him not long after the accident. She rode her rusty bike all the way out to take them to him. It touched him very deeply.'

Amy felt tears prickle at the back of her eyes. How like Lindsay to reach out to someone drowning in despair in spite of her own desperate struggle to keep on top of things.

'Well, I'd better get going,' Helen said. 'See you in the morning.'

'Yes… See you…' Amy said vaguely, as her eyes went to the desktop folder on the computer containing the list of patients' names and addresses. The Kentons lived a short distance from Marraburra Point and she quickly jotted down the address before locking up for the evening.

The road leading to the Kentons' house was smoothly tarred and landscaped on either side with flowering native plants. The house itself was large and modern and a shiny-top model BMW was parked in the open four-car garage. Amy couldn't help re- calling the scruffy clothes and unkempt appearance of Shontelle when she had come to the clinic the day before. Amy had been expecting the girl's home to be a reflection of the same level of neglect, but nothing could have been further from the truth. She hadn't expected a fisherman to live so comfortably, but, then, Shontelle had said her father owned a couple of fishing boats. There were obviously a whole lot bigger than she'd realised.

A man in his early fifties came out as soon as she arrived, his face open and friendly as he came to greet her. 'Hello, I'm Barry Kenton. You're Amy Tanner, the new locum, aren't you? I've heard all about you.'

Amy gave him her hand. 'Yes, I am. Nice to meet you, Mr Kenton.'

'What can I do for you, Dr Tanner? And, please, call me Barry.'

'Thank you, and my name is Amy,' she said, and then added,

'I was wondering if your daughter was home. She, or at least the receptionist, said you had cancelled her appointment this afternoon and I was worried about her. Is she here?'

A bleak look came over his features. 'I'm sorry, Amy. My daughter is totally unreliable, as you have no doubt noticed. She's gone off somewhere with my grandson, I don't know where. She's like that—a bit wild, if you know what I mean. I do what I can but she's a law unto herself.'

'I understand.'

Barry's expression looked pained. 'I wish I knew what to do. Ever since my wife left when Shoni was thirteen, things have gone downhill. I can't control her. I lie awake at night, worrying about little Nathan, but what can I do?'

Amy felt deeply for the man's distress. How many times had she heard the same story from other parents who, in spite of the loving upbringing they had given them, their child was hell-bent on rebellion?

'I wish I could say something to help you,' she said.

Barry moved his lips upwards into a loose version of a smile. 'I appreciate you coming out all this way to show your concern. I hear you're only here for three months. You're not thinking of extending your stay?'

'Not at this point,' she said.

There was an almost immeasurable silence.

'I'm so sorry about your cousin,' Barry said. 'She was a lovely lady. I had a lot of time for her.'

Amy was so used to concealing her surprise it came almost naturally this time. 'You knew her personally?'

'Yes,' he said. 'I often gave her a lift to town whenever I was going past. It's nice that you've come all this way to see where she lived. Were you very close to her?'

'No, not as much as I used to be,' she confessed. 'She... We grew apart over the years.'

'It's understandable,' he said. 'Drugs can do terrible things to people, can't they?'

Amy looked at him for a moment. 'She told you about her drug history?'

There was another infinitesimal pause before he answered. 'I've seen it before. It's a pathway to hell. But what can you do? I'm terrified my daughter might get into it, if she hasn't already.'

'I'll try and speak to Shontelle when I get the chance,' Amy offered. 'You never know, I might be able to help in some small way.'

Barry gave her a grateful smile. 'I'd really appreciate that. She's not been the same since my wife left. A girl needs her mother, especially when she becomes a mother herself. I've tried to be the best father I can, but it's never going to be enough.'

'None of us can do more than our best,' Amy said, and held out her hand. 'It was nice meeting you, Barry.'

'And you, Amy,' he said with a firm, friendly grasp. 'And thank you for your concern. It's greatly appreciated.'

What a pity there weren't more fathers like that in the world, Amy thought as she drove away a few moments later.

'Where's my mother?' Amy asked when she encountered Angus in the kitchen on the return to his house.

'She's taken a bus trip up north to Monkey Mia,' he informed her. 'She left a note on the bench. She'll be back in two days' time.'

Amy frowned as he handed it to her. It was there in black and white…bright pink and white actually, she noticed with an inward smile. Unlike her father, her mother had never been a black-and-white person.

'What would you like for dinner?' Angus asked.

Amy put the note to one side. 'I don't expect you to cook me dinner.'

'I have to cook for myself so I may as well do enough for two,' he said. 'We can make up a roster if you like—that is, if you can cook.'

She sent him a withering glance from beneath her lashes. 'For your information, I happen to be a very good cook. My mother and I went to classes. We even went to Italy to a cookery school in Tuscany.'

'I'll look forward to seeing what you can do. How about we alternate nights, unless one of us gets called out?'

'Fine.'

Amy watched as he began to slice some vegetables, his movements so deft and assured she couldn't help being impressed. Simon had barely been able to open a can, let alone prepare a meal from scratch.

'Carl Haines is coming in to see me tomorrow,' she said into the silence.

He looked up in between transferring the stir-fry vegetables to a bowl. 'He's not really an alcoholic,' he said. 'He's just a man who's had a bit too much tragedy to deal with at one time. He'll pull himself out of it eventually.'

'Helen told me Lindsay had done some paintings for him, of his wife and daughters.'

He resumed slicing carrots and shallots into slivers. 'It was a nice gesture. It showed she understood a bit of what he was going through.'

'It's hard what life dishes up sometimes,' Amy said as she fiddled with a stray strip of carrot skin and began curling it round her finger. 'People get up and go to work the same as usual and then in the blink of an eye everything changes. Their loved ones are snatched away from them. I don't think I'll ever get used to it, you know…death and dying.'

Angus put his knife down and looked at her. 'You have to toughen up or it will take you down,' he said. 'Especially in a

place like this, where a lot of the people you treat are know
to you personally.'

'How do you switch off?' she asked. 'I just can't do it.'

'You have to do it.'

'I'm not sure I want to stop feeling for people,' she said.
need to be able to feel for them so I can help them.'

'I'm not saying don't feel for them, but unless you develo
some clinical distance you'll skew your judgement and end u
doing more harm than good.'

'You sound like Helen,' she said. 'She told me I was wastir
my time with Shontelle Kenton, but I can't help feeling that gi
really needs a guiding hand.'

Angus's hands stilled on the wok he'd just taken from th
cupboard. 'You've met her?'

'And her little boy. They came to the clinic late yesterday-
he had a bead up his nose. I was going to see them whe
I…er…almost ran into you. Shontelle agreed to come bac
today to have a chat with me about parenting techniques, b
she didn't turn up. Her father cancelled the appointment. I we
out to their house before I came home.'

His eyes held hers. 'Did you meet Barry?'

'Yes,' she said. 'I thought he was lovely. He was terribl
worried about his daughter and his grandson. He's worrie
Shontelle might be into drugs. He was quite open about it.'

'Did he mention his wife?'

'Only that she left when Shontelle was thirteen,' she said. '
was funny, you know. After meeting Shontelle and Nathan in th
clinic, I was expecting her to be living in a shabby council hous
but the Kenton place is like a mansion. Barry's car is the late
model BMW. I didn't realise there was so much money in fishing

'Yes, well, there's fishing and there's fishing.'

Something about his tone brought Amy's eyes back to hi
'You think there's something shady about him?'

'Did I say that?'

'You didn't have to. I can see it in your eyes.'

'Look,' Angus said, deciding to be up front about it, 'I think ou should stay well away from Barry Kenton and, yes, even s daughter. Your Mother Teresa mission is not going to get ff the ground with people like that. Anyway, you'll be gone a matter of weeks and they'll go back to what's familiar efore you've driven past the Marraburra turn-off.'

'But what if I didn't leave when my time's up?' The words me out before she'd known she was going to say them. 'What I decided to stay a little longer?'

His dark brown eyes pinned hers. 'How much longer are you lking about?'

'I don't know…six months, a year maybe.'

'I think you should leave as planned.'

Amy stared at him in affront. 'You don't think I'm doing good job?'

'I don't think you belong here. Besides, you came here for l the wrong reasons.'

'Only according to you,' she threw back. 'You don't like me king questions about my cousin, do you? You've made it ear right from the word go, but it makes me all the more de-rmined to prove you wrong.'

'You're wasting your time.' His voice tightened in anger. Your cousin took her own life. Get over it.'

Amy got to her feet and, slamming her hand on the bench, ared at him. 'I will not get over it. I know there's something spicious about her death and I also know you're trying to stop e from finding out what it is.'

'You're a doctor, not a detective,' he said. 'Stick to what you ow. This is not the sort of place you can wander about voicing spicions without some sort of backlash.'

'Is that what you're worried about, Sergeant Ford?' she

asked. 'That there's going to be some sort of backlash yo
can't handle?'

'No,' he said, moving from behind the bench to take her b
the upper arms and pull her towards him. 'This is what I'
worried about not being able to handle.' And his mouth swoope
down and captured hers beneath the scorching heat of his.

CHAPTER FIFTEEN

HE thought of resisting Angus never once entered Amy's head. he returned his kiss with the same fiery fervour he was bestow- g on her, his tongue diving into her moist warmth with electri- ing expertise. Every nerve in her body vibrated with need and ery pore of her skin opened to receive his touch. His hands oved over her with urgency, moulding her to him, leaving her no doubt of his arousal.

His mouth left hers to devastate her senses even further by nding the tender curve of her breast his hands had uncovered. er spine shuddered with the first warm glide of his palm over r fullness, her tight nipple prodding him. She whimpered in e back of her throat when his mouth closed over her breast, e rasp of his tongue and the teasing, tantalising scrape of his eth making her writhe against him.

Her body was screaming for more of him, all of him. She anted to feel him in every secret dewy place, anointing her ith the essence of his being, making her feel like a woman in e most timeless way of all.

It was a hit-and-miss scramble to his bedroom but Amy ardly noticed. Furniture toppled over in their wake, and Fergus elped and backed away at one point as Angus misjudged the istance from the hall to the bedroom door.

They landed in a tangle of limbs on his bed, the mattress springing with their weight, bringing her into closer contact with the rigid heat of his body.

Clothes went in all directions, and for the first time Amy gave no thought to the consequences of sleeping with a man just for the sheer irresistible force of out-of-control desire that was storming through her being like a tumultuous tide.

She vaguely registered the tearing sound of a condom being unwrapped from its tiny package, and then her senses soared when Angus's hard strong body entered hers in a smooth but spine-arching movement that left her totally breathless.

Her climb to paradise was faster than any she'd ever experienced. It was as if every cell of her body had been preparing for this moment for years and now it was heading towards cataclysmic release that had no equal.

She felt herself lift off as he drove harder, as if he too was chasing an exhilarating release that had so far escaped him. Her body tightened around him, her panting breaths rising in tempo as she reached the pinnacle of pleasure. A thousand lights exploded in her head, the tiny cascading particles dancing around the perimeter of her consciousness as she felt his final plunge into oblivion…

Amy must have briefly drifted off as she woke to the sensation of one of his hands stroking up and down her arm. She turned and looked at him, her fingers going up to his mouth, tracing its contours. He captured her finger with his mouth and sucked on it, his eyes holding hers.

She gave a little giggle and tried to pull her finger out. 'Let go.'

'No,' he said, holding her with his teeth.

'Are you taking me as your prisoner, Sergeant Ford?' she asked, her stomach kicking in excitement when he rolled her under him again.

'Damn right I am,' he growled, and took her on another fast

and furious ride to fulfilment, leaving her boneless and weak in his arms.

Amy had never been good at this part, the moment after the madness. Even with Simon she had felt awkward and self-conscious. She lay very still, breathing in the clean male scent of Angus as he lay relaxed over her, his face buried in the soft skin of her neck, the whisper of his breath like a teasing feather against her.

Angus lifted himself off and looked down at her. 'I don't know about you, but I never really know what to say at times like this.'

'I guess, thanks for the memories sounds a bit tacky, huh?'

His brows moved together slightly. 'Yeah, it does.'

'How about let's enjoy this while it lasts?' she said after a tiny pause. 'I mean, that's all you're offering, isn't it? A short-term fling?'

His expression clouded even further as he looked down at her mouth. 'I'm not sure what I'm offering,' he said. 'Up until a few moments ago I would have said we had nothing in common and that the sooner you left town the better, but now I'm not so sure.'

She gave him a twisted look. 'What are you saying, Sergeant Ford, that you might want me to stay around a bit longer after all?'

His dark brown eyes glinted as they homed in on hers. 'I'm not sure what I'm saying but I certainly know what I'm feeling right now.'

Amy could feel it too…

She woke to the sound and feel of her stomach growling with hunger. She pushed herself up on her elbows to find Angus standing by the bedside, watching her.

'I've made dinner. Are you hungry?' he asked.

She brushed her wild hair out of her eyes. 'I'm starving.'

He held out a hand and she slipped hers into it, his strength as he pulled her upright thrilling her as her naked body brushed against the hard frame of his. He lowered his mouth to hers, kissing her lingeringly, the taste of his lips and tongue sending her into a maelstrom of feeling.

He pulled away to look down at her, his hands still cupping the sides of her face. 'I think I should tell you that this sort of thing didn't happen with my previous boarder.'

She smiled at his dry tone. 'I'm assuming the engineer from Broome wasn't female, then?'

'No, definitely not.' He stroked his thumbs along the curve of her cheeks for a moment as his eyes held hers.

'Angus?'

His thumbs stopped. 'Yes?'

Amy took a shaky breath. 'I think I should tell you that this sort of thing has never happened to me before.'

'You mean falling into bed with your landlord?'

'No, I mean falling in love with a man I only met a couple of weeks ago.'

There was a moment or two of air-tightening silence.

'"Love" is a very strong word,' he said. 'Aren't you confusing it with physical attraction?'

'I'm not sure…' She sank her teeth into her bottom lip, releasing it after a second to add, 'I never felt anything like this with my ex-fiancé. I didn't respond to him like I do to you, not ever. I feel something so powerful and electric every time you touch me. Do you feel it, too?'

'Amy.' He let out a sigh that sounded rough around the edges. 'I'm not sure I can promise you anything other than here and now. I've already gone down the permanent track and it didn't work out. My fiancé wasn't prepared to live the life I've been called to live. I know this probably sounds a bit crazy, but I didn't choose to be cop, not in the way others do. And, no, it has nothing to do with my father being a cop and his father before him. It was about me. My world view, my convictions, my need to contribute to the community in such a way as to make a difference.'

'But I feel like that, too!' she said. 'That's why I'm a doctor. I love helping people and making a difference.'

'I realise that, Amy, but my job requires certain sacrifices, gut-wrenching sacrifices that most women find hard to cope with.' He released her to rake a hand through his hair. 'When Dan died, I saw what it did to his wife. She lost her entire world, her purpose for living. She's still not on track. Her kids are traumatised, and will be for the rest of their lives. How could I do that to someone I cared about? It might not appear to be so out here, but sometimes my job is extremely dangerous. I've already had several death threats and I have no reason to believe they weren't serious.'

'Is that why you're here at Marraburra?' she asked.

It was a moment or two before he answered, and even when he did, Amy wondered if he was being straight with her. His expression had that keep-away look to it again, and it hurt her to have felt so close to him physically but so far away emotionally.

'I'm here to get a job done, simple as that.'

'And after that job is done?' she asked.

'I have a few options open to me,' he said. 'But I'm not prepared to discuss them right now.' He handed her a bathrobe with a small smile that should have softened the blow of his words but somehow didn't. 'You'd better put this on, otherwise I might forget that I've got dinner simmering on the cook-top.'

Amy slipped into the soft folds of the robe and tied the cord around her waist, her heart feeling as if it had been squeezed inside her chest as she asked, 'So what you're saying is we only have this time together?'

Angus lifted her chin to look into her dark blue eyes, the tug of temptation so strong he had to call on every gram of resistance to counteract it. 'Better to spend three months with someone you like than thirty years with someone you hate, right?'

'Ten weeks,' she said flatly. 'That's all we've got…'

He took the cord of her bathrobe and untied it, letting the garment drop to the floor at her feet. 'Then let's not waste a minute of them,' he said, and pulled her back into his arms.

Amy had just finished treating a woman with biliary colic the next day and organised a gall-bladder ultrasound for her to Geraldton when Helen informed her that Carl Haines had cancelled his appointment.

'Did he give a reason?' Amy asked as she handed the receptionist the last patient's notes to be filed.

'He said he's too sick to drive into town,' Helen said. 'But that could mean he's been drinking and didn't want to risk being pulled over by Angus or one of the other cops.'

'I'll go and visit him at home,' Amy said. 'What's his address?'

Helen gave it to her on a piece of paper. 'He lives on a pretty rough road. I hope your car won't get a stone chip.'

'It doesn't matter,' Amy said as she pulled out her keys. 'I'm thinking of selling it anyway. It's totally unsuitable for out here.'

Helen's brows lifted. 'So are you thinking of staying longer?'

Amy gave her an inscrutable look as she swept past. 'I haven't quite made up my mind.'

Carl was sitting on the front verandah of his house when Amy pulled up, his bloodshot eyes narrowing as she came towards him.

'Hello, Carl, I thought since you weren't feeling well enough to come to see me, I'd come and see you,' she said.

'You shouldn't have bothered,' he said, looking away. 'I

don't really care if I live or die anyway, so what need do I have of a doctor?'

Amy sat on the edge of the verandah next to him. 'You might not need a doctor but surely you could do with a friend?'

He turned his head to look at her, his expression so racked with pain she had trouble containing her emotions. Lines of grief roadmapped his face; his eyes were like murky hazel pools of bottomless grief and his skin had a sallow look to it as if it had grown tired of containing the sadness he was carrying in his body.

'I miss them so much...' He spoke after a long aching silence.

She touched his hand with one of hers. 'I know you do, Carl. You'll always miss them.'

'I want to get myself together but I can't face the years ahead without numbing the pain.' He gave a grunt of humourless laughter and continued, 'Funny thing is I wasn't even a drinker before I lost my wife and daughters. I had the occasional beer but I never really got into it in a big way, not like some of the other guys around here.'

'Bill told me you were on an antidepressant,' she said. 'Are you taking it regularly?'

'Not really... I guess I should, right?'

'Might be better than the drink,' she said. 'You really shouldn't be having both.'

'I know. Angus said the same.'

'He's a good friend to you, isn't he?'

'Yeah...' He gave her a little smile. 'So, are you his girl-friend now? I heard you moved in with him.'

'Just because I share his house doesn't necessarily mean I will be sharing his bed,' she said, hoping the colour of her cheeks weren't giving her away. *Or not for long anyway.*

Carl looked down at his dusty workboots for a moment. 'I'm glad you came out here to see me,' he said without looking at her. 'I have something to show you, you being Lindsay Redgrove's cousin and all.'

'I heard she was friendly with you.'

'She was,' he said. 'She gave me paintings and stuff. She even gave me one the day before she died.'

Amy blinked at him. 'Have you still got it?'

'Course I have,' he said. 'I just wish I'd been here when she dropped it off… I might have been able to talk to her, you know, to stop her doing what she did.'

'Can I see it?'

He got to his feet and beckoned for her to come inside. Amy stepped over the threshold and her eyes went immediately to the three portraits on the wall. Her cousin had never done anything so beautiful. The face of Carl's wife Julie showed warmth and love and a sparkling personality, and the two little girls had doll-like features and bright blonde curls, their engaging smiles bringing tears to Amy's eyes.

She vaguely registered the sound of Carl opening a cupboard and the crackle of a canvas being unrolled. She turned as he handed it to her.

'I'm not much of an abstract art lover myself,' he said. 'The portraits she did of Julie and Katie and Meg were the only realistic things she did, so I don't really know what this is meant to represent. But I kept it because she left it on the doorstep, I guess as a sort of goodbye.'

Amy looked down at the painting in her hands and felt a shiver of something indefinable pass over her skin. The painting was as Carl said, abstract, but even with the crude slashes and strokes of the brush she could make out the figure of a woman on a beach, running away from what looked like hundreds of rectangular white shells.

Amy swallowed and, lowering the painting, looked at Carl. 'Have you shown anyone this? The police, for instance?'

He shook his head. 'No. I didn't even think of it until someone said you were her cousin the other day. I just thought you might like to have something of hers to keep.'

'I would love to keep it, if you're sure you don't mind?'

He gave her another sad little smile. 'Why would I want that when I have these three?' he said, and pointed to his family on the wall.

Amy squeezed his hand and fought back tears. 'Thank you, Carl,' she said. 'You don't know how much this means to me or to Lindsay.'

Amy was on her way back to Angus's place when she received a call from Barry Kenton, who informed her Shontelle and Nathan were now at home if she wanted to drop by and check on the little boy's nose.

'I offered to drive Shoni and the boy into the clinic to see you, but she refused,' he said with a frustrated sigh. 'I thought if you just dropped around casually, it might be easier. I hope you don't mind. I know you're probably busy and it is the end of the day but I thought it was too good an opportunity to miss.'

'Not at all, Barry,' she said. 'I'm only a few minutes away. I've just finished a house call nearby.'

'And here I was thinking doctors didn't do house calls any more,' he said. 'See you soon.'

'Where's Dr Tanner?' Angus asked Helen as he came into the clinic with quick urgent strides.

'She's on a house call to Carl,' Helen answered. 'Have you tried her phone?'

'It keeps going to the message bank,' he said, trying to stem the panic flooding his system. 'It must be turned off or out of range. I'll give Carl a call to see if she's still there.'

'What's wrong, Angus?' Helen asked. 'I've never seen you so on edge before. Is it something to do with Amy?'

'I can't talk right now,' he said as his fingers pressed the rapid dial on his phone. 'But if you see her, don't let her out of your sight and, whatever you do, don't let Barry Kenton anywhere near her.'

'B-Barry?' Helen put a hand up to her throat. 'Oh, dear... He called not two minutes ago, asking for Amy to call in at his place to see Shontelle and Nathan. I told him to call her on her mobile...'

Angus let out an expletive and flew out the door.

CHAPTER SIXTEEN

THE Kenton residence looked deserted when Amy first drove in but almost as soon as she had got out of the car the front door opened and Barry appeared with a welcoming smile on his face.

'Amy, I don't know how to thank you for taking such a special interest in my daughter and grandson.'

'Hi, Barry,' she said, taking his outstretched hand. 'It's my pleasure, really. I'm glad you called as I've been a bit worried about Nathan's nose. I want to make sure it hadn't become infected.'

'Come inside and make yourself comfortable and I'll call them both,' he said, leading her into the luxurious lounge area overlooking the ocean.

Amy turned to look at the view cast in an orange glow from the setting sun. She heard Barry call his daughter's name but as far as she could tell there was no answer. He came back into the room a short time later with an apologetic look on his face.

'I'm sorry about this, Amy, but I can't seem to find her anywhere. She's not answering.'

'Could she have slipped out without you noticing?' Amy asked. 'She drives, doesn't she?'

'Her car is in the garage,' he said, scratching his head.

'Maybe I should come back later.' She reached for her bag

but he put his hand over hers and the bag fell back to the floor
with a little thud.

'No,' he said with another smile as he stepped back. 'Please,
don't leave just yet. I'm sure she's just taken Nathan for a little
walk. Why don't we sit and have a drink until she returns?'

Amy would have refused except it had been hours since
she'd had anything to drink and the thought of a tall glass of
iced water was just too tempting to resist. 'All right,' she said,
returning his smile.

Before she could stop him he bent down and picked up her
bag. 'I'll put it on the bar over here,' he said. 'Nathan was
eating a biscuit in here the other day and we've had ants ever
since. I wouldn't want them to get in your bag.'

Amy inspected the floor at her feet as he took her bag away.
Ants were OK as long as there were no spiders. She gave a little
shiver and turned to face him again.

He held up a bottle of red wine and two glasses. 'How about
a smooth red to finish the day?'

'I'm the only doctor in town at the moment so I'd better stick
to water or something soft,' she said.

'Surely one little glass won't hurt?'

She shook her head. 'Sorry, Barry, but you go ahead. I'll be
happy with a soda water.'

She watched as he opened a bottle of fizzy water and poured
it into a glass, the chink of ice falling into the liquid suddenly
sounding loud in the silence.

'You have a lovely home,' she said. 'Have you lived here long?'

'Ever since Shoni was a toddler,' he said. 'My wife and I
moved here from the Northern Territory.'

'Shontelle told me you're a fisherman,' she said once they
had sat down with their drinks. 'Are you away a lot?'

'Not as much as I used to be,' he said, taking a sip from a
full glass of red wine. 'I'm at a time of life when I want to sit

back and relax a bit, enjoy the benefits of all the hard work I've put in over the years.'

'I guess it must be quite a tough life, going out for a week at a time, leaving family and loved ones behind.'

'Yes.' He stared into the contents of his glass for a moment. 'That's why my wife left. She couldn't handle the loneliness.' He lifted his eyes back to hers and smiled. 'But that's old history. Tell me about you. How are you enjoying your stay in Marraburra? Have you settled your concerns over your cousin's suicide?'

Amy gave him a self-conscious look. 'So you've heard about my real reason for being here.'

'It's hard to keep a secret in a place the size of this,' he said with another smile. 'I heard you were interested in the details of your cousin's death.'

'Yes, so I decided to come here and do a little background research for myself.'

'And what have you found?' he asked.

Amy put her glass down and met his interested gaze. 'I don't actually think my cousin committed suicide.'

He held her gaze without blinking. 'You think she was murdered?'

'It's got to be one or the other, hasn't it? For one thing, she didn't leave a note…' She let the sentence fall away as she thought about the painting in her car.

Barry's brows rose slightly. 'Do you have any evidence to suggest foul play?'

'Not really,' she answered, 'although Carl Haines gave me a painting earlier today that made me wonder…'

'A painting?' His tone sharpened a fraction. 'A painting of what?'

Amy had hoped to speak to Angus before anyone else about Lindsay's canvas but she couldn't see any harm in telling Barry

who, as a local, would surely be well aware of the drug
problems along the coast.

'Lindsay left a painting on Carl's doorstep the day before
she died. I might be wrong about this but I think she may have
seen something suspicious along the beach—you know, drugs
being dropped off or something.'

'Where is this painting at the moment?' he asked.

'It's in my car.'

'Can I have a look at it?' he asked. 'I might be able to help
you solve your little mystery.'

Amy put her glass to one side and, picking up her keys, left
him to go to her car, returning a few moments later with the
canvas and rolling it out for him to look at.

He looked at it for a long time, the silence stretching and
stretching until he broke it by saying, 'I think you're wrong
Dr Tanner.'

'What do you mean?'

He met her eyes with the ice blue of his own. 'Your cousin
did commit suicide. There's never been any doubt of that. You
have only to ask the police who investigated the circumstances
of her death.'

'But this painting seems to suggest—'

His eyes hardened as he interrupted her. 'Your cousin had a
drug problem since she was a teenager. This painting is just
about what was going on in her head.'

'I don't agree,' Amy argued. 'Lindsay did have a drug history
but she never touched a thing after she went to hospital. She was
terrified of having another relapse into psychosis—the thought
of being institutionalised again petrified her. I've heard along the
Western Australian coast there are drop-off points for South-East
Asian drugs. Boats go out to meet container ships and the drugs
are offloaded, and some of the drug packages can go astray.
What if Lindsay found some packages on the beach where she

lived? It would be her worst nightmare that the one thing she'd travelled so far to avoid landed virtually on her doorstep.'

'That's an interesting theory, Amy. Maybe you should raise it with the police?' he said. 'It sounds a bit fanciful to me. I've never seen any drug drop-offs along this part of the coast.'

'I guess you wouldn't have, would you Barry?' Angus's voice spoke from the doorway.

'Sergeant Ford.' Barry was all politeness as he got to his feet. 'Would you care to join us in a drink?'

Amy felt the tension in the air as if someone had charged it with high-voltage electricity. She looked from one man to the other, her mind distantly assembling comments, thoughts and vague observations that hadn't fitted together before. Barry had said Shontelle's car was in the garage but when Amy had gone to get the painting only Barry's black BMW had been there. Why had he lied about something like that?

Now there was no sign of the urbane host of earlier. He was like a cornered dog eyeing up an opponent, his body tense, hands opening and closing as if preparing to do battle.

'It's over, Barry,' Angus said.

'Over? What's over, Angus? I'm not following you,' Barry said, still with that cool polite smile in place.

'Your fishing business is over. Except it's not fish you've been hauling in, is it, Barry?'

'I'm really not with you, Sergeant,' Barry replied, moving to a closed cupboard next to the bar. 'We haul in our quota off the coast, nothing more—you can check the log.'

'Step away from the cupboard, Barry. The coastguard has already intercepted your latest catch. You've got your quota all right—pure heroin. Your men are all being charged by the drug squad down at the docks as we speak.'

'You're lying!' Barry threw back, all attempts to remain polite fading. 'You've got nothing on me. I've been here all along. I've got nothing to do with what those creeps have on those boats.'

'Haven't I?' Angus asked with a chilling smile. 'I have your daughter and grandson in protective custody. Josh Brumby brought her and Nathan in earlier today. She'd gone to him for help. She told me less than an hour ago how she overheard a phone conversation between you and one of your men about the guy you pushed over the cliff at Caveside Cove. Brent Handley was the hit man you engaged to murder your wife. He woke a couple of hours ago from his coma. Your wife didn't run away as you led everyone, including your own daughter, to believe, did she, Barry? You had her killed in cold blood because she wanted out of your operation. She threatened to spill the beans.'

Barry opened and closed his fists again, and backed away from the bar. Amy could tell he knew he was beaten. Angus had his gun trained on him and James and Tim Greenaway, the other junior constable, had already silently entered the room with guns at the ready.

'Dr Tanner was partially right, wasn't she, Barry?' Angus continued. 'Lindsay Redgrove probably would not have taken her own life except you put pressure on her when she found those packs of heroin on the beach after the last drop-off six months ago. Brent Handley didn't appreciate his assisted flight over the cliff—he's given a full account of your operation. He said you got him to threaten Lindsay. You knew it wouldn't take much to tip her over the edge. She killed herself the next day, frightened out of her mind that she would be institutionalised again if the drugs were somehow connected to her.'

Barry's mouth thinned into a hard tight line. 'You're making all this up to force a confession out of me. I'm not saying a thing until I speak to my lawyer.'

'We don't need a confession, Barry,' Angus said. 'Your

daughter has told us everything we need to know. You've been controlling her with your fists for years. And you've been doing the same to her son. That's why you lured Dr Tanner here this evening, wasn't it? You couldn't find Shontelle and Nathan and it got you worried. You didn't like the fact that your daughter trusted the new doctor in town—couldn't have her blubbering to her, could you? I guess Dr Tanner not being convinced of her cousin's suicide must have topped it off for you, eh? That was just too risky, wasn't it, Barry? You had to do something and do it tonight.'

Barry sent a filthy glance towards Amy as the two other officers clipped handcuffs on him. 'You just had to come up here poking your nose around, didn't you? Well, you won't get away with this, I swear to God.'

'Make all the threats you like, Barry,' Angus said as he directed his men to take him out to the police van. 'But if ever you want to get to Dr Tanner, you'll have to deal with me first, because I won't be letting her out of my sight.'

Amy would have given anything to have had a chance to speak to Angus right then and there about that heart-stopping statement, but apart from a few parting words about how she was feeling, and her getting back home, the formal arrest and transfer of Barry Kenton, together with the rest of the drug squad operation, necessitated her having to wait.

She filled in the time checking her phone for missed calls. She hadn't realised that Barry had turned off her phone when he had taken her bag to the bar. There were ten missed calls from Angus and three from her mother. She listened to the messages, her heart swelling with hope when she heard the frantic tone of Angus's voice recorded there. She decided she was never going to erase them.

'Angus?' She came up at him at as the others were finally leaving.

CHAPTER SEVENTEEN

AMY looked up at Angus a couple of hours later in amazement. 'Did you really mean it when you said you'd never be letting me out of your sight?'

He smiled as he pulled her closer. 'Of course I meant it. How else am I going to ensure you keep out of trouble unless I put you under permanent police guard?' He tapped her on the end of her up-tilted nose and added, 'You came speeding into town and very nearly undid two years of police work with all those questions about your cousin's death. I was so close to cracking the case, just waiting for the next big drop-off. We thought Barry might take the operation elsewhere because of the sudden interest you had in your cousin's suicide. He's been under close surveillance, but we've never had the proof. We called him the Chess Player—always a few moves ahead—a very smooth operator, as you found out for yourself.'

Amy winced in embarrassment. 'I'd practically nominated him for father of the year, he seemed so convincing about his worries over Shontelle and Nathan.'

'He's been more like the father from hell. It's probably why Shontelle got pregnant in the first place in a desperate attempt to get away, but it backfired when the father of her baby deserted her. We're investigating whether Barry had something to do with that, too—the father's vanished at this point. Maybe he got a little too close to stumbling onto Barry's operation.'

'What will happen to Shontelle and Nathan now?'

'I've already organised a police social worker to meet with her. If support can be arranged, she might be able to complete her high-school education and make something of her life for Nathan's sake. She has you to thank for that, you know. She now realises the cycle of violence could stop if she makes the right choices.'

'I'm glad I was able to help, even if I did nearly jeopardise your investigation in the process.'

'We both got the answers we were after,' he said. 'You found out the truth behind Lindsay's suicide and I closed down one of the biggest heroin suppliers in the country.' He pulled her closer, his voice deepening with emotion. 'I nearly went out of my mind when you didn't answer your phone. I realised then how much I loved you. I know I said I wasn't interested in anything long term, but nearly losing you made me have a rethink, which leaves me with just one other question I want an answer to.'

'Oh,' she said, smiling up at him rapturously. 'What question would that be?'

'Amy Tanner, will you spend the rest of your life by my side, to be my love, my companion, my strength and my purpose for living, no matter where our careers take us?'

Amy's eyes started to sparkle. 'Is that a proposal, Sergeant Ford?'

'It is indeed, Dr Tanner,' he said with a sexy smile. 'And is the doctor I love more than life itself by any chance saying yes?'

'Well, *of course* she is,' Grace said as she came into the room with her overnight luggage in one hand, a beaming smile splitting her face. 'Aren't you, darling?'

Amy rolled her eyes and groaned. *'Mu-um!'*

FREE ONLINE READ!

Outback Crisis

by Melanie Milburne

Don't miss this short story linked to
Melanie Milburne's novel in
Masters of the Outback

To read your free online story, just go to:

www.millsandboon.co.uk/mastersoftheoutback

www.millsandboon.co.uk

M&B™

THE

Balfour
LEGACY

*E*IGHT SISTERS, *E*IGHT SCANDALS

VOLUME 1 – JUNE 2010
Mia's Scandal
by Michelle Reid

VOLUME 2 – JULY 2010
Kat's Pride
by Sharon Kendrick

VOLUME 3 – AUGUST 2010
Emily's Innocence
by India Grey

VOLUME 4 – SEPTEMBER 2010
Sophie's Seduction
by Kim Lawrence

8 VOLUMES IN ALL TO COLLECT!

www.millsandboon.co.uk

M&B

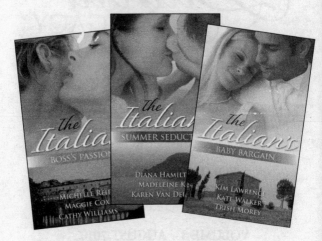

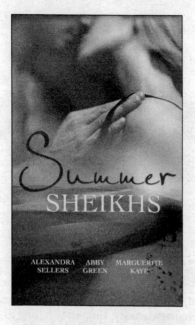

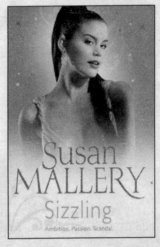

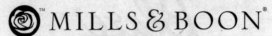